JACK MURPHY WON'T BACK DOWN

The headlines scream the ghastly news of an abandoned truck filled with murdered immigrants. Detective Jack Murphy and his partner Liddell Blanchard are on the case. They've got a lone survivor, rumors of a witness, and the feds getting in their way. Jack's gut tells him there's a connection with a local killing—and the bloodshed is far from over. He's going up against a butcher who commits the unspeakable in the name of protecting America. Some say the worst crime is to look the other way. Jack Murphy only looks for justice . . .

Visit us at www.kensingtonbooks.com

Highest Praise for Rick Reed's Thrillers

THE DEEPEST WOUND

"Reed gives the reader a genre story worth every minute and every penny spent."
—*Book Reporter*

"Whew! The murders are brutal and nonstop. Det. Jack Murphy tracks killers through a political maze of lies, deception and dishonor that leads to a violent, pulse-pounding climax."
—**Robert S. Levinson**

"The things Reed has seen as a police officer make for a great book."
—*Suspense Magazine*

THE COLDEST FEAR

"Everything you want in a thriller: strong characters, plenty of gory story, witty dialogue, and a narrative that demands you keep turning those pages."
—**BookReporter.com**

THE CRUELEST CUT

"Rick Reed, retired homicide detective and author of *Blood Trail,* the true-crime story of serial killer Joe Brown, brings his impressive writing skills to the world of fiction with *The Cruelest Cut.* This is as authentic and scary as crime thrillers get, written as only a cop can write who's lived this drama in real life. . . . A very good and fast read."
—**Nelson DeMille**

Books by Rick Reed

The Jack Murphy Thrillers
The Cruelest Cut
The Coldest Fear
The Deepest Wound
The Highest Stakes
The Darkest Night
The Slowest Death
The Deadliest Sins

Nonfiction
Blood Trail
(with Steven Walker)

Published by Kensington Publishing Corporation

The Deadliest Sins

A Jack Murphy thriller

Rick Reed

LYRICAL PRESS
Kensington Publishing Corp.
www.kensingtonbooks.com

LYRICAL UNDERGROUND BOOKS are published by
Kensington Publishing Corp.
119 West 40th Street
New York, NY 10018

All Kensington titles, imprints, and distributed lines are available at special quantity discounts for bulk purchases for sales promotion, premiums, fund-raising, educational, or institutional use.

Special book excerpts or customized printings can also be created to fit specific needs. For details, write or phone the office of the Kensington Sales Manager: Kensington Publishing Corp., 119 West 40th Street, New York, NY 10018. Attn. Sales Department. Phone: 1-800-221-2647.

Lyrical Underground and Lyrical Underground logo Reg. US Pat. & TM Off.

First Electronic Edition: October 2018
eISBN-13: 978-1-5161-0456-7
eISBN-10: 1-5161-0456-0

First Print Edition: October 2018
ISBN-13: 978-1-5161-0457-4
ISBN-10: 1-5161-0457-9

Printed in the United States of America

"Two urns by Jove's high throne have ever stood,
The source of evil one, and one of good."
—Homer, The Iliad

"Without a sign his sword the brave man draws,
And asks no omen but his country's cause."
—Homer, The Iliad

This novel is dedicated to ICE, Immigration and Customs Enforcement, for the very necessary work they perform in these difficult times. And to the local, state and federal officers involved in cracking down on terrorism, whether it be by gangs, lone-wolf, international, or the homegrown variety.

I would also like to dedicate this seventh book in the series to Michaela Hamilton, my editor at Kensington Books, who believed in me and gave me a chance. I consider her my friend and mentor. And to my excellent team at Kensington who are experts at publicity, marketing, proofing, editing, legalese, cover design, distribution, and so many other things. Without all of you this book would still be a file on my computer.

Chapter 1

The "Coyote" sat in the booth, drinking stale coffee, eating a crust of cherry pie, and writing in a five- by nine-inch ring notebook. He had to record his thoughts, his feelings. That's what his shrink said. His shrink was an asshole, but at two Benjamins a session Coyote didn't want to waste the advice.

The gray-haired waitress shuffled over in dirty house shoes. She was wearing faded gray sweat pants and a shirt with stains and smudges of flour.

"Coffee?" she asked.

Coyote looked around the shabby café. It was narrow, with a six-foot counter on one side and two ramshackle booths on the other—one of those had duct tape holding a leg together. There were no other customers. The varnished seat of the booth had turned to a gummy residue, but the top was worn smooth. Mounted in one corner of the ceiling was a defunct surveillance camera, its wires disconnected and hanging. The coffee in the bottom of the carafe was black and thick as syrup. *She calls this drain cleaner coffee?*

He was polite. "No," he said. His voice was gruff, deep for a man barely five and a half feet tall. He was wearing a charcoal-colored Burberry coat, black leather gloves, black Western Stetson, crisp white shirt with imitation-pearl snap buttons, creased blue jeans, and Western boots. He wasn't a big man by any standard, but only a few men had made the mistake of seeing him as "small."

The woman said, "Closing in five."

He ignored her as her shoes scuffed across the stained black-and-white tiles. He dug deep in a pocket and pulled out a crisp twenty-dollar bill. He slid the twenty under his cup and read what he'd written so far:

I'm tired. Tired of everything and everyone. People disgust me. Food doesn't taste good. No happiness anywhere for me. I see people pretending to sing, their words full of hate and anger and violence. They dance with faces showing hate and confrontation. What are they so unhappy about? Why do they want to disrespect everything they got for free? They won't work. They think they can be rich and happy taking drugs. They dishonor their parents and each other. They fight from a safe distance with texts and computers and phones. Cowards.

Everyone is out for themselves and the only thing they can agree on is that their elders were wrong, racist, or homophobic. They don't see why "elders" always talk about the past, about the lessons that took a lifetime to learn. They are confused about who they are, who anyone else is, angry that their elders didn't give them more. Why should they take any blame or responsibility?

This is where my mind goes when I'm on the road. Alone, thank God. My dreams are visions, premonitions of things to come. Slackers, drug addicts, and alcoholics, irresponsible, arrogant pretenders surround me. They have created a world where they matter. They don't. If the last three or four generations were wiped from the face of the earth, we wouldn't notice. They contribute nothing. They do nothing. They want everything. They're using my air.

"Time," the old woman said.

Coyote got up. He couldn't wait to leave. The smell of putrid coffee mixed with the odor of fried onions was enough incentive to go. He walked out the door, his boots crunching on rock salt. He pulled his coat tighter against the frigid air, looked down the street at the car with the fogged-up windshield. The asshole had made Coyote wait. Coyote respected that.

He tugged the coat collar up around his neck and face. He pulled a cigarette from inside his jacket and lit it. Holding it between his lips, he slipped his hands into his pockets and turned down the alleyway.

* * * *

The stolen VW sat halfway down the block from the Coffee Shop. It was an older VW, a '73 or '74, puke-green where it wasn't primered. Its lights were off, but the unmistakable burbling exhaust noise came from the engine. The driver was stuffed into the driver's compartment, knees touching the dashboard, upper body bent forward, hands on the wheel, head almost touching the roof. A black-and-white dog sat in the passenger seat, mimicking the driver's focus through the windshield.

He'd made the delivery over the same route dozens of times in the last five years. Each time, they gave him a new burner phone with one pre-programmed contact number. He was told the phone was for incoming calls only. He'd never gotten a call until today.

The caller identified himself as Coyote. Coyote said there was a change of plan. He was to deliver his cargo in Evansville, Indiana, and turn the truck over to Coyote. He was given a location. He'd never been told to leave the truck with someone he didn't know at a different location than where he'd been headed.

He told Coyote so and asked how he was supposed to get back to Texas. He asked if he'd done something wrong. Coyote assured him he would have transportation waiting for him in Evansville. He would still be paid and with a big bonus on top because he might not be making deliveries for a few months. Coyote said his employers were being careful and he shouldn't ask any more questions. That made him worry even more. All kinds of scenarios played through his mind. What if the big boss had been arrested and gave him up? What if this guy, Coyote, was a Fed?

He didn't trust anyone he didn't know, and he didn't know Coyote, so he'd deliberately missed the meet and drove around a few hours. Coyote called him again. This time Coyote was outright threatening and ordered him to do as instructed, not to call or talk to anyone or there would be hell to pay. He believed Coyote.

Not calling anyone was easy. He didn't have his employer's phone number, and even if he did he wouldn't have called. Only one other person knew he was driving, and they wouldn't be any help if the Feds were involved. He needed this job. He was stuck. He couldn't make the delivery with any confidence he wouldn't be arrested, and he sure as hell couldn't drive around aimlessly. Coyote had made it clear that he had no choice. But that didn't mean he couldn't improvise a little. Protect himself. Meet with Coyote on his own terms. No one would get the cargo until he got paid.

He'd picked the time and location for the meet, but he was deliberately late again. One thing life had taught him was caution. He'd parked the truck clear across town, stolen a car, and drove to the location early enough to see the small man in the cowboy hat go inside. It must be Coyote. Coyote sat down in a booth by the front windows and didn't move except to drink coffee, and it looked like he was writing on something. Maybe a check ledger? Maybe this really was the guy who paid the drivers?

The meeting place wasn't perfect, but he was driving a stolen car and didn't need to attract police attention. He'd picked the place by the University of Evansville, with its sweeping lawns, water fountains, concrete benches, fraternity houses, bookstores and libraries and labs because he'd thought the place would be crawling with students and similar junky cars.

Not so. He'd only seen two or three tiny groups of people on the street since he'd arrived. Watching them, he thought of his own dream of going to school once upon a time. He'd given up those ideas before he made it to high school. He'd been forced to join his father in the family business of stealing and stripping cars. It brought in money and you didn't need a degree to do it. That's how he was in possession of this car. He wondered how different his life would have been if he hadn't...

Coyote came out and looked down the street at the VW. He put a cigarette in his lips and walked into the alleyway. Coyote must have seen him driving by and was watching him. He had to run the heater while he watched Coyote. He hadn't been as careful as he thought, but he had to get his money. All of his own was spent keeping his mom in that goddam nursing home in Florida. He'd only taken the job to take care of her. He owed her. She'd kept him alive in between the beatings his drunken bum of a father had given him and had always encouraged him to do something with his life, even knowing hers would never amount to anything but abuse.

The old woman who had waited on Coyote came out wearing a sweat suit. She was thin as a rail, and he could see her S-shaped spine pushing against the back of the shirt when she turned to look up and down the street. She looked directly at him and went back inside. The shop lights went out, and the street was swallowed up by darkness, with the only light coming from the campus parking lots a block away. He'd picked this neighborhood during the day specifically because of the university campus with its raucous crowd of college students always running to and fro. The cold hadn't seemed to bother them during the day, but now it was dark and the streets deserted. He didn't want to go down that alleyway in the dark, but he had no choice.

He turned to the dog. "Stay, uh..." He didn't know the dog's name. It wasn't his, but maybe he'd keep it. He'd never had a dog. Wouldn't have this one but he couldn't leave it behind in the cold truck. He couldn't do that to the mongrel. It was his soft spot. "Spot. I'll call you Spot, okay?" he said to the dog. "You like Spot?"

The dog was a shepherd mix or a terrier. It cocked its head to one side and looked at him.

"Stay," the man said.

The dog cocked its head to the other side, and its dark, seemingly pupilless eyes locked on his. It gave a short whine, as if to say, "Are you crazy? Take me with you."

He exited the VW. The dome light came on, the door hinges creaked long and loud, and he had to slam the door twice to keep it shut so the dog wouldn't run off or mess up the meeting.

Noise wasn't a problem. Coyote knew he was there and knew he would come to meet him in the alley. He looked around again. He didn't want some asshole stealing the car and his dog. An unlocked car was like a bug light. It attracted thieves.

The dog whined.

He leaned down and put a finger to his lips, and it settled back in the seat. "Smart dog. Good dog."

He approached the alleyway, and a cold wind smacked him in the face. He pulled his coat collar up for all the good it did and stepped into the dark. He saw something near the end of the alleyway. A small glow at waist level. *The cigarette.*

He stopped ten feet from the glow. "Mr. Coyote?"

No answer. The cigarette didn't move.

"It's me. I want my money, or you can tell the boss he don't get the truck. Pay me and I'll tell you where to find it."

Coyote said nothing.

He took a few steps forward. He had to be firm. He might be out of this business for good, and how would he support his mother? He could drive the VW as far as it would take him, sell it, and take a bus to Texas. He still had friends there. He still needed the money.

He said in a loud voice that echoed in the cold confines, "You'd better make your mind up quick, Mr. Coyote. That *cargo* won't last long in this cold. I just want what's owed me." He took another step and realized the glow was from a cigarette sitting on top of a crate. He backpedaled two steps when he felt a sudden pressure in his side and an arm tightened around his throat. His knees gave, and the arm pulled him backward and downward. He felt a face next to his and smelled coffee and cigarettes. The side of his chest felt as if he had just been punched in the ribs. It was on fire.

Pain found its way deep into his chest until his legs turned to jelly. The arm around his throat tightened even more and lowered him to his knees, holding him upright.

"Tell me where the truck is," Coyote said.

The point of a weapon burrowed into the shoulder muscle beside his neck. "You're making a mistake." He reached up to grab the blade, but it dug deeper.

"I wouldn't do that," Coyote said in his ear. "One push and this goes through your heart. Tell me where the truck is." Coyote pushed the blade a little deeper.

He let out a weak scream, and Coyote pushed the blade deeper still until the man's muscles went slack and he slumped against Coyote's legs like a puppet whose strings had been cut.

"You'd better tell me quick," Coyote said.

"They'll freeze," he said with difficulty.

Coyote had no intention of going to the truck unless he needed to help Mother Nature along.

"That's the point, asshole." Coyote drove the long blade down through the man's lungs and chest until he was sure he was dead. He pulled the blade free and let the body slide to the ground.

He knelt beside the body, checked the coat pockets and found the keys to the truck and pocketed them. He took the wallet and found a flip phone. He threw the phone and wallet up on the roof. The police would eventually find them, but he'd be long gone.

"You've been paid." Coyote walked away.

Chapter 2

Detective Jack Murphy, third generation Irish American cop, ducked under the yellow crime scene tape blocking the mouth of the alleyway while his partner, Liddell Blanchard, aka Bigfoot, went to interview the first arriving officer.

Jack stood six feet tall. He was sturdily built, with short dark hair that was spiked in the front, and gray eyes that could turn stormy if he was provoked. He liked redheads, Scotch, Guinness, the beach, and long walks, minus the long walks.

His partner, Liddell Blanchard, stood over six and a half feet tall and weighed in at a full-grown yeti. Liddell was a transplant from the Iberville Parish Sheriff Department in Louisiana. He was part French, part Creole, and all muscle.

Once a month Jack and Liddell worked weekends in the detectives' office. This weekend was their turn. If this run had come in thirty minutes earlier, it would have been a third-shift detective standing here, but such was the luck of the Irish.

The air was frigid. Jack covered his mouth and nose with a gloved hand. On the street behind him an ambulance was pulling away. Its emergency equipment was silenced. The coroner would be needed, not a medic.

In front of him, crime scene techs in winter gear covered by white Tyvek coveralls and hoods worked around a body lying in the alley like a crumpled piece of paper. Even from the sidewalk Jack could see dark splotches of red on the light-colored quilted jacket.

Sergeant Tony Walker approached him. Walker was fifty years old, but except for his salt-and-pepper hair, he could pass for twenty years younger. He didn't have an ounce of fat on his frame. He had been Jack's mentor and partner when he first made detective a decade ago, but then Walker was promoted to sergeant and transferred to Crime Scene. Since Tony had taken over, the Crime Scene Unit ran much more smoothly. The brass was afraid to cross him, and the other detectives respected him. It was the best of both worlds, as far as Jack was concerned.

Walker was bundled against the cold under an oversize Tyvek suit with the hood pulled up on a white sock cap. It made him look like the Stay Puft Marshmallow Man in the *Ghostbusters* movie, or a fat, white commando.

"It's a mess back there, Jack," Walker said.

"What have we got?" Jack asked.

Walker tilted his head toward the body. "White male, possibly in his late forties. He was stabbed once in the side of the chest. Multiple times in the trapezius strap of muscles up here on top of the shoulder." Walker patted the top of his own shoulder. "And at least once in the throat, through and through. The owner of the Coffee Shop found the body this morning. I heard she thought he was a drunk. She told Magary she didn't touch the body. He was first officer on the scene. My guess is the victim has been down overnight, ten to twelve hours. It takes that long for blood to freeze, and some of the blood pooled under him is frozen. No identification on the body. Nothing in his pockets so far."

Jack pointed to the end of the alleyway. "What's back there?"

"Trash, boxes, the back door to the Coffee Shop, and the back of the barber's place next door. A small alleyway connects with Lincoln Avenue. We have everything roped off, and there are officers posted on Lincoln Avenue to keep people out of the back alley."

Liddell approached them and said, "I just talked to Officer Magary. Magary said he'd found homeless people, drunks, and some college students sleeping in the alleyway. His first thought was that the guy was a drunk. He got closer and saw all the blood, checked for a pulse, backed out, and called for detectives and Crime Scene. Freyda Rademacher, the owner of the Coffee Shop here, called in the original run as a mugging. He said she swears she didn't go near the body."

"That would have been...?" Jack asked.

"Seven o'clock sounds right, pod'na," Liddell answered.

Walker said, "The killer made sure this guy was dead." He pointed to one of the punctures in the fabric of the coat.

"Some kind of blade," Liddell said.

Walker said, "See the shape of the tear in the jacket. It's star shaped. I'll run it through our database after we get the autopsy. Maybe Dr. John has seen this before." He was referring to Dr. John Carmodi, the forensic pathologist for the Vanderburgh County Coroner.

Corporal Morris interrupted them. "One of his shoes came off, and I found this in the shoe." He held up a clear evidence bag that contained a brass key. "Can we turn him over, Sarge? I want to see what's under him. We haven't found any identification, but we haven't been able to search him."

"Let's do it," Walker said. "Coroner's on the way?"

Corporal Morris said, "It's a balmy five degrees. It was three below overnight. This guy's a popsicle."

Morris and another tech turned the body on its back. The once-tan quilted jacket was splotched with deep red blooms around the left shoulder and left side of the chest, but there were no obvious injuries to the front. He was dressed in tan desert-style military boots, no gloves, no hat, and a Black Watch plaid scarf tucked down inside the jacket. No jewelry. His hair was blond, going on gray, going on bald, and crusted with frozen blood. His cheeks were sunken. His lips were deeply lined. The middle and index finger of his left hand were yellowed. Ice crystals had formed on the ridges of the jacket. Tony and Morris were right. He'd been down a while.

Jack had worked some stabbing deaths less than a month ago where the cold was a factor. Those bodies displayed frozen blood, too. He remembered from the autopsy report that blood contained chemicals that slowed the freezing process. He was sure this guy was killed here and left here.

Jack asked Morris, "Were his shoes scuffed like he'd been dragged?"

"No. One just came off. I figure he was struggling with whoever killed him. It happened right here where he is," Morris answered.

The victim's face was flattened like a coin on the side that had lain against the ground. Morris patted down the victim's clothing and said, "We'll have to wait until the coroner gets him to the morgue to search him better, but he doesn't have anything on him except the key."

"We can't rule out robbery as a motive," Jack said. He knelt beside the body and examined the victim's hands. "I don't see any marks on his hands."

Walker agreed. "No scrapes or defensive wounds. He didn't fight his attacker."

Jack asked, "Any idea what kind of lock the key goes to?"

Morris took the evidence bag out again. Imprinted in the metal were capital letters. ABUS. He pointed to the letters.

"Tony, can you take a few pictures of this guy's face with my phone?" Jack asked.

Walker took the photos and handed the phone back to Jack. "One day you need to learn how to use this. Technology isn't your enemy, Jack."

"That's easy for you to say," Jack replied, and he and Liddell walked back to the sidewalk.

Liddell said, "The university bookstore is just across the street, I peeked in the window and didn't see any surveillance cameras. The sign says it's closed Saturday and Sunday. The bank next to it faces Lincoln Avenue. I know there are some on the bank that face Lincoln Avenue and the university. There's one in the back looking over the parking area."

"Let's go talk to the woman that found the body," Jack said.

"Her name is Freyda Rademacher."

Jack opened the front door of the Coffee Shop. A bell over the door tinkled, and warm air blasted them. The place was empty except for a woman wearing gray sweats behind the counter. The sweats were old, like the woman. The cuffs were frayed and the butt was translucent from wear. It was impossible to guess her age, but her thin gray hair said it was safe to assume she was past her prime.

She paid no attention to the men and poured water into an old-fashioned stainless-steel coffee percolator. Two glass coffee carafes sat nearby, one with an orange handle for regular, the other green for decaf. A five-pound bag of coffee beans was on the floor beside a small table. Two bags of what might be roasted peanuts sat on top of the table with a coffee bean grinder.

A restaurant-size gas oven was by the sink with all four burners turned on high. She put the coffee pot on one of the burners and lowered the flame. Jack's mother had one of these coffeemakers when he was a kid. She would grind her own coffee beans and add a dash of salt instead of peanuts. You knew the coffee was finished brewing when the liquid that perked up in the glass bubble on top of the coffeemaker turned the right shade of brown.

Jack cleared his throat, but the woman continued to ignore them and opened the oven door a crack. The shop was filled with a mouthwatering smell of freshly baked apple pies.

She used a folded kitchen towel to take two pies from the oven and set them on the counter. Satisfied, she turned to them and wiped her hands on her flour-streaked apron. "More cops."

Liddell said, "Mrs. Rademacher, I'm Detective Blanchard and this is Detective Murphy. We'd like to ask you a few questions if you have time."

"I don't," she said. "I'm busy trying to run a business."

The Coffee Shop was empty. "Mrs. Rademacher..." Jack began, and the woman's shoulders dropped.

"Oh, go ahead. I guess you people won't leave me alone today. I didn't see anything. I don't know who killed that guy out there. It wasn't me. No,

I didn't see anyone. Yes, I found the body, but I don't have a police record. Now can I get back to work?"

"Why would you think you're a suspect, Mrs. Rademacher?" Jack asked.

She grinned and showed some of her top teeth were missing. "I watch *Cold Case Files* and *CSI New York*," she said. "I know the last to see 'em alive or the one that finds 'em is the prime suspect."

Jack had experienced *CSI*'s effect on the public. Crime show addicts were a different breed of people.

Jack said, "We don't think you killed anyone. You're not our prime suspect."

"Unh huh," she said as if she didn't believe him.

"But you are our best witness. You might be able to break this case wide open."

"You think so," she said, feigning surprise.

"What time do you open your business, Mrs. Rademacher?" Jack asked. He hoped to enlist her, but civic duty to help the police was a thing of the past.

"Depends," she said and offered nothing else.

Time to change tactics.

"What time did you open this morning?" Jack asked again in a less friendly manner.

"Why?" she asked. "I told you I didn't kill him. Are you going to arrest me?"

Jack said, "It's warm in here. This building is maybe eighty years old."

"Ninety-two," she corrected him.

"I can see you don't have central air or heat because there are no air vents or steam heaters. Even in a building with good insulation it would take that stove of yours several hours to heat this place. I'm guessing you've been open since five this morning."

"Five thirty," she said. "Stove's a good 'un. They don't make 'em like this no more. Don't need central heat. I open the doors, front and back, for air."

"You got in at five thirty. You called the police at seven," Jack pointed out.

"You want to know why it took me two hours to call the police. It's none of my business who's drunk. I keep myself to myself."

"But you *did* call the police," Jack said.

"I took trash out back, and he hadn't moved since I opened. I told your dispatcher I didn't want to be involved. She said I didn't have to give my name."

"That's right," Jack said. "We got your address from the phone call." Jack didn't have to pretend to be impatient. "Ma'am, we can do this here, or we can do it downtown. Start talking or I'll take you to lockup for failure to assist an officer in the performance of his duty."

She snorted. "That's a good 'un. Cops have to read you Miranda rights first." She put an age-spotted hand to her mouth to suppress a grin.

"Are you gonna talk or do I have to get rough?" Jack asked and winked at her.

She crossed her arms as if in thought. "Take a seat." She pointed at one of the booths nearer the stove and came out from behind the counter. She was wearing a ratty pair of cloth house shoes, and her bare ankles showed. Her sweatshirt and the thighs of the pants were flour spattered. Considering there was a dead man just outside her shop, Jack didn't understand how she could be enjoying this encounter.

"You boys might as well have coffee and a piece of pie. I don't have any donuts," she said with a mischievous wink.

Jack remained standing, and Liddell considered the rickety wooden booth.

"Mrs. Rademacher," Jack said, and she interrupted.

"Name's Freyda. I never did like being called by my married name. Mr. Rademacher, curse his hide, is dead. Dying was the only good thing he ever did. He used all our savings and bought this damn place, and I've been stuck here since."

Jack found a sturdy chair and pulled it over to the table. He motioned for the woman to sit. She ignored him and went behind the counter again. She came back with two mugs of black coffee and handed them to the two detectives.

"Want some apple pie?" Without waiting for an answer, she went back around the counter, got plates and silverware, and brought one of the piping-hot pies to the table.

"Thank you, ma'am," Liddell said. He slid into the booth and scooped half of the pie onto a plate.

Freyda Rademacher sat on the chair. "Ask your questions."

"Okay. Freyda," Jack said. He remained standing. "If you were the detective, what questions would you ask such a fine, observant woman as yourself?"

Freyda snickered. "Fine woman. That's a hoot. You must be blind as a bat, but let me think. I guess I'd ask about that car down the street. And I guess I'd ask who the customer was that left here at closing last night."

"That's good thinking," Jack said. "Tell me about the car and the customer from last night."

"You haven't tried your coffee," she said.

"You aren't drinking the coffee," Jack said.

"Are you kidding?" she said. "This is way too strong for a 'fine woman' such as myself."

Jack took a sip. She was right. He could strip paint with this stuff.

She said, "If I was a detective I could ask the questions, but she wouldn't say anything to the cops. She, or he, would be afraid of getting whacked. Killers always return to the scene of the crime. That's what that hunk on *CSI New York* says. Gary Sinise knows killers." She pronounced his name "Sin-ci."

Chapter 3

Liddell asked for seconds on the pie and a second cup of coffee.

Freyda said, "You like my pie."

Liddell grunted with a mouthful and scooped the other half of the pie onto his plate.

"That guy last night didn't like my pie, and he barely touched his coffee. Just sat there writing in that little notebook. What do you think he was writing?"

Jack asked, "You said you saw a car down the street with the engine running. Did he come in that car?"

"I was in here when he came in. Can't see down the street from here, can I?"

"Tell us about your customer. Anything you can remember," Jack said.

She got up, brought the steel coffee pot to the table, and warmed up Liddell's coffee. "It grows on you." She sat back down. "He was a white man. Younger than me. Older than you two. He was shorter than me, and I'm five feet ten. He was wearing a dark-colored spy coat. You know? A trench-looking thing like they wear in spy movies. He had on a cowboy hat and cowboy boots. He never took his gloves off," she said and looked at Jack eye to eye. "You need to know what color his eyes were? I don't know."

"A Burberry coat?" Liddell suggested.

"It wasn't a berry-colored anything. Just a dark color. Dark gray maybe," Freyda said.

Liddell took out his phone and punched a few letters, bringing up pictures of Burberry coats. He held it where she could see and flipped through. She stopped him at one.

"That's it. That's the coat. It was shiny. Like leather."

Liddell showed the picture to Jack. The coat cost over a thousand dollars. "Expensive taste."

Freyda slapped her hand on the table. "That's what I'm saying. I guess my coffee wasn't good enough for a big spender like him."

"What color was the hat?" Liddell asked her.

"Dark like his clothes. Brown, black, I don't know."

Jack had a thought. "Did he pay in cash or with a credit card?"

Freyda said in a practiced spiel, "I don't take credit. Cash only." She crossed her arms. "These kids bring in spare change and wadded up dollar bills. Most of 'em don't have two nickels to rub together. I don't take mommy and daddy's credit cards. But this guy was a big tipper. Gave me a twenty for stuff he didn't even touch and didn't ask for change."

"Do you still have the twenty-dollar bill?"

Freyda got up and went behind the counter. She came back carrying a metal lockbox. "I got college kids and professors in and out all the time. They don't pay in twenties. I only got one twenty in here."

On top of a very small stack of paper money was a twenty-dollar bill.

Jack took a plastic evidence bag from his pocket.

"There goes a day's earnings," she said. "I guess you're gonna take that twenty and fingerprint it. All you'll find on it probably is my fingerprints because I already told you he was wearing gloves."

"The whole time. Are you sure?" Jack asked.

"Of course I'm sure. I'm old. I ain't blind. Come to think of it, he was like a cowboy spy."

"Cowboy spy," Jack said to Liddell. "Better write that down."

"He don't have a sense of humor, does he?" she asked Liddell.

Jack used a napkin to pick the money up and put it in the envelope.

"I want a receipt. And I want it back. Can you do that? It costs money to run this place."

Liddell handwrote a receipt on a napkin and gave it to her. "We'll get it back to you as soon as we can, Freyda."

She took the napkin and stuffed it in the cashbox. "Can't spend a receipt, can I?"

"What else do you remember?" Jack asked.

Freyda took the box back behind the counter. She took a corroded plastic cup and filled it with cold water. Jack watched as she popped out her upper denture, swished it around in the water, and brought the cup to the table.

"He was undernourished. Should'a ate my pie. He was hard looking. Like he'd seen some things. Done some things. You know what I mean? He was odd."

"Could he have been someone from the university?" Jack asked.

She chuckled. "He wasn't a college student, I can tell you that. And he wasn't a professor. I would have seen him before. His voice was froggy, deep, like one of them chain-smokers. He gave me the creeps. Not that most of them from the school don't."

Jack pulled up the picture Walker had taken of the victim. "Do you know this guy?"

"No. Never seen him. Is that the guy that's in the alley?"

The victim looked taller than she'd described. He was wearing different clothes and his face wasn't visible from the sidewalk, but Jack didn't believe she hadn't seen him before.

"Did the customer talk to you? Say anything you can remember?" Jack asked.

"He ordered coffee. Black. I brought it and a piece of my pie. I asked if he wanted anything else. He said no. Later I told him I was closing. He didn't say anything. Just up and left a twenty under his coffee mug to pay a three-dollar tab. Only one reason a man gives you that much money. I was scared he was after something else."

The thought of what she was suggesting made Jack vomit in his throat just a little. "I can see why you would think that," he lied.

"You're so full of it," she said and gave that mostly toothless smile again.

"Did anyone else come in?" Jack asked.

"Too cold," she said, motioning toward the university dorms. "Them kiddies stay inside smoking their wacky weed and fornicating all day like rabbits. Bunch a' dummies. I hired one or two of them over the years, but they couldn't even make change without getting on them damn phones."

Jack changed the subject. "Tell me about the car."

"Yeah. I locked up and checked the street after he left. The car was halfway down the block. That way." She pointed south. "The engine was running and someone was in it. Maybe two people. I couldn't see if they was man, woman, or child."

Jack asked for a description of the car and was surprised at how succinct the answer was.

"Seventy-four puke-green Volkswagen Beetle," Freyda said.

"You seem sure," Liddell said.

"I oughta be. My asshole husband owned one. I sold the damn thing the day after he died. Got me a Cadillac convertible. Always wanted one, but *asshole* said it wasn't in the budget. He was so tight he'd squeeze a penny until old Abe's gums bled."

Jack remembered seeing a faded green older model VW down the street when they arrived. He was getting on his radio when an officer came in. Jack recognized him as one of the newbies. His nametag read: S. Hurt.

"Detective Murphy, we've got a stolen car out here," S. Hurt said. "It was overnight from the west side."

"Green older model VW?" Jack asked.

"Yeah. I've called a wrecker," Officer Hurt said.

"Don't tow the car until either Sergeant Walker or myself tell you to. It might be related to this murder. Tell Sergeant Walker I want to see the car after I finish here."

Officer Hurt took out his portable radio, and Jack said, "Don't put anything on the radio. Use your phone if you need dispatch."

"I don't have the number for Sergeant Walker."

Jack said, "He's right outside, Officer Hurt. If he's not, one of his people can call his cell, but I want you to talk to him directly about the car. Did you notify the owner yet?"

"Dispatch probably sent someone over there last night," Officer Hurt said.

"Call dispatch—on your phone—and get the owner's information. I want you to call the owner and get what information you can. When did they last see their car? Did they recently sell it to someone? That kind of stuff, Officer Hurt. Report back to me."

"Have you got dispatch's phone number?" Hurt asked, and Jack gave it to him, sending him on his way.

"Ma'am, we might need to talk to you again," Jack said. He took out a business card, wrote his cell phone number on the back, and gave it to her.

"Wait a minute." She went behind the counter again, came back with the second apple pie wrapped in foil, and handed it to Liddell.

"For me?"

"You might as well take it. Won't be many customers today with all that commotion outside my place."

Jack asked, "Where was the customer sitting?"

"The booth near the window," she said. "Ain't cleaned it yet. You think there might be some latent fingerprints you can run through that automatic fingerprint machine?"

"What's back there?" Jack asked, indicating the back of the shop.

"Supplies," Freyda answered. "My rooms are upstairs."

"Freyda, is there any chance you didn't wash the dishes from last night?"

Her eyes widened. "DNA? You guys are almost as good as Mark Harmon."

"Don't touch anything you think he might have touched. I'll have a crime scene detective come in, and you can let him do his thing."

"Will there be a reward?"

"I don't think so," Jack said.

"Well I want my twenty back at least."

* * * *

Jack and Liddell followed Officer Hurt down the street to a faded-green '74 VW. The car matched the description Freyda gave, except for the dog inside this one. A black-and-white border collie jumped at the driver's window, snarling and showing impressive teeth.

"I'll call the car's owner to see if the dog belongs to them. I've called Animal Control," Officer Hurt said and checked his cell phone, typed some text, smiled, and put the phone back in his pocket.

Wires were hanging under the broken steering column cover. "Be sure no one touches anything before Crime Scene gets what they need."

"You really think this car is involved in the murder?" Hurt asked.

"It's possible," Jack said. "Call me if you get anything from the owner."

To Jack's disappointment, the officer replied, "I don't think they'll know anything except the car got stolen." He checked the screen of his cell phone again.

"Do you have something else important to do, Officer Hurt?"

As if on cue the officer's phone dinged, indicating a new message or email.

Hurt said, "I got off an hour ago, Detective Murphy. My wife's pregnant, and she's sick, sir. I'm sorry but I didn't think I'd be here this long."

Jack said, "That's the job you signed up for. Wait until Animal Control gets the dog. Give me the owner's information and be sure Crime Scene gets the car. Contact the owner and tell them it will probably be towed and held for a day or so. Tell them I'll want to talk to them. Turn in your supplementary report, and you can go home. I'll tell your sergeant I dismissed you."

Officer Hurt handed Jack a page from his notebook. "The car owner's name is Samantha Lee."

Jack saw Hurt had written down the offense report number, the victim's name, address, and phone number. Hurt probably hadn't called because he didn't want to get any more involved and not get to leave. It was understandable given his wife's condition.

"If someone relieves you before Animal Control gets here, be sure they tell Animal Control to keep the dog by itself. Don't hurt it. Got it?"

"You think the dog has something to do with the murder?" Hurt asked.

Jack couldn't decide if Hurt was being a smartass or was really that dense. "Officer Hurt, did you understand the orders I just gave you, or do I need to write them down?" He shouldn't have needed to say the dog might have a chip, or that the dog had left evidence all over the car so why not on the victim or his transportation prior to stealing the VW.

"I got it, Detective Murphy," Hurt said.

Jack and Liddell headed back to the Coffee Shop when he heard loud cursing behind them. He turned in time to see Officer Hurt on the ground and the collie bouncing off his chest. It was coming their way fast.

"What the hell?" Liddell said as the dog flew past and turned down the alleyway.

Officer Hurt ran after the dog. "Sorry, detectives. I was just checking to see if the car was unlocked. I wanted to get the registration papers for my supplementary report, and the damn thing jumped me."

Jack chased after the dog and rounded the corner to find it sitting beside the body with its haunches up against the dead guy, teeth bared at the crime scene techs, who had wisely backed away.

"I guess we know whose dog it is," Liddell said.

Hurt put his hand on the butt of his gun, and Jack put a hand on Hurt's arm. "Do not shoot the dog, Officer Hurt. Animal Control will be here and I need the dog."

Officer Hurt said, "Well, I guess you don't need me here then."

Jack said, "Get the owner of the Coffee Shop and have her ID the car. Her name is Mrs. Rademacher."

"This is my district, detective. I know who she is." Hurt turned to leave.

Jack yelled at the retreating officer's back, "The dog does not get hurt. I need it segregated from other animals."

Officer Hurt raised an arm and waved without looking back.

Liddell muttered, "You old softie."

"Bite me, Bigfoot."

Jack's cell phone buzzed. He answered, and the dispatcher said, "Jack, you and Liddell are wanted behind the old sheet metal works off Fountain Avenue. That's near the railroad tracks by Pigeon Creek."

"We're kind of busy here," Jack said. "Call Captain Franklin and tell him what's going on. Ask him to call someone in. I need Liddell here."

"Captain Franklin is the one that said to send you and Blanchard."

"Okay. We'll leave here in five or ten minutes," Jack said.

"Captain Franklin said to go now, Jack. There's multiple dead, and—"

Jack hung up on her and nudged Liddell toward their car. "We need to go."

"What's up, pod'na?"

"When it rains, it pours, Bigfoot."

"Another murder?"

Jack said, "Give me the keys."

Liddell tossed them over, and they got in the Crown Vic. "Who's going to work this one?" Liddell asked. It was Saturday. They were the only detectives working.

Jack said, "Sergeant Walker is pulling double duty here I guess until they call someone in from home. We're going to a multiple victim scene, authority Captain Franklin. I'll drive. I want to get there before the earth cools. You drive like an old maid."

"Do not," Liddell said.

Chapter 4

Jack drove west toward Fountain Avenue and called dispatch from his cell phone. "Have the crime scene officer at the Fountain Avenue scene call my cell phone."

Seconds later his phone rang.

"What have you got?" Jack asked.

The female officer's voice was trembling. "This is Joanie Ryan. God, Jack! Just get here quick." The call ended.

Jack stepped up his speed and was in the area in just minutes. He crossed Pigeon Creek and drove over railroad tracks. A police car was blocking a gravel drive off to his left. It backed up to let Jack turn in. Two more police cars were parked a hundred feet ahead blocking three news vans with dish antennae raised like ants surrounding their prey.

A uniformed officer was talking to the driver of the nearest news van, making gestures that brooked no argument. The van's driver pulled off in the grass, and the officer moved on to the next van, shooing them away while motioning to Jack with the other hand to proceed ahead.

Jack squeezed around the news vans and drove over the grass to get behind the building. Even in dead of winter with the car windows up he could smell the stench that was Pigeon Creek. Just ahead, yellow-and-black crime scene tape was strung up in two semicircle perimeters, one inside the other, radiating from a docking bay. Inside the smallest perimeter was a fourteen-wheeler tractor-trailer. Inside the larger perimeter was an ambulance, another police car, and the motor patrol sergeant's car.

Jack stopped outside the string of crime scene tape. He got out of the car and felt a presence behind him. Claudine Setera, investigative reporter for Channel Six, was a few feet away and running to catch up.

Claudine was mid-twenties, dark hair worn down on her shoulders, dark eyes, and immaculate olive skin. Her news-anchor figure was partially hidden by her tight fur-lined jacket. She was as capable and treacherous as she was beautiful. She wasn't supposed to be inside the crime scene tape.

Jack and Liddell ignored her and ducked under the crime scene tape. They didn't slow their pace.

"Hello, Jack. Liddell," Claudine said, ducking under the tape and jogging to keep up. "Can you slow down please?"

They stopped abruptly, and Claudine bumped into Liddell.

"Where's your cameraman?" Liddell asked.

"Where's the knife?" Jack asked.

Claudine let out a laugh that was somewhere between a bray and a snort. Her laugh wouldn't be a deal breaker on a blind date, but it would take the steam out of your "little engine that could."

"No knife," she said. "Want to pat me down?" She struck a flirtatious pose.

"Be nice," Jack said.

"I am being nice, Jack," she said and batted her eyelashes.

At almost zero degrees, the flirting didn't work. Mr. One-Eye was safely tucked away from the cold and didn't want to play.

"You're not supposed to be inside the crime scene, Claudine," Jack said. "Whoever let you come back here is fired or under arrest."

"Or both," Liddell added.

"You know me." She smiled, and out came the reporter's notebook. The kind with a steel wire spiral at the top used to hold the pages together, or as a garrote. The journalist's motto was "Always be prepared to lie."

Jack did know her. In Jack's world there were two different sets of constitutional rights, one for law enforcement and one for the news media. If a law enforcement officer stood on someone's porch and filmed through the window of their house, they could be sued and criminal charges filed. The news media did this routinely and called it "informing the public."

"C'mon Jack. It's cold and I'm freezing. Give me something and I promise to go away." Claudine tried for a pout that came out as a grimace with her teeth chattering.

"Okay," Jack said. He reached inside his coat, took out a business card, and handed it to her.

"Okay what?" she asked, looking at the card.

"Okay. I gave you something," Jack said. "Now go away." He caught the eye of one of the uniformed officers and inclined his head toward the journalist. The officer came trotting over and corralled her.

"Is the body by the University of Evansville involved with these multiple deaths?" she called out as she was being led away. "What can you tell my viewers? How did he die?"

Jack said, "Who says it was a male victim?"

"I have sources, Jack. I just need you to confirm...."

"Since when did you confirm anything?" Jack said under his breath as the uniformed officer escorted a disappointed Claudine Setera out of the crime scene.

When she was out of earshot Liddell asked, "How does Claudine know there's more than one death here, pod'na?"

"I'll give you one guess."

"Well, there are too many leaks to pick just one. Larry Jansen, Deputy Chief Dick, and three hundred other officers and civilians and their friends and families and..."

"Shut up, Bigfoot," Jack said. "It has to be Double Dick. I'm surprised she wasn't carrying him in a papoose baby thingy."

"It's called a baby carrier, Jack," Liddell said. "Marcie got one for Jane. It's kinda neat." Liddell was a new father. Marcie had picked out the name Jane. Jane Blanchard. Jack had pouted for a while that they hadn't named the baby Jackie or Jaclyn.

"Who ever heard of a yeti named Jane?" Jack asked.

"Are you still sore? It's been a month, pod'na. If the baby had been a boy, I would have insisted on a different name."

"Yeah?"

"Yeah. I was thinking Boris, or..."

"Just shut up," Jack said.

They ducked under the inner perimeter tape. The factory's service parking was vacant except for the lone tractor-trailer where crime scene tech Joanie Ryan waited for them. Joanie, for all of her one year of experience, was in charge of this crime scene. Her eyes were red-rimmed, and the tops of her cheeks were chafed from the cold, or from rubbing her eyes with the sleeve of her coveralls.

"Are you okay, Joanie?" Jack asked.

"I've never... I can't... Jesus, Jack!"

"Does Sergeant Walker have someone coming to help you out?"

"He does," she said.

"Show me what you have," Jack said.

She pointed to a brass padlock lying on the ground. "The security guy for the factory called dispatch forty-five minutes ago to report an abandoned truck. He thought it was suspicious because this place used to make some kind of vehicle parts for the military."

Jack remembered the news. The factory closed due to a drawdown in military troops the last couple of years. More than a hundred people had lost their jobs.

The outside of the truck and trailer were coated with frost. The back doors of the trailer showed smudges in the grime and frost from when the officers opened the doors.

Joanie continued. "The responding officer called Sergeant Mattingly when he saw that." She indicated an uneven crust of something frozen and brownish that had leaked from the bottom of one of the doors.

"Is that blood?" Liddell asked.

"It wasn't, but it looked like it. Sergeant Mattingly arrived and cut the lock off the door," she said.

"Well, let's have a look," Jack said.

Joanie pulled the door on the right open wide. The sickening smell of feces and urine washed over them. The sky was overcast but with just enough light for Jack to make out forms of literally dozens of unmoving bodies.

"I got here ten minutes ago. Sergeant Walker called me in on account of the other murder. Sergeant Mattingly had already gone inside to see if anyone was alive. They weren't. I closed the doors to keep the smell down and to keep out people like that reporter you were talking to. I called the coroner."

"When will Tony get here?"

She shrugged. "Sergeant Walker said you can take a quick peek but not to let you go inside. I've taken some pictures from outside, but no one's been inside except Sergeant Mattingly."

Jack could see streaks and smears of blood on the edges of the door where someone had tried to claw it open. The gummy material coated the bottom of the door and the threshold. Three bodies—two men and a woman—lay just inside. Dozens more were scattered across the floor. A pile of bodies filled one corner in the back.

Jack took out a small flashlight and trained the beam on the nearest body. It was a huge man. He lay on his side facing the door, one arm behind his back, the other spread out in front. He wasn't wearing a coat. His long-sleeve button-up shirt sported two bloody holes in the front of his chest. Blood pooled around him on the floor. He died right there. Was stabbed, fell down, bled out.

Next to him a woman was spread-eagle on her stomach, arms up over her head as if she was swimming. Her coat was also missing. Her head was twisted at an unnatural angle. She had on a man's black-and-red plaid shirt with the cuffs and neck buttoned up. She wore skintight jeans and cheap half boots. There were no visible injuries other than the broken neck.

Another man's body completed this grouping of the dead. He was curled into a fetal position near the dead woman, arms around his knees, knees tucked under his chin. He wore military-type pants, combat boots, wool shirt, but no coat. He may have died from exposure.

Jack put the light on the woman's face. She was dark-skinned with thick, dark hair and dark wide-open eyes. He moved the light down her arms. Her hands were clinched and bloody. The skin on the tips of her fingers was shredded to the bone. Jack trained the light on the threshold. In the goop, he saw a fingernail.

"Joanie, can we open the other door?" Jack asked.

"You don't want to do that," she said firmly and showed him some digital photos she had shot behind the door. "That was their toilet."

"Okay, thanks," Jack said and turned his attention to the guy in semi-military clothing and no coat. Something glinted in the man's hand. "Joanie, can you tell what that is?"

She moved up behind Jack's shoulder while Jack directed the beam onto the dead man's hand.

"Looks like a knife," she said.

"A military knife, pod'na," Liddell added.

"Let me get a picture," Joanie said.

Jack shined the light around the three bodies and could see the footprints and smears in the toilet goo and blood on the floor. Down inside the trailer, several single bodies slumped against the walls. Larger groupings huddled together. He didn't see any other signs of violence.

"These three must have been trying to get out and got into a fight," Joanie said.

"Possibly," Jack said. "If the guy with the knife killed these two, he did it quick and clean. She was clawing at the door." Jack pointed at the fingernail stuck on the threshold.

Liddell said, "The woman's neck looks broken."

Jack said, "I think we know who was driving this truck. Corporal Morris found a key on the body in the alleyway over by the university. The key was stamped ABUS just like this padlock, and we have a car that was stolen about six blocks from here."

"The dead guy parked the truck here, stole a car, drove clear across town, and was killed in an alley. Why?" Joanie asked. She pulled heavy mittens over her latex gloves and tucked her hands under her arms.

"Very astute question, my dear Watson," Liddell said.

Joanie said through chattering teeth, "Why would he leave them here?"

"We answer that question and we'll find the killer," Jack said. "The body was found in the alley beside the Coffee Shop. Walker thinks the guy was killed late last night, and the owner of the shop said she had a customer that left when she closed up. She thought the customer was waiting for someone. He was in the shop an hour and didn't eat or drink anything."

"You think he's connected. The customer, I mean?" Joanie asked, and Jack shrugged.

Jack played the light around inside the trailer. "I don't see any source of heat. Have you checked the truck's cab yet?"

Joanie said, "It's locked. Sergeant Mattingly saw food wrappers and to-go cups on the floorboard."

"I don't see any water bottles or food wrappers back here," Jack said. "I count at least twenty-five bodies. This guy didn't give a shit what kind of shape these people were in when they got to wherever it was they were headed." He wondered how it would have felt to be closed in this dark moving coffin with the smell that was already making his eyes water.

"Who's keeping the crime scene log?" Jack asked.

"Officer Fellwock should be here," she said.

"I had to put him on the perimeter," Sergeant Mattingly said from behind them. "Officers Maxwell and Johnson got here first and talked to the security guy that called it in. They said the hood of the truck was cold and no one was around. They ran the plates, and it came back to a rental company in New Jersey. We tried to call them, but it's a weekend. I used bolt cutters and found what you see there."

Frost still covered the ground, and a number of boot prints with the lug sole pattern of Rocky brand boots were everywhere. He suspected every officer that arrived at the scene had come by to see.

Mattingly saw where Jack's attention was focused. "Those prints will be mine, Fellwock's, Johnson's, and Ryan's. I had to send Fellwock to run off gawkers with camera phones. He'll be back in a minute. Joanie was temporary crime scene log officer. I'll have everyone here do a report."

"I'm not accusing you of doing anything wrong, Sergeant," Jack said.

"I understand," Mattingly said. "Chain of custody can be a bitch."

Joanie slowly played her light over the frozen bodies. "A couple of them back there are naked," she remarked. "I studied this in class. In severe hypothermia cases, some victims feel like they're burning up and take off their clothes. I think they were in here a couple of days, Jack."

"We'll have to wait for the autopsy to be sure," Jack said.

Sergeant Mattingly said, "We don't know how long the truck was parked here either. According to the private security guard, there hasn't been any activity here for a month or longer. He said the security company was hired to check the building's doors a couple of times a day, but he admitted that was hit or miss. He said some of the guys, including himself, would just drive by the front of the building and visually check. He said it was 'possible' that no one had come back here for a week or more. Here's the guy's information." Mattingly handed Liddell a sheet from his notebook.

Trees and thickets of shrubs lined the banks of Pigeon Creek across from where they were. A baseball field and a skateboarding area were over there as well. Behind that were picnic areas with access to Evansville Greenway and paths that ran the length of the creek. It was too cold for anyone to be using the Greenway, but it would be tempting for reporters to set up cameras.

"Can we block the Greenway to foot traffic?" Jack asked.

Mattingly said, "I sent an officer over there."

"Tell the reporters there are snakes in the woods," Jack suggested.

"That'll only scare the snakes." Mattingly's portable crackled, and someone told him a news van was driving across the baseball diamond on the other side of the creek.

"Now there really *are* snakes in the woods," Mattingly said and moved away.

Jack called after him, "Hey Sarge, I told Officer Hurt he could take off and go home to his sick wife."

Mattingly said, "Hurt isn't married."

"That lying little shit," Liddell said.

Jack said, "Shhh. Listen."

They all went quiet, and Jack directed the flashlight at the pile of bodies in the back of the trailer. The fingers of a small hand poked out, and a weak voice said what sounded like, "Poppy."

"Someone's alive!" Jack shouted and hoisted himself into the opening.

Chapter 5

Jack hadn't waited for an ambulance. He and Liddell had loaded the survivor in their car, and Sgt. Mattingly escorted them, Code 3, to Deaconess Hospital Emergency. Sgt. Mattingly was needed back at the scene and left. A few minutes later Captain Franklin showed up at the ER.

"I've called in more detectives. Detective Chapman will be your liaison. He will keep you updated on anything they find and pass on your requests."

"Who is taking the murder by the university?" Jack asked.

"Detectives Melton and Jordan will take the truck scene. Chapman will stay at headquarters as the hub. He'll be available if we need to pull him. You two will be lead on all of this. Do you need a detective to take the coffee shop murder?"

It was an early Saturday morning, but Captain Franklin was dressed in his usual black suit without a speck of lint or a wrinkle, starched white shirt, and red tie as if he were going to a business meeting. *Commendable. Anal.*

"We need some guys to start doing neighborhood checks," Jack said. "We're already working that scene, so we might as well stay with it. Is Deputy Chief Dick coming in, Captain?"

Jack had no more than said this when he heard Deputy Chief Richard Dick's voice coming from the ER registration desk, telling the nurse who he was in the condescending tone he reserved for those beneath him. Seconds later the Dickster strode into the ER treatment area.

If Captain Franklin was a bit obsessive with his clothing, Double Dick was a clothing Nazi. Full dress uniform, chest full of ribbons, go-to-prom shiny shoes, and the ever-present eight-point cap with gold braids adorning the bill. He was, of course, in full dress uniform now in anticipation of a Kodak moment. Double Dick was also what the troops called a media whore. If a reporter was nearby, Dick was always ready to be interviewed.

"Where are we?" Dick asked no one in particular.

Liddell said, deadpan, "We're in the emergency room at Deaconess Hospital, sir."

Dick didn't smile. He crossed his arms and waited.

Franklin nodded toward a treatment room with the door closed. "We're still waiting for the ER doctor to come out, Deputy Chief."

"Only one survivor?" Double Dick asked, but it was obvious by the excited dance in his eyes and the twitch of his upper lip that he already knew the answer.

The word "survivor" set Jack's teeth on edge. He'd seen a lot of violent murders, but he'd never experienced anything as callous on a large scale such as this. The victims were abandoned, locked up in a remote area where even if they screamed and kicked the walls of the trailer, there was no chance they would be heard and rescued. They had been left, murdered by the negligence of the truck's driver. That the driver himself was killed was little compensation.

"How many deaths?" the Dick asked.

"Thirty-one at last count, Deputy Chief," Captain Franklin answered. "Crime Scene is working with the coroner's office to document, tag, and bag the bodies."

Dick seemed to swell up. "Don't you think I know how this works, Captain?"

"Yes sir," Captain Franklin said.

"I mean, I am the Commander of the Investigations Unit," Dick said loudly, but no one seemed to notice.

"The call I received indicated higher casualties," Dick said to Jack. He sounded disappointed.

"What number did Claudine give you?" Jack asked.

Before Dick could stop the words, he said, "Miss Setera told me a trailer full of bod..." He cut the statement short and gave Jack a sharp look. "Detective Murphy, your job is to catch this maniac, not to question me. My job is to liaise with the news media and keep them friendly. Claudine Setera is an important part of the news community and a friend of this department."

Deputy Chief Richard Dick had earned the nickname Double Dick not just because of his two first names—Richard Dick—but because he was known to repeatedly punish someone for a perceived transgression against the department or any personal slight to himself. Hence the name Double Dick.

The door to the treatment room opened, and a doctor emerged from the patient's room, calling for a nurse.

"Talk to me, Doctor," Double Dick said.

The doctor stepped around Double Dick and went directly to Jack. "Hi'ya, Jack. *Short time* no see." He patted Jack's arm. "You're a shit-magnet, buddy. It just follows you around. You're like a can of 'whoop-ass' dragging the can around. You're like..."

Jack stopped the doctor from going on. "How is he, Doc?"

"It's a miracle the boy's alive," the doctor said. "He's suffering from hypothermia, frostbite, dehydration, malnutrition. We're bringing his temperature up slowly, and we've got him on an IV to get his fluids up. He'll be with us..."

Jack held three fingers up where Double Dick couldn't see.

"For at least...well, I estimate three days. Maybe as much as a week," the doctor said, and Jack nodded. "I'll be able to give you a more accurate assessment tomorrow morning. He's going to ICU tonight."

Jack raised his eyebrows at the doctor and mouthed "No visitors."

The doctor continued. "Of course, I will have to insist on no visitors except with my express approval. No phone calls and absolutely no news media."

The disappointment on Double Dick's face was obvious. There would be no pictures of Dick taken with the survivor.

Dick said, "Doctor, I'm the deputy chief in charge of this investigation. Are you telling me I can't see a witness to a mass murder?"

"Jack is the lead investigator, am I right, Deputy?" the doctor said.

"It's Deputy Chief. Jack may be the lead but..." Dick said, and the doctor interrupted him.

"This kid doesn't need a bunch of people talking to him right now. Jack's the one that brought him in. Maybe Jack can see him in a bit—for a few minutes. The kid doesn't need any unnecessary stimulation."

Dick's jaw worked as he thought of something to say.

The doctor ignored him and said to Jack, "He may have brain damage." He said this while casting his eyes toward the deputy chief. "I've ordered a psych consult, and of course we'll monitor him closely."

Jack had just worked a case where a person of interest had been dumped in the icy Ohio River. In that case the person had severe hypothermia and had the symptoms the doc had just described. In this case the doctor was deliberately laying the diagnosis on a little thick for Dick's benefit.

Captain Franklin said, "Deputy Chief, I think we should let Jack take care of interviewing the boy. I'm sure you're needed to monitor the entire situation since we have multiple scenes. Decisions will need to be made, sir."

Deputy Chief Dick picked at a piece of imaginary lint on his uniform jacket. "Captain Franklin, I'll leave this to you, but we want to be informed the minute we can talk to him. The very minute." He didn't wait for a response and swept out of the treatment area.

After Double Dick left, Liddell asked, "Was he using the royal 'we'? Or did he mean the news media?"

"That's enough of that, Detective Blanchard," Captain Franklin said.

"Yeah. I'm ashamed of you, Bigfoot," Jack said.

"Good one," the doctor said.

"When can I talk to him?" Jack asked.

The doctor looked cautiously at Captain Franklin.

Jack said, "Go ahead, Doctor."

"He's in pretty good health considering what he's been through. He is mildly hypothermic and definitely dehydrated, but both are not life-threatening. He has the beginnings of frostbite on some of his fingers, and that will bear watching. He hasn't spoken or answered any of our questions. If you can get him to talk, we need to get a medical history."

"You talk to him, Jack," Captain Franklin said. "I'll check on the progress and call Chief Pope back. Liddell comes with me."

"Deputy Chief Dick?" Jack asked.

"I'll talk to Chief Pope and suggest Dick take charge of any news release," Franklin said.

"Thanks, Captain," Jack said.

"Double thanks, Captain," Liddell said.

Chapter 6

Jack followed the doctor into a room that smelled of hospital antiseptic and freshly laundered linen. The temperature in typical hospital rooms is a standard seventy degrees, but this one was cranked up to full sauna. The boy that Jack had pulled from the pile of bodies was propped up in the bed with a Bair Hugger blanket wrapped around his upper body and connected to an air/heat pump. A heavy salve had been applied to the tip of his nose. An IV line was taped to the back of one hand.

The boy looked to be no more than ten years old. His skin, hair, and eyes were dark-colored. He wasn't emaciated like the doctor had described, but he was thin, like most kids.

"Hello," Jack said.

The boy didn't react except to pull the blanket tighter.

"You saved his life, Jack."

The boy's eyes grew wide, but he still said nothing.

He understands us.

"Doc, I need a couple of favors."

"When don't you, Jack?"

"I do need you to keep him a couple of days for real. Maybe longer. I'll need access to him, but I don't want anyone except medical staff getting near him. Don't notify anyone yet. Can you do that?"

"In other words, you want me to lie and put him in a private room?"

"Yeah."

"And you don't want me to notify Child Protective Services."

"Yeah."

"You'll owe me," the doctor said.

"And I need you to do something else for me," Jack said.

"That's three favors."

Jack said, "Until I know what we're dealing with, I don't want his condition released by anyone to anyone. Can you pass the word to your staff to keep mum?"

"Well, we have a privacy policy that will keep most of the employees from talking, but I can't promise you anything."

"Thanks, Doc. I'd give you a Junior G-man's badge, but I'm fresh out."

The doctor said, "I expect a bottle of McCallan's 50-year."

"Not a problem."

"Let me know when you're through with him," the doctor said. "I'll be out here treating a gunshot wound, two broken bones, and a stab wound from last night."

"Bar fight?" Jack asked.

"Domestic dispute. The wife beat his car with a hammer, and started beating him. He ran to the kitchen, stabbed her with a butcher knife, and chased her to the bedroom. She got a gun and shot him twice. Now they're back in love and refusing to press charges."

"You always hurt the one you love," Jack said.

The doctor left the room, and Jack sat on the side of the boy's bed.

"I know you understand me," Jack said.

"You are a detective?" the boy asked.

"Yeah. I'm a detective. Feel up to talking?"

The boy started to answer, but the door to the room opened again and a nurse entered with two plastic mugs of something steaming. To Jack she said, "Coffee for the hero. You look like you can use it."

"A compliment and insult in the same sentence," Jack said. "Good for you."

She smiled and handed the other mug to the boy. "This is chicken broth. You need to sip it." She imitated holding a cup to her lips and taking small sips. "Understand?"

The boy took the mug but didn't answer.

"If you can keep this down, we'll discuss food," the nurse said. "Food." She made like she was putting something in her mouth and chewing. "Okay?"

The boy just looked at her.

Jack said, "I'll make sure he sips it."

"I'm sure you can get him to do whatever you want. You have a way of doing that. How have you been, Jack?"

The nurse seemed familiar to Jack, but he couldn't put a name with the face.

"Tammy," she said. "You don't remember me, do you? I moved here from Ohio a few years ago. We met at a party at Two Jakes Marina."

Her words said they'd merely met, but her eyes said they'd done more. "Tammy. Of course," Jack said, pretending to remember.

She picked up the call button and clipped it to the boy's pillow. "If you need anything, hon, just push the red button. I'll take good care of you. And don't let this guy talk your pants off." She smiled at Jack when she said the latter.

The boy smiled at Nurse Tammy from Ohio, and she patted his leg.

"Sip the broth. It's hot and you need it." She turned and left.

Jack watched the boy watching the nurse leave the room. He could swear the boy's face flushed. He was all boy. His mind was working just fine.

"I'll make you a deal," Jack said. "You answer some questions, and I'll buy you a cheeseburger. Lots of cheese, bacon, pickles, the whole works."

The boy set the drink on his side table. "Can I have the cheeseburger now please, detective?"

"Hospital food's not my favorite either. I'm Detective Murphy. What's your name?"

The boy sat up straight and offered a small hand. "Jose Alejandro Bogran. I'm nine years old. You're the one that found me."

"I am," Jack said.

The boy released the blanket and wrapped his arms around Jack's neck, spilling Jack's coffee. He hugged Jack fiercely and said, "Thank you, Detective Murphy."

Jack patted the boy's back. "You're very welcome. You're safe now, Jose."

"Call me Joe," Jose said.

"You can call me Jack."

The boy released his grip on Jack and sat back against his pillows. "No. That is disrespectful. I cannot, Detective Murphy."

"Okay... I'll call you Joe," Jack said. "Like my mom always said, 'You can call me anything as long as you call me for dinner.'"

Joe asked, "Why would your mother call you something that is not your name when she calls you to eat?"

I'm getting old. "Never mind. Do you feel up to talking?"

Joe didn't answer.

Jack got up, pulled a rolling stool over to the bed, and set his coffee on the bedside table. He'd ask something simpler. He picked up a napkin and took out an ink pen. "Can you spell your name for me Joe?"

Joe did.

"Were you traveling alone?"

"With my grandfather. I think I will not see my grandfather again." Tears welled in Joe's eyes, but he didn't cry. He breathed slowly through his nose, his lips clamped tightly shut. He got it under control and said, "I heard the nurses and doctor. They called me 'the survivor'."

"I'm truly sorry, Joe," Jack said.

Joe sipped the hot broth, and he seemed to go away.

"What was your grandfather's name?" Jack asked.

"I was named after my grandfather. We are the same."

"Do you know where you are?"

"In a hospital," Joe answered.

"I mean, do you know what city and state?"

"The nurses say 'this never happens in Evansville.' We are in Evansville. I don't know what state. We are in America."

"That's right, Joe. You're in Evansville, Indiana, in the US."

"I studied geography in school. We learned about America. Indiana means 'land of the Indiana.' It was part of your Northwest Territory. It is where much corn is grown. Yes?"

"That's right," Jack said. He had forgotten the history associated with the naming of the state, but it sounded right. "Where are you from? Where did you live before you came here?"

"Puerto Lempira."

"Where is that?" Jack asked.

"Honduras," Joe said. "Puerto Lempira is a small village on the sea."

Like many Americans, geography was never Jack's strong suit, but he knew Honduras was somewhere in Central America near El Salvador and Nicaragua or thereabouts. This kid had come a long way to end up in Evansville locked in the back of a semitrailer with dozens of dead.

"Did you know the other people traveling with you?" Jack asked.

"Only my grandfather. Grandfather wanted me to go to college in America. He said we would work here in America."

"What kind of work did your grandfather do?"

"He owned a business at home, but now it is gone," Joe said.

"Joe, what was your destination? Where were you and your grandfather going to work? What city? State?"

Joe didn't hesitate this time. "A small city like Puerto Lempira. Grandfather said our new home would be on a lake as big as an ocean."

"Do you know the name of the city?"

"Fort Gracious in Michigan," Joe said.

Michigan made sense to Jack if the truck was coming from Texas. It would possibly pass through Indiana. He'd never heard of Fort Gracious.

"Did your grandfather know any of the people traveling with you?"

"I was told..." Joe's words trailed off. He seemed uncertain what to say.

"You were told what, Joe?" Jack prompted.

"Grandfather said I wasn't to look at them."

"Who weren't you supposed to look at?" Jack asked.

"You saved me, Detective Murphy. Please don't ask these questions. My grandfather said not to speak of this."

"I have to ask these questions, Joe. It's my job. Understand?"

Joe said nothing.

"A fight broke out near the doors. Did you see it?"

Nothing.

"Are the people who were in the fight the ones your grandfather told you not to look at?"

Joe put the broth down, pulled the blanket tighter, and looked toward the door to the room.

Jack said, "I'm trying to help you, but you're going to have to talk to me, Joe. I need to know some things. You understand that, right? Can you help me?"

Joe raised his face. "You saved me. I will try, Detective Murphy."

Jack decided to go at it from a different direction. "You can nod or shake your head instead of talking. Were the people you weren't supposed to look at men?"

"No."

"Men and women. Good. How many men?" Jack asked.

Joe held up two fingers.

"Women?"

Joe didn't answer.

"Was there a woman with the two men?"

"Yes."

"Were they in a fight?"

"Yes," Joe said.

"Were they fighting other people, or were they fighting each other?" Jack asked.

Joe kept his eye on the door. He was clearly uncomfortable talking about this, but Jack had to know what went on in the trailer.

"The man with the knife," Jack said. "Did he kill the man and woman?"

"Grandfather said don't look," Joe answered.

"Did you hear what they were fighting over?"

Joe picked up the broth and sipped at it slowly. Jack could hear the boy's stomach growl and gurgle in retaliation of the invasion of sustenance.

Joe warmed his hands on the mug and changed the subject. "We traveled for many days from Honduras to Mexico. We walked sometimes for a long way. Sometimes we rode in the backs of pickups." His eyes lit briefly when he spoke of this, as if it were an adventure. "My grandfather arranged transportation to America, but we had to leave Puerto Lempira very quickly and take nothing. Not even grandfather's vehicle. We were smuggled out in the trunk of his friend's car. It was very warm for most of the journey, but it was very cold when we reached the border.

"The men we met there said they would give us blankets and food in the trucks. They lied. The men took everything from us except our papers. Some people had hidden American money in their shoes. You can't eat money."

"I'm truly sorry, Joe. It was wrong to treat you that way," Jack said.

A pained expression crossed Joe's face. "I will never see my grandfather or Shadow again."

"Shadow?"

"She is my dog." His eyes came alive again. "When the men put us in the truck, they said Shadow could not come." He raised a small hand and made a gun out of his finger and thumb. "One man said he would shoot Shadow if I did not get in the truck. I said, 'Do not hurt my dog.' Grandfather whispered something to the man, and the man said to the others to put Shadow in the front. A different man said he will give Shadow back to me when we arrive at Fort Gracious."

The fire seemed to go out of him, and he slumped back against the pillows.

Jack held a hand a couple of feet above the floor. "Is Shadow a female dog, black and white, yea big?"

"Yes!" Joe sat up quickly. "She has curly hair. One ear is black, the other is white. Her tail is bent, and the tip of one ear is missing. I told her to ride with the man and not to bite him. The man liked her."

Jack didn't want to get the boy's hopes up. "Would you recognize the man that said he would give Shadow back when you reached Michigan? The one that liked Shadow?"

"Do you have Shadow? Did the man hurt her? Is she here?"

Jack visualized the dog from the stolen car. It was a female, black and white, kind of a border collie mixed mutt, and the last few inches of her tail might have been bent. He definitely remembered seeing a difference in her ears. One of them didn't come to a point.

"Joe, the dog I found is unharmed, but it might not be Shadow. I have other important things to ask. Okay?"

"I know it is her," Joe said, and Jack hoped that was true for the kid's sake.

"Let me show you a picture. Tell me if this person is familiar. Can you do that?"

"I will try."

Jack showed Joe two close-up face shots of the dead man from the Coffee Shop.

Joe said, "That is him! He is the one that took Shadow."

"Was anyone with this man when he took Shadow to the front of the truck?" Jack asked. Freyda said she'd possibly seen two people in the VW. It might have been the driver and the dog, or two people. The dog may have been in the back seat.

It would make more sense to have more than one driver to trade off on the long drive from Mexico to Michigan. Maybe Mrs. Rademacher's customer was the other driver. Maybe one had tried to quit. The two had gotten into a dispute and one killed the other. Maybe there was another body waiting to be found.

Joe said, "Five men were loading the trucks with people. I counted three trucks. The men had long guns. The one you showed me had no gun."

Jack asked, "Did you see a man about this tall talking to the guy in the photo?" He stood and held his open hand at chin height. "He would have been older than me and wearing a cowboy hat and dark-colored long coat."

Joe shook his head. "It was dark, Detective Murphy. I only know I saw guns like on television. The kind soldiers carry. You must take me to Shadow." Joe pulled the covers back, swung his legs over the side of the bed, and winced as he put his feet on the cold tile floor.

Jack helped Joe back onto the bed. The boy's legs were stick-like, and even with his dark skin you could see they were covered in bruises and healing cuts. The soles of his feet had scars of old burns.

"Where did you get those burns and bruises, Joe?"

Joe didn't answer.

"How long were you and your grandfather in that trailer?"

"I slept three times. It was always dark, and the sound of the truck made me sleepy."

"Did you ever stop anywhere to use the toilet, get food or water?"

"No," Joe said. "The truck stopped many times and the driver would knock on the wall and warn us to stay quiet."

"Are you sure it was this man?" Jack held up the photo of the driver.

"I don't know, Detective Murphy. It was a man's voice. American. But the picture you showed me is the man that took Shadow."

"How long was the truck stopped before I found you?"

"A long time. Many people were sleeping."

Already dead, never to wake again in this world.

"I was scared that we would never be let out. Grandfather told me this wasn't true. He was keeping me warm and covering me with coats."

This explained the missing coats from some of the bodies.

"You heard the fight near the doors, Joe. Tell me again about the fight. Why were they arguing?"

"I could not hear their words," Joe said, but Jack could tell this wasn't true.

"What did you hear, Joe?"

Joe took a deep breath and let it out. "The truck wasn't moving, and I could hear a woman and man were angry with someone. I heard screaming. It got quiet. Grandfather told me to sleep. Someone brought extra coats to me. I went to sleep and now I am here."

"Okay," Jack said. The boy was suffering from hypothermia, so he probably hallucinated some of what he was telling.

"Where is your family, Joe? Do you have someone in the United States?"

The boy said quietly, "I have no one. You will send me back to Honduras. Grandfather told me this is true."

"I can contact your family there, Joe."

"No family now. There was just Grandfather."

Jack was sad for the boy. He would undoubtedly be deported, and Jack had a rudimentary idea of what that entailed. He'd taken an in-service class at the police department regarding the new immigration rules, but had only half listened. Evansville wasn't exactly a town to attract immigrants. If he couldn't deport the mayor and city council, what good was the class.

Jack couldn't think of anything else to ask Joe. "Do what the doctors and nurses say. I'll be back soon. I promise. No one will take you anywhere unless they notify me first. Okay?"

Jack could feel the boy's eyes on him as he left the room. He walked outside in the ER drive to make some calls. He failed to notice the woman watching from a doorway down the hall. When Jack was gone, Claudine Setera and her cameraman entered Joe's room.

"Hello," she said.

Chapter 7

Liddell's Crown Vic pulled into the emergency room drive when Jack came outside. The Crown Vic rose several inches when Liddell lifted his ample frame out.

"Good timing, Bigfoot. I just finished talking to Joe. You get anything?" Jack asked.

"Joe?"

"I can't remember his entire name, so it's Joe for now," Jack said, and his cell phone vibrated. It was Franklin.

"Yes, Captain."

"Liddell's on his way to you," Captain Franklin said.

"He's here."

Franklin said, "Tell me about the boy, and I'll fill you in on what we found."

"I'm going on speakerphone, Captain." Jack punched an icon on the phone. "He's a nine-year-old from Honduras. He will probably be able to be moved in a week or so," Jack lied. He didn't want to keep Captain Franklin in the dark, because he was one of the good guys, but what he didn't know wouldn't hurt him.

Jack said, "He was traveling with his grandfather. He has burns and bruises all over his lower legs and the bottoms of his feet. He heard an argument after the truck stopped here. A woman and some men were near the doors of the trailer where we saw the homicides, but he says he didn't see the fight. He says he didn't know anyone in the trailer, but he also said his grandfather said not to talk about any of this.

"His grandfather sheltered him, and he went to sleep. Grandpa probably saved his life." Jack said this, but it didn't jibe with what his gut told him at the scene. If Joe was being sheltered by Grandpa, and even covered with extra coats, it didn't explain the other bodies piled on top of the boy and the grandfather. Someone else must have dragged the bodies over and piled them up.

"Spell the boy and grandfather's name for me," Captain Franklin said.

Jack reached into his pocket and pulled out the napkin on which he'd jotted the boy's name. He gave it to Captain Franklin.

"The victim from the Coffee Shop is at the morgue," Captain Franklin advised. "Dr. John has been called in. Lilly Caskins brought an intern with her and is still performing triage at the truck scene. Some will go to the morgue freezers; the bulk will go to Swonder Ice Rink. The chief got the mayor to agree to close the ice rink until we can sort this out. I called the State Police, and they've agreed to put a rush on any lab stuff we collect. The sheriff volunteered some deputies to stand guard at Swonder Ice Rink."

Jack groaned inwardly. He'd hoped to keep the investigation in-house, but this plan was going to shit quickly. The more agencies that were involved, the more supervisors involved, the more supervisors, the more political interference. Soon there would be meeting after meeting, and handwringing, the gnashing of teeth, and nothing would get done.

"Captain, we can handle this by ourselves," Jack said.

"No can do, Jack," Captain Franklin said. "Joanie Ryan found some identification cards on the bodies. Green cards and passports. She thinks the green cards are forged."

"Makes sense, Captain. If they were legitimate green cards they would have passed through a border checkpoint legally. And they wouldn't be traveling locked in the back of a truck for God knows how long."

"I've notified someone in Immigration. Maybe ICE will be able to help you put names to the bodies," Captain Franklin said. ICE is the acronym for Immigration and Customs Enforcement, which replaced the former INS, or Immigration and Naturalization Service. INS was eaten up by Homeland Security, as were other agencies that it was believed would work more efficiently under the same roof. The mission was the same except now ICE had more bite to their bark.

"We'd better be prepared to be in the crosshairs of every news agency in the country," Jack said.

"In any case, the survivor is Honduran. He's in the country illegally, and police SOP and the law says we contact the State Department and notify the Honduran Consulate."

"I'm not ready to do that, Captain," Jack said. "I showed him a photo of the victim by the Coffee Shop, and he identified the man as the driver of the truck. I need him to identify his grandfather's body. Plus the ER doctor won't release him for several days. He's nine years old, Captain. He's convinced that if he's sent back to Honduras he'll be killed, and we both know that he'll be sent back. I want to do the right thing here," Jack said, "and I think the right thing is to protect the boy for the time being. At least until he's well."

Franklin said, "Jack, we can't sit on this. You know we have to..."

"Captain, the boy had healed burns all over the soles of his feet and some recent burns and bruising on his legs. Someone tortured the kid. Honduras doesn't sound like a healthy environment. Maybe he could request temporary sanctuary?"

"That's not your job, Jack. We just follow the law. You'll have enough on your plate with this investigation."

"I haven't finished interviewing him, Captain. He was feeling ill, and the doctor made me leave. I'll interview him again when he's feeling better."

"Okay, Jack. Maybe we can keep him as a witness, but this isn't my field of expertise, or yours. Anything else?"

Jack said, "We still have to talk to the owner of the stolen car. The VW was reported stolen this morning from a trailer six blocks south of the abandoned tractor-trailer. Joe described the dog we found in the VW down to a crook in its tail and the tip of one ear missing. Joe said the driver or someone else claimed they were going to put the dog in the front cab."

"You can connect the dog to the truck? That's good," Captain Franklin said.

"Walker will check the body for dog hair and check the cab of the truck for a match. We may be able to use the dog and the boy's identification to prove our dead guy was the driver."

"The chief will be glad you're making progress."

"There's a possibility the VW wasn't really stolen. Maybe the owner knew the guy and let him take the car. We'll talk to the owner and show the victim's picture around the trailer park. Maybe someone's seen him before."

"Any idea where they were headed? Please don't tell me the destination was Evansville," Franklin said.

"Joe's grandfather told him they would start a business in a city on the Great Lakes. Grandfather was a business owner in Honduras but had to leave it behind. I haven't found out why they fled, but it may have something to do with the fight in the back of the trailer. He said something like Fort Gracious."

Captain Franklin said, "I think he meant Fort Gratiot. It's in Michigan on the lakes. I've got a cousin that lives near there. You say the grandfather was going to open a business?"

"Yeah."

"Usually these migrant workers pay the mules to bring them here and have to work off the debt. It's slave labor basically."

"He was being optimistic," Jack suggested.

Captain Franklin said, "There's something you have to do right now, Jack. Call FBI Assistant Deputy Director Toomey."

Shit! A month back, Jack had come to the attention of Assistant Deputy Director Toomey when FBI Special Agent Frank Tunney had proposed Jack as a recruit for a newly formed federal joint task force called Unsolved Serial and Organized Crimes. USOC. The Feds love their acronyms. Jack had a different name for the unit—USUCK. The task force was comprised of FBI, Homeland Security, ICE, DEA, ATF, and some other agencies of the kind that existed in dark closets or under beds in the dead of night.

Toomey was recruiting active and retired police detectives and forensic experts from all over the United States. He had presidential authority to conscript any other federal experts he needed. The task force's mandate was twofold. Investigate serial violent crimes—which included organized and international actors—and apprehend or stop said actors. Jack had asked Toomey what the definition of "stop" was and received a blank stare for an answer. Maybe Toomey wasn't so bad after all. Or maybe that was a warning.

"Is USOC taking these cases from us, Captain?" Jack asked.

"They're not taking the cases, they're taking you and Liddell *and* the cases, authority of Chief Pope. You and Liddell are to report to Assistant Deputy Director Toomey this morning for reassignment. He's in charge now. Of course, the Evansville Police Department will be supporting the effort, but as of right now you work for the FBI."

Liddell whispered to Jack, "Should you decide to accept this mission, Detective Murphy, you and your team will be working for the Feds, dealing with cutthroat politicians, media pimps, and earning nothing more than a paid suspension from duty. As usual, if you screw the pooch, the FBI will disavow any knowledge of you. This tape will self-destruct in..."

"Can it, Bigfoot," Jack said. "Captain, we weren't supposed to be sworn in as federal officers until Friday. I don't want to do anything illegal."

Translation: I don't want to work with the Feds.

When Captain Franklin stopped laughing, he said, "I'm going to hang up now, Jack. Call Director Toomey."

"Got it. Call Director Toomey," Jack said, but the connection was gone.

Liddell slapped Jack on the back. "I can't wait to get one of those fancy FBI badges, pod'na." Liddell whipped his badge case from his coat pocket and held it out comically. "Blanchard. FBI."

"Yeah," Jack said. "Can't wait." He didn't like working *with* the Feds, much less working *for* them. He didn't care for the snail pace and the mountains of paperwork and permission slips required to chase down some turd and flush him. When he had to work side by side with a federal investigation, he'd always been able to cut through the red tape and get the job done because he didn't answer to them. Now he would be expected to play nice, wear a suit, shine his shoes, get a *GQ* haircut, and stop drinking Scotch during lunch. *Not.*

When he'd first learned that he was being hijacked by the FBI, he'd argued that the chief of police didn't have the authority to make working on the task force a condition of Jack's continued employment. Jack and the chief had finally compromised. Jack would do exactly what he'd been told. Negotiations with upper brass sucked.

Liddell said, "The Feds are taking lead. That means we'll be doing all the grunt work and they will take all the credit. I'm okay with that, but I don't understand us not being sworn in yet. I mean, what if you do something un-FBI-like?"

"Me? What about you, Bigfoot?"

"You're the one that always sticks *his* foot in *our* mouths."

"This is just Toomey's way of establishing his alpha dog position," Jack said.

"There's a bright side, pod'na. At least he didn't hike a leg and pee on our desks."

"It's not official yet," Jack said, and they got into Liddell's Crown Vic. "It was one hell of a trip across Honduras for a nine-year-old, catching rides and walking. It must have taken weeks. All to end up in a cargo of dead bodies."

"We know we have the driver of the truck? Now we just have to find out who he is," Liddell said.

"And why he was killed and by who," Jack added.

"Piece of cake, pod'na."

"Let's go to the morgue. Walker texted me while the captain was neutering us. Dr. John is ready for the autopsy."

Liddell pulled out of the parking lot and headed toward the county morgue. "I bet you we'll get sworn in as federal agents today."

"You think?" Jack said.

"Well, yeah. Toomey wants you to call him this morning. On a weekend. I mean this case is going places besides little old E-ville."

Jack said, "Your point?"

"Well, as Feds we'll have more cooperation with other agencies, broader arrest powers, more jurisdiction."

"Leap tall buildings in a single bound and stop bullets with our teeth. Bigfoot, when did we let jurisdiction stop us?"

"I was talking legal, pod'na. Are you going to call Toomey?"

"We've got some other things to do before we get tied up," Jack said. "On the other hand, we're out of our element here. Maybe Toomey can give us an idea who to contact to start identifying all the victims."

"Should we head for the Federal Building? I'll get out my Secret Squirrel Decoder Ring, pod'na."

"Keep it in your pocket, Bigfoot. Morgue first. Federal vasectomy second. We need an accurate count of victims, cause of death, all that boring flatfoot cop kind of stuff. I'll call Toomey when we get some answers so we know what questions he's going to ask."

Liddell turned right onto Walnut Street. Another right onto John Street. In the side mirror, Jack saw a white SUV with the Channel Six logo following at a distance.

"Stop a minute," Jack said, and Liddell pulled to the curb.

Jack got out and flagged down the SUV. It stopped. He approached the driver, twirling a finger, telling the driver to roll down the window. The driver's window powered down. A young man with John Lennon–type glasses and a sparse goatee smiled at Jack.

"Detective Murphy," the young man said. "I'm Bart. Bart Hiller."

"You're Claudine Setera's cameraman," Jack said. "Bart, Detective Blanchard and myself are going to the morgue. You won't be allowed to come inside, but if you park right down there at the corner, you can get some good photos of us entering the morgue."

"I don't think I can see the morgue very good from there," Bart said.

Jack said, "Just pull up on the grass in front of the body shop. They won't mind. It's a weekend, and I know the owner if anyone gives you shit."

"That'd be great, Detective Murphy. Thanks."

"Not a problem, Bart," Jack said.

"Will you give me an interview?" the man asked.

Jack grinned. "Not on your life. But I might need a favor later."

Bart asked, "Why would I do you a favor?"

"Because it's all about connections. Right, Bart?"

"Got it, Detective Murphy."

Jack thought Bart was going to salute. Jack said, "Hey, we'll be thirty to thirty-five minutes, but I promise we'll look grim for the camera, going in and coming out. Maybe I'll even point at you and motion for you to go away."

The young man was gripping his steering wheel so tight his knuckles turned white.

"You can tell your bosses that I screamed at you if you want. Now go. We've got police work to do."

The window powered up, and the Channel Six SUV drove away. Jack returned to the car.

"I heard that, pod'na. Are we really going to do that?"

Jack said, "Screw him. We'll sneak in and out the back way."

"A life lesson."

"Right. Park behind the morgue."

Liddell said, "A shrink might say this is your way of striking out at someone because you feel powerless."

"Screw the shrink too," Jack said.

Liddell parked where the car wouldn't be seen from the street. If Bart parked where Jack indicated, he wouldn't even see the Crown Vic drive away. They walked around to the front door of the coroner's building, and Jack angrily stared across the street at the SUV before ringing the buzzer. No answer. He pointed at the cameraman's car and saw the guy fumbling with his camera. He pushed the buzzer again. Still no answer. Now he didn't have to pretend to be angry. He pounded on the front door with the side of a fist and rang the buzzer again.

A female voice from inside said, "I have PMS and a gun. Go away." It was Little Casket, the Chief Deputy Coroner for Vanderburgh County. She was known for her lack of compassion for the living and the dead. She probably wasn't kidding.

Chapter 8

It was a little after four in the morning when Coyote stopped in the parking lot of the Interstate 64 rest stop near the Missouri state line. He hadn't tried to find the truck and wondered if that was a mistake. He wasn't concerned about the contents. Not his problem. Mother Nature would do her thing. He just didn't want it to be found before she'd done her job.

He went through a mental list. He'd left no fingerprints or evidence linking him to the murder. The old lady in the shop saw his face. The VW the driver had come in was most likely stolen. Coyote had left it. There was a dog in the car, and that might draw attention to it, but it didn't really matter. His own car was parked several blocks away from the Coffee Shop. He hadn't seen anyone out. He didn't think anyone had seen him walking to the Coffee Shop. He hadn't passed in front of any businesses where there would be cameras. He'd done the deed and left Evansville without being stopped by police. All was well, but he had a nagging in the back of his mind that he should have found the truck. Made sure the cargo was eliminated. Too late now.

He stayed on the road as much as possible. He seldom slept in roadside motels. He preferred to sleep in his car in truck stops, highway rest areas, anywhere a man sleeping in a vehicle wouldn't arouse suspicion. State Troopers who were otherwise nosy thought nothing of a car during morning hours with the occupant sleeping. But during the night, with nothing else needing their attention, they were likely to roust him, check him out, and that could lead to nothing good. For them at least.

He was dead tired by the time he'd made it across the Missouri state line. He needed sleep, but he dreaded sleep. He stayed up most nights when he was on the road and slept during the day. He had what his shrink called night terrors. She told him the terrors were repressed memories, and if he could make himself remember and write it down, they would eventually go away. Two years now with this quack. The terrors hadn't gone away.

He drove a newer Dodge Dart, the kind and color of car you saw and forgot. It spoke of a middle- to lower-class businessman who traveled to make ends meet. He'd changed out the standard engine, a 1.7-liter four cylinder, for a 3.6-liter six cylinder. The standard engine was no more than a lawn mower engine that touted 40 mpg on the highway. The Dart would burn rubber. He'd traded mileage for power and speed.

He parked near the restrooms, left the engine running, pulled his coat tight, tipped his hat over his face, and relaxed. The droning sound of the engine and the hiss of the car's heater soon became one sound. He drifted off and dreamed.

The .50 caliber machine gun spit hot shell casings so close to his face he could feel the heat and sting of occasional contacts with his skin. He was too busy trying to stay alive to worry about the burn. His M-14 rifle was set on full-auto, and he was emptying magazine after magazine into the tree line where he thought enemy fire was coming from. It was hard to pinpoint their direction in the fading light, and they would be moving. The pounding of the .50 caliber machine gun next to him stopped. The expected call for ammo didn't come from the gunner, and he turned his head to see the machine gun and the gunner were still there but the top of the gunner's head was missing.

He laid his M-14 down to get the .50 caliber going again. It was his best chance. He pried the dead man's hands from the machine gun's stock and tried to move the gun. The tripod legs it rested on were buried in the mud, and it wouldn't budge. He shoved the body away and knelt in the gunner's position. His knee came down on something sharp. He reached down and felt something slick and jagged and recognized it as part of a skull.

He felt a sharp pain in his shoulder and heard a bloody scream, or it might have been the scream first and then the pain. He didn't remember in what order, or if he was the one screaming. He remembered thinking he'd been shot and that he was going to die. He remembered hearing the crunch in the bones of his shoulder, his body driven back and pinned to the hard clay of the foxhole. He tried to feel for the .45 semi-auto handgun he'd carried since the first day his foot had touched Vietnam soil, but he couldn't feel his arm or his hand. He saw the rifle bayonet protruding from his upper chest and looked up into the face of a boy. The boy was yanking and twisting the rifle, trying to free the bayonet where it had gone through his shoulder and buried in the clay. The boy was still trying to pull the blade loose when he used his good arm and pressed the muzzle of the M-14 into the boy's shocked face and blew the head up like a ripe melon.

Coyote woke from the day-mare drenched in sweat. He had drawn his bayonet while asleep. One hand clenched the hilt, the other hand pressed tightly against his upper chest. He could feel the metal plate the Army surgeon had used to mend his collarbone. He ran his fingers over the old healed wound on his chest. The skin felt numb under his finger, like touching a cadaver, but his shoulder still ached sometimes. He swallowed, expecting to feel the click his throat made when the wound was fresh.

It was a dream, but he could still taste blood on his lips, smell the stench of his own body, soaked in his own blood and that of the boy soldier. He had lain in that foxhole, the dead soldier on top of him, for a day before he was found.

His hands slowly moved to the top of the steering wheel, and he pulled himself up straight in the seat. A slow breath escaped his lungs, and he could feel the ghost itch and electrical tingle in the strap of muscle beside his neck. That part never felt numb. He remembered a medic working on him as he was medevaced out of the kill zone. Remembered the pulsing *whomp, whomp, whomp* of helicopter blades, the medic placing Coyote's hands against the bleeding wounds and yelling over the noise, telling Coyote to keep pressure on them. He learned that he'd been stabbed twice. Once in the upper chest, and once in the muscle strap and through his shoulder. Mostly he remembered the feel of the steel blade that remained protruding from his body, his fingers surrounding it, pressing down, staunching the bleeding.

The next thing he remembered was briefly waking in a field hospital, and again on a hospital ship. The bayonet had nicked his jugular vein and collapsed a lung, but somehow he had lived. The surgeon removed the bayonet, sewed him up, and presented the weapon to him as a "memento" of his narrow escape from death. During his three tours of duty, he'd been wounded several times. Nothing like this. This was a one-way ticket stateside if he wanted it. He didn't. He didn't run from a fight.

The horror faded, replaced by anger, and last, a practiced calm. He glanced around. It was daylight. The clock on the dash of the Dart showed he'd been asleep two hours. It seemed longer. It would have to do. He needed to get another hundred miles behind him.

A tricked-out dually pickup with loud mufflers started up beside him. The driver was checking him out, grinning, racing the engine, no doubt hoping his toy had the desired effect of startling someone. It didn't. Coyote said, "You're wasting my oxygen," but his words were lost in the rumbling and revving beside him. The dually beeped a backup warning and eased out of the parking space.

Every kid needs his toys. He reached inside his coat and found the notebook where he recorded his thoughts. The shrink had told him to write his dreams down if he could remember them. He'd told the shrink that he didn't have trouble remembering the damn dreams. He was paying the shrink to help him stop remembering.

He slowly recorded the dream, leaving nothing out, describing as well as he could the pain and excitement of killing up close. The more he wrote, the more his anxiety eased. When he was done journaling, he loosened his coat and got out of the car. The frigid air was a slap in the face. He was tired, both physically and mentally. He debated with himself whether to continue driving or to make the call. He decided to make the call.

He saw the dually driver parked beside a minivan with a family inside. The man driving the minivan was yelling at the driver. Coyote walked on. Not his problem.

He picked up the pay phone receiver, dropped some coins in the slot, and dialed the number. A sleepy voice answered.

"Who is this?" the man asked angrily.

"Nap time's over, Miles," Coyote said.

His gravelly voice was unmistakable. "Coyote?"

"Give me Indy."

"Indianapolis is still a go. Got a pen?" Miles said.

"Go." Coyote wrote in his journal the next delivery date, driver name and burner phone number, and the route the truck would take. He hung up.

Chapter 9

Chief Deputy Coroner Lilly Caskins, aka Little Casket, stood in the doorway with her hands on her hips. She wasn't armed, but her thick-lensed horn-rimmed glasses were trained on Jack like a sniper scope. She had earned the nickname Little Casket because of the grim nature of her profession and her lack of compassion for both the living and dead. Instead of a scowl, her mouth was twisted into a maniacal smirk. She was in her element.

"Hi, Lilly," Jack said.

Little Casket turned and stalked away toward the autopsy room without responding. Jack's cell phone buzzed. He checked the screen. It was Assistant Deputy Director of the FBI Toomey. Jack disconnected.

"Aren't you going to talk to Fearless Leader?" Liddell asked.

Jack thought that was as good of a nickname as any other. "Fearless Leader isn't in town. He can leave a message like other telemarketers."

Little Casket held the door to the autopsy room open for the detectives. "You almost missed the party."

The smell of strong disinfectant in the autopsy room made Jack's eyes water. Another smell, too. Liquor. Cheap whiskey. Jack sniffed Little Casket. It was awfully early to be drinking.

"It's not me," she said. "It's Dr. Frankenstein's idea." She was referring to Dr. John Carmodi, or Dr. John, the forensic pathologist who would likely be performing victims' autopsies for the next week or longer.

Dr. John was pouring whiskey over the pubic area of the corpse lying on the stainless-steel autopsy table. The feet were nearest the sink; the head was propped up by a curved piece of plastic. Another empty bottle of rotgut whiskey sat atop the stainless-steel sink tray by the table. Sergeant

Tony Walker stood to one side, snapping digital photos of the body. Two clear plastic bags with the tops tied tightly were on the floor near the door to the garage. Jack recognized the victim's coat in one of the bags.

Dr. John emptied the bottle. "Greetings and salutations, my friends. It's a wonderful day, isn't it?"

"Why the whiskey?" Jack asked.

"Phthiriasis," the pathologist answered. "Common spelling."

"Hir-ri-a-what?" Liddell asked.

Dr. John smiled. "It's pronounced 'hi-rye-a-see'. In layman's terms, his clothing is infested with mites and he has crabs in his pubic hair."

"Oh," Liddell said and stepped back.

"You won't catch anything," Dr. John said. "Not unless he was a really *close* friend, if you know what I'm saying."

"Looks like you were the one drinking with him," Liddell said.

"Whiskey is the quickest way to get rid of the crabs," Walker said.

"I've never heard of using whiskey," Jack said.

Liddell stepped further back.

Walker said, "I couldn't disinfect the clothes with that stuff."

Now Jack took a few steps back.

Dr. John grinned. "This guy probably hasn't bathed in a year. Most of his teeth are rotted out of his mouth."

"Summer teeth," Liddell said. "Sum'r there n' sum ain't."

Little Casket said, "If the comedy routine's wrapped up, we have work to do."

Little Casket had taken the requisite X-rays and prepped the body before Jack and Liddell arrived. She clipped three X-rays to the light box.

"Join me, gentlemen," Dr. John said. "You too, Liddell."

Jack, Liddell, and Walker stood around the light box on the wall while Dr. John explained what they were seeing.

"Three narrow, deep stab wounds," Dr. John said. "Without measuring the wounds themselves, I'm going to guess the object used was twenty to twenty-three inches in length."

Jack asked, "A spike?"

"I don't think so," Dr. John said. "I'll show you on the body in a minute."

Jack saw two vertical lines entering at the shoulder strap near the neck. They continued down into the mid-chest. A third line, this one horizontal, crossed the side ribs and intersected the other two lines in the mid-chest.

"Punctured his heart?" Liddell asked.

"We won't know for sure until we open him up, but that's in the right area."

"We?" Liddell said. "Not me. I'm staying over here. Marcie wouldn't believe I got crabs from this guy."

"Please continue, Dr. John," Jack said and nudged Liddell.

"Three stab wounds. Two of them downward through the left trapezius strap as you can see. They angle inward to the heart. This one broke the clavicle on its path," he said, pointing to one line that seemed to pass through the bone. Pieces of bone could be seen near the break. "This one"—he pointed to the horizontal line—"entered the left side of the chest through the ribs. I suspect it punctured the heart. There's evidence of cardiac tamponade—fluid around the heart. You can also see the left lung is smaller than the right. When a lung is punctured, the air escapes and it deflates. Any of these wounds could have caused death. The entry wounds are shaped in a cruciform design. I'll show you."

They followed Dr. John to the autopsy table where he pointed to one of the puncture wounds. "See the marked edges of the skin where the blade entered There are four striations, but it's not exactly a square. See where the flesh between the ridges is curved."

"A star shape," Jack said.

"That's close. Cruciform is the term for that wound pattern," Dr. John said.

Walker said, "I'll go through my weapon books." He was referring to the forensic books depicting and describing various penetration wounds caused by guns, knives, animal bites, animal attacks, or other objects and what made them.

Dr. John picked up one of the dead man's hands. "There's no abrasions on his palms." He turned the hand over. "Nothing on his knuckles. He has a fresh scrape on his right cheek bone just below the eye. Tony showed me photos of the body from the scene, and I'd guess this scrape is from his falling face forward. No scrapes on his hands tells me he was unconscious or dead when he fell forward. It's instinct to put your hands out if you're falling." He held his hands in front, palms facing forward, to demonstrate. "Either that, or the killer held him up," Dr. John concluded.

Jack saw a slight abrasion on one of the victim's knees. "Can you tell which of the stab wounds came first?"

Dr. John said, "Most likely, the stab wound in the left side. It didn't penetrate as far as the other two."

"Would a wound like that bring a man to his knees?" Jack asked.

"Maybe."

"Stand in front of me, Bigfoot," Jack said.

"What are you thinking, pod'na?"

"This guy is around five feet ten inches. Right, Doc?" Jack asked.

"Five feet eleven," Dr. John corrected.

"The owner of the Coffee Shop said her customer was shorter than her by about five inches. She's almost my height," Jack said.

Liddell let Jack stand behind him.

Jack pretended to hold a weapon in his left hand and stab Liddell in the left side. "The wounds are all on the left side of the victim. Here's what I think. He stabs this guy in the side. The victim drops to his knees. The killer is standing behind him and stabs downward twice."

Dr. John said, "Sounds about right. If he was standing behind the guy that is."

Jack stood in front of Liddell and imitated stabbing him in the left side again with the pretend weapon in his right hand. "There were no defensive wounds on the victim. If the killer was facing him, he would have tried to defend himself."

Dr. John said, "I think you're right."

Liddell said, "So the killer is left-handed and possibly smaller than the victim. That makes Freyda's customer sound plausible. I'm playing devil's advocate here. For all we know, the killer could be a woman. Let's not be gender biased."

"A knife isn't usually a woman's weapon of choice, Bigfoot," Jack said. "Maybe in domestic violence situations, but unless this guy's ex-wife caught him cheating on her with the dog, my money is still on the customer."

"Did this woman say her customer was left-handed?" Dr. John asked.

"I didn't ask." Jack called Freyda, asked the question, and hung up. "She said he was writing in that notebook with his left hand. Doc, you think this guy was trying for the heart?"

Dr. John went back to the X-rays. "The wound in the side was placed very exact, and there's fluid around the heart to indicate bleeding. One of the other wounds hit the clavicle, so it may have deflected the blade. He may have been trying for the aorta. The second wound took out the lung, and if I'm reading the X-ray correctly it pierced the aorta."

Walker said, "Morris fingerprinted the VW and got a match with the victim's fingerprints. He was definitely in the VW."

"Can you give us a time of death?" Jack asked.

"Midnight is close," Dr. John said.

"This wasn't a robbery. It was an execution," Jack said.

Liddell said, "The victim parked the truck, stole a car, and drove across town. He must have been meeting someone."

"But why steal a car to do it?" Jack asked. "Why not drive the truck and park in one of the vacant parking lots near the university? Or at the university, for that matter. And why would he hide the key to the truck in his shoe?"

"He didn't trust the guy he was meeting," Dr. John said.

"Maybe it was me," Little Casket said. "Liddell thinks the killer is a woman. Maybe I got tired of men being so damn stupid and just went off." She walked toward the hallway door. "I'll be in my office. Come get me when you're going to stop yapping and get this autopsy going." She went out and slammed the door shut.

"What the hell?" Walker said. His cell phone beeped. "It's Corporal Morris. I've got to take this." Walker moved a short distance away. He disconnected and said, "Morris said Mrs. Rademacher let him collect plates and cups, but she wouldn't submit to being fingerprinted. She said it was government intervention and a violation of her constitutional right to privacy."

"She and a million criminals agree," Jack said.

"Morris also said Animal Control came to get the dog and she threatened to throw a pot of hot coffee on them. She said to tell you that we'd better not send the dog pound out again or there'd be another body lying in the alley."

The thought had crossed Jack's mind to take the dog to his veterinarian friend, Dr. Branson, to get her cleaned up enough to find a home for her. It wasn't very likely that the pooch would be returned to Joe. "We need to take her to a veterinarian friend of mine. We don't want her to bite someone."

Liddell said, "Do you mean the dog or Freyda?"

Walker said, "I forgot how much of a dog person Jack is. You never told me how Katie is getting along with your rescued pooch now that you're back home?"

Jack had rescued a dog during a case a year or so back. The dog had been injured defending her master from a psycho killer. A redneck police chief had threatened to shoot the injured dog, and Jack had to threaten the chief. He'd taken her to his friend to get treated, but he ended up adopting her. The dog's name was Cinderella, and she wouldn't answer to any other name. Her last owner was a gay man, and she didn't like men who weren't. She'd bare her teeth when Jack was around, and she'd pee on his pillow and in his shoes when he wasn't home. "She's in restraints, muzzled and tied to a backboard."

Walker's eyebrows rose, and Jack said, "Cinderella. Not Katie."

"Let me know if you can definitely put the victim in the truck," Jack said.

"We should be able to do that with fingerprints and the dog's hair," Walker said. "Joanie said she found dog hair all over the front seat in the cab of the truck. It's the same color as the pooch. Morris took hairs from the car, and I collected some from the victim's clothing. We'll run the fingerprints through AFIS and IAFIS." AFIS is the Automated Fingerprint Identification System maintained by the FBI. IAFIS is the Indiana version of the FBI system. The FBI system is the most comprehensive database in the world. "Chief Pope has arranged for the other bodies to be stored at Swonder Ice Rink when we can get them all moved."

"It'll put a crimp in ice hockey for a bit," Liddell quipped.

"The mayor's assistant is coming up with a story for why it's closed. The City Event Manager is resisting because people might not want to skate where dead bodies were stored," Walker said.

Liddell said, "I'd think that would be a draw."

Walker said, "Well, I guess they'll have to come to a decision soon. Joanie said some people are showing up at the scene carrying placards protesting our treatment of immigrants."

"I knew this would start eventually. How the hell did they get organized so quick?" Jack asked, and answered his own question. "Claudine Setera. Shit!"

Lilly Caskins said from the doorway, "You boys might want to see this."

Jack, Liddell, and Walker followed her to the conference room where she had a television on and tuned in to Channel Six news.

Chapter 10

People say that if you want good food, go where the truck drivers go. From experience, Coyote knew that wasn't true. But big places, like the Flying J Truck Stop and Café just outside St. Louis, had a place for the truckers to take showers and change clothes. After he showered he put the hat, boots, and Burberry coat in his duffel bag and pulled on a Green Bay Packers sweatshirt and clean blue jeans. He slipped on a beige nondescript parka and scuffed loafers, and discovered The Flying J Café was temporarily closed. Just as well. He'd been stationary too long.

He found another little café just down the road that resembled a train's caboose, but with windows running across the front so customers could see outside. He could see the waitress. She was young, still a teenager. Her elbows were on the countertop, face propped on her hands, chewing gum. He wasn't expecting much in the way of service, but he had to eat.

He parked the Dart and went inside. The inside of the café was set up like a soda shop from the '50s with booths lined across the front under the windows. Four chrome barstools with red Naugahyde seats were lined up at the counter. The waitress wore a pink uniform with wide white lapels and pockets. The resemblance ended there. The waitress was on her cell phone, tapping the screen, giggling, and totally ignored him.

He found a seat in the back corner where he could watch the door and the counter. The waitress still didn't move. Behind her was a door leading to the kitchen and the back. Next to that was the serving window where there would undoubtedly be a grill his father had liked to call a fry and die because they served fried everything. His dad liked fried food. Especially anything with bacon. Ironically his dad didn't die from a heart attack from all the grease. He died at the ripe age of forty-two from lung cancer. Maybe it had something to do with a four-pack-a-day habit.

The waitress pushed herself up to a standing position with a sigh. She grabbed an order pad and walked over to Coyote's booth.

"There's plenty of seats near the counter," she said accusingly. "What'll you have, mister?"

Coyote pointed to the breakfast special and put the menu down on the not-too-clean table. She scribbled briefly on the pad and walked away with another heavy sigh meant to convey her displeasure with having to walk ten feet extra.

He was somewhat rested and feeling good about last night's mission. He took out his notebook and pen. The waitress came back with his order, set the plate in front of him along with a coffee mug stained on the rim with lipstick. At least the coffee was hot. He used a gloved finger to wipe at the red baked-on smudge.

There was nothing special about the "special." The bacon was limp and greasy, the eggs were burnt, and the toast wasn't toasted.

He opened the notebook.

Feeling good today. Was down last night. The meeting didn't go as smoothly as I would have liked. The guy I was meeting with was merely a pawn, a driver, obviously not in a good place in his life because he was late. He was being cautious. I couldn't blame him given the current political climate. He would be out of work if things continued as they were. I don't think he ever considered another job, or that this one might cost his life. If you shovel shit for a living you get some on you. But we resolved that issue. By the time the meeting ended he was in a better place.

I'm still disappointed—no, I'm disgusted—with everything I see. People are lazy, expect everything will be given to them, everything will be okay, their stupid lives will go on as usual and they call that normal.

I have lost my appetite. I know I need food to keep functioning but this food looks like it came out of a trashcan, which is where it's going. The cook needs a serious attitude adjustment.

It's like you said, doc, I'm always in the "on" position when it comes to anger. In the past, I would have walked back in the kitchen and shoved the son of a bitch's face on the grill until his flesh was as done as the bacon should have been. But today I'll give him a pass. He should thank you for his life. I want you to write that down at our next session. Write down that I didn't hurt the cook. And I'll leave a good tip. The workers get away with what management lets them get away with.

Coyote pushed the plate away, dug a roll of twenties out of his pocket, peeled one off, and put it under the coffee mug. He continued writing.

My business contact is supposed to call about the Midwest mission. Business is good. I'm keeping busy. You said that was a way to deal with my issues. Traveling is the hard part, but life is about sacrifices. Right? My country makes heavy demands, but I've never said no. This country needs men like me. My old boss was too worried about his own ass to see what needed to be done. My country didn't desert me. He did. He hung me out to dry. Humiliated me. Had me dismissed from service. But like they say, karma's a bitch. I'm working for myself now. I've got all the contacts I need. I can make this all work. The rules I have to obey are my own. Taking people's lives is wrong. I know that. But taking the lives of people trying to ruin my country is forgivable. I'll kill them all to protect the people I love.

You spend your soul and...

He heard Evansville mentioned, and his attention was drawn to a television on the wall behind the counter. A male news announcer with a smug look said something else about Evansville. Coyote heard "gruesome discovery."

"Turn that up," Coyote told the waitress.

She was once again slumped against the counter. She looked over, saw the twenty-dollar bill peeking out from under the coffee cup and said, "We don't keep it loud, mister. The other customers don't want the noise, but since there ain't no one here..."

What customers? Coyote ignored her. He was barely registering the spoken words on the television, concentrating on the video taken of a dark-skinned young boy in a hospital bed, raising rail-thin arms to hide from the camera. The caption at the bottom of the picture read: "Survivor in Evansville."

The waitress turned the volume up. The picture changed to the smug-looking man again, saying, "Claudine Setera from our sister station in Evansville has more on this breaking story. Claudine?"

A beautiful dark-haired woman's face filled the screen. The camera backed up and showed her standing in front of an emergency room. Behind her, through sliding glass doors, a uniformed policeman could be seen leaning against a counter, and the backs of two well-nourished nurses in mint-green scrubs walking down a hall.

The female reporter said, "I'm here at Deaconess Hospital Emergency Room in Evansville, Dan, where the lone survivor of what can only be described as a shocking mass murder was brought in by Detective Jack Murphy just hours ago. We have a video from the scene where the bodies of more than thirty victims were discovered by police this morning. The victims all appear to have died of exposure after being locked in the back of a semitrailer with Texas plates. Police are speculating the truck may have been abandoned days ago behind a vacant warehouse on Fountain Avenue."

Male Anchor:
"We'll share those photos with our audience, Claudine."

The picture changed once again to an outdoor crime scene shot from the Channel Six helicopter, showing a semitrailer sitting with the back doors open and white-clad workers carrying body bag after body bag from inside.

Claudine:
"As you can see, Dan, the police were ill-equipped to deal with a tragedy of this type. At last count, twenty-three of the victims' bodies have been taken by ambulance to a hastily arranged cold storage area at Swonder Ice Rink."

Male Anchor:
"Claudine, have the police identified any of the victims or the survivor?"

Claudine:
"I asked that question of Deputy Chief of Police Richard Dick this morning, and he had this to say."

The picture changed to a uniformed police officer. The emblem of the Evansville Police Department was displayed on the brick wall behind the officer. A microphone was clipped to the starched and pressed shirt of Deputy Chief Richard Dick's dress blue uniform. With his blond hair, blue eyes, and posture he could be the poster boy for the Aryan Brotherhood. He looked appropriately stern for the camera.

Deputy Chief Dick:
"Claudine, this morning police were notified of a suspicious vehicle, a tractor-trailer, parked behind an abandoned business near the Pigeon Creek Bridge. Upon investigation officers found the trailer doors were locked, and upon probable cause, forcibly opened the doors to discover the dead bodies of thirty-one men and women. The victims all appeared to have succumbed to the elements. At my direction, the trailer was searched for signs of life, and one boy was found alive. He was rescued from the piles of bodies and is currently receiving medical treatment. The investigation is ongoing, so names will not be released, but I can assure you I am doing everything in my power to identify the victims and bring the perpetrator to justice."

The screen filled again with the woman's face.

Claudine:
"Deputy Chief of Police Richard Dick is the Commander of the Detectives Unit and in charge of this ongoing investigation."

Male Anchor:
"Police haven't identified any of the victims or the survivor, Claudine? Do they know why the victims were in Evansville?"

Claudine:
"I understand Detective Jack Murphy is the lead detective and has identified the survivor, but given his age, the police haven't made his name public, Dan. The victims are believed to be illegal immigrants. Deputy Chief Dick speculated the victims were part of a failed human trafficking operation. He didn't have information on the possible destination. Another source close to the investigation has revealed that another murder victim was found early this morning near the University of Evansville. The

male victim in that case had no identification on him, but the police have evidence to believe he was the driver of the semitruck."

Male Anchor:
"Were you able to speak to the survivor, Claudine?"

Claudine:
"The boy was taken to Deaconess Hospital as Deputy Chief Dick said. He was too traumatized to speak to us."

Male Anchor:
"Have the police interviewed the boy?"

Claudine:
"Detective Jack Murphy spent some time talking to the boy, and I understand he was able to get a name and other information pertinent to the investigation. A source in the police department has confirmed the survivor and victims were illegally being brought into the United States and that the State Department is being notified."

Male Anchor:
"Were you able to interview Detective Murphy?"

Claudine:
"The short film clip you're seeing is the attempted interview with Detective Jack Murphy."

The screen changed to a shaky film clip showing Claudine approaching two serious-looking detectives. Both were big; one was huge. A semitruck and trailer were in the background. A white-clad technician stood outside the back door of the trailer talking to a uniformed policeman. Claudine could be heard asking questions before she was led away from the scene at the direction of the smaller of the two detectives. The female reporter had called the smaller man Detective Murphy. She came back on screen.

Claudine:

"As you can see, Detective Murphy refused to comment, but the public has a right to know if a dangerous criminal is loose in Evansville, Dan."

The news continued, but Coyote had lost interest. He'd made a mistake. If the lady on the news was telling the truth, he'd made more than one mistake. The police had found the cargo much quicker than he'd thought possible, and someone in the truck had survived. He was sure the driver was dead when he left him, so it had to have been dumb luck on the cops' part. But what if it wasn't? What if the driver had kept the boy up front in the truck? What if the boy heard the driver's plans to meet with Coyote? That information alone wasn't enough to lead them directly to him, but it was more than Coyote wanted to be known.

The policeman giving the interview was chatty and full of himself. Either this Deputy Chief Dick was a complete fool, or he thought he was being shrewd by using the news media to try to draw Coyote out. He wasn't being shrewd. He was just another self-important prick. If he was an example of the best Evansville had to offer, there was no need to worry. But the other guy—Murphy. He was a hard man.

Coyote had killed many people, both in the war in Vietnam and in the war here in America, but he had his limits. He wouldn't do a cop. He was a patriot. He had conflicting feelings. He had to protect himself so he could continue to do his work. If the cop, Murphy, threatened all that Coyote had done—would do—he had to be dealt with. Coyote would return to Evansville and...

He felt a presence and turned instinctively. He'd been so immersed in the news story he hadn't noticed the waitress had come up behind. She was reading what he'd written in his notebook and turned away quickly. He judged by her expression that she was disgusted, scared, didn't understand what she was reading.

"You a writer or something?" the girl asked.

Coyote said, "Thrillers." He closed the notebook and put it back in his coat.

She eyed the twenty dollars on his table. "You don't want this stuff, I'll get you something else, mister."

Coyote's response was to push the plate toward her. She cleared the table, snatched the money, and headed for the counter. Coyote followed.

Chapter 11

"Just shoot me?" Jack said after Channel Six Breaking News ended.

"Looks like your friend Claudine let the cat out of the bag, pod'na. And she got Deputy Chief Dick to give them a sound bite," Liddell said.

"First of all, she's not my friend, Bigfoot," Jack said. "Second, Double Dick can give me a 'sound' bite. He'll be giving tours of the crime scene next."

Walker said, "Claudine got into the boy's room at the hospital and scared him off. If he wasn't traumatized before, he is now. He'll be afraid to go outside."

Little Casket said to the detectives, "I guess we'll just stand here and watch this guy decompose. Stay or leave. Some of us have things to do."

"I talked to Joanie Ryan while you were watching the news and got an update for you," Walker said.

Dr. John grinned and made a shooing motion at them. "You boys talk. I'll go ahead and begin so Lilly can take her anger out on the body."

"We'll be in the hall," Walker said.

"What do you have, Tony?" Jack asked.

"Remember the three bodies just inside the back doors of the truck," Walker said. "The one with the knife had a Honduran passport and a green card. His passport and green card had different names. The passport wasn't stamped for the United States, so he didn't go through customs. He had over a thousand dollars US and a wad of Honduran money in his pocket.

"The stabbing victim and the woman had Columbian passports. Their passports were stamped in the US last week at LAX. They didn't have green cards or money, but they had new burner cell phones. Joanie checked the call log, and there weren't any calls or numbers listed in the history on the phones. Did you say the boy's last name was Bogran?"

"Yeah," Jack said.

Walker made a call. "Joanie. Did you tell me you found a passport for someone named Bogran?" He spelled the name for her, listened, and said, "Send me pictures of the passports and green cards you have so far."

"What?" Jack asked when Walker disconnected the call.

"Joanie said two Honduran passports with the name Bogran were found on one of the victims in the trailer."

"Joe and the grandfather," Jack said. "We'll have to run all this by Toomey and see what the Feds can find out for us."

"You're referring to our new bestest friend and boss, Deputy Assistant Director Toomey of the USOC federal task force," Liddell said.

"We'd better go to Deaconess and do damage control, Bigfoot. We'll call your friend Toomey after."

"Toomey liked you first, Jack."

"It's interesting the three that were fighting had passports. It makes me think that some of these people were hiding among the sheep. Sneaking into the US for other reasons than working for a living."

"How does the boy fit into this?" Liddell asked.

"You tell me, Bigfoot. Better yet, we can let him answer that question. Let's go."

"Immigration is going to be all up in this," Liddell said.

"Lucky for us, we don't work for Immigration. Our job is to find the assholes responsible. We've got the driver. Now we have to find his killer. If that guy turns out to be an illegal alien, I'm going to 'beam him up,' not deport him."

They left Sergeant Walker at the morgue and headed back to Deaconess.

"Do you think that news guy is still waiting?" Liddell asked.

"I hope so," Jack said, and his phone rang.

"Jack, you need to get back to Deaconess right away," the dispatcher said.

"We're headed there now. What's up?"

"Security called and said the boy you were talking to earlier has disappeared."

"Shit!" Jack said.

"Detective Jansen will meet you at the hospital to take the missing person report," the dispatcher added.

"Step on it, Bigfoot," Jack said, and disconnected.

Chapter 12

Jack kept his eyes peeled for Joe. A boy in a hospital gown and no shoes should stand out, but there was no sign of him. They pulled into the ER drive, and Jack was glad the Channel Six news wagon wasn't there. The last thing a traumatized nine-year-old boy needed was Claudine Setera shoving a microphone in his face and asking, "How does it feel to be an orphan? Did you see the others die? Did your grandfather say anything before he froze solid? How did that make you feel?"

They parked behind the unoccupied Crown Vic that belonged to Detective Larry Jansen, the missing person detective for EPD.

"Maybe the captain called him in to help with this?" Liddell suggested.

"You're a glass half full person, Bigfoot."

"You're a glass needs to be full of Scotch guy," Liddell retorted. "Marcie says if you think positive, good things will happen."

The heavy glass doors whooshed open, and they saw a security guard waiting for them inside.

"Okay. I'm positive we'll have to run that greasy little bastard off," Jack said, half kidding. Larry Jansen had been on the EPD since Moses floated down the Nile in a basket. He was politically connected to unknown parties, and this connection had saved his slimy hide more than once. He was also a part-time protégé or snitch for Double Dick when it suited him, so he could be dangerous. Like a snake hidden in the grass, you never know when it's going to bite you in the ass.

The hospital guard was from Powers Private Security, and he was built like an NFL linebacker. He sported a dark goatee, but his head was shaved. Jack had seen the man at the hospital a time or two. With great effort, the guard pulled his eyes from the nurse's cleavage. His nametag read: COFFEE. The name was appropriate to his skin color. Captain bars adorned the epaulets of his starched white shirt.

Jack and Liddell introduced themselves, and Jack said, "Fill us in, Captain."

Captain Coffee said, "Two of my people are out checking the floors, and one of your detectives is here. No word yet."

"Detective Jansen?" Jack asked. "Short older guy that could be an evil twin of Columbo?" Murphy's Law says: "Shit in one hand and wish in the other and see which one fills up first." The guard's answer indicated the former hand.

Coffee laughed. "I knew he reminded me of someone. Columbo. That's good." He laughed again. "This kid isn't officially missing yet. The nurse discovered he was gone maybe ten minutes ago."

"Did anyone see the boy leave?" Jack asked.

"We're still talking to people, but so far the answer is no. I checked with all the ER staff, and they were busy. We had a domestic violence couple that we were dealing with. I was going through security footage before you got here."

The security footage must have been on the nurse's cleavage, Jack thought.

"If you come back to my office we can talk there."

"He couldn't have gone far," Jack said. "Okay, let's go."

Coffee led them into a small office crammed with filing cabinets and one large desk. Atop the desk was the video surveillance system. The monitor showed a split-screen view of four exits. Coffee punched a button, and the picture changed to four views of hallways. The system was outdated.

Jack asked, "Captain, can you play the footage starting five minutes before he went missing?"

Coffee said, "I'm doing that now. This is a big place, and the monitors switch to four different views every five seconds. I can freeze a camera if I see something."

"Did you get a description of the boy?" Jack asked.

"Dark-skinned, dark hair, Hispanic, and skinny. I think he'll stand out, don't you?" the guard said.

"Did he take his clothes?" Jack asked.

Coffee was still.

Jack asked, "Has anyone reported missing clothing?"

"Detective Jansen said he would check on that," Coffee said. "But even if the kid took clothes, it might not get reported right away. And if he took medical scrubs or any of that, we probably wouldn't know. There's a supply room just outside the back entrance to the treatment rooms. I'll call ER and ask if he took his clothes from the room."

"Do that. Do you have a camera back there?"

Coffee was embarrassed. "Been trying to get the hospital to put one in since I been here." He called ER and spoke briefly. "He took his clothes, but the nurse I talked to said she didn't remember what he was wearing."

Jack knew. "He was wearing jeans, a dirty T-shirt with some type of logo on the chest. The logo was round with spikes. He had cammo boots and a beige bomber jacket that was too big for him."

"I'll have to go back through the footage. I was told he was in a hospital gown," Coffee said. "I put out a Code Yellow for a missing ER patient."

"Good work," Jack said. "If you see Detective Jansen tell him to call Jack Murphy. If you find anything, and I mean anything, call me." Jack gave him a card.

"Will do," Coffee said.

"Captain Coffee," Jack said, "are you going to check the footage from the..."

"Parking lots. I'm on it," Coffee said.

Jack and Liddell headed toward their car.

Liddell said, "What about Jansen? Want me to have Coffee put a Code Columbo out on him?" He cupped his hands beside his mouth and yelled, "Code Columbo. Code Columbo! Lost detective, short, squat, wearing a rumpled coat, head up his ass. Consider him unarmed and languorous."

Jack said, "I don't think Jansen can hurt anything now."

Liddell said, "I'll call dispatch and put a BOLO on Joe?" BOLO is Be on the Lookout.

Jack said, "Not yet," and called dispatch. He asked the dispatcher, "Did anyone ask you to put out an alert on this missing person from Deaconess?"

"Not yet," the dispatcher answered.

"Don't. Contact me or Liddell first." He hung up.

"Where are we going, pod'na?" Liddell asked.

"Let's stop and ask the nurse if Joe said anything before he left."

They stopped and talked to the doctor and to Nurse Tammy from Ohio but gained no further information except that they saw Claudine Setera and the cameraman in the boy's room and made them leave. Security wasn't called. The doctor said Joe was in a state, and the nurse was getting something to help him relax. Tammy said when she came back to the room Joe was gone. They called security right away, and a Code Yellow was put out.

Captain Coffee stopped them as they were leaving. "That pretty newswoman was thrown out by our ER doctor. Do you want footage of any of that?"

"No," Jack said. "She didn't do anything illegal. We can't arrest people for being assholes."

"Too bad," Coffee said. "It might make good viewing at the FOP Club some night."

Liddell said, "Make us a copy. I'll come back and get it."

Chapter 13

Jack pulled out of the Deaconess Emergency Room drive and turned west on Columbia Avenue.

"He wouldn't have gone far in this cold," Liddell said. "I think we should check the convenience stores. There's a CVS down the street and a couple of gas stations. He'll need to get warm. He'll want real food. There's that greasy spoon down by St. Vincent's Day Care."

"I have a better idea," Jack said.

Three blocks from the hospital, St. Anthony's Catholic grade school building had been turned into a homeless shelter, but the church was still in use, as was the convent and rectory. Because Jack's parents, especially his mother, were of the Catholic faith, Jack had been sentenced to St. Anthony's for eight long years. When Jack was thirteen he was transferred to the maximum-security version called Rex Mundi High School. The nuns at Rex Mundi were better armed and better trained than corrections officers. They carried throwing stars made from rosary crucifixes, sharpened rulers, and it was rumored among the inmates that the nuns carried Uzis under their habits. Some of the girls called the nuns penguins. The boys called them *nunjas*.

Few cars were on the road and even fewer people on the sidewalks. Jack parked illegally on First Avenue in front of St. Anthony's church, and they climbed the worn stone steps. The three sets of double front doors surrounded by arches of carved Bedford stone were tall and wide enough that even Bigfoot was small in comparison. Each door was made of three-inch-thick solid walnut that was worn smooth around the iron handles. Liddell tried the left side door, and it swung easily, a testament to the craft of the builders back in the 1800s.

"What makes you think he's here?" Liddell asked.

"He's in a strange country and in trouble. He'll be wanting sanctuary."

They entered the church. The heavy door swung shut behind them. Liddell whispered, "Looks empty to me, pod'na. I mean, no people."

"Let's walk through anyway, Bigfoot. This is a big place. There are rooms behind the altar and upstairs in the choir loft," Jack said. "Did I ever mention that I went to school at St. Anthony's?"

"No," Liddell whispered.

"You don't have to whisper, Bigfoot. Maybe Joe will hear us and come out."

"Hey, Joe," Liddell called out.

"Joe. It's Murphy," Jack said.

A head that looked like a cotton ball on a stick popped up behind the altar. The woman attached to it was old enough to predate the church. Her wispy hair was so white it shone like a halo in the light coming through the stained-glass windows. She appeared surreal, angelic, and with a granny apple frown. The heavy wool sweater she wore was hanging from her thin frame, and if she was standing, she was four-foot-tall because only her head showed above the altar.

"This is a church," she admonished them.

"Sorry," Jack said. "We're looking for a young boy."

The woman stared at him. "Well you won't find a boy of any age here. You should go home and pray. This is a house of God."

Liddell came up beside Jack and chuckled. "What my partner means is that we're looking for a boy who is..."

She stared from Jack to Liddell. "Your partner?"

"Yeah. We're partners. He's Jack. I'm Liddell." Liddell quickly added, "I'm married and have a baby."

The old woman continued to stare disapprovingly.

"Not me and Jack. Me and my wife have a baby."

"There's no young boy here. Now I've got cleaning to attend to." Her head disappeared down behind the altar without another word.

"Come on, Bigfoot. He's not here."

They walked out and down the stone steps in front. Liddell asked, "Do you think she thought we were 'partner' partners, pod'na?"

"What do you think?"

Liddell nudged Jack's arm. "Well, you did tell her you were looking for a 'young boy.' You started it."

"Did not."

"Where to next?" Liddell asked. "The bus station?"

"You're very funny, Bigfoot. You should take those big feet on the road. Let's go to the convent."

"Why are we wasting time here, pod'na? We should just drive around and check places that are open like I said."

"St. Anthony of Padua is the patron saint of the lost, Bigfoot. The church was named for him. Joe is lost. Let's check the convent first. I promise we'll find somewhere you can get food after we find him."

St. Anthony's church grounds included one square block facing four different streets. German immigrant Anthony Reis had built a mansion on the land that became the rectory upon his death. He also bequeathed the remaining land to the Catholic Church. The church was built and named St. Anthony, and soon after, work was completed on a two-story grade school and a convent. They walked up the steps to the front door of the convent.

"We used to call this the nunnery," Jack said to Liddell. "We used to dare each other to sneak inside because we thought this was a gateway to another world where the aliens wore penguin suits and ate kids."

"That explains a lot of things, pod'na."

Jack knocked, and after a short time the door was answered and a sister stepped into the opening. She was pushing five feet, with a heavily wrinkled face and stick-like fingers. She was wearing a black floor-length gown with a flowing scapular and a black-and-white veil covering her head and part of her face. Jack remembered her being more vital with a commanding presence that could stop fights and freeze angry words in your throat. He didn't remember her being the frail and shrunken woman standing before them.

"Jack Murphy," Sister Aquinas said with delight in her eyes. "What kind of trouble are you in now?"

"I'm surprised you remember me, Sister Aquinas. It's been a while."

"Not so long that I've forgotten your daily presence in detention for fighting. Come in."

They stepped inside the narrow foyer, and Liddell had to stand sideways as she closed the heavy door. The men followed as she moved at a surprising pace down the hallway. The temperature warmed as they neared the back of the house.

"You didn't answer my question, Jack."

Jack was chagrined but not surprised that trouble was what she associated him with. He was, after all, a shit-magnet.

"I've tried to stay out of trouble. It's good to see you again, Sister Aquinas."

"I don't watch the news much anymore because my eyes aren't what they used to be. But I read the newspaper. All the fistfights you had seem to have prepared you for your chosen profession. I can't say I approve of some of the stories I've heard."

"Yes, Sister," Jack said.

"But in your own way you seem to be doing His work."

"Yes, Sister," Jack said again. He felt he was back in grade school in the principal's office.

"How are Kevin and your mother?" Sister Aquinas asked.

She's still got a mind like a steel trap. "They're fine, Sister. My mother's in Florida and Kevin is—well he's still Kevin."

"I was sorry to hear of your father's passing. He and your mother were in Mass every Sunday with Kevin." Jack had missed mass whenever possible. "I'm glad you are back with Katie. Such a sweet girl," she said, once again surprising Jack with her knowledge of his life. Time to change the subject.

"This is my partner, Liddell Blanchard."

Her wrinkled face turned skyward to take in Bigfoot's towering figure. Bony hands wrapped around Liddell's massive hand like roots around a tree. Her smile was warm. "Hello, Detective Blanchard. Liddell is a fine name."

"Yes ma'am, erm, yes Sister."

Sister Aquinas patted his hand and smiled. "Sister is just fine," she said. "Aquinas for Saint Thomas Aquinas, the patron saint of Catholic education." She studied his face. "Liddell is Scottish."

"Cajun," Liddell said. "Creole to be exact."

"Originally it was Scottish," Sister Aquinas continued. "The Scots, French, and English settled in what would become the Louisiana Territories. They mixed with slaves and freeborn alike from other countries and the indigenous Indian tribes here. Blanchard is French. It means 'one who rides a white horse.' You have an interesting ancestry. We should talk sometime."

Liddell stood openmouthed. "The Saint of Education definitely suits you, Sister."

Jack said, "Sister Aquinas taught Geography and World History."

"Latin, French, Spanish, and Math," Sister Aquinas said with a smile and turned to Jack. "And detention."

Liddell said, "Jack's Irish. His name means 'one who steals a white horse.'" He punched Jack on the arm. "Stay away from my horse, pod'na."

Jack didn't think it was funny. His dad had hinted there were horse thieves in his family tree before coming to America. Maybe afterward as well. Dad said the family turned to law enforcement to keep from going to prison or being hung.

"We're on the job, Sister, and..."

"You might as well come in the kitchen," she said, interrupting him. "I've just made a pot of tea. Have you had breakfast?"

"I'm afraid we don't have time, Sister. A patient is missing from Deaconess and..."

"I know. Ruth called me from the church. She's a widow and spends most of her time cleaning. She said you were quite rude."

"We weren't rude. We told her we were looking for a..."

"Yes. I know what you said. She's a crime story fanatic and thinks all men are rapists and child molesters. Please, come in and have tea. Policemen may never get cold, but I'm old, in case you haven't noticed. It's much warmer in the kitchen."

Jack and Liddell followed the diminutive nun to the room at the back.

"You're searching for a runaway," she said.

"How did you hear our missing kid was a runaway?" Jack asked. They hadn't mentioned that to Ruth of the Cleaning Obsession.

"You'll want that tea," Sister Aquinas said.

They passed between stacks of boxes on each side of the hallway. More boxes ran along one side of the stairway leading to the second floor. It brought back a memory of a grade school classmate. Crazy Bobby Sanders.

Crazy Bobby had made it as far as the first-floor hallway in the nunnery before he was caught by Sister Aquinas and escorted to the rectory. The rectory was an even scarier place than the nunnery. It was where the priests lived, and the rumor was that several kids had gone in and never came out again. The lucky ones had been forced to wear gowns and carry burning pots of incense and become altar boys. Bobby Sanders had made it out with wild stories of being tied in a chair and pummeled by the nuns. Of course, Bobby Sanders had lied. He became a journalist when he grew up.

When Jack and Liddell entered the kitchen, they saw Joe sitting at the table. A glass of orange juice, a large glass of milk, and a half-demolished plate of scrambled eggs, bacon, and toast sat in front of him. "Hello, Detective Murphy."

"Bigfoot, this is Joe. Joe, Bigfoot."

Liddell said, "Glad to finally meet you. My name is Liddell."

Joe asked with a serious expression, "Does Detective Murphy call you Bigfoot when you are going to eat?"

Jack said, "It's a long story, Bigfoot." To Joe he said, "I promised you a cheeseburger. You didn't need to leave the hospital, Joe."

"I must go now," Joe said to Sister Aquinas.

"I think that's up to these policemen," she said.

A bomber jacket, two sizes too big for the boy, hung on the back of a chair. Joe was wearing hospital scrubs over his own clothes and old army boots.

Jack asked Sister Aquinas, "Do any of the boxes in the hallway have clothing in them?"

"I was just going to find something when you knocked," she said and left the kitchen.

Jack said, "I guess you were hungry."

Joe shoveled the last scraps from his plate into his mouth.

Jack asked, "Why did you leave the hospital, Joe?"

"People with cameras came in my room. The woman said she is a newsperson. I left to find Shadow," he said. "You are a good man, Detective Murphy, but your president doesn't let people like me come here. My grandfather told me this. I will be sent back."

"What would happen if you went back to Honduras, Joe?" Liddell asked.

"I would be killed. Made an example by Mara Salvatrucha."

Jack pulled up a chair and sat. "Is that why you left Honduras? MS-13?"

"I'm not to talk of this. My grandfather told me they hear and see everything."

"I can promise you that MS-13 can't hear or see anything in here. You're safe with us." Jack inclined his head toward Liddell. "Bigfoot here would stomp them like bugs."

"Grandfather couldn't protect me or my family," Joe said in a whisper. "I will never be safe."

"I'm not going to lie to you, Joe. I said I'd try to help you stay here, and I will, but I don't know if I can do that." Jack could sense the boy shrinking away.

"I would rather die here, Detective Murphy."

Jack didn't know what to say. Joe's grandfather was right. If Joe was turned over to ICE, he would be deported. If MS-13 was after him, they would end him. The kid had already faced things most grown men would never experience.

Jack asked, "Joe, do you know what honesty means?"

"Lying. To tell a lie is a sin," Joe said.

"Why did you and your grandfather leave Honduras? Why did you come here to live?" Jack asked.

"Grandfather has a business..." Joe began and hesitated before saying, "Detective Murphy, I told a lie and I am ashamed. My family lived in San Pedro Sula. My mother, my father, my sister. Grandfather owns a small printing shop in San Pedro. Another one in Puerto Lempira. One day some men come to our house. They tell my grandfather that he must work for them now. My grandfather told the men no, and they laughed. They said Grandfather must work for them or bad things will happen."

"MS-13?" Jack asked.

"That is what you call them."

"Is that why you left your home? Because your grandfather was being threatened by MS-13? Mara Salvatrucha?"

"Grandfather says they are everywhere. He says they are killers of women and children. Even babies. I have seen what they do. Grandfather says we must stand up for what is right and be brave, honorable. He tried to bring others together to resist Mara Salvatrucha. But everyone is afraid. Mara Salvatrucha killed my mother, my father, and took my sister when they learned of Grandfather's talk. They came back and took me and told Grandfather he will work for them or I will die." Joe looked down at his feet.

"Is that where you got the burns, Joe?" Jack asked.

Joe didn't answer.

"How did you get away from them, Joe?" Jack asked.

"Grandfather and his man found me. They killed the one watching me and said I had to leave with them. Grandfather said other people from San Pedro will follow. But I know MS-13 is angry. They will kill everyone. They will find me."

Claudine Setera had painted a big target on the boy's back with her "public has a right to know" type of excuse for getting her face on television.

"This other man you say came with your grandfather to find you. Did he travel with you?"

Joe's eyes remained downcast. "I did not tell you all, Detective Murphy. I'm sorry. My grandfather says not to tell anyone because Mara...MS-13 will find us. It doesn't matter if I tell now because the ones that found us are dead and I will be sent back."

Joe said a word in Spanish.

"What does that mean, Joe?" Jack asked.

"Bodyguard," Joe answered. "Grandfather always had one or two personal bodyguards protecting him."

Sister Aquinas stood motionless in the shadow of the kitchen doorway, listening to the boy's story.

"I have no one now. My mother and father were killed. My sister was with them, so she must be dead."

Jack asked, "The fight you heard in the truck trailer was your grandfather's bodyguard protecting you from the man and woman?"

"Yes," Joe said. "He died so that I might live."

"Who were the man and woman he was fighting with?" Jack asked.

"MS-13," Joe answered. "But they were not Honduran. That is all I know."

"During the fight did you hear any words spoken?" Jack continued.

"They called my grandfather by his name. The man and woman who were killed did. The bodyguard rushed toward the man and woman, and they fought. Grandfather took me away from the sounds of fighting, and I heard a man cry out. A woman screamed. The bodyguard came to Grandfather and brought coats. Grandfather put them on me. I remember nothing else, Detective Murphy. I am sorry."

Sister Aquinas said, "I have some warmer clothes for this young man." She put the clothing on a chair.

Joe didn't take the clothes. "Thank you, Sister. You are kind, but I cannot take them."

"Nonsense," she said. "We need to get you warm. I'll make another breakfast. You must be starving. The second door on your right is a restroom where you can change clothes. Hurry, or you'll hurt my feelings."

"You don't want to hurt her feelings, Joe, and to be honest, you stink to high heaven," Jack said.

Joe sniffed at his shirt-sleeve and made a face.

Joe gathered up the clothes.

Chapter 14

Jack left the boy with Sister Aquinas. He wanted to keep Joe away from the press, and he knew no reporter was a match for the tough little nun. Plus, he wasn't ready to turn the boy over to ICE and make further contact with him difficult. As they were leaving the convent Captain Franklin called.

"You should have let me know the boy was missing," Captain Franklin said. "I don't like hearing things from the deputy chief."

The deputy chief knew Jack had found Joe because Jack had called Deaconess Hospital and dispatch to call off the search. The captain had probably heard dispatch calling the search off, but Jack should have called him directly. The deputy chief probably had been informed by Detective Jansen, who was at Deaconess Hospital sniffing around the case. He hoped Jansen hadn't called the news media, too.

"Joe was missing for twenty minutes tops, but you're right. I should have called you when I found him." If Double Dick knew where Joe was, he would be arranging a well-televised search and rescue event, with himself at center stage.

"Captain, the boy is safe and having breakfast," Jack said.

"I'll call the State Department, Jack," Captain Franklin said. "We have a duty to report this. Not to mention that the boy's embassy needs to be made aware of his involvement to protect his rights."

"Involvement in what? Captain, he's just a scared kid. After what he's been through, I say we cut him a little slack," Jack said.

"He's not *just a kid,* and you know it. Let the State Department do their thing. He won't go to jail, Jack. He most likely won't even be sent back to Honduras for a long while. If he has family here in the US, he'll go through Immigration procedures and they'll take care of him. It's out of your hands. You don't want to screw with Assistant Deputy Director Toomey. Need I remind you this is exactly the type of thing Deputy Chief Dick can use to have you fired?"

Jack knew, but he'd promised Joe he'd do what he could. Besides, maybe not jumping through federal hoops was the best impression to give Toomey. The man should know what he was getting. Hopefully Toomey wouldn't have Jack sign a prenuptial promising not to screw the Feds.

"I'll call the State Department and tell them we have the boy in custody," Jack lied. "I'm pulling up their phone number right now."

"Bring the boy in, and I'll make some calls to see where we can house him until State or ICE decides what to do with him. No messing around here, Jack. And when you're done talking to State, you need to call Assistant Deputy Director Toomey. He's called here twice and said you're not answering your phone. Don't let me catch you screwing around."

"You won't catch me screwing around. I mean I won't. I promise," Jack said and ended the call.

Jack pulled in to Donut Bank on First Avenue where even on this cold morning the lot outside was full and the inside was packed, but they were in luck. An older couple had just gotten up and left an empty table in the corner.

As they sat down, Liddell asked, "Do you even have the State Department's phone number, pod'na?"

"Why would I have that?" Jack said. "I'm going to call Anna Whiteside. Apparently the captain has already called them. Maybe she can help stall this."

He found her number and called.

Anna Whiteside, special agent with Immigration and Customs Enforcement, or ICE, was part of a task force dealing with human trafficking when Jack and Liddell had met her in Louisiana. Whiteside had used them as bait to take down some members of the law enforcement community who were involved in a sex trafficking ring. Jack considered her a ruthless friend with federal benefits. She considered Jack a loose cannon just one step this side of illegal. It was a match made in heaven.

"Whiteside," the phone was answered.

"Anna. It's Jack Murphy. I need a favor."

"The last time I did you a favor a historic mansion burned to the ground, hundreds of acres of sugar cane fields went up in flames, and lots of people died, Jack."

"Only the right ones," Jack responded. "And the mansion wasn't my fault. They tried to kill me and Bigfoot first."

"That's your story and you should stick to it," Anna said. "By the way, congratulations on being selected for USOC. I'll be at your swearing-in ceremony next Friday. I'll be the one dressed in total body armor in case you get excited. Now what can I do for you?"

"We have a situation here that ICE might be interested in," Jack said.

Anna said, "You have a nine-year-old Honduran boy, the survivor of an illegal entry into the US via Mexico. You have thirty-one dead in a truck trailer, and the driver of the truck was murdered across town."

Jack didn't say anything.

"Your captain and Assistant Deputy Director Toomey called me. Apparently neither of them trusts you to keep anyone informed. I feel the same, by the way."

Jack came back with, "You seem to know everything, so tell me what I need from you."

"You need lots of things, Jack. But you should tell me what you haven't shared with your other bosses. When I know everything, I can tell you if you're going to federal prison."

Liddell snickered. "She's on to you, pod'na."

"As a sworn officer of the law, you are under an obligation to report his presence and custody to the State Department through his embassy. As a federal agent you are doubly obligated."

"I'm not a federal agent yet, Anna," Jack said.

"You will be soon. I won't believe it until I see it, but there it is. I've got to tell you, Bobby Troup was a little concerned that you and Blanchard would be working for us," Anna said.

Bobby Troup had been a detective with the Vice Unit for Iberville Parish Sheriff Department in Louisiana during the days Liddell worked there. Bobby had become a suspect in a suspicious death and subsequently resigned under a cloud. Liddell was the sheriff's detective that had investigated Troup. There was no love lost between Bobby Troup and Liddell.

"I'm sure Troup will live," Jack said. "At least he won't be working with us, so there shouldn't be an issue."

Quiet from Anna's side of the conversation.

"Shit," Jack said. "What?"

"Director Toomey assigned Troup and yours truly to your investigations," she said. "I've put Troup on hold, but I'm considering sending him to Evansville. I will if you give me any reason."

"Anna, you don't have to send Bobby Troup here. I'll keep you informed. I promise."

"Why don't I believe you?"

"I'm calling you now," Jack said.

"You weren't going to until you needed a favor, Jack. Now, tell me everything you know."

"Okay," Jack said, and he did. Sort of. He told her about Freyda Rademacher, the customer, the stolen car with the dog inside. About the key they found hidden in the dead man's shoe and how it fit the padlock on the truck, and finding Joe half buried beneath a mound of frozen bodies.

"I interviewed Joe at the hospital," Jack continued. "He was traveling with his grandfather. The grandfather had a bodyguard with them. Apparently, the grandfather was confronted by MS-13 in Honduras. He was being threatened to work for them."

"What kind of work?" Anna asked.

"He owned a couple of small printing businesses," Jack said.

"And they wanted to take over his business," Anna said. "I'm guessing he refused and fled the country."

"MS-13 killed the boy's parents, kidnapped him and his sister to force the grandfather to play ball," Jack said. "The grandfather pulled a fast one on them. He and his bodyguard freed Joe, and they fled to the US. During the trip, a fight broke out. Joe said the grandfather's bodyguard killed a man and a woman. We found Columbian passports on the man and woman who were killed by the bodyguard, who was carrying a Honduran passport. The Columbians had burner phones."

"Okay. Did Joe tell you where he and his grandfather lived in Honduras?"

"Puerto Lempira and San Pedro Sula. Along the coast. Why? You looking for an all-inclusive beach vacation complete with machetes and beheadings for an activity?"

"Do you know what Puerto Lempira and San Pedro Sula have in common, Jack?" she asked.

"I don't know," Jack said. "Bananas?"

"Close, Jack. But the answer is MS-13. These people make Hitler seem like a sous chef at a McDonald's. If they were fleeing MS-13, it was a smart move. If they've killed gang members during this little trip, the boy will be hunted down."

Jack hoped she was exaggerating, but Anna wasn't prone to do that. Lie, yes. Exaggerate, no.

"Let me do a little digging to see if this MS-13 angle is related to what we have," she said. "MS-13 could use a small newspaper to create propaganda and make fake passports. These guys are branching out, Jack. They're into selling weapons, drugs, human trafficking, assassinations, and they're taking over a lot of small businesses here and in Central America to launder their money. It's not your typical gang."

"I wasn't aware we had that large of a problem here in the US," Jack said.

"Our president wants MS-13 eliminated and has declared war on them. Where they once flaunted their activities in the face of the authorities, they are now taking it underground or hiding it behind businesses. It hasn't slowed down the violence, but they are smart like rats. If the route is blocked one way, they find another."

"You seem to know a lot, Anna. Any chance you can cut to the chase and tell me who my murder suspect is?" Jack asked.

Anna said, "Let me guess. Joe and his grandfather were headed for a small town on one of the Great Lakes, Ft. Gratiot in Michigan."

"Yeah. Ft. Gratiot. How could you possibly know that?"

"Most of the people in that trailer were most likely recruited or were being forced to work the docks for MS-13," she said. "Your captain says you had some dealings with mercenaries mimicking MS-13 killings last year."

Jack remembered the two hired ex-military mercenaries he'd dealt with a year ago. They had beheaded a half dozen people and left the heads on public display.

"They are like any other terrorist group," she said. "They rely on fear and their reputation for violence, but they don't take credit for their acts. They don't need to leave a calling card. They've adapted. Wherever they're small in numbers they use weapons at hand: rifles, handguns, knives, even garrotes. They never leave a survivor, Jack." She let that sink in. "I'll send you some of our material so you can catch up."

"That would be appreciated, but I don't have a lot of time to sit and read."

"You're kidding. You can read?" she asked sarcastically. "I was going to send you the picture book."

"Bite me, Anna," Jack said. "We haven't had a lot of gang activity around here. The closest we have to a violent gang is called a City Council. They eat their wounded."

Anna chuckled. "I can see why you have so much support, Jack. Director Toomey said he practically had to threaten your mayor to keep you on the police department while you work for the task force. The mayor wanted you gone."

"I'm hurt, Anna. Let's get back to the reason I called. I need a favor."

"Okay, I'll listen to your favor, and in return you have to do some things for me."

"Deal," he lied.

"What do you want to ask me, Jack?"

"I want to keep Joe on ice for a while. I have him somewhere safe, and before you ask where, I'm going to refuse to tell you. He's all I've got, and I'm not sharing."

She surprised Jack and asked, "Is that it?"

"Yeah. For starters. And I want you to keep this quiet with your people until I'm ready, because I don't want Feds swarming all over me. I don't like to be touched."

"I can do all of that, except all of that," Anna said. "Jack, you called me. You need my help. Here's what I want in return for not doing any of what you want. I want good photos of all of the evidence collected from the truck, the car, the dog, the boy, the bodies, all of it. And you need to tell me where the boy is."

"I guess you didn't hear me," Jack said.

"Typical," she said. "How much of this has gotten out to the public already?"

"Your guess is as good as mine," Jack said. He hoped Anna was wrong about MS-13 pursuing the boy until they killed him. Claudine had spilled the beans, so Jack was more determined than ever to hide the boy away. The fewer people that knew where Joe was, the safer the boy was.

"The media was at the truck scene. I didn't see anyone around the Coffee Shop where we found the other body. But our deputy chief knows most of this, and he is really an undercover journalist in a policeman's uniform."

"Your captain told me that. Sounds like a dick."

"That's goes double," Jack said. "And there's this television reporter that asked me if the first murder and the deaths in the truck were connected."

"Who's the reporter?"

"Channel Six. Claudine Setera."

"I'll take care of her," Whiteside said.

"Okay," Jack said. "I've got to call my new boss at the FBI. Got to go."

Anna said, "I'll call Toomey. I don't think he wants to talk to you for the time being. I'm your new boss, so you report directly to me. And don't get all sulky. I won't try to get you or that yeti friend of yours killed again. By the way, tell Liddell congratulations on the baby girl. Jane's a good name. My aunt's name is Jane."

"We don't work for you until Friday," Jack said. "Anna, don't take this wrong. Well, actually I don't care how you take it. I'm uncomfortable working with you until my kidnapping is official or until you're having my baby."

"I'll have your baby, Jack, but Katie's not going to be too happy."

Touché.

Anna said, "I'll leave this kid, Joe, alone for now, and I'll see what I can do. No promises. For that, you have your crime scene people get my stuff together. So, get your head out of your ass and get busy. Your local FBI has access to a light plane. They'll transport. I need it yesterday, Jack."

"The Feds have all the toys, Anna."

"Are you still talking?" Anna asked sarcastically.

"Okay. I'll get this started. I'll have the coroner's report sent as well."

"And Jack... You'd better answer your phone for me or I'll have you picked up, packaged, and delivered on that toy plane of the FBI's. Got it?"

"I promise," Jack said into a dead connection. "She hung up on me."

"You do that to everyone else, pod'na," Liddell pointed out.

"Will you call Sergeant Walker and tell him what Anna wants? I don't trust myself," Jack said.

Liddell called Walker and passed on ICE Agent Anna Whiteside's request. When he finished he said to Jack, "You don't trust the ICE Queen with Joe's whereabouts?"

"What she doesn't know won't screw us, Bigfoot."

Chapter 15

When Jack and Liddell arrived downtown, Deputy Chief Dick was waiting at the back entrance to the detectives' office.

"Murphy and Blanchard. Chief's office. Now," Dick said. With that he turned and marched away.

"Murphy and Blanchard," Liddell said smoothly. "Has a television series ring to it, pod'na? Like Butch and the Sundance Kid. Blanchard and Murphy. That's better."

"Coming from Double Dick it has a 'shit storm is coming your way' kind of ring to it. A Butch Casualty and Sumdunce Kid."

"You a funny man, pod'na. What did you do to get us called to the principal's office?"

He hadn't done anything. At least Jack didn't think he had.

They followed Double Dick through the front lobby to the chief's complex. An unsmiling Judy Mangold, the chief's secretary, buzzed them in and ignored them while she talked to an older man sitting in the waiting area. Dick led them past the chief's office and straight into the conference room without a word.

Sitting around the large mahogany table were Chief Marlin Pope, FBI Deputy Assistant Director Toomey, Captain Franklin, county attorney Bob Rothschild, Channel Six investigative reporter Claudine Setera, the station's attorney David Wires, Sergeant Walker, and a stern man Jack had never before seen.

Double Dick walked around the table, stopping briefly to put a reassuring hand on Claudine's shoulder and accepting a toothy smile from her. He took the empty seat on the other side of Chief Pope. No chairs remained, so Jack and Liddell were left standing at the end of the table with all eyes on them as if they were truant children.

Jack checked out the unknown man for signs that he was a cop or an attorney. Maybe another federal officer.

Chief Pope spoke first. "Most of you know each other, so I won't waste time on introductions."

"I know everyone," Jack said, "but I have to wonder what Channel Six is doing here? Is she filing a complaint because I threw her out of a crime scene?"

Dick said, "You're here to brief us, Murphy, not ask questions."

Chief Pope said, "Jack, Channel Six has agreed not to air anything until I or Deputy Assistant Director Toomey give our permission. They will stop airing the photos they have of the survivor and will take that video down from their website."

"Swell," Jack said.

"What did you say?" Dick said.

"I said this is great, Deputy Chief Dick," Jack said, emphasis on Dick. "I assume another part of the deal is that Channel Six gives us any witnesses or evidence they come across?"

Dick came out of his seat. "I won't tolerate this insubordination from..."

"Sit down, Richard," Chief Pope said.

Channel Six's attorney, Wires, said, "We're not required to give you our sources, you understand. The Constitution says..."

"Not a big deal," Jack said, interrupting the law lecture.

The unknown man in the room was barely covering a grin.

"I'm assuming you've told them what you already know?" Jack asked. "I called ICE and gave them everything." *Except where the boy is staying.* To Claudine he unnecessarily explained, "ICE is Immigration and Custom Enforcement." He continued, "They've requested green cards, passports, and photos along with any reports." He directed his next words to Dave Wires. "We'll need Claudine and her cameraman to give a statement to one of our detectives. They were both at the scene and at the hospital talking to the survivor from the truck."

Claudine stiffened and turned to her attorney. Wires's cheeks reddened.

"Get on with it, Jack," Captain Franklin said.

"ICE is assisting in identifying the bodies. I assume the autopsies will be done here, Chief?"

Toomey said, "A mobile facility is being sent here. We'll want our own medical examiners involved of course."

Of course. "We're ninety percent sure the body we found by the Coffee Shop is the driver of the truck. We've seen the body. Dr. John—our pathologist—will do the autopsies for our team. This victim was stabbed three times with a bladed weapon twenty to twenty-two inches in length." He didn't tell them about the star shape of the blade. The shape Dr. John had called cruciform. If Double Dick or Claudine Setera knew details about the weapon, "Crucifix Killer" would be in the headlines.

Jack continued briefing the room, with Liddell adding or clarifying a fact here and there. When he was finished he braced himself for the inevitable question and didn't have to wait long.

"Where is the boy now?" Claudine asked.

Jack said, "He's safe. That's all I'm going to say for now. This is a nine-year-old child, Claudine. He won't be giving interviews." *Or crying on camera.*

Jack fielded a couple of questions from Double Dick and both attorneys, but the unknown guy said nothing, and for whatever reason, Claudine Setera didn't ask him why he was present.

When the meeting wrapped up, Chief Pope said, "Jack. Liddell. Stay." He thanked everyone for coming and pressed flesh as the civilians left the conference room. Double Dick kept his seat, and Chief Pope said, "Richard, you don't need to be here for this."

Dick got up, started to say something, thought better of it and left the room, shutting the door hard behind him.

Assistant Deputy Director Toomey introduced the man who was apparently working for Toomey.

"I've already introduced Lieutenant Sanchez to the captain and chief." To Sanchez he said, "The big one's Liddell Blanchard. The mouthy one is Jack Murphy. I hope you can work with them."

Toomey continued, "Everyone else in this room thinks Lieutenant Sanchez is my aide. He is, sort of, but he's also with the St. Louis PD Homicide Unit."

Chief Pope said, "Jack, Anna Whiteside advised that she told you she would be leading your team."

"That's what she said, Chief. But she didn't tell me squat on the St. Louis thing."

Chief Pope said, "She didn't tell you a lot of things. Agent Whiteside said you had some concern of not being sworn in as a federal agent."

"Chief, I..."

"Don't interrupt," Chief Pope said. "Captain, can you bring him in?"

Captain Franklin left the room and came back with the man Jack had seen talking to the chief's secretary.

Chief Pope said, "Pete, this is Detective Jack Murphy. And this is Detective Liddell Blanchard."

"Peter Swaim," the man said. "US Marshal for this region."

"Pete's here to swear you in early," Chief Pope said.

Director Toomey added, "We'll still have a brief ceremony in the Federal Building on Friday. We'll announce your addition to USOC to the press at that time."

The press. Of course.

"Do we get badges?" Liddell asked, and Sanchez smiled at Jack.

"I must have left them in my other suit," Toomey said, deadpan.

Swaim said, "You'll get the badges next Friday when we do this again."

Jack was grateful Liddell didn't say something stupid like, "We don't get no stinkin' badges?"

The US Marshal said, "Raise your right hands and repeat after me."

Jack and Liddell were sworn in with no pomp, ceremony, cameras, family, or throwing of police hats into the air.

It was over in two minutes, and Toomey said, "Thanks for coming on such short notice, Pete."

Swaim replied, "And on a weekend. You owe me," and left.

"Any more complaints, Jack?" Chief Pope asked, obviously not expecting an answer. "EPD will support you in any way we can, but as of now you're working for Director Toomey."

Toomey said, "Since you don't seem to want to talk to me, Lieutenant Sanchez will fill you in on why this is a task force issue. You'll need to go home, kiss your wives, pack, and report to St. Louis HQ today. Why so surprised, Detective Murphy? The FBI can move fast when it needs to. Can you?"

"Yes sir," Jack said.

"Sanchez, they're all yours," Toomey said.

Chief Pope, Double Dick, and Captain Franklin left the room, and Sanchez stood.

"Walk to the Federal Building with me, and we'll talk on the way," Sanchez said, tore a page out of his notebook, and handed it to Jack. "You don't have to rush over to St. Louis, but when you get to a stopping point, call me and come to this address."

Chapter 16

The chill wind kept the conversation to a minimum.

"Can you tell us what's going on, Lieutenant?" Jack asked.

"I'll tell you how I'm involved. I've been a street cop, detective, and then a lieutenant with the St. Louis Police Department's Homicide Squad. A few weeks ago, this guy Toomey shows up, and bim-bam-boom I'm on his task force. USOC stands for Unsolved Serial and Organized Crimes. Toomey said that was just the beginning, because this task force is just getting its wind."

"So, are you permanently working for Toomey now?" Liddell asked.

"I don't know how it'll work for you two, but I'm on it for special assignments, and afterwards, right back to homicide."

"That's pretty much what our chief told us," Jack said.

"Okay. Now let me tell you why you're coming to St. Louis. Last August we found a truckload of dead illegal immigrants behind an abandoned warehouse."

Jack and Liddell exchanged looks.

"Yeah. Our case is similar to yours, except ours happened in August and they'd been locked inside in triple-digit temperatures for about three weeks. The driver was found about a mile away from the truck, and he was killed like yours was. The weapon he used sounds the same. Whoever did this is one sadistic son of a bitch. This wasn't my case originally, but I was assigned by Toomey and my chief a couple of weeks ago. There's more of these."

Jack asked, "How many?"

"Five events that we know of. Florida, Texas, and Louisiana all had similar events. All in the last six months. With your body count, we're over two hundred murders." Seeing their reaction, Sanchez said, "Yeah, it's a lot to swallow. I'm still trying to get my arms around it. Missouri was the first case. Texas in September, Florida in October, Louisiana in November..."

Jack said, "And Indiana in January."

"Yeah. You're last, but we don't think this guy is done. He took Christmas off. Maybe he has a family and he wanted to spend Christmas with some semblance of sanity," Sanchez said.

"We think our driver was killed last night or early this morning," Jack said.

"The St. Louis driver was found a mile or so from the truck two days after the bodies in the trailer were discovered. The drivers' bodies in the Florida and Texas cases were found with the trucks. The one in Louisiana is still missing."

"Swamp?" Liddell asked.

"Yeah."

"Alligators," Liddell said.

"That'd be my guess. Our case is the oldest," Sanchez said. "We've had the most time to work on it, but we haven't gotten very far. We weren't aware of the other states' cases until a few weeks ago when Toomey came to my chief. And here I am. Lucky me."

"What does Toomey want from us?" Jack asked.

"You'll be getting everything that we drug up over the last six months, but it will all be new to you. Maybe you'll have a different perspective since you're not invested in a theory."

Jack said, "I don't think we'll be welcomed with open arms by your detectives. Hell, I know I wouldn't want someone coming in and stepping all over my investigation."

"It won't be like that," Sanchez said.

"Are you saying the St. Louis Homicide Squad is going to cooperate?" Jack asked.

"Nah. They'll bitch and moan. They always do, but they'll leave us alone because I'm one of them. We won't be working directly with them unless we need them."

"My question again. What are we supposed to do for you?" Jack asked.

"Toomey wants fresh eyes on this. The St. Louis case is stalled big time. They get stuck on one suspect after another and each time, the suspect has an ironclad alibi. I know that don't mean much normally, but these are all local assholes that I doubt had time or money to travel to all the locations, murder a bunch of people, and come home to the Show-Me state."

Jack said nothing. This sounded like the Feds were grasping at straws to him. If they didn't have more to go on than getting a fresh set of eyes, it meant they wanted someone to blame for the case not being solved. It was an ideal case for him.

They passed the Winfield K. Denton Federal Building and crossed the street to the YMCA parking lot.

"I hope you didn't park in here," Liddell said. "The Meter Nazis will have your car towed by now."

"I've got an FBI placard in the front," Sanchez said.

"That's just chumming the waters in the downtown area, Lieutenant," Liddell said. "These people eat FBI for breakfast. Out-of-state plates make you a meal deal."

Sanchez stopped at a black GMC Yukon Denali 4X4 with heavily tinted windows and a push bar on the front. An FBI placard was on the dash in the front window.

"Ain't she a beauty? The downside is I have to stop every other block or so to gas up."

"Don't complain," Liddell said, still in awe. "We're driving Fords almost old enough to vote. Do you think Toomey will get us both one of these?"

"Sure, Bigfoot," Jack said. "And maybe you'll have Double Dick for a driver."

"Double Dick?" Sanchez asked.

"We'll explain later," Jack said.

Sanchez got in the SUV and drove away.

Jack said, "Let's go back to the detectives' office and see if Chapman has anything yet."

* * * *

"We should have driven him to his car," Liddell complained by the time they climbed the steps to the back door of the detectives' office. Detective Larry Jansen was waiting for them.

"Hey, Jack. Hey, Liddell," Jansen said.

Even in the zero-degree weather, Jansen was wearing a summer-weight tan trench coat and brown felt hat. All that was missing from the Columbo image was the ever-present unlit cigar that Peter Falk favored for the role as the not-so-bumbling detective. Jansen's strategy for interviewing suspects—when he was inclined to do police work—was to act stupid but be cunning. Jansen *was* stupid and *acting* cunning.

"Larry," Jack said. They headed to the detectives' office at a brisk pace.

Jansen hurried to catch up. He pulled out a tattered notebook. "Well, I've gone through the entire hospital, every person, every floor, and no one saw your boy leave. I know he's already been found, but I got a list here, names, where they work, who they were visiting, room numbers, other stuff if you need it. So where is the boy anyway?"

"That's swell, Larry," Jack said. His gut told him to have Captain Franklin order Jansen to stay out of the investigation. Two reasons for not doing so presented themselves. Jack could feed Jansen info that would leak to Double Dick and/or the news media; and more importantly, something this big would require all the help they could get. "Give your report to Detective Chapman. He's the central hub on this."

"The pivot man in a circle jerk," Jansen said, smiling, holding the door for them to enter. "Is that where you're headed?"

Jack stopped and turned to face Jansen. It wasn't like the little man to be so "helpful." It definitely wasn't like him to do real detective work to give it to Jack for free. Something smelled.

"That's where we're going," Jack said. "Why?"

"Good. That's good," Jansen said and rubbed the skin of a cheek lined deeply from years of chain-smoking. "I just had a thought. The list I made might come in handy after Channel Six told everyone the kid was in the hospital. You know. In case the killer came to the hospital to finish what he started."

Jack felt his face flush. He'd been so pissed at Claudine and so focused on finding Joe he hadn't thought of that. He hadn't posted a guard on the boy at Deaconess and allowed the boy to take off. That Claudine was able to get in to see Joe so easily was his fault as well.

"Good thinking, Larry," Jack said.

"I was just wondering if—you know..."

"What is it, Larry?" Jack asked.

"I was wondering if you want me to keep an eye on the boy for you. I don't mind," Jansen said. "I want to help out."

Then you'll know where Joe is, and that's information you could trade or sell. "Why don't you come with us and tell Chapman what you have? I'm sure there's other things that need doing. I've got the boy covered for now. Maybe later. Thanks." *Asshole.*

Jansen gave Jack a resigned sigh.

"Nah," Jansen said. "I'll get with Chapman later." The notebook disappeared back inside his coat. "I just remembered I got other things to do. Important things."

Chapter 17

Detective Earl Chapman had taken over a sergeant's office in the basement of police headquarters. When Jack and Liddell came in he said, "What have you gotten me into, Jack?"

Chapman was Jack's go-to detective if he needed something done right the first time with minimal whining. The magnitude of this investigation made it a monumental task, so Jack needed someone he could trust not to cut corners. Chapman was running the scut work for this investigation, anything that needed done—door to door contacts/interviews, running license plates, running records on all the neighbors, verifying information—it was like running an emergency room with one doctor after an airplane crash.

"Aren't you retired yet, you old geezer?" Jack asked.

"Well, I was going to and then some asshole killed a bunch of people. Why? You want me to leave? I will, you know," Chapman said, smirking.

"I'll owe you one," Jack said.

"You'll owe me more than one. How about you loan me your boat for a week in July? I promise to bring it back, and I'll split the fish I catch with you."

Jack had a 25-foot cabin cruiser called the *MISS FIT* in dry dock for the winter months. He owed a bottle of Scotch to the Deaconess ER doctor, and now this.

"I'll go with you," Jack said. "What have you got?"

"Two things. Diddly and squat," Chapman answered. Piled in front of him was a small stack of reports created by officers and other detectives working the case.

By tonight the inch-thick stack of papers would be a foot high.

"We're going to St. Louis, Earl," Jack said.

"I hear you two are real G-men now," Chapman said. "What's in St. Louis? Is that where the FBI Secret Hideout is?"

"Bite me, Earl," Jack said. He wasn't surprised that Earl had already heard they'd been sworn in by the US Marshal. Earl probably had seen the guy come in the building and put two and two together.

"You think this guy got whacked by someone in St. Louis, Jack?" Chapman asked.

"We can't rule anything out this early," Jack said. He remembered Sanchez said the St. Louis case was stalling out. It had been six months. It wasn't always a hard and fast rule, but if a case didn't come up with some leads in the first day, it was difficult to solve at best. Some people—the FBI—thought it was all over after twenty-four hours. Jack thought it was over after twenty-four years, give or take a decade.

"You got a lead? I know you're FBI and shit, but you can tell your old pal, can't you?" Earl asked.

Before Jack could answer, the phone on Chapman's desk rang. It was Sergeant Walker for Jack.

"Tony," Jack said.

"We have the pictures and other things your girlfriend, Anna, asked for. One of my detectives is bringing it upstairs to you."

"She's not my girlfriend, Tony," Jack said, and a crime scene detective named Suzie came into the office with two thumb drives and a mailing envelope stuffed tight.

She handed Chapman the mailing envelope and one of the thumb drives. "You need to put a copy of all your paperwork in that, and an FBI agent is coming to get it." She handed Jack the other thumb drive. "From Sergeant Walker. Do I need to keep copies of any updates to forward to your girlfriend?"

"She's not my girlfriend," Jack said.

"Sure," Suzie said. "I hear you're real Feds now. I heard they're flying all this stuff to your girlfriend." She winked and left.

"Your girlfriend?" Earl asked.

"Yeah. Jack's a stud-muffin, Earl. Men fear him, women love him," Liddell said.

"Shut up, Bigfoot."

"I thought you were back with your ex," Earl said.

"I am. I don't have a girlfriend, Earl."

Chapman's phone rang again. He answered and said, "No. No. Not yet, Mrs. Raymond. No, that won't be necessary, ma'am. I won't need to talk to you again, Mrs. Raymond. Yes. I'll let you know if there's any cause for alarm. Okay. Bye, ma'am."

Chapman said to Jack, "That woman has called a dozen times. She was interviewed during a neighborhood check, and she insists she saw the killer drive past her house. She didn't see shit. Just a car that she thought was suspicious. Everything over by the university looks suspicious to me. She won't stop calling."

Jack raised an eyebrow.

Earl said, "She's a widow. She's lonely. She wants to be needed. Channel Six has created a monster with their bullshit news specials. Now the Civic Center switchboard is transferring calls from anyone asking for information or leaving tips on the murders straight to us. Not witnesses. Just the curious."

"We were told that Channel Six will cease and desist," Jack said. "It should slow down in a little while. Need some help?" Jack asked. "I'll call the captain and..."

"I've already talked to him. He's putting together some guys and phone lines to field this crap," Earl said.

"Where does this woman live?" Jack asked. "Mrs. Raymond, I mean."

"Four blocks north of the Coffee Shop on Weinbach Avenue. I'm telling you, Jack. Don't waste your time. She's as nutty as a Payday candy bar."

"I believe you, Earl, but I need to talk to her just so I can say I followed up."

"Really?"

"You never know. She's a widow, lonely, probably up all night watching out her window and dreaming about you," Jack said.

Earl wrote her name and address on a piece of scrap paper and handed it to Jack. "Her name and address. If you talk to her, it's like feeding a stray. You'll never get rid of her."

"Thanks, Earl. I'll take the risk."

Jack and Liddell headed toward the parking lot. Jack said, "Maybe Earl really *should* retire. He's getting burned out."

"He's done this longer than the both of us, pod'na. He might be right about the widow, but I guess it won't hurt to run by there on our way to St. Louis."

Jack handed the car keys to Liddell. "We're in no hurry, so you drive."

"You saying I drive like an old lady again, pod'na? Ooh, that hurts."

They drove down Walnut heading east. Mrs. Raymond's house was on a narrow corner lot four blocks from the murder scene. Two picture windows partially covered by sheers gave a perfect view of the street. The house was white-wood-sided and badly in need of paint. A low brick wall enclosed a small front porch decorated with two black rockers like Cracker Barrel furniture. Stone lions guarded the three steps onto the porch. The steps were covered with that hideous green indoor/outdoor carpeting that was popular when Nixon was president. Around the front foundation were flowerbeds, now thick with frozen plants and weeds. Jack expected to see the traditional collection of concrete yard gnomes belonging to an old woman, but the yard was neat and empty.

They stepped onto the porch, and a woman in her late 20s or early 30s opened the door before Liddell could knock. She was Jack's height with a runner's physique that matched her orange and purple running outfit, fluorescent pink running shoes, and ear muffs that hung around her neck. A blond ponytail protruded from the back of her Otters baseball cap.

"Is Mrs. Raymond at home?" Jack said and opened his badge case.

"Detective Murphy and Detective Blanchard," she said. "I knew you'd come. Please come in. Make yourselves at home. The front room is to your left."

Jack and Liddell didn't move. Mrs. Raymond was a little young to be an eccentric widow, as Chapman had led them to believe.

"I'm Mrs. Raymond," she said and stepped back to allow them to enter. "Please come in and let me shut the door. This is an old house, and it takes an hour to heat once it gets cold."

Jack and Liddell came inside. "You're the Mrs. Raymond that talked to a detective?" Jack asked.

"Yes. Detective Chapman and I have talked quite often this morning. Would you like coffee—or tea? I have instant coffee, but I make the tea strong and sweet. My grandmother taught me how to make it. You see, my mother and father died in a plane crash coming back from a church mission to Haiti, so I was raised here by my grandmother. I married, but my husband passed away, and I moved back in with my grandmother. She's gone now too, and I just can't give this place up."

Jack said, "Nothing for us, Mrs. Raymond. We just have a few questions, and we'll let you get back to whatever you were doing."

"Are you sure you don't want anything?" she said. "I just made fresh canapés, and then I remembered I shouldn't eat so many... Well, I'm sure you don't want to hear all that. I was getting ready to go for a run, but it can wait until I answer your questions. I know you'll want to 'pick my brain.' At least that's what Detective Chapman called it. He's so nice. Don't you think? His wife is very lucky, but he doesn't seem too happy. I don't know if he even has a wife. Does he?"

"Yes, ma'am," Jack said. "Yes, he's a nice man. Now, you told him you saw the killer." Before she could launch into another long monologue, he said, "We've heard what you told him, but we need to see for ourselves how you saw this person, and what makes you think it was the killer."

"I didn't really see the killer," she said. "Come in here." She led them into an adjacent room with a huge picture window. The room was devoid of furniture but was crammed with fitness equipment. The allowance for furniture was a well-used leather recliner in one corner, facing the window.

"Wow. This is awesome," Liddell said.

"This isn't what I wanted to show you. I know that as investigators you have to ascertain if a witness could see what they claim to have seen. A lot of what you get is people's idea of what they really saw, when in fact they were in another room or peering through a bush, or something else had their attention."

"That's correct," Jack said, thinking they had another fanatical fan of crime scene shows. *CSI* was giving prospective criminals a training they wouldn't get in college, and it was giving real investigators a pain in the ass.

"Sit there," she said, pointing to the recliner in the corner.

Jack sat on the edge of the seat, and from there he had an unobstructed view of the street all the way to the corner.

"You can see the street and the intersection, can't you?"

"Yes."

"My grandmother would sit in that chair all day, watching her television shows, and watching out the window. She was what you would call a nosy old woman. Sorry, Grandma."

"Sorry for your loss," Liddell said.

"Thank you, Detective Blanchard. My point is, I have a clear view of this street and the corner. I haven't been sleeping well, so I get up and work out in here. I just light a candle. Something about the dim light helps me exercise, and helps me go back to sleep. Grandma Raymond always said I burned the candle at both ends. But anyway, I was just finishing my sets with the weights. I do the arm curls on the edge of the recliner, which gives me a clear view of the street. I saw a car creeping down the street with its lights off."

"What time was this?" Jack asked with a renewed interest.

"About eleven or so. Before midnight anyway. Sorry I can't be more precise. I know I should have because details count in a murder investigation."

There were sheers covering the sides of the window, but maybe at night, with a low light, she could see enough. "Can you describe the car?" Jack asked.

"There's a streetlight on the corner and another halfway down the block toward the crime scene," she said. "I know the crime scene was down beside the Coffee Shop by the University of Evansville. It was on the news. Anyway, I didn't go outside, but I went to the window and saw the car continue south on Weinbach Avenue with its lights off. At first, I thought it might just be a college student. But the car slowed to a stop several times, like he was casing the neighborhood."

"Okay," he prompted her to continue. She hadn't answered the question about the car's description, but he hoped she would get around to it soon.

"It didn't feel right to me. There are a lot of young people in this neighborhood going to the university. Most of them are on foot, but some drive, and they like to speed. This car wasn't speeding. I called the police and reported a suspicious vehicle and..."

"You called the police?" Jack asked.

"Yes. Did I do right?"

Liddell was on his cell phone calling dispatch.

Jack said, "You did exactly right, Mrs. Raymond."

"Lucy Raymond is my full name in case you need that for your report, Detective Murphy."

"Go on," Jack said.

Liddell disconnected the call with dispatch and said to Jack, "Dispatch says they got two calls from here. One at eleven ten last night and another at eleven forty."

"Should I continue, Detective Murphy?"

"By all means," Jack said.

"The car came by here several times. It was always going in the same direction, toward the university. Like they were circling the block. I called 9-1-1 again, but I never saw a police cruiser come by. I watched for a while, and when the car didn't come back I went to bed. That was around one in the morning. Of course, that doesn't mean the police hadn't searched the neighborhood, but they never came down my street, or came to my house."

"Officer Hurt was dispatched to both runs last night, pod'na," Liddell said.

Jack gritted his teeth. The same Officer Hurt who lied about his wife being pregnant and sick. Hurt was probably sleeping all night. If he'd patrolled the area and found the car, he might have prevented a murder.

"Can you describe the car, Lucy?" Jack asked again.

"Of course," Lucy said. "It was a VW Beetle, '70s model maybe. It was an ugly green, like a mint but faded. And the front and back had chrome grills. I didn't see the license plate. Sorry."

The stolen car. What was he doing sneaking around the neighborhood? The answer was, he was getting himself murdered.

"And something else, too," Lucy said. "I saw a dog in the front. A black-and-white dog. I couldn't tell what kind, but it was medium-sized. I didn't get a clear view of the driver, but I'm pretty sure it was a man."

"You did good, Lucy. You're very observant," Jack said and made her smile.

"I'm trying to work on that," she said. "I've started paying attention to people's faces when I'm on my run. I run five miles each morning, so you see a lot of cars, people, kids, things like that. I can tell you who's home all day and who works, what they drive, whose kids belong where, that kind of stuff. I only run twice a week during the evening now that it's so cold."

"Can I ask you something, Lucy?" Jack asked.

"Sure. Anything, Detective Murphy."

"How did you know our names? Have we met before?" He didn't think so, but he'd been surprised by the nurse at the emergency room.

"I've seen you both on television, and you've been in the newspapers. You're kind of famous. I know Detective Blanchard's married, and you're not. Earl said you were the detectives working the case."

Earl? "And how do you know I'm not married?" Jack asked. He didn't think that kind of information had ever been on the news.

She grinned. "He's wearing a wedding ring. It looks a little faded, so it's older. You're not wearing a ring, and you have no line around your ring finger. If you are married, you don't wear your wedding band." Her cheeks reddened. "And that's none of my business, Detective Murphy."

Jack laughed, and she explained, "I'm finishing a master's degree in criminology, and I'm on the hiring list for the Evansville Police Department. My husband always wanted to be a policeman, but he had a bad heart. That's why I'm doing this."

Jack knew where he'd seen her before. Her picture was on the bulletin board in the hallway of the police department with forty or so other pictures of police applicants. The pictures were mug shots—front and profile. The bulletin board allowed the sworn officers to peruse the new police applicants' pictures before they were hired in case the background checks had missed something.

Jack said, "Well, Lucy, good luck on the hiring list. Thank you for the information."

As they were leaving, Lucy asked, "Detectives, was that the killer I saw?"

Jack thought how to answer. "Between us?"

"Yes. Between us, Detective Murphy."

"You just described the car and the dog we found," Jack said.

"Was the car stolen?" she asked.

"Yes," Jack said.

"Is his murder connected to the ones you found behind that warehouse?" she asked.

"You'll make a fine detective someday, Lucy," Jack said. "Keep this to yourself."

"I promise, Detective Murphy."

Chapter 18

Jack and Liddell drove toward headquarters.

"Too bad she doesn't live across the street from the Coffee Shop," Liddell said.

"I wonder if Chapman knew she was an applicant?" Jack said. "Anyway, the timing's about right. If she saw the stolen car, it would jibe with what Freyda told us about the customer waiting to meet someone. We need to put a rush on the evidence taken from Freyda's place."

"And speaking of Freyda," Liddell said, "we should stop by there again before we go to St. Louis. You know, in case she remembered something."

Jack thought Liddell's motivation was to get some pie for the trip, but in any case, Bigfoot was right. Sometimes a witness knew or saw more than they remembered. Memory was a slippery thing.

Freyda was behind the counter pouring two cups of coffee when they entered the shop. Next to the cups was a pie wrapped in foil. The dog lay on the floor at the end of the counter with its head up and alert.

Freyda said, "Have a cup on the house."

Jack and Liddell sat at the counter, and she set a carton of Half and Half in front of them along with two spoons and sugar. The dog put its head back on the floor, but its black eyes remained focused on the men.

"Who does the dog remind you of, pod'na?"

Jack didn't have to think. Cinderella, the Wicked Witch of the Shoes. Dogs were supposed to be man's best friend, but unless Cinderella was baring her teeth or had just done something wrong, she would give him the same attitude as this dog. He'd even installed a doggy-door so she could go out in the backyard to do her business. The door had been a success, but now he was retrieving chewed-up shoes from the yard. He'd had to force her out the door this morning because it was so cold. It was a battle, but he'd won in the end. Maybe.

Freyda pulled up a wooden stool by them and asked, "What can I do you for this time, detectives? You need more money? Well, I don't have any. Someone took my last twenty dollars this morning."

"Just following up," Jack said. "Is there anything you remember from last night that you haven't told us? Or that I haven't asked you?"

Freyda gave him a blank stare. "Let me think. Oh yeah. The guy said he was going out beside the store to kill someone. He said his name was John Egghead and gave me his address too. Then he pulled a big gun and walked outside. He comes in all the time. He knows the police don't patrol out here. They don't even come in for free coffee and pie, except for you two."

Jack made another mental note to have a talk with Officer Hurt's Sergeant.

"Did the guy say, 'Am I happy to see you or is this gun in my pocket?'" Jack asked Freyda with a straight face.

Her face crinkled up, and she let out a loud cackle. "You're a smartass. Like me."

Jack took a sip of the black coffee. With a little Scotch it might be okay. "Seriously, Freyda."

"Well, there is one thing. Hang on a second," she said and went into the back.

He heard her climbing the stairs and coming back down. She came in with a VHS tape. The case of it was worn to a matte finish from years of handling.

A surveillance camera was in the back corner of the ceiling. Jack saw it the first time they were here, but he had assumed it was a fake because of the disconnected wires sticking out of the back of it. He had wondered why she even bothered to keep it.

She tapped her temple with a finger. "Not so old and stupid, am I?" she said. "The recorder is up in my place. I figure a camera's not gonna stop someone if they want to misbehave. But it'll make them think they got away with it, and smart cops like you two will bust their asses."

Jack took the cassette from Freyda. The tape was wound halfway through.

"I already watched it. It's wound to the time the guy came in. It doesn't have a correct time and date. I'm not so smart I figured out how to set it. That thing's nigh as old as I am."

Jack felt butterflies in his stomach. "Thanks, Freyda. This might be very important," he said, silently cursing her for holding it back and cursing himself for not being more thorough.

She must have noticed the change in his expression. "I'll say I forgot the camera was working if anyone makes a federal case out of it. I'm old, so no one can prove different."

They thanked Freyda and left. While Liddell drove, Jack called Sergeant Walker.

"Tony, you're not going to believe this, but I've got a VHS video tape from the Coffee Shop."

"Really?" Walker said. "Timmons said he saw the camera but she said it was a prop to keep people from stealing."

"The recorder is upstairs. She said she watched the video and wound it back to when the customer came in. You want to watch it with us?"

"I'll meet you downstairs in CSU's workroom," Walker said.

Jack disconnected and called Lt. Sanchez, who was still on the road. "Lieutenant, we're going to be just a little while." He told Sanchez about the videotape.

* * * *

Walker met them in the basement Crime Scene lab at Police HQ. An old-style TV equipped with a VHS player sat on his desk.

"Let's see what you have," Walker said. He slipped the VHS cassette into the television, and a perfectly clear image from inside the Coffee Shop came on the screen. The view was toward the front door and taking in the register on the counter and one booth.

Jack said, "Freyda said he sat in that booth near the window."

"Too bad she doesn't have a camera outside," Liddell said.

The view didn't take in the street, but some of the sidewalk could be seen if you squinted hard enough. It was pitch black outside. The time and date on the video was from last October and showed it to be nine in the morning.

"Did you see her recorder?" Walker asked.

"We didn't ask to see it. She just gave us the tape. Do you need it?" Jack asked.

"I'll need to take a VHS tape to her anyway to replace this one. If I can even find a blank. I'll use her recorder and hold something with the correct date and time in front of the camera so we can compare the date and time with this tape," Walker said. "We'll need that for court if this turns out to be evidence."

"Why didn't you think of that, pod'na?"

"Just watch, Bigfoot," Jack said.

Vehicle headlights could be seen growing in intensity through the window and dissipating again.

"Looks like it was going south," Walker said.

The booth was still empty, and Jack was thinking Freyda hadn't rewound the tape like she'd claimed, until she appeared. She swiped at the top of the booth table with a rag. Just as she walked away, a shape could be seen approaching from outside.

A person wearing a dark-colored coat and a Western-style hat opened the door and entered. The camera angle wasn't enough to catch the face because his head was down.

"He knows the camera is there," Jack said.

The person went to the booth Freyda had cleaned and sat with his back to the camera.

"That's a Burberry coat and a dark cowboy hat," Liddell said. "Just like Freyda said."

Walker turned up the volume, and a loud scratching noise came through. "Did she say there was sound?"

Jack said sheepishly, "I didn't ask, and shut up, Bigfoot."

Walker adjusted the volume. They could hear a faint voice say, "What'cha havin', cowboy?"

Walker turned the volume up all the way. The man said something inaudible. Freyda turned and walked out of the picture. They heard clinking, and Freyda came back into the picture with a plate and a mug and set them in front of the person.

"Man or woman?" Jack asked.

They all agreed the person was a man.

She came back with silverware, and they could hear her say, "You want creamer or sugar?" The man said nothing. "I've got Sweet'N Low?" He didn't move. She walked away.

The man picked up the mug and smelled it before setting it back down.

"He's wearing gloves," Walker said.

The man pushed the plate away, took something from his pocket, and put it on the table in front of him. It was a small spiral notebook. He took out a pen and began writing. His face remained down, never turned toward the camera or Freyda.

He wrote for several minutes, but his hat would tilt up as the headlights from a vehicle passed going south.

"He's watching for someone," Jack said. "Do you think you can get the video enhanced, Tony?"

Walker answered, "I can try. Are you thinking we might be able to get his reflection in the window glass?"

"Possibly," Jack said and continued watching the video. The man didn't move for the better part of an hour except to tilt his head when an occasional vehicle passed.

"I make that five cars that have passed," Liddell said to Walker. "He's looked up each time. We have a witness that lives four blocks away. She said the stolen VW cruised down her street a couple of times. Maybe the stolen VW was scouting the Coffee Shop."

"Freyda said she closed at midnight and the guy came in around eleven. Tony, can you play it forward a little faster?" Jack asked.

Walker did. Freyda could be seen moving about, and in one instance she stepped outside but stayed in the doorway. The man in the booth never moved. Walker slowed the video. "It's close to midnight now if Freyda is correct on when he came in."

Freyda came back in, went to the booth, and said something to the customer that wasn't quite audible, and if he replied they couldn't hear it. Another minute or two passed. He stopped writing and put the notebook back in his coat. He took something from his pants pocket, slid it under the coffee mug, got up, and left. He turned left outside the door. Walker stopped the video.

"Play it a few minutes more, Tony," Jack said, and Walker did.

Freyda could be seen going outside. She had told them she checked up and down the street after the customer left. She came back inside and locked the door. She picked up the plate, mug, and unused silverware, and walked to the back room. Walker played the video for ten more minutes. During that time, the lights went out and there was nothing else.

"The guy must have come from across the street," Walker said. "He didn't come from the right or left into view. He must have parked across the street or down Lincoln Avenue somewhere."

"He went to his left when he exited," Jack said. "He's our guy."

"Yeah," Liddell said.

"I'll go through the video more carefully. It looks to be several hours of tape set on LP—long playing," Walker said.

"Does the video from the bookstore show the Coffee Shop at all?" Jack asked.

Walker answered, "It's pointed toward Lincoln Avenue away from the Coffee Shop."

"Shit," Jack said. "Dr. John said the first stab wound didn't kill the victim. Let's go through another five minutes."

Walker played the video forward another fifteen minutes. The Coffee Shop went dark in the first few minutes. Nothing. Not even headlights in the background.

"Tony, can you find out if your tech has delivered all the stuff to the FBI? I want this to go, too, and mark it attention Anna Whiteside. They might be able to enhance the video for us."

Chapter 19

While Jack and Liddell were viewing the video from the Coffee Shop, Coyote was in Missouri, sitting at a café table. He knew what he had to do. The one thing he felt about killing them was his lack of feeling. He didn't enjoy it. It was just necessary.

Coyote's mind was moving ten steps ahead. The television reporter said there was a survivor in Evansville. She said the kid was found alive *inside* the truck trailer. Coyote hadn't considered that anyone would live long in this cold. He knew traffickers didn't think of their cargo as people. They were merely something to be delivered. According to Miles, the truck had left Texas three days ago. No one could have lasted that long without heat or water, and he knew the trucks only stopped for gas.

Now he had to wonder if this idiot driver had brought the kid and the dog along to the meeting. He'd seen a dog in the VW with the engine running. The kid might have been asleep in the car, and Coyote hadn't gone near it because of the dog. It was the damn dog's fault.

The pompous cop on the news hinted there might be more evidence, and he didn't seem smart enough to be planting false information. What other evidence might they have? He'd left nothing behind. Touched nothing except maybe the tip he'd left that old woman.

The waitress stood behind the counter, punching buttons on her cell phone, smiling, ignoring him.

In his deep gravelly smoker's voice, he said, "Excuse me, miss. Can you tell the manager I need to speak to him?"

Her smiled faded. "I don't know if the manager's here."

Coyote knew she was lying. Coyote pulled a badge wallet from his back pocket, flipped it open long enough to show a small gold badge. "Health Department."

Now she was paying attention. "Are you gonna complain about the breakfast? Because if you are it's not my fault. I've been telling Billy to do 'em right. He's such a jerk. He's quitting anyway, but this time he's gone for sure. Listen, you don't have to pay nothing."

"Let's go talk to this cook. If the manager isn't here, we'll call him in. You aren't in trouble, but I need to talk to you, too."

She was mildly concerned now. "I guess the manager's here. I don't like working here noways."

Coyote pulled on his leather gloves. He hadn't touched anything except the coffee mug. He picked the mug up and went around the counter, his other hand going to the bayonet sheathed at his back. He let the waitress lead the way through the swinging café doors and slipped the bayonet from its sheath. Her back was to him. His eyes took in the kitchen. Billy, the short-order cook, was scrubbing the iron grill top with the blade of a heavy spatula less than ten feet away. He turned to smile at the waitress.

Coyote drove the bayonet down into the strap of muscle beside the girl's neck. She flinched and gave a little grunt. He shoved the bayonet down a second time and severed her aorta. She gave a gasp and dropped like a rock. There would be little blood, except what was filling her chest cavity.

Billy's smile vanished, and Coyote could see confusion and a question forming in that slow mind. Coyote slammed the coffee mug into Billy's face, smashing his nose.

Billy's eyes widened when his mind registered what was happening. He tried to raise the heavy spatula to fend off Coyote's next blow, but he didn't make it. Coyote smashed the heavy coffee mug into the side of Billy's head hard enough to shatter the mug and leave a bloody gouge just under the cook's eye. The spatula dropped and bounced off Billy's grease-stained Keds sneakers.

Coyote grabbed a fistful of the front of Billy's shirt and drove the bayonet through his throat twice. By reflex the cook's hands went to his throat, and he was swaying but somehow remained upright. Coyote scanned the room quickly and saw an office, the door open, twenty feet away. So far, he'd made very little noise.

He pulled the bayonet out of the cook's throat and drove it through his left eye hard enough that the tip skittered across the bone at the back of the man's skull. Billy's dying legs went rubbery. Coyote helped him to the floor.

The waitress lay still as if asleep. Her order pad had fallen out of her smock pocket and was lodged under her hip. Coyote took the order pad, put it in his coat, and stepped over the waitress's body. She was young and pretty. She was dead. He felt nothing. He'd write it in his journal later. His lack of feeling seemed important.

Off to his right, the sounds of someone typing loudly and slowly and muttering obscenities came from an open door. He stepped in the room and saw a middle-aged woman hammering at the keyboard of a laptop. Her pink sweater stretched tightly over large breasts and an even larger stomach. She was sitting at a cheap steel desk, her side to him, concentrating on beating the laptop into submission with two fingers. She heard him and turned her head his direction. He moved in quickly with the bayonet raised overhead. She threw an arm up to stave off the blow, but it was too late. The point of the bayonet drove through her wrist and pinned her arm to the center of her chest. The blade struck something hard and lodged tightly. He tried to free it but wasn't able to twist or yank it loose. He used the other hand, striking the butt of the handle, driving the blade through her back and into the chair. He twisted it and pulled it free.

Blood filled the woman's mouth; her eyes were open and staring at him. She sputtered, coughed up blood, and Coyote stepped aside. She grabbed his arm, but she was weak. She said, "You don't have to do this." He drove the bayonet down a second time, through her shoulder and deep into her chest. This time it did its work. Her eyes were open, staring, but stilled. She slumped in her chair. Her arms fell to her sides.

He stepped back and examined himself for blood. He saw none, but there were scratches in the sleeve of his coat, and the heel of his hand throbbed from pounding it on the butt of the bayonet. He used her shirt to wipe the blood from the bayonet and sheathed it. A nameplate on the desk said her name was CINDI. "Sorry, Cindi," he said, "but everyone has to make sacrifices. Thank you."

The office was small, not much bigger than a bathroom really, but every inch was crammed with boxes and bags and papers. The screen on Cindi's laptop was an order for a bunch of food and napkins and other café type shit. A row of program icons spread across the bottom. Coyote clicked on one that looked like a camera. The screen changed to a four-way split view. One was the front door to the café. One was directly over the register. One pointed toward the booth where Coyote had been sitting. The last view was of the office. On it he saw a safe tucked under the desk. He could see himself.

Cindi's purse hung from the back of her chair. He took her wallet and cash and keys and went to the front of the café. He turned off the red neon OPEN sign, turned off the inside lights, and locked the door. He left the blinds open. He considered taking his dirty dishes to the back, but it wouldn't really matter since he hadn't touched the crap.

Behind the counter, he began punching buttons on the cash register until the drawer opened. He collected the bills in the drawer, left the change, and went into the kitchen. He found a suitable box by the grill, tossed the cash in it, and took it into the office. He pulled the cords loose from the laptop. The laptop went in the box. He shoved papers and binders and a couple of miniature cactus plants to the floor. In the side desk drawer, he found a small lockbox. It rattled when he picked it up. He tossed it in the box. He pulled the remaining desk drawers out and dumped some of them on the ground.

He searched the waitress and cook like a junkie or a robber would have. The waitress didn't have any cash. He wasn't surprised. She was a horrible waitress. The cook had an ID that showed he was on work release, no driver's license, no money. He put the ID in the box and closed the top.

He went to the front door, pulled a blind aside, and peeked out. The parking lot was still empty except for one older model SUV and his own Dodge Dart. He unlocked the front door, walked out, and used Cindi's keys to lock the door. As he crossed the parking lot, a dark gray Dodge Charger with Missouri State Highway Patrol markings turned in and came directly toward him. Coyote put the keys in his pocket, and his hand slipped under the back of his jacket to rest on the handle of the bayonet.

The trooper stopped not ten feet from him, and the driver's window powered down. Coyote smiled at the female state trooper.

"You coming or going?" she asked.

Coyote knew she'd watched him pocket the keys. Her eyes were sharp. She'd seen his face. There was nothing for it. Coyote knew what he had to do. He drew the bayonet, hiding the action behind the box he'd taken from the office. He took a couple steps toward the trooper, talking to keep the driver's focus on his face and words.

"I got here just in time," Coyote said in his deep voice. "Problem in the kitchen freezer last night I guess. Got me a box of patties before they went belly up though." He held the box out where she could read the printed 48 ALL BEEF PATTIES on the side.

He was five feet from the car. He was smiling at his supposed good fortune, and she was smiling along with him, but the smile began to falter and the eyes were once again sharp. The hand on the steering wheel disappeared down to her side.

He continued to move in on her and said, "You ought to get some."

Her hand came back up, and she was holding her Smokey hat. "I hope you got a good deal. The woman in the office is a tough cookie. By the way, did you see the waitress? Young girl, seventeen, blond hair?"

Coyote was at the car's window. "She's in there. The cook and manager too." Her gun wasn't on her right hip. She was left-handed just like him, which meant her gun was on her left side, against the door. Bad mistake. Instead of leaning into the window, she should have leaned away. Free up her gun hand. He asked, "The waitress in trouble, officer?"

"Trooper," she corrected him. "Maybe. I'm just making sure my daughter showed up for work. I can't reach her on her cell. You know how kids are. Guess I'll go in. Thanks."

She popped her seat belt, and Coyote heard the door click. She reached for the window control. Coyote dropped the box and grabbed the fur collar of her Tuffy jacket. He yanked her up against the window opening and drove the point of the bayonet down at her shoulder. Her heavy jacket stopped the blade from sinking in more than a few inches. He pulled the bayonet free and drove it down again with more strength. This time he aimed the bayonet beside her collar, into the throat, and the blade dove deep. The door latch popped, and the door opened an inch. She grunted, and he could hear her hand scrabbling for the gun that was trapped between her body and the door. Coyote pulled the blade free and drove it downward through the front of her throat with all of his strength. Her body shuddered, her legs kicked out. She stopped moving.

He shoved the door shut with his hip, reached through the open window, and moved the body into a sitting position. He wanted any blood to stay inside the car. He opened the door just enough to power the window up. Her Smokey hat was lying against her leg. He put it on her head, tilted it slightly forward, and let her head rest against the seat as if she were taking a nap. The engine was still running. He left it. He didn't think anyone but another trooper would approach the car and risk waking her.

Chapter 20

"It's a three-hour drive to St. Louis, Bigfoot," Jack said. "Do you want to run by your house?"

"I already called Marcie, pod'na. You want to check in with Katie?"

"I think Katie is at some event at school right now. I left her a voice mail," Jack said.

Katie taught sixth graders at one of the toughest middle schools in the city. These kids were on their "last" school before permanent expulsion. Instead of getting a degree, they got pardoned or paroled. She seemed to love teaching there, and he had to admit she did a good job of turning some of them around. One of her students had turned eighteen and was now a Reserve Vanderburgh County Deputy. Jack worried that the kid did it to carry a gun, but they didn't get guns until they turned twenty-one, so maybe it would be okay.

He drove west. He didn't give a shit about the drivers of the trucks. They were transporting humans like cattle. They deserved what they got. But the immigrants had been sold a bill of goods. They didn't deserve to die like they had.

In past years millions of people had come into America illegally. Some had come to build a better life for themselves and their families. Others had come to deal drugs, flee from imprisonment in their own countries, or just to get lost in the crowd.

This killer was carrying out his own agenda. Sanchez said there were five such incidents of mass murder now. All illegal aliens, all carrying phony green cards, and at least four of these were carrying foreign passports. Three of them were among the dead in Evansville. Two had burner phones. There was more to that, but he didn't know what. Yet.

And kids like Joe were caught up in greed on one side and hatred on the other. He was so lost in thought he didn't notice his phone was vibrating in his pocket until Liddell said, "You going to get that?"

It was Katie.

"I heard about the deaths on the news, Jack. I'm so sorry. Are you okay?"

Her words made him pause. He hadn't thought about how he felt, and no one had asked. That was police work. You did what you had to do until it was all over, and then you reacted internally. You made sacrifices. Other people, like Katie, made sacrifices so the job could get done. He didn't want to think about how he felt right now.

"I'm fine, Katie. I love you," he said, and he meant the last part. She was the sunshine in his darkness. He wondered, and not for the first time since they'd divorced, how he could ever have given her up. He guessed he never had. This was where he was meant to be. She was...

His thought was interrupted by barking in the background and Katie scolding Cinderella, his mutt.

"That doesn't sound good," Jack said.

"I'm home, as you can hear. She had a pair of your underwear in the backyard burying them. Don't worry, I'll keep her in and fix everything."

"Fix what?"

"I've got to go, Jack. She's gone back to the bedroom. Call me when you have a chance. I love you. Be safe and come home soon," Katie said, and the line went dead.

"I heard most of that, pod'na. Isn't it cute your dog misses you?" Liddell said. "And here you thought she didn't like you."

"Maybe the mutt's just wanting me to leave," Jack said.

"You're so negative. You need to think happy thoughts. Maybe things will turn out better if you do," Liddell said. "Look at me. I'm positive."

Jack *was* positive. Positive things would go to shit before they got better. Murphy's Law says: "Anything that can go wrong will always screw you sideways."

* * * *

They didn't know enough to know what to question, but they were both energized by the enormous scope of the cases they were now involved with. Jack hated to admit it, but he liked the idea of not being stuck in Evansville city limits. Criminals had no restrictions and every advantage. Jack had gone outside his legal jurisdiction more than a few times before, but now he could do so legally and not have to worry about Double Dick's wrath.

The address Lt. Sanchez gave them skirted north of St. Louis proper and took them into the countryside. Even with the trees stripped of their leaves and patches of snow on the ground, the empty spread of land was breathtaking.

Jack said, "You own land in Louisiana, Bigfoot. Have you ever considered moving back to Louisiana with your brother and niece? Or maybe moving out in the sticks somewhere around Evansville?"

"All the time, pod'na. All the time."

"Why haven't you?"

"Why haven't you?" Liddell asked.

"I asked first," Jack said.

Liddell grunted. "I guess we just never got around to it. We've talked. Played with the idea. But now with the baby and school districts and the drive to work, I guess we stopped talking until we have a plan."

"Stopped talking about it, or stopped dreaming about it?" Jack asked.

"Maybe both. Maybe family is what it's all about. Maybe I want to be anywhere Marcie and Jane are, no matter where that is? I never put that in words before, but I guess that's it. Now you," Liddell said.

Jack thought that over before saying, "I love my river cabin. I love the freedom I feel on the water and knowing that no one lives near me. I love the freedom to decide what to do and when to do it and not having to answer to anyone for the why or where. I love all that. I love Katie more than any of that. I'll tell you something if you can keep it to yourself, Bigfoot."

Liddell sat quietly.

"I'm going to ask Katie to marry me. Again," Jack said.

Liddell punched Jack on the arm. "That's great, pod'na. It's about damn time too, if you ask me."

"I didn't ask you, but you're right. It is about time."

Jack was quiet and Liddell asked, "What's the matter, pod'na? You didn't already change your mind, did you?"

"Not a chance. It's just that I don't know if she'll have me back. I don't know if she wants to risk it all again. I mean, part of me left her when the baby died. The divorce was just putting us out of our pain."

"Losing the baby was no one's fault, pod'na. God called her home," Liddell said.

"Yeah. God. How could I forget?" Jack knew he'd been a horrible husband, and thought he would have been a horrible father. The job was his life. He gave it all he had. Thinking about it made him sick, but thinking about Katie, about starting over, that made him glow inside. He was a better man now. He'd learned from his mistakes. He could put the job second now. He wanted to be with Katie forever. They both wanted children. But...

"I don't know if I'm ready for it, Bigfoot," he said.

"What do you mean? Ready to marry Katie? Of course you are. You're back home with her the way it's meant to be. Hell, Marcie will be tickled pink if you two tied the knot. So am I."

Jack chuckled. "A pink Bigfoot. I'd like to see that. To be honest, I don't know if I'm ready to try to be a father again."

"Hell, pod'na. That's the fun part. The hard part is getting up all hours of the night and walking them around rocking them until they go back to sleep. The hard part is being interrupted by crying when you're right in the middle of..."

"Shut up, Bigfoot. I don't need to hear that."

They rode in silence for a while until Liddell asked, "Well, what are you going to do? You going to pop the question? Have you bought a ring? Where are you going to do it?"

Jack said, "You writing a book? I'm sorry I shared."

"Can I be your best man?"

"You know it," Jack said.

"Can we be little Jack's Godparents?"

"Only if you promise not to eat him," Jack said.

"Jack?"

"What?"

"I'm proud of you, pod'na. I'm honored to work with you. You're a good man, and you'll be one hell of a father, pod'na."

"Quit it before you make me change my mind," Jack said.

The GPS on Jack's phone announced they had arrived at the address given to them by Lt. Sanchez, but the stretch of road they were on was devoid of any connecting roads or driveways or houses.

"The last turn I saw was about half a mile back, Bigfoot. Siri is a lying bitch."

"I think I see a mailbox up ahead," Liddell said.

He was right. A quarter mile up the road, a rusty mailbox was wired to a steel pipe directly across from a gravel driveway. The driveway trailed off into the trees and disappeared around a bend.

They'd driven six or seven hundred yards when Liddell said, "I don't think we're in Missouri anymore, Toto. There's nothing back here. Maybe it goes to a hunting cabin. Or maybe it just leads to a field?"

Another five hundred yards and they spotted a rust-colored metal roof over the tree line of dead limbs. They came to a narrow concrete road that turned toward the structure and followed it to a 1950s-style farmhouse, two-story, wood-sided, with padded gray paint and blue trim. A covered porch wrapped around the house.

The concrete drive continued behind the house to a barn. The barn was a new construction with a new coat of red paint and a new corrugated metal roof. A carport was attached to the side of the barn. Under the carport sat a Gator 4-wheeler and a Harley motorcycle.

"Have you got Sanchez's number?" Jack asked. "This can't be..."

Lieutenant Sanchez came out of the barn and crossed to the house with a beer can in his hand. He motioned them to come over.

Jack and Liddell walked up to the porch.

"A little early for beer, isn't it?" Jack asked.

"That's from last night," Sanchez answered. "We had a little party and drank all the beer. Sorry."

"We?" Liddell asked.

A black Lab came trotting from behind the house and nosed Liddell's hand.

"Meet Cutie," Sanchez said. "I didn't name her. My ex did."

Liddell nudged Jack's arm. "You should see Jack's dog. She's..."

Jack cut him off. "You were drinking with the dog all night before you drove to Evansville and back?"

"Drinking was Cutie's idea," Sanchez said. "She's a lush, but she's the only thing I kept from my last marriage...my fourth one. The dog loves me more than my ex did anyway."

"Where are we going to work?" Jack asked.

"You're looking at it."

"This house?" Jack said. *If I sneeze it'll fall down.*

"We're working in the barn," Sanchez said and threw the empty beer can toward the barn. Cutie raced off and snatched it before it hit the ground.

Sanchez opened the barn door, and the stark transformation from barn to modern office/living space was shocking. Cutie trotted to a trash bin and dropped the empty beer can inside.

"Good girl," Sanchez said, scrubbing the top of the dog's head. "I'm trying to teach her to pick up after herself."

The barn's floor was shiny hardwood. The ceiling was at least twenty feet high and crisscrossed with silver central air and heat ducts and PVC pipes and wiring. At the back of the room was a ladder leading up to a spacious loft. Jack could see a dresser and four-poster bed. The space under the loft was walled off into two rooms. The one on the left had a half-moon carved into the door. Bathroom. The other room was partially walled in. It had the makings of a kitchen, with the oven and cabinets stored along the wall. On that same wall was a full-size freezer/refrigerator.

"Bathroom on the left," Sanchez said, following Jack's gaze. "Got a refrigerator with a freezer and ice maker. I'm still working on the kitchen. I don't really need it because I grill out most of the time. Upstairs is the bedroom. It's home."

"You live out here and not in the house?" Liddell asked.

"The house is a money pit. I keep it because it was my grandparents' place. At one time, there were three generations of Sanchezes living in that house. Four thousand square feet and a basement that's little more than a root cellar. I put heat and a/c in the barn, insulated it, and it's comfortable, so I live out here."

Jack remembered doing basically the same thing when he and Katie got divorced. She kept the house—which was his childhood home—and he'd moved into his grandfather's old river cabin. He'd poured money into the cabin to make it livable, added a dock, boat, and a hot tub. He couldn't put a refrigerator outside because he feared his beer would get stolen.

Sanchez had set four army surplus desks in the middle of the main space, two desks facing two more, office chairs, filing cabinets, a printer, and laptops. On top of two of the desks were thick stacks of manila file folders. A small table in the corner was equipped with a coffee maker and condiments, coffee mugs, and four boxes of donuts. Sanchez had brewed a fresh pot of coffee and pointed to the mugs and donuts.

"Get a coffee, donut, pick a desk, park it, and let's get to work," Sanchez said.

Chapter 21

They loaded up on coffee and carried it back to the desks. Lieutenant Sanchez sat at the messier desk with a stack of folders twice as thick as those on the other desks. On top of Sanchez's desk someone had placed a wooden name plaque that read: C. A. W. A. I. C.

Liddell brought coffee and a box of the donuts, and he pointed at the name plaque. "That some new FBI task force title?"

Sanchez said, "My partner put it there. It stands for Chief Asshole What Am In Charge."

Liddell got seated. They did what most cops do when meeting another cop they haven't worked with. They drank coffee, ate donuts, and told stories.

It didn't matter what kind of case a detective worked, murders included, every detective carried their own interpretation of right and wrong. If you go into battle with a man, you want to know if he's got grit, if he's honest, how far he will bend the rules. Most importantly, will he have your back?

Police work was a battle. Jack didn't write traffic tickets or play basketball with kids in the projects. He was always up against the most vile and dangerous scumbags with one goal, to protect his city. Good versus evil wasn't just a random headline, and he didn't really give a shit what the news media said.

Normal people aren't wired to think in those terms, but Jack was chasing a monster. He had to know who was chasing the monster with him.

They were running out of stories when Liddell asked, "How'd you score that primo SUV you're driving, Lieutenant?"

"The Denali came from a narcotics seizure. I had to promise not to sleep with the chief's wife to get it. The land, everything else you see, is mine. This is my war room." Sanchez turned to Jack. "Your captain told me you had a war room a little nicer than this."

Jack said, "The captain talks too much."

"How much land?" Liddell asked.

"Six hundred and thirty acres of woods and farm fields. No one's worked the land since my father died a long time back. It'll go to scrub and volunteer trees. If either of you hunt, let me know when you want to come and I'll give you a map so you don't shoot up the barn. I live here, remember."

"Is someone else joining us?" Jack asked, indicating the unoccupied desk.

"When my chief assigned me to USOC, I was told I might be working with other detectives. I got to bring my partner in the Homicide Squad on board. She's busy on a related assignment at present. You'll meet her today. Kim's a damn fine detective, but she plays it strictly by the book and can be a pain in the ass sometimes. I think she was a little ticked off that Toomey didn't send her with me this morning. Truth is, I could have taken her, but she drives like a crazy woman. And before we start, I want you to call me Lou, not Lieutenant."

"Lou—as in Lieutenant?" Liddell said.

"No. Lou, as in my name. Louis Sanchez. Lou. No more rank stuff, okay?"

"Okay, Lou," Liddell said.

"Do either of you have any experience with these damn computers? For all I know, they're expensive paperweights."

"Jack's threatened by technology, Lou," Liddell said. "I know how to turn one on. We usually have our computer guru do the research stuff."

"Well, shit. I was hoping one of you was a computer geek. Kim requisitioned the laptops from the PD. She's the one that does all that kind of computer shit for me. Well, I guess we'll have to find some twelve-year-old."

Jack said, "Let's start with why the St. Louis case is stalled."

"Not stalled exactly," Sanchez said. "The Homicide Squad thinks they have it solved, ABA."

"ABA?" Liddell asked. He'd never heard that term in police jargon.

"Yeah. All But Arrested. ABA. You guys don't use that one? Anyway, we had a witness that claimed she saw the murder. She went through our mug shots and identified a guy. He turned out to be a mental case and in the psych ward when the murders happened. Later on, she was ninety percent sure it was another guy, a gang member who happened to be a suspect in some other murders. Turned out he was in jail in Oklahoma at the time. But one of our detectives still likes him for the killings and is stuck on proving he could have been here and not in the showers with Bubba in Oklahoma."

Jack sputtered hot coffee back into his mug. "That's all you've got? No offense, Lou, but we've got a fresh case on our plate, so what are we doing here picking the bones of an old one. Toomey seemed to think we could help you or you could help us."

Sanchez was unperturbed. "It wasn't my idea to bring you here. I know how hopeless this looks. I was brought in three weeks ago and haven't come up with much of anything, but I've made some connections to other cases. You didn't even know about the cases in Florida, Texas, and Louisiana until I told you."

Jack said, "Sorry. You're right." Jack didn't want to piss Sanchez off, but this seemed like a waste of time.

Sanchez said, "Sorry. I guess I'm a little touchy right now. I've spent the last three weeks bleeding ideas and not much to show for it. Maybe Toomey thought a fresh set of eyes might see something I missed. You're here. I'll answer questions, but you should form your own opinions. If you still think we have shit for a case, I'll buy you dinner and send you home. How about that?"

What Jack thought was that this was typical Fed foot-dragging and he was losing some of his good opinion of Lieutenant Sanchez. But he said, "Okay. Point made. Sorry I went off on you."

Seeing the fighting was over, Liddell tucked a donut in his mouth.

"The important stuff is in these folders," Sanchez said. Three sets of identical file folders lay one on each desk. Sanchez opened the top folder and took out several eight-by-ten color photos that were paperclipped together. Jack and Liddell did the same.

The photo on top was an aerial photo taken by a drone of a semitrailer parked close to the loading dock of a large warehouse-type building. The back doors of the trailer were open, and an ambulance was backed in near the doors.

The next photo was the inside of the trailer. Piles of bloated bodies covered the floor. Jack skipped through the remaining photos. He'd already seen his share of decomposition and various stages of death.

Sanchez continued. "Back in August we got a suspicious circumstance call. The suspicious circumstance turned into a semitrailer full of bloated bodies. We don't have an exact date the trailer was left there, but the coroner put the date of the deaths at about three weeks prior to our guys finding it. That would be the first week of August. The temperatures that month ranged from the high nineties to three digits.

"Forty-seven dead including two baby girls. All of the dead had hot-off-the-press green cards, except for one. He had an Egyptian passport showing he came into the country through JFK airport three weeks ago. He was carrying a Russian-made semi-auto, 7.62-millimeter TT-30 pistol. I'll tell you why the caliber is important in a minute.

"These aerial shots will give you an idea of the area where the semi and trailer were found, and the condition of the bodies," Sanchez said.

Liddell said, "The picture is marked Drone #3. You've got drones?"

Sanchez asked, "You guys don't use drones? Huh. The other photos in that set are of the inside of the trailer." He said to Liddell, "We didn't need a drone for those."

Jack said, "I believe our Honduran guy was trying to pry the doors open with the knife. There are MS-13 connections."

Sanchez said, "There's evidence that some of ours tried to claw the doors open. The Egyptian never used the gun. You found your driver right away, but the driver in our case wasn't with the truck. He was found a few days later stabbed to death like your driver."

Sanchez continued. "Nothing out of the ordinary inside the truck's cab, but we did find a gas receipt. Someone, maybe the driver, gassed up in Fort Worth exactly three weeks before the truck was found. We didn't find any food or water in the trailer, and no signs there had ever been any. They were using the floor as a toilet.

"If he came up from Mexico, he would have had to gas up around Fort Worth. That would take him to Oklahoma City, where he could get on I-44 and straight into St. Louis. No blood or signs of a struggle, so we figured he just parked and walked away or got a ride. We thought the bastard just left them to cook, and he may have done just that."

"Maybe he was delivering them to St. Louis and was getting paid?" Liddell suggested.

Sanchez's hands clenched into fists. "Anyway, we found that asshole's body in a little wash this side of the Mississippi River. He was a mile north of the Queen Casino. The next set of photos shows the body in relation to the truck location."

This view was from higher up. The body was circled in red, and the location of the truck was circled in blue.

Liddell asked, "Do you think your driver knew his killer or thought he knew him and left voluntarily?"

"Whatever, it still comes out the same. There has to be a reason the doors were left locked," Jack said. "The doors were locked in our case as well. We found the key to the padlock hidden in the driver's shoe."

"I put the photos of the driver's wounds in the next folder."

Jack and Liddell opened the manila folder marked "Driver" and immediately saw the connection between the St. Louis and Evansville cases. The wounds were cruciform in shape and in the same area of the body in each death. Jack focused on one of the wounds of the St. Louis driver. "Have you got a magnifying glass?"

"You saw the same thing I did," Sanchez said. "Our coroner said it was a bolster mark, and our forensics confirmed it." A bolster is a collar where the blade meets the handle of a knife. Its purpose is to keep the hand from slipping down the handle onto the blade. That's particularly helpful if the hand is slick with blood.

"Open the next folder," Sanchez told them.

Jack and Liddell opened the next folder marked "Weapon." Inside were photos of a bayonet laid out next to a tape measure. The handle was short, wooden, four inches in length. The blade measured eleven inches. The bolster was designed with a hole bored into the metal at the top.

"Just a minute," Sanchez said and went to a filing cabinet, reaching behind it. He came back holding a rifle with a bayonet folded back against the side of the wooden stock. "Check this out," he said and unfolded the bayonet. It clicked into place alongside the barrel, and he laid it on the desk.

"That's it," Liddell said.

"Our forensic guy says he's ninety percent sure this is like the weapon that was used. It's an old bayonet of Russian design made specifically for a Mosin-Nagant M44 7.62mm Russian rifle. The blade is twenty-two inches of hardened steel. It's been in use since WWI and is still in use some places. And believe it or not, this isn't a rare bayonet. My forensic guy found this one online. I bought this rifle and bayonet off the internet for three hundred dollars."

Sanchez used a screwdriver, removed the bayonet from the rifle barrel, and handed it to Jack. Jack balanced it in his hand. It was heavy. The cruciform blade was dull.

Sanchez said, "The coroner said the edges of the blade were razor sharp. This one is shit, as you can see. This guy must keep it sharp. Remember I told you about the Russian-made semi-auto 7.62 millimeter pistol the Egyptian was carrying? It was made in the '30s like the rifle. Maybe a coincidence? Anyway, our Homicide Unit is all over this. They're running down everything they can related to Russian-made weapons, but I think they are concentrating mostly in the area around St. Louis. And I think they aren't giving up on their main suspect, who was in jail in another state at the time. I gave Anna Whiteside a copy of all this. She's checking."

"What do you make of the Egyptian passport?" Jack asked.

"Whiteside says the passport is forged," Sanchez answered. "She's running pictures of the Egyptian and all the others through her database and the Interpol database."

"Any luck identifying your driver?" Jack asked. "So far we've got nothing on ours."

"We did. The wallet and money were gone, but so were his shoes and belt. For all we know, some homeless bastard found the body before we did and helped himself. The driver's fingerprints were a goldmine. We got a hit, or rather, Anna got a hit, on the driver's latent prints."

Jack and Liddell opened the next folder marked "Driver"—Hank Brown. Last known address, Cincinnati, Ohio. He had a commercial driver's license issued in Ohio. He was thirty-one years old, and the physical description on the license was of a big man, six-four, two hundred forty pounds.

Sanchez had included copies of handwritten notes reporting Brown had a bachelor's degree in criminal justice and an MBA from the University of Dallas. The notes added that after graduation, Brown was hired by US Border Patrol. He attended training at the Federal Law Enforcement Training Center in Glynco, Georgia, worked the Mexican border for two years, and resigned. The notes didn't give a reason for the resignation.

"He was ex-Border Patrol?" Liddell said.

"Yeah. Brown disappeared after resigning and made no contact with family, friends, school chums, or past co-workers for the last four years."

"This is all accurate?" Jack asked.

"Yeah. Anna had some of her people run this stuff down. He hasn't been seen or heard from for four years, except to get the Ohio CDL license, and he used a phony address in Cincinnati to get that. His family thought he'd run off and joined the Peace Corps," Sanchez said.

"Why the Peace Corps?"

"He was always talking human rights."

"Sounds more like he was preparing himself for a lucrative job than protecting human rights," Jack said. "His education and two years working for the Border Patrol must have given him some good contacts. He started hitting for the other side."

Sanchez agreed.

Jack suggested, "He may have had a partner in his new business. Maybe someone went to the dark side with him."

"Damn!" Sanchez said sarcastically. "See, that's the kind of stuff Toomey was talking about. Fresh eyes. You are good, bro."

"You already ran that down," Jack said.

"First thing I did when we got his name. In fact, Anna gave me some contact numbers for ex-coworkers and friends. He wasn't married. No girlfriend that we could identify."

"Disciplinary actions in his personnel file?" Jack asked.

Sanchez's grin faded. "I'll check."

"Roommates in school? Favorite bar?" Jack persisted.

"I'm running down what I can. But he's not our suspect. There have been five of these cases. He was a random victim. Wrong truck, wrong time."

Jack said nothing. He didn't want to make enemies.

"Sorry," Sanchez said. "It's hard enough working with the Feds and pissing my own detectives off. I'm embarrassed that I didn't hit all the corners. You got good instincts, Murphy. I'll pass some of those leads on to Toomey, and he can have someone start checking. Just for my dead driver, we'll want to talk to a lot of people in Dallas and Ohio. That will take boots on the ground. I've been working strictly by telephone."

Jack agreed that it wasn't something they could do on the telephone. But he believed that sooner or later they would have to follow their guts to wherever that would take them. Tracking a serial killer through five states wasn't something he'd had to do.

"Let's move on," Sanchez suggested. "Like I said, we have a witness. Her name is Libby Quinn. She's homeless, a semi-hooker depending on if she's eaten or shot up that day. She was squatting in one of the abandoned warehouses that would have a view of the abandoned truck, and she's the darling of the Homicide Squad at present."

"You don't think she's credible?" Liddell asked.

"She's desperate. A week ago, she walked up to officers in a squad car and propositioned them. Both of them. The female officers didn't think it was funny. They arrested her and turned her over to Vice. That's when she came up with the 'I saw the whole thing' bit. They knew she was full of shit, but they still had to check it out. Right? They took her through her story a couple of times and showed her mug shots of known traffickers, murderers, and people with a record for violence. The guy she picked out was dead for two years."

"Are you still talking to her?" Liddell asked.

"Me? I never talked to her. Last I heard she said she didn't actually see the driver get whacked, but she saw him park the truck and start talking to a dude. She thought the other guy came up in a mid-size dark-colored car. The description she gave of the guy that came up talking to the driver could be anyone. But she did come damn close to describing the driver. That's why I'm telling you about her."

"Are we going to talk to her?" Jack asked.

"I'd say why waste our time. But Toomey wants you to take a shot."

Chapter 22

The three detectives were in Sanchez's beast, heading east on Interstate 70. Interstate 70 turned into I-44, and they headed into downtown St. Louis.

Sanchez said, "Our witness is scared to stay at the warehouse where she was squatting. She's afraid the killer will come back for her because—and this is another phase of her story—the killer saw her watching them. You see where I'm going with this?"

"She's not too dumb," Jack said.

Sanchez continued. "Homicide gets all excited that they might have a witness. They get a sketch artist, put her up at the Hyatt, feed her, round the clock protection, cable TV, and...get this. They get her absolved of all charges. It's a win-win for her."

"You really haven't talked to her yet?" Jack asked.

"A team in Homicide was—is—handling it. I wasn't involved until Toomey kidnapped me, so I didn't want to interfere in Homicide's investigation. That's one of my crews when I'm not on loan to the Feds. These guys have worked hard on this case since August, and they don't take well to outsiders—that includes me—coming in and asking questions. You know how it is."

Jack knew how it was. He would have felt the same way if someone got up in his investigation. It would feel like he was being second-guessed. It was bad enough that Double Dick interfered and screwed things up more times than not.

"Did the sketch artist do any good?" Liddell asked. Liddell was stretched out in the back seat.

Sanchez gave a snort. "I saw the sketches. The picture of the dude in the dark car looks a little like me when I'm drunk and mean. But the sketch of the guy she said was the driver is damn close, like I said. She's either turned a trick for the guy before, or did after he parked. Or she's a lucky liar. But she's all they got. It's been three weeks now, and she's still living on the county's tit. Every time they question her she remembers something else. Something that conveniently has the ring of truth. Probably because it's been on the news or she's overheard her protection detail talking about. I think one of my guys is doing her and giving her tips on what to say next. Strike that. I'm sure one of the guys is doing her, but I can't prove it and I've got more important things on my plate. Who cares if a hooker is getting a free ride? But she's tying up valuable resources."

Jack knew Sanchez had other reasons for wanting Jack and Liddell to be there for the first official federal interview of this witness. Sanchez didn't want his guys to be pissed at him. He could blame the interference on Evansville and Toomey. He asked Sanchez, "You want us to talk to her, or are you going to do the questioning?"

"I want you to interview her. I hear you have a certain charm."

"Bite me, Lieutenant. Sir," Jack said.

"None of that rank crap. Well, maybe you should defer to me in front of any of my officers who might be present. I don't want them forgetting who the boss is."

Sanchez turned off I-44 and onto Chestnut Street. The top of the Arch was visible over the tops of the buildings from I-44. He slowed down for the garage entrance to the Hyatt at the Arch Hotel.

"She's staying here?" Liddell asked.

Sanchez answered by pulling into the parking garage. He held his credentials out of the window for the gateman.

"The witness got a pretty sweet deal. The Hyatt Regency," Jack said.

"Yeah. The Homicide Squad has a deal with the Hyatt. We do a lot of business with them because we get stuck with presidential details and visiting dignitaries and such. They figured she'd be safer here than anywhere else, and they would be more comfortable here than anywhere else."

"Good thinking," Jack said and thought about the run-down twelve-dollar-a-night motel rooms he'd been stuck in with various witnesses.

Liddell got out and stretched. "Where our department puts us up, a continental breakfast is something you find on another continent. You have to cross the street to a McDonald's to get food."

No one said anything, so Liddell continued his rant. "Room service is when the manager goes through your stuff while you're out and only steals a little of it. The front desk is behind shatterproof glass and the concierge is..."

"I think he gets the picture," Jack said.

Sanchez parked, stuck the FBI placard on the dash, and they went up the elevator. The doors opened on the ninth floor, and Sanchez led the way. Jack didn't see anyone in the hallway. He put a hand on Sanchez's arm, and the other hand rested on the butt of his .45. "Where's the guard," Jack whispered.

Sanchez chuckled. "Probably inside the room banging the maid."

They stopped at a door marked 919, and Sanchez knocked. "Police. Open up."

"What's the password?" A female voice came from behind the door.

"Hell, I don't know," Sanchez said. "Open the damn door, Kim."

The door cracked open, and a pretty blond woman in a tracksuit said, "Good enough, I guess. What'chu want, Lou?"

"World peace, Kim," Sanchez said. "But I'll settle for talking to your 'charge.'"

"I don't mean to be insensitive," Kim said, "but I don't know these guys, so get stuffed."

"You're Kim?" Liddell said. "Lou's—I mean, Lieutenant Sanchez's—partner?"

"Has he been talking about me again?" Detective Kim Burdick said and grinned.

"They're with me dammit, Kim," Sanchez said.

She stepped back, letting them enter the suite. She gave Sanchez a quick hug and said, "Where you been, Pops. You never call. You never write. I thought the Feds put you in a suit and stuck your ass behind a desk to rot. Or worse yet, stuck a suit up your ass like the rest of them."

"We just talked yesterday. Kim, these are the Evansville detectives I told you about. The big one's Liddell."

"Play football?" Kim asked Liddell.

Liddell said, "A little. College."

"Lou said your partner calls you Bigfoot. I can see why. Lookit them feet! What'chu wear? Michael Jordan hand-me-downs?" She laughed at her own joke.

The living room looked like a tornado had hit it. The door to the bedroom was partially shut, and he could hear loud snoring coming from that room. A small kitchenette, a bathroom, and a full-size refrigerator created an ambiance that said, "My boss gets the penthouse suite and I get this shit."

"The Princess is still sleeping. She gets up around noon and takes frequent naps for getting up so early. She's like a damned cat. Sometimes I swear..." she said, mimicking a strangling.

"Wake her up," Sanchez said.

"Okay, but you've got to put her back to sleep when you're done," Kim said and slapped the palm of her hand on the bedroom door until the snoring stopped.

"Get up, Libby. You got visitors," Kim said loudly.

"I'm not decent," a young-sounding voice said.

"You're tellin' me," Kim muttered.

Lou asked Kim, "Are you working this alone? I was told there were two of you round the clock."

"Are you seeing two of me, Lou?" Kim asked and chuffed. "You were up drinking all night with Cutie again, weren't you?"

"His dog had a beer can this morning," Liddell interjected, and Kim chuckled.

"Dog's a lush," she said. "They deserve each other. And he gets gas so bad from beer the damn dog's the only one stupid enough to sleep in the same bed."

The bedroom door opened, and Libby Quinn came out wearing a Hyatt Regency robe that completely swallowed her thin body. "Who's this?" she asked and stumbled on the hem of the plush hotel robe. The robe was pulled so tightly that all that showed was a head and toes sticking out of the top and bottom. She smiled hesitantly and extended a hand toward Jack.

"Libby Quinn," she said, and they introduced themselves.

The heat in the room was cranked up to "smelter," but Libby was shivering and her skin was pale. Her eyes were sunken and the whites were yellow. Jack imagined the arms underneath the robe's sleeves were marked with enough needle tracks to make a map of St. Louis.

She's in withdrawals.

"Are they taking care of you, Libby?" Jack asked.

"As can be expected," she said. "Did you catch him?"

"No, ma'am," Liddell said. "We're from Evansville, Indiana."

"Evansville?"

"Yes, ma'am."

Sanchez said, "They're here to ask you some questions that might relate to a case they're working. Do you feel up to it?" His tone brooked no reply but a *yes*.

"Can't I have coffee first?" Libby asked.

"I'll get it," Kim said. "While I'm at it, maybe I'll go out for croissants. You guys hungry? I'm sick of room service." Without waiting for an answer, she grabbed her coat and was out the door, leaving them alone with Libby.

Before Jack could ask a question, Sanchez told the woman, "Have a seat, Libby."

She sat on the sofa, arms snugged across her middle, eyes staring into another dimension. She had entered the twilight zone.

Sanchez said, "I don't care why you're here or how long you stay. Understand?"

"I don't..."

"Don't talk," Sanchez said. His tone wasn't angry, just determined. "The St. Louis PD has you here, and I imagine it's a sweet deal compared to where you were living. But I have to warn you that if you lie to us the deal goes in the toilet. We're sworn federal agents. You get it? If you lie to us, it's a federal crime. I'll take you straight to prison. You will go away for a very long time. No money. No privacy. No skag."

She slumped forward and let her breath out. Sanchez winked at Jack.

"You're a heroin user, aren't you?" Sanchez asked.

She nodded.

"Agent Murphy is going to ask you some questions, and on my mother's grave, if you lie, I'll let the big one use you for batting practice. Got it?"

She nodded again.

Jack and Liddell asked Libby questions, and she gave the expected vague answers until Kim came in with a bag of bagels and four cups of Starbucks Komodo Dragon coffee in a holder.

"You got nowhere," Kim said.

Sanchez shrugged. "Had to try. Now we've got to go. Good luck with this. I'll keep trying to get you off this detail and back where you belong."

"On a beach in Hawaii? You sweet-talker you," Kim said. "I've got a master's degree in criminology and I'm being a damn babysitter. Now go before I jump out the window."

Liddell asked Sanchez in the hallway, "You're not going to tell Kim?"

"I told Libby I didn't care what deal she had with Homicide. I keep my word. If she'd lied to us, I would gladly rip her throat out and feed it to my dog."

"You should tell Kim she made most of her testimony up," Jack said. "I believe her about the driver, because I believe she turned a trick with him. She may or may not have seen a dark-colored car. She could have been hallucinating that part."

"Yeah. I believe she saw the driver and the truck," Sanchez said. "One look at her and you know she's a junkie. She's going through withdrawal. She'll be in a psych ward detoxing by Monday. Probably a good thing she lied to the Homicide detectives. It's probably all that's kept her alive in this cold."

"We're back to square one?" Liddell said.

"I was never past square one," Sanchez answered. "Let's hope Anna comes up with something we can investigate."

Jack said, "We'll be heading back to Evansville when we get to your place. That is, unless you have something else?"

"Nada. I really hoped we'd get something from her, catch a break and be home in time for some really good Scotch," Sanchez said.

Liddell said, "The only thing we'd get from her would *be* catchy."

Murphy's Law says: "The degree to which you look on the bright side is directly proportional to the amount of misfortune that will befall you."

An FBI agent once told Jack that a case is either solved in the first twenty-four hours or it will never be solved. That type of thinking was part of Jack's lack of willingness to join the task force. However, knowing he could work with guys like Sanchez made it more palatable. He knew Sanchez would never give up.

Sanchez drove twice the speed limit, pulled in his driveway, and stopped beside the Crown Vic. Cutie was lying on the porch with two empty beer cans between her paws.

"OCD," Sanchez said about the dog.

"I'll go get the boxes, bwana. I c'n fetch 'n tote, suh," Liddell said and headed for the barn.

"We'll go through all this stuff and call you," Jack said to Sanchez.

"Toomey's a dick, but I'm hoping you see something I've missed."

The radio in the SUV came to life. "Hey, Lou. You there?" It was Kim calling on a side channel used by detectives on special assignments.

Sanchez said to Jack in a sarcastic tone, "Maybe the 'witness' remembered something important after we left." He pulled the mic from the holder. "Go."

"This is gonna blow your socks off, Lou. You still got those two Evansville guys with you?" Kim said.

Sanchez said, "Yeah. Why? Did she identify one of them as the killer now?"

"You need to call dispatch. Right now, Lou," Kim said. "I think it's your guy."

"We have another truck?" Sanchez asked.

"No. Just call dispatch. I don't want to say anything else. Get me?"

"Will do. Thanks." Sanchez knew she was worried about Libby overhearing and changing her story again. He replaced the mic and said, "This might involve you guys." He called dispatch on his cell phone.

Sanchez's side of the conversation made Jack's stomach drop. Sanchez hung up and honked the horn until Liddell came out. Liddell threw the boxes in the back of the Crown Vic and got in the Denali. Sanchez put it in gear and made a U-turn.

"Shit!" Sanchez said.

* * * *

Det. Larry Jansen of the Missing Person Unit knocked on the door.

"Come," Deputy Chief Richard Dick said using his royal voice, the one he reserved for talking to peasants, which was anyone below him in rank, including most of the public.

Jansen entered the spacious office and waited to be told he could sit. He wasn't, so he remained standing to deliver his report.

"I tried to get some information on the survivor's whereabouts, but Murphy shut me down," Jansen said. "I checked with my niece. You remember me telling you she's working in Senator Young's office as an intern?"

Dick rolled a finger in the air and said nothing.

"Yeah. Okay. My niece checked with her boyfriend, who's working as an intern for Homeland Security, and he knows someone in..."

"Larry, I trust there's a point to your interrupting my work?"

Dick's desk top was bare except for a cell phone that lay screen up. He was playing *Scrabble with Friends*. Dick turned the phone over and cleared his throat.

"Anyway, my niece said the State Department has never been notified of the existence of an illegal alien in custody of the police in Evansville. That's against..."

"Department policy," Dick finished the sentence. "I already knew that. Did you locate the boy? Yes or no?"

"No," Jansen admitted. "I've been pulling out all the stops on this, but I don't see how finding the boy is going to get us any closer to solving these murders? I mean, he's just a kid. He was lucky to survive. According to everyone I talked to, the truck trailer was locked shut. They froze to death. And the other guy they think was the driver was found clear across town. I think we're barking up a dead tree."

"I want the boy," Dick said. "Do what you do best, Larry. Get information and pass it on to me. Just me. Understand?"

"If I do all this, do we still have a deal?" Jansen asked.

Dick sat stone-faced, but Jansen wouldn't be deterred. "Do we?"

Dick picked up his cell phone, indicating the meeting was at an end.

Jansen held his ground, and Dick flapped a hand toward the door. "I keep my word, Larry. Now go, but keep in touch. I want you to report even the smallest piece of information you dig up, even if you 'think' it's nothing. We're a team on this. I should know what you know."

As Jansen walked through the door, he muttered under his breath, "That goes both ways, asshole."

When the door shut behind Jansen, the deputy chief took a file folder from his desk drawer. It contained photos of both crime scenes. He had a complete file on a thumb drive, but he'd printed several pictures that he thought would be snapped up by the news media.

He knew he had a reputation. Media Whore they called him behind his back. Double Dick. It rankled him to be made fun of, but then, he'd risen to the rank of Deputy Chief because of who he was. He was at the top of his career, merit-rank-wise, but he still had one more step, Chief of Police. That was an appointed position, but he had friends on the city council, friends that were big tax contributors, even an ex-congressman. It didn't matter if the rank and file of the Evansville Police Department hated him. He could still become chief of police and a high-profile, hell, a national-profile case like this could be just the ticket.

He perused the reports he'd ordered Detective Chapman to supply, and he had copies of the initial police crime reports. The thing he didn't have was that damn Detective Murphy's notes. Murphy didn't do reports until the deed was done. It always infuriated him that he wasn't kept in the loop like Captain Franklin or Chief Pope. Hell, even Sergeant Walker was privy to much of the current progress of a case, and he always played ignorant. Dick swore that when he became chief of police he would clean house. The ones loyal to him would hold all the positions of power. It would be good for the city. Good for the police department. Most of all, it would be good for him. When he retired he wanted to be able to say he'd risen to the top. He was so close.

He held a particularly heart-wrenching photo taken of the huddled frozen bodies in the back of the trailer. He placed it on top of the pile and dialed a number on his desk phone.

"You've reached Claudine Setera, Channel Six. Leave your message at the beep," came the voice over the line.

Deputy Chief Dick hung up before the beep. He wasn't ready to go out on a limb quite yet. He needed to know where the boy was first. He'd find a way to make Murphy tell him.

Chapter 23

The Dream Lodge in Evansville was anything but that. The bed was as hard as a cinder block, the same stuff as the unpainted water-stained walls. Coyote had left the truck stop café after killing the state trooper. He wasn't concerned about being stopped by the police. He was invisible as far as the cops were concerned. He'd thrown the stuff from the café into the Mississippi as he crossed the bridge, and no one had slowed to watch him park on the bridge. They were all sheep. How would they survive without men like him to protect them?

The cops weren't bad people, just stretched too thin and under too many political edicts. He wasn't. He'd seen the light and made his own path.

Room ten at the Dream Lodge smelled like stale cigarette smoke, the stink of sex, mold, and rotting wood. He dropped his gym bag on the bed and took off his Colts jacket. He'd bought it in a thrift store when he'd gotten into Evansville. The jacket would draw attention away from his face. The Indianapolis Colts football team were like gods in Indiana.

He'd need solid information on the whereabouts of the boy. He didn't think his source would have anything on the kid. He needed to know more. He needed background on Detective Jack Murphy and the big guy, Blanchard, his partner. He'd learned the hard way that you never underestimate your opponent. Murphy exuded determination. Cleverness. The big guy was a rock wall that would take some climbing. Together they were more of an obstacle than they first appeared.

He played with the idea of approaching Deputy Chief Richard Dick for the information he needed. He could show Dick a badge. He had several of them. Or he could say he was with the Indianapolis newspaper. Dick liked to talk. A talking dick. Coyote smiled, but the smile faded quickly.

Bad shit happened when you weren't focused. Plus, showing his face to the deputy chief would mean he'd have to eliminate the arrogant man. Another cop would raise too many eyebrows.

He had a source where he could get the information he needed, but he hesitated to call them. If his source wasn't aware of his failure to eliminate a target in that hick town, they would soon work it out. They might even try to turn it to their own advantage. He didn't think his source would want him caught. Killed, but not caught. Coyote knew too many secrets.

His shrink had said, "Don't ruminate. Write." He scooted back on the mattress until his back was against the wall and opened his journal:

It's all turned to shit. Yesterday, I was looking forward to the next mission. Now I've got to clean up a mess. I was careful but I made a mistake. That worries me.

I left the old woman alive. She was no threat to my mission but the boy shouldn't have survived. That's the way mistakes played out. One problem leads to another and pretty soon the shit hits the fan. I take no pleasure in killing a boy. Any boy. But he's a sacrifice. I can't afford to fail.

Lost my appetite. My sleep is filled with the past. The jungle. The medic. The chopper lifting off. The pain in my chest. Can't breathe. It's real to me. But then I'm home. My home. Not the jungle. I see my wife and little boy. His face is dirty and smeared with tears because Daddy is going to work. Waving Daddy goodbye. Then dirt of the border trail kicking up dust, thick choking dust even with the windows up. The two men in the Explorer's headlights, not running, staring us down, one of them gives us the finger. Shots. Blood. I scream at my partner but nothing comes out. I am helpless to stop what's coming but I enjoy it all the same. I feel alive.

My past was the mistakes of youth. Why won't it end there? It follows me around like sewer gnats. My country's enemy is growing in numbers every day. It's like trying to empty the ocean with a spoon. I can't kid myself. I'll never stop the spread of this disease alone. But who can I turn to? The government is a joke. They play at being a soldier. I'm the real deal. They complain. I act.

He put the notebook away and unzipped the gym bag. He took a bottle of peroxide and a sharpening stone from the bag and went to the rust-stained sink in the bathroom.

He poured peroxide on the bayonet blade and put the bottle on the side of the chipped porcelain tub. He scrubbed all the blood away and scrubbed it again. His dad always said, "You take care of your tools, and they'll take care of you." He was right about that at least. He went to work with the whetstone. Soon, the four-edged bayonet was gleaming.

He wiped the blade clean with toilet paper and slipped his Indianapolis Colts team jacket back on over a clean Black Watch–patterned flannel shirt. He pulled on a faded baseball cap, a pair of faded Cat boots, and slipped the bayonet in the sheath behind his back.

He saw a library a few blocks away when he came into Evansville. Libraries had internet. He'd start there. He needed a clue to where the boy was being kept. If the newswoman could be believed, the kid wasn't taken by Immigration. Murphy had shown his soft spot. The kid. That was Murphy's mistake. Everyone makes mistakes.

Chapter 24

Sanchez stopped the Denali short of the yellow-and-black crime scene tape that was blocking the entrance to the café parking area. Four gray Missouri State Highway Patrol cars were positioned carefully in the parking lot to maintain the required crime scene integrity. A trooper sat in one of the vehicles up front near the café entrance, head down, most likely doing a report. A fifth marked vehicle, their crime scene wagon, was parked back near the perimeter tape.

A tall trooper was pulling perimeter duty and watched them closely as they exited the Denali. He was wearing a fur cap with the straps snapped under his chin instead of the traditional Smokey Bear hat associated with State Police.

A second trooper stood at the foot of the café's entrance with a clipboard stuffed under one arm. He was dressed similar to the perimeter guard but with the addition of sergeant's chevrons sewed on his Tuffy jacket. He was stamping his feet in a futile effort to keep warm but stopped while he sized up the three newcomers. He must have made them for cops and went back to doing what crime scene log officers do. Nothing.

Jack couldn't see the other troopers that must be on the scene and assumed they were inside the café.

As he approached the trooper on perimeter duty, he realized that Bigfoot was right about the federal agent badges. Having federal identification would have made this much easier. Sanchez took his badge case out and was about to show his to the perimeter guard when a female trooper came out of the café. She was tall with dirty blond hair tucked under her Smokey hat. Her Rocky boots made no sound as she moved quickly toward them. Her mouth turned down at the sides as if she were angry to be interrupted.

Rick Reed

"This is a crime scene," she said in a tone somewhere between incredulous, curious, and challenging. "You have no business here. Turn around and get back in your car."

Sanchez approached the crime scene tape and in a deft move slid underneath while holding his leather credential case open and out. "Federal agents, Lieutenant," he said.

The trooper's nametag identified her as Lt. J. Battle, and there were silver bars on the epaulets of her jacket to confirm that. Battle ignored Sanchez's credentials and asked Jack and Liddell, "You two federal agents too?"

"They're with me, Lieutenant Battle," Sanchez said, slipping his badge and his hands in his pockets.

"Show me," Battle said to Jack.

Jack's badge identified him as an Evansville PD detective, but he showed it anyway. Liddell followed suit.

"Indiana, huh? What's two Indiana detectives doing at my crime scene? Matter of fact, what are you doing in my crime scene?" she said to Sanchez.

"Maybe Lieutenant Sanchez should explain," Jack said.

"Lieutenant now, huh? I didn't know the Feds had lieutenants," Battle said. "Let me see that badge again."

Sanchez said, "We're part of a newly formed federal task force." He handed her his credentials again. While she examined the ID carefully, he said, "We were told by the St. Louis police dispatcher that this might be connected to a mass murder we're investigating."

The words "mass murder" got her attention.

"You mean the truck trailer in August?" she asked. "The illegals? You're working that?"

"Yeah," Sanchez said. "These men are Evansville detectives but have been sworn in as federal officers and are assigned to the task force. They have a similar case in Evansville. You can call FBI Deputy Assistant Director Toomey, who's in charge of our task force." He wrote a phone number on the back of his business card and handed it to her. "That's the local FBI number. Ask for Toomey."

Battle returned Sanchez's badge case. She watched their faces to judge whether they were telling the truth and said to Sanchez, "Well, I could turn this 'mass' murder scene over to you guys, but even if you prove it's connected to yours, I won't do that." She pointed toward the State Trooper vehicle where the driver hadn't yet moved. "I got a dead trooper, and as much as I appreciate your interest, you don't have jurisdiction here, so bye bye."

Sanchez straightened to his six-foot-three height. "We can play rock-paper-scissor all day, Jill, but we have to confirm that we don't have an interest in this case. We won't know that until you tell us what you've got."

Jack thought, *Jill. They know each other, so why's she being such a hardass?*

Lt. Jill Battle took a deep breath without speaking.

Sanchez continued, "If this is connected to our cases, we *will* be involved in your investigation and you can bet your Smokey-hat-wearing ass that we're not leaving here until we find out."

"Uh oh," Liddell muttered.

Battle met Sanchez eye to eye, lips tight, and then said, "You understand that I don't know any of your friends personally or professionally, and I've never heard of this task force. I'm going to call this guy Toomey." She turned to go to her car. Over her shoulder, she said to the perimeter guard, "Don't let them go anywhere."

After she was out of earshot Liddell said, "Should we assume the position?"

Sanchez tapped the butt of his .45. "We're better shots, but in a fistfight, you don't want to mess with Jill," Sanchez said, causing the perimeter guard to chuckle.

"She's just doing her job," Jack said. "She doesn't understand the dynamics involved here. We're police from two different jurisdictions telling her we're Feds and asking to involve ourselves in a State Highway Patrol investigation that's her jurisdiction; plus, one of her own was murdered."

"She's just being a bitch, Jack," Sanchez said, surprising them. "She's trying to act like she doesn't remember me. A few months back I met her at a club. I guess she's still sore that I didn't tell her my real name."

"Give her a break," Jack said. "They've lost someone."

When they'd first arrived on scene, Jack had assumed the occupant of the Highway Patrol cruiser was doing paperwork. A sick feeling crawled into the pit of his stomach. The dead trooper's cruiser was nearest the café door. The parking area was gravel that was frozen hard and ran around both sides of the café. On the left side of the café, he could see the side of a red Dumpster. There didn't appear to be any other vehicles, and he didn't see any tire tracks, but the cruiser's tires hadn't left tracks either.

He turned his attention back to the dead trooper. "The trooper didn't have a chance to get out of the car." The sick feeling Jack felt turned to barely contained rage. "What the hell is happening to this world?"

"Pod'na, this is a screwed-up mess," Liddell said and asked Sanchez, "Lou, were there any unexplained murders at the time of the incidents in Florida or any of the others?"

Sanchez said, "I know what's in the reports from the other states. That's all. I'll see if Anna can get us a list of murders that happened around the date of death in the other states."

Liddell said, "We don't know if the killer is male or female or if there's more than one. I read your coroner's report, and they didn't even offer a guess. We probably need to talk to your coroner again and get an opinion."

Sanchez said, "If the killer is female, she's one hell of a strong female. The wounds are twenty or more inches deep, but I see what you're saying. You said your video shows a man in the Coffee Shop."

"The video is poor," Jack said.

Sanchez said, "Could it be a woman? There are some strong women. That pig sticker would even the odds. It wouldn't take that much to push that bayonet in deep. Take Trooper Battle for instance. You don't think she could kick your ass in the blink of an eye?"

Battle came up quietly behind Sanchez. "In your case, Lieutenant Sanchez, you might not even have to blink. Director Toomey verified your story. Come on. I'll show you around. Crime Scene is inside, and I've notified him we're coming. Don't touch anything."

They followed her across the lot, and when they came even with the dead trooper's car, Jack stopped to look inside.

Lt. Battle turned and said, "The crime scene tech is waiting for us."

"Just a minute," Jack said.

The victim was a female state trooper. Probably in her early to mid-thirties. The Smokey Bear hat was shoved onto her head at a crooked angle. Something a trooper would never do. The collar of her jacket was pulled up on the side near the driver's window. The OPEN sign was turned off, and a CLOSED sign hung in the front door glass.

She spotted someone either coming out or already in the parking lot. She saw the CLOSED sign. She would have known the place shouldn't be closed, but for whatever reason, that fact wasn't suspicious enough to get out of her car. She was left-handed. Her gun is still holstered. The killer surprised her? Yanked the door open, grabbed her, killed her, and left her in the seat with the engine running to make it appear she was working or asleep?

"Is this the way she was found?" Jack asked Battle.

"More or less. A regular customer found her and came to the State Post to report it. He said Jeanie—I mean Trooper Battle—was in her car with the engine running and she was bloody."

Jack saw the nametag: J. Battle.

"Is she related?" Jack asked.

"My sister," Battle said.

"Lieutenant Battle, I think you should excuse yourself from the scene," Jack said.

Sanchez said, "I'll call the Post."

Battle's expression hardened. Her eyes settled on Jack.

"Is there anyone we can call for you? Someone who can stay with you?" Jack asked.

"Go to hell, Murphy! I'm not going anywhere. Lieutenant Sanchez—or whoever you are this time—that's my sister. My niece is inside. Murdered. Everyone inside is dead. And I'm..." Her words trailed off, and she turned her back to them, arms hanging limply by her sides, head bowed.

Sanchez stepped away and called his dispatch. He spoke for a moment and came back. "Dispatch is calling Highway Patrol. They're going to send a captain and a team out here. We'll stand by."

Battle glared at Sanchez, but her resolve was weakening. "You don't have the authority to relieve me here. This is still a Missouri Highway Patrol investigation, and I..."

Sanchez yelled at the sergeant with the crime scene log and motioned him over. The sergeant came trotting up.

"Sergeant, you take charge here until your supervisor and a team of investigators arrive."

"That's my supervisor," the sergeant said, nodding toward Lt. Battle.

The man's nametag read Sgt. L. Ringo. Sanchez said, "Sergeant Ringo, you need to put the lieutenant in your car and stay with her. We'll help out until the team arrives from Highway Patrol."

"She outranks me," Ringo said.

"I don't give a shit if she's your mama. She's a liability in a murder investigation. Lawyers would have a field day with that. They may anyway because no one knew she was working on the murder of her sister and niece. Did you know?"

Sgt. Ringo said nothing.

Sanchez pulled his badge and held it out. "I'm a federal agent, and I'm assuming control of this crime scene. That includes you and everyone here. I'm ordering you to take the lieutenant to your car and stay with her until help arrives."

The sergeant looked relieved and trotted off to corral the lieutenant, who was now sitting on the front fender of her dead sister's car. She pushed his hand away but followed him to his car and got inside.

A few minutes later another Highway Patrol vehicle pulled into the lot and drove up to the taped perimeter. The driver left the car there and approached them on foot.

"Major Maddox," he said but didn't offer his hand. "My dispatcher explained your credentials. I've spoken with Assistant Deputy Director Toomey, and he vouched for you. I didn't even know we had a new federal task force, but nobody tells me anything. I appreciate you boys calling this to my attention. I just wish you hadn't said anything to our dispatcher. Oh well, the deed is done. What have we got?"

Jack motioned for Sergeant Ringo to come and explain what they had found, which was good, because Jack hadn't heard all of it yet. Lt. Battle remained in the sergeant's car, facing forward.

Ringo said, "I got here first, Major. A regular customer came to eat lunch and saw the CLOSED sign in the door and the blinds were shut. He said he noticed the Highway Patrol car sitting there when he pulled up." Ringo motioned toward the car with the dead trooper inside. "It's Jeanie Battle. Anyway, the witness said he went to ask her what was going on. He thought maybe there'd been a robbery. This place is robbed at least twice a year. Anyway, he tapped on the window and saw the blood. He swears he didn't touch anything. He just got in his truck and came straight to the Post. He's still at the Post as far as I know," Ringo said. "He was told to stay put until someone took his statement."

Major Maddox's face was unreadable, but he said, "No one stayed with the witness?"

"The lieutenant made the decision, sir," he said.

It made sense to Jack. She somehow knew her sister and niece were in trouble and like any family member, especially someone with enough rank to control the police response, would try to go and see things for herself. She probably realized she was in over her head when she found her sister was dead and not just wounded. She panicked and went inside to help her niece. But the girl was already dead.

Jack thought she was giving them such a hard time because they were encroaching on her jurisdiction, or because she was angry with Sanchez. In fact, she was already in shit up to her neck and drowning for messing the case up.

Major Maddox said, "Sergeant, we'll discuss this later. I want you to answer these men's questions. I'll have some of my own."

Chapter 25

Sanchez drove west on I-64 like he was in the Indy 500. The Denali had emergency lights in the grill and back window, and a siren, but he didn't need them as he bullied his way through traffic. Jack approved.

"It's our guy," Liddell said.

"I'm glad Major Maddox took charge of the scene," Sanchez said. "Maybe they can salvage the investigation."

Sergeant Ringo had told them the witness came to the Post and their dispatcher called Lt. Battle instead of sending a trooper to the café. The dispatcher had been trying to contact the lieutenant's sister, Trooper Jeanie Battle, to send her to a vehicle accident on the interstate. When Trooper Jeanie Battle didn't respond to several radio calls, the dispatcher called her sister, Lieutenant Battle.

Lt. Battle told the dispatcher to send another car and to let her know when she made contact with her sister. Lt. Battle was on the other side of the city when the customer came to the Post and reported an injured trooper at the café. From there it turned into a comedy of errors.

Sgt. Ringo said he'd volunteered for the run to the café because he was familiar with it and he was close. Lt. Battle had called him on his cell phone and asked him to keep her updated on the café run. She was going to her sister's house to check on her.

Sgt. Ringo arrived at the café and immediately knew it was more than an injury. He went to the dead trooper's car and opened the door. He saw blood and called for an ambulance. He checked for a pulse and found none. He called dispatch and asked for backup assistance.

Lt. Battle heard Ringo's call for an ambulance and advise it was for a code ten-zero, which means deceased. She had called Sgt. Ringo, and he told her that her sister, Jeanie, was dead.

Lt. Battle did one thing right today. She didn't allow every trooper on the road to crowd into the crime scene. She responded to the run herself, along with one other trooper, and told the other cars to remain on patrol. She arrived and found the door of her sister's car still standing open. She checked for signs of life, shut the car door, and ran to the front door of the café. Sgt. Ringo had gone to the back door and found it open. He came to the front door and let the lieutenant in. They both searched the back of the café.

Major Maddox had allowed Sanchez, Jack, and Liddell to do a walk-through of the scene inside the café.

"The wounds on the bodies appear identical to our cases," Jack said. "Neither of you think it was a robbery, do you?"

"No way," Liddell said.

"The money and identifications were stolen. The manager had a laptop computer, but I didn't see one, just the power cord," Sanchez said. "He kills three people and stages the scene. That didn't happen in any of the other murders. All the other murders followed a pattern. Maybe this guy is just killing for fun now. He's completely unhinged."

"But why these three people?" Jack asked. "That bayonet is his signature. He's gotten away with five mass murders and left no trace. Why do this now?"

"Maybe this one was personal," Liddell suggested.

Sanchez pulled into the grass of the highway divider, did a U-turn, bounced up on the eastbound lanes, and picked up speed. He called dispatch and asked them to have Major Maddox call ASAP. Maddox called, and Sanchez told him what he wanted.

When Sanchez hung up, he said, "He's still with Lieutenant Battle at the State Post. He said she will talk to us."

* * * *

Sanchez parked behind the State Highway Patrol Post, and they met Major Maddox at the back doors. Maddox led them to his office, where Lieutenant Battle sat, eyes red and puffy from crying. She had changed into a clean uniform. Forensics had taken hers.

Maddox said, "Lieutenant Battle has agreed to talk to you, but I have to remind you that we are conducting our own investigation of the matter and anything she says will be recorded for a disciplinary hearing. Tread carefully, gentlemen."

Battle grimaced slightly at that but was otherwise composed. She said nothing, which was probably smart given that she'd screwed the pooch at a homicide scene involving an officer.

Jack said, "I have a few questions, Lieutenant. Could this have been personal? Would anyone want to hurt your family? Or you?"

The question seemed to take her by surprise. "Jeanie has been divorced for ten years," she said. "Her ex wasn't in the picture for years before that. He travels. A truck driver. She didn't want support, and he has no interest in being a daddy, so I can't see..."

"Enemies?" Jack asked.

"My sister and I are cops. What do you think?"

"Anyone in particular we should know about? Spurned lovers? Stalkers?" Sanchez asked.

Battle took a deep breath before answering. "My sister is married again. This time to a wonderful and caring woman who is always present in their lives. They've been together for a very long time, and there are no problems at home. Jeanie would have told me. We shared everything. Her wife helped raise Benny—that's my niece—as if she were her own child. You're barking up the wrong tree, Agent Sanchez."

"Is there any reason you can think of?" Sanchez asked.

She said to Jack, "You had a trailer full of dead immigrants in Evansville this morning. I saw it on the news here. Now you're wanting to see if your case is connected to the case in St. Louis. The St. Louis case is like the one in Evansville. Am I right?"

"Yes," Jack said.

"Was it connected? Is it the guy you're after?"

"We're not sure." Jack said, although he was ninety-nine percent sure. "You said Jeanie's ex-husband is a truck driver. Do you know who he's working for or how we can reach him?"

"He's a truck driver, but he's not capable of killing a fly. I'll give you his information, at least what I know, but you're wasting your time." She wrote the ex's information on a scrap of paper and gave it to Jack.

Jack said, "Lieutenant Battle, I can't begin to understand what you're going through, but I can promise you we'll find the person responsible."

Her hands tightened into fists, and her voice filled with emotion. "Not if I find the bastard first."

Major Maddox turned his face away.

They started to leave, and Battle said, "Will you at least keep me updated?"

Jack assured her they would and left her with Maddox. She was his problem now.

Outside the Post as they climbed into the Denali, Sanchez said, "She didn't do herself any favors in there."

Jack agreed. Major Maddox would have no choice but to suspend Lt. Battle and maybe even suggest dismissal from service. She could fight it, but that would be like pissing into the wind. Some of it always comes back on you. He felt for her, and he'd meant what he said about catching this guy. He decided he'd do his best to keep her updated.

"I'll get you back to your car. I don't guess there's much you can do here for now. You'll need a little time to get familiar with all of the cases, and that might take a few days," Sanchez said.

Jack thought he was right. There were at least three full Bankers Boxes of case file information. He had no doubt they could add the café to those cases after the autopsies of Jeanie Battle, her teenage daughter, the cook, and the manager. Their wounds were identical to his case. *Three civilians now and a trooper.*

Chapter 26

The trip from Evansville to St. Louis had seen little conversation because Jack and Liddell had so little information. The trip back to Evansville, so far, was anything but quiet. Jack turned the conversation back to the café and the killer's change in his selection of victims.

"The killer has been consistent with the bayonet. It means something to him. It's a signature, and this guy seems to be smarter than that," Jack said.

"He's getting careless. That's good for us. Right?" Liddell said.

"We've been focusing on the murders of the immigrants when we needed to be looking at the drivers. Why the trucks were parked where they were."

"I'm not following you, pod'na."

"I'm saying, the drivers are killed near their trucks. The killer knew just where to find them. The driver in Evansville was the only one that met this guy away from the truck. That sounds deliberate. Did the driver suspect something? Did he know the other drivers were being killed?"

"Or the killer commandeered the truck," Liddell suggested.

"I don't think so, Bigfoot. Why would he steal a car and kill the driver across town? Our case, Texas, and St. Louis had some evidence the drivers were on their knees when they were executed."

"Okay."

"The Florida driver was stabbed in the cab of the truck. The first wound, according to their medical examiner, was through the right side of his neck, and again through the right temple."

"The killer was in the truck with the driver," Liddell said.

"That doesn't mean he was in the truck with the other cases," Jack said. "But he seems to have a lot of knowledge of how human trafficking is done. And he has some way of contacting the drivers. The drivers have some reason they would stop for him, or go to meet him."

"And he's pretty skilled with a bayonet. He doesn't just stab them repeatedly. All the wounds are near fatal."

"We think he's left-handed, and most of the autopsies of the drivers indicate the same thing. Let's say he's not very tall, because he gets the victims on their knees or kills them where they can't avoid the bayonet," Jack said.

"Like the people at the café," Liddell said.

"Yeah. I didn't think of that one, Bigfoot. Let's get to that next. Right now we have a left-handed, not-too-tall killer with easy access to his victims. Let's assume the trooper was in the wrong place at the wrong time, and he didn't mean to kill the people in the café."

Jack and Liddell were quiet for the next five miles.

"I'm going to call Anna," Jack said.

"The ICE Queen?"

"Don't let her hear you say that, Bigfoot. I'm going to ask her to bring Angelina in on this."

Angelina Garcia was a computer genius. She started her career as the IT person for the Evansville Police Department fixing glitches in the data systems that linked EPD to other law enforcement agencies in the state and to the federal database. It was supposed to be a temporary job, but the chief of police discovered the police department needed her and hired her full-time. She was soon assigned wherever needed when she wasn't patching a system.

She was working with the Vice Unit when she came to Jack's attention. He was searching for a serial killer that was using nursery rhymes to select and kill children. She had proven herself invaluable in digging up information and using her connections with other agencies and in the cyber-world.

After that case Angelina got engaged to Mark Crowley, a deputy sheriff from a neighboring county. She semi-retired from EPD and moved into her fiancé's cabin on Patoka Lake and was now on a consulting basis with the Evansville Police Department and several other law enforcement agencies. He and Liddell had worked a human trafficking and murder case in Louisiana early on in the summer. Angelina had given them a hand with that, and she ended up getting chummy with the FBI, ICE, DEA, and ATF. Jack suspected she was now consulting for the Feds, but Angelina wouldn't admit it.

"She's probably still on her honeymoon, pod'na."

"I happen to know she's back home. Mark was called back home to stop a war between the County Council and the Sheriff's Department." Mark Crowley was now the sheriff of Dubois County.

"His dad starting trouble again?" Liddell asked.

Mark's father was Tanner Crowley, who was the previous sheriff, but had stepped down. Tanner was in early stages of dementia. Sometimes he was okay, and sometimes he forgot he wasn't sheriff anymore and would stop cars or go back and start interrogating people from cases he had closed. The County Council was threatening to have Tanner put in a secure nursing facility. Tanner was threatening them, and Mark was trying to keep peace.

"Mark can take care of it, Bigfoot," Jack said. He called Anna Whiteside to have Angelina brought into the case.

ICE Special Agent Whiteside answered the phone. "What?"

"I need something from you," Jack said.

"What a surprise, Jack. Go ahead and ask."

Jack had to laugh. Pretty on the outside and, like an ice sculpture, cold on the inside. "ICE Queen" definitely fit her.

"We're going to need some computer support on this," he said.

"Have you gone through the other case files completely?" she asked.

"Yes. But there's a ton of paper, and I don't think we have time to connect all the dots thoroughly. Can you get..."

Anna interrupted with, "Angelina's already at work on this. I sent her everything. You need to send me what you found at that café in St. Louis. I understand the Missouri Highway Patrol is still on scene, so there will be more, but send me what you can and I'll share it with Angelina," Whiteside said.

Jack had the call on speakerphone, and Liddell was listening. "Anna, this is Liddell. Since you have Angelina on this, do you think you can just put her on our task force after this is over?"

Jack had the same idea.

"No," Whiteside said. "Who says you'll even have a job when this is over?"

"Bite me, Anna," Jack said.

"We're tracing the trucks' owners, any log books, tickets issued, that kind of stuff, but it's a mess," she said. "The license plates on your truck were stolen. The truck was listed as sold for salvage. All of the trucks were listed as salvage and sold for parts or destroyed. We're talking to people at the salvage yards where the trucks were supposedly scrapped, but it looks like a dead end. The salvage papers are phony like everything else about this. We're dealing with human trafficking, so it's not surprising they are creating dead ends between the big bosses and everyone else."

Jack thought that if ICE couldn't trace the truck owners, he didn't have much chance of doing so. That was one thing he could cross off his list.

"Anything else?" Anna asked.

"Just an observation," Jack said. "This guy covers his tracks like a professional assassin. We think he has special military training, or maybe was, or is, law enforcement. Can you check into that angle?"

"Already being done. You know the driver in St. Louis was ex-Border Patrol. We gave Sanchez what we found, but we're still digging. Or I should say, Angelina is digging. You think it's an ex-Border Patrol guy?"

"Maybe," Jack admitted. "But the bayonet thing is off. He may have a grudge against illegal immigrants, but why kill civilians?"

"Why does anybody kill anybody?" she asked. "Freud would say the bayonet was an extension of his penis or something like that. We know we have to consider that all of this is a rivalry between trafficking organizations. MS-13 is always expanding territory. Anything else you want?"

"Yeah," Jack said. "Do I need to call Toomey?"

She was laughing when she hung up.

Chapter 27

Willard Library looked like an old river mansion to Coyote with its brick walls and Bedford stone pillars and steps. The cold air cleared his mind and made him pick up his pace. He didn't get enough exercise these days. He was still strong, but he was getting older and could feel the change even if he couldn't see it.

He trotted up the eight stone-slab steps and admired the craftsmanship. The steps were worn, polished down three inches or more each from tramping feet of the curious, students, children, and more likely now—in this weather—the homeless.

The doors were made from solid slabs of mahogany, four inches thick, with roses and vines ornately carved inside the wooden panes. He opened one door and stepped into what should be a museum. His cowboy boots clacked across the marble tile floor. Ahead was the checkout counter with a very attractive woman scanning and stacking a dozen books. On his right were rows of tables, all empty except for one young girl, maybe twenty to twenty-five years old. She was sitting at the end of a table nearest the old-fashioned heating radiators that were as old as the building. A thick book was open on the table in front of her. She wore a fatigue jacket, pulled up, with her chin stuck down the front, arms holding the jacket tight and her head lolling down and then jerking upright. She was obviously stoned.

The woman at the counter smiled and asked, "Can I help you find something, sir?"

Coyote pointed to the bank of computer terminals.

"Help yourself," the woman said and continued scanning books.

There were eight computer stations, all with wooden dividers for privacy from the sides, but all with the monitor facing the front desk. Coyote took the computer station nearest the girl, keeping her between him and the librarian. She smelled ripe. *Humanity at its weakest*. He pushed it out of his mind. He didn't want to start down that path.

He followed the directions on the card taped to the table and logged on to the internet easily. He typed in Channel Six and brought up the one he wanted. He moved the cursor over "Channel Six Live News" and clicked the mouse. A menu popped up. One of the headlines was titled "Immigrants Abandoned to Die." Another was titled "Immigrant: Survivor." He clicked on that one.

He made the video wide-screen and watched with interest. The volume was too high, and he hurriedly turned it low. He glanced behind him. The stoner and the librarian didn't notice.

He watched the video twice, pausing, focusing his attention on the face of the boy. The lone survivor. He was young. The woman reporter said he was. She didn't have a name for him or an age or where he came from, but she made the most of the boy's startled expression when they had confronted him in a hospital room. *Bitch.*

The end of the video showed a tractor-trailer in the distance, and you could see by the shaky view that the camera was moving toward the scene at a brisk pace. He guessed the reporter had a camera on her clothes or in her purse. She was approaching the two detectives he'd already seen on the video at the little café in Missouri. She called one of them Detective Murphy. The conversation between them was muted except for her asking Murphy what they were investigating.

"She don't know squat," Coyote muttered. He wrote the number for the station down in his journal. He typed Jack Murphy into the computer. There were more than a hundred hits. He scrolled through the newest dozen and found what he wanted. Two stories. One was from the Evansville newspaper and titled "Hero or Killer?" He tried to pull that story up, but it required him to open an account and log in. He hated computers. He scrolled through the other headlines, and a pattern emerged. Jack Murphy was a dedicated cop. He wasn't someone who could be intimidated or bought. Even the mayor didn't seem too pleased with him. In several Instagram photos, Murphy was seen with his partner, Liddell Blanchard, or at a murder scene.

He shut he computer down and wrote one word under Jack Murphy's name. "Dangerous."

Coyote walked to a foyer where a set of stairs led down to something called the Walnut Room. At the bottom of the stairs a heavy wooden door led outside, and a similar one into the Walnut Room.

A landline was on the librarian's desk upstairs. Another landline was down here on the podium in the Walnut Room. He considered using the one down here, but he didn't want to be overheard. He didn't want another bloodbath on his hands.

He heard footsteps coming down, and the librarian passed him. "We're very proud of this addition," she said. "Have you been here before?"

Coyote was careful to keep his face turned away, which wasn't hard. The librarian was tall, he was short. He held his thumb and little finger to his ear, mimicking a phone.

"We're not very busy, as you can see," she said. "It must be the cold keeping them home. You can use the phone in the Walnut Room if you like. Just no long-distance calls," she said with a smile and opened the door to the room for him. "The phone is on the podium. Just dial nine to get an outside line."

He decided to chance using the library phone. If that nosy waitress hadn't been reading his journal, he wouldn't have had to leave things like they were at the café. No one knew who he was. Here, he was just another schmuck in a library.

He picked up the receiver and opened his journal. He punched in the telephone number for Channel Six. A woman answered. He asked who the reporting team was on the truck murder that morning. She gave him the names. Claudine Setera was one of them. The other was a guy. Bart Hiller. The cameraman.

"I remember talking to him out at the scene," Coyote lied.

"I can connect you if you wish. Can I tell him who's calling please?"

"Tell him the guy he talked to at the truck scene. He'll remember me," Coyote said. It rang twice before being picked up.

"Bart Hiller, Channel Six, can I help you?" said the man's voice.

He sounded young. Eager. Coyote said, "This is Bobby John. I saw you at that horrible truck thing over there on the west side." Claudine Setera had reported the name of the street it was near, but he didn't want to be too specific. "You're that cameraman, aren't you?"

Bart said, "Yes. I was there. Who is this again?"

Coyote said, "Bobby John. I talked to you at the scene, but I guess you was too busy running errands for that woman reporter."

"Oh yeah. I remember you," Bart said. "What can I help you with, Bobby?"

"I think it's me that c'n help you, Bart," Coyote said. "I want to tell you something that I bet will get you out from under that woman. She was snitty with me. Like I was dirt under her feet."

Bart didn't quite take the bait. "She's an okay person. I don't really work for her. I work for the station."

"Okay. Sorry if I said somethin' wrong. Maybe I should talk to her. I got information. I might've seen the truck park there."

Coyote could hear Bart's breathing increase and his voice took on an urgency. "No. You don't have to do that, Bobby. Was it Johns?"

"Close enough," Coyote said. "If you want to transfer me to one of them reporters that's fine. I thought someone would want to hear what I got to say. The cops at the scene didn't seem too interested. Assholes."

"Why don't you tell me what you saw, sir. I'll make sure it gets to the right person," Bart said.

"Well. Okay. What I saw was a big semi with a trailer drivin' real slow down the street and pull in behind one a them empty warehouse buildin's."

"What time was this, sir?"

"Last night. I don't know, maybe just after dark. I don't have a watch."

"Did you see the driver leave the truck, sir?" an excited Bart asked.

Coyote said, "Yeah. He walked away. Didn't go in one of the buildings or get in a car. That's why I thought it was strange. You know?"

"That is strange, sir," Bart agreed. "What else did you see?"

"Well. I didn't see anything else there." He could imagine the disappointment Bart was feeling, but he'd be happy again. "But after I saw that report from the hospital. You know? The survivor."

"Yes. I know. I filmed it," Bart said.

Coyote could hear the pride mixed with impatience in that sentence. He'd set the hook. Now it was time to reel in the fish.

"I just saw that boy. Saw him plain as day. He was just walking down by the hospital."

"Wait! What?" Bart said.

"I seen that survivor you had on the news. Little guy. Eight or ten years old, right? Dark skin, dark hair?"

"That's what the kid looks like, yeah, but..."

"He was walking down the street, heading north. He kept looking over his shoulder like."

"Mr. Johns, sir, I don't think you could have seen the boy. The detectives found him a while ago. By now he's with Immigration."

"No, he ain't," Coyote said mustering some anger. "The police are liars if they said so. They ain't got him. He's gone. That's the way this damn government works. I just saw him. You calling me a liar, Bart?"

"No sir. I just..."

"Damn right I'm not a liar. I'm telling you that boy is out there in this cold-ass weather. The decent thing would be to find that boy and get him in a home or something so he can go back to wherever he came from. Right?"

"You're absolutely right about that, sir. I'm not calling you a liar, Mr. Johns, but are you sure you saw him?"

Silence.

"Sorry, sir," Bart said. "What would you like me to do?"

"Well, that's it, ain't it. What are you going to do? You're a reporter. Well, I mean, you're not a reporter yet, but if I was you, I'd check on the kid. Maybe the police just found him. But if they did, I think the public has a right to know. Maybe there's a good story in it for you. Maybe next time you'll be in front of the camera instead'a using it."

Bart was quiet for a moment. "Okay. Which way he was walking again?"

Coyote chuckled. "Now you ain't gonna catch him on foot, are you? It's been an hour or so since I saw him. I just now worked up the nerve to call someone about it. I didn't call those detectives I saw on TV because they don't give a shit. And they're liars. Who were the detectives again?"

"Jack Murphy and Liddell Blanchard, Mr. Johns."

Coyote said, "I heard about those two. If you can't find the boy, maybe they got him stashed away. Murphy don't seem honest if you ask me."

"I've had some dealings with Jack Murphy just this morning, sir. He is a liar, just like you said. You can't trust him. But if I can't verify the boy is or isn't in their custody, I really can't do anything with this. I'm sorry, sir, but..."

"You got a phone, don't you?" Coyote asked.

"Yes, I..."

"You call them immigrant people and ask where that boy is at. If they won't tell you, threaten them with that right to know stuff."

"The Public Information Act?"

"Yeah, that. An' if that don't work, you call the police and demand to know about the boy. O' course they'll lie, but you keep the pressure on 'em. You call those welfare people. You know. The ones that take kids away from poor people."

"Child Protective Services?" Bart said.

"You call them and say you're doing a piece on how they fell down in their duty to protect that boy from the cops. You lay it on heavy like. That's all these public workers understand. Ain't it?"

Bart said, "You know, it might work. It just might work. Thanks, Bobby, I mean Mr. Johns. Can I get you on camera saying what you told me about the truck and the boy, sir?"

"Well. I don't know about that now. If those cops see me saying something against 'em they'll be harassin' me. But, maybe I will. You just find the boy. When I see it on the telly, I'll call you back. Bart Hiller, right?"

"Where are you calling from..." Bart was saying when Coyote hung up.

Coyote would go back to his room, watch the "telly" and wait. If he'd told Bart there were some similar cases all over the South, the kid would have shit himself. If Bart struck out getting any information on the boy's whereabouts, he'd think of something else.

He was hungry, and it was getting dark.

Chapter 28

The detectives drove past the Federal Building. A few office windows on the upper floors were lit, but the halls were dark. The same with the civic center except for the police department, where every light was on. Police departments and Walmarts never closed.

Liddell pulled in to a parking space where a metal sign on the back wall declared the space reserved for "Deputy Chief of Police Richard Dick." The metal sign was twice as big as any of the other parking markers, but needed to be, as it included Double Dick's name and rank.

"If I see Double Dick, I'll back out over him, pod'na," Liddell said without much humor. "Twice." He was tired. Jack could see it in his eyes.

Jack was wiped out, too. It had been one hell of a day. "I'm going home, Bigfoot. A double Scotch, with a Scotch chaser, seems to be in order."

"Marcie saved me a plate of roast turkey, mashed potatoes, and gravy. I can't let it go to waste. There are hungry children in China," Liddell said.

"My dad used to say, 'Finish your beer, Jack. There're sober kids in China.'"

"Wise man, your dad."

"Yeah." Jack wondered what his dad would have thought about the death toll this crazy bastard was leaving in his wake. Back in his dad's day if someone killed a couple of people they were called "mad dog killers." Now, if they don't kill at least a dozen, they don't get many "Likes" on Facebook. It was a competition.

"Going home," Liddell said. "See you early unless something comes up."

"Go on," Jack said. "I'm going to make a few calls before I head out. We need to give the stuff Sanchez gave us a going over. I feel like we're missing the tree for the forest."

"Want me to stay and help?" Liddell asked.

"Roast turkey. Gravy, mashed potatoes..."

"Okay. You had me at roast turkey," Liddell said, and Jack got out of the car.

Liddell went home, and Jack went to the detectives' office and made a phone call.

"I'm busy," an inebriated-sounding Anna Whiteside said.

Jack said, "The dead Missouri State Trooper's ex-husband is a truck driver. I've got his information if you want to have someone run him down. It's a waste of time. I think the guy is a cop or a federal employee."

"I'll take it under advisement in the morning, Jack. Did you have a vision?" she asked sarcastically.

Jack had a vision of a drunken ICE Queen melting in a hot bath. "Just have your people focus on that angle. I'm right. There's one guy, and he's on a mission or evening a score. Look harder at the dead Border Patrol guy from St. Louis. You missed something."

Jack heard a man in the background asking who was on the phone.

Anna said, "Absolutely no one. I'm hanging up now, Jack. Call in the morning." The connection ended.

The detectives' office was empty. It was almost shift change time, with the exception of Jack and Liddell. They could go home, but they would still be on call until this was over.

He headed for his car and hoped Anna would concentrate the search efforts toward law enforcement or military. He'd call the ICE Queen again in the morning. Maybe she'd listen better when her BAC wasn't over legal limits and her hormones were balanced.

He was halfway home when his cell phone rang.

"Is there anyone you haven't pissed off, Jack?" Angelina Garcia asked.

"Did Whiteside tell you to call me?" Jack asked.

"No," Angelina said. "She called you some names I won't repeat, but I wanted to call and thank you for having her spoil a perfect evening for me."

"Glad I could help," Jack said.

"I guess you're making up with Katie now that you've moved back home. Planning on spending some quality time together? A little cuddling in front of the fireplace? Drinks? Sex?"

"I get your point, and I'm sorry. If it wasn't important I wouldn't have called the ICE Queen."

"Well, I might have something you'd be interested in, but I think I'll wait until two a.m. and wake you up. I'll set an alarm. See you."

"I'm sorry, Angelina," Jack said, but she was gone. She didn't really have anything to report, or she would have told him. Fifteen minutes later he was welcomed at his door by Cinderella. The house felt empty. "Katie, you home?" he said before he saw the note taped to the inside of the door.

The note read: "Food is in the oven. 350 degrees for ten minutes. At Moira's. Be home soon."

Moira was Katie's younger sister, and was also a deputy prosecutor. Moira had just broken up with a young detective that had seemed to dote on her. Jack didn't know what that was about and didn't care to find out. Katie was probably hearing all about it from Moira. He'd drink his supper and hit the sack.

He hung his coat on the coat tree by the door where Cinderella lay on her side, ignoring him.

"Fetch me a Scotch, girl," Jack said.

Cinderella rose and padded away to her bed near the heat vent.

"Stay out of my bed, mutt," Jack said to her.

Chapter 29

When Katie came home Jack was out to the world, so she had let him sleep. When he woke in the morning, he returned the favor. Jack was back in the office early. Captain Franklin was even earlier and waiting in Jack's office.

"Call Anna Whiteside," Captain Franklin said.

"Good morning to you too, Captain," Jack said. He saw no coffee was made yet. "I'm going to make coffee first, Captain. I'll call her. Do you want a cup?"

"Call Whiteside first, Jack. I'll go to Records and get coffee."

"Black is okay," Jack said.

"I didn't say I'd get you coffee, but I will," Captain Franklin said and left.

Jack sat down at his desk and pulled out a yellow legal pad and pen. He made the call thinking Anna must have something big for the captain to be in a twit.

Whiteside picked up on the first ring. "Get something to write on," she said.

"Go ahead," Jack said.

"Take down these numbers." She gave him two phone numbers. One was an overseas number.

"Where does that last number...?"

"Ireland," she interrupted. "Your ancestry has been declared enemies of the state. Forget that number. I didn't mean to give you that one. Just shut up and listen. You were on my last nerve last night, but Angelina worked most of the night and found several persons of interest. You're close to Mt. Vernon, Indiana, right? One of these people lives in Mt. Vernon."

"Okay. Give me what you have on him. I don't want to call and warn them I'm coming. I'll check it out as soon as my partner gets here," Jack said.

"It's a woman, Jack. You think a woman can't be a suspect? Her name is Karen Stenger." Anna gave him the address. "The first address is her home. She's lives outside city limits on a tract of land she's turned into a militia training camp."

"Why her?" Jack asked.

"Angelina said this Karen Stenger was very vocal about illegal immigration. Facebook, LinkedIn, all the online stuff. She was the subject of a newspaper article a couple of years ago when her son was murdered by a Costa Rican illegal that had fled his own country after he committed a couple of murders. This guy was deported instead of imprisoned for the boy's murder."

"Sounds like she has good reason to hate illegal immigrants," Jack said.

"Yeah. Well, when he didn't go to prison she withdrew from public life and began recruiting for her little militia. Next thing you know, the Costa Rican met his death in Mexico. Two witnesses claimed he tried to rob them, ran, fell off a chain-link fence, and impaled himself on—guess what?"

Jack said, "A bayonet."

"Not exactly the same type of bayonet as we have on our murders, but her members train with all kinds of weapons, including bayonets."

"Are you going to re-interview the witnesses?" Jack asked.

"That will be hard because they gave the Mexican police false IDs."

"You said several persons of interest. Who are the other two?" Jack asked.

"We're still doing the workups, but one of them stood out."

Anna didn't continue. Jack didn't interrupt her silence. He didn't like being controlled. Or hung up on.

Anna said, "The ex-Border Patrol driver from Sanchez's case has an interesting history."

"You mean besides having a master's degree in business and criminal justice and a couple years of experience working for Border Patrol? We already have that."

"Angelina dug deeper. While he was with Border Patrol he and his partner were accused of murdering an illegal alien. The victim was murdered at a border control crossing point. The investigators weren't sure which side of the border the murder took place on, but the body was found on US soil. The investigation ended when he and his partner resigned. The case was deep-sixed along with all record of it, but Angelina somehow got the whole file. That girl had better be careful digging around in Homeland Security computer systems. Anyway, guess what weapon was used?"

"A bayonet," Jack said.

"Okay. Guess what happened to the two Border Patrol agents?"

"Just tell me, Anna. It's early and I haven't had coffee," Jack said.

"Well, as you know, one of them was Hank Brown, who ended up working for the other side and got himself killed in St. Louis. But his partner just dropped off the grid after resigning. We, and I mean Angelina and all the king's horses and men, can't find anything after that date. No tax records, driver's license, voter's registration, library cards, Starbucks card, nothing."

"You're going to tell me the name any time now," Jack said.

"Cody Samuel Coté," she said. "White male, age sixty-two, five-five. Angelina checked military records and his personal history prior to his resignation, and bingo. The guy is ex-military. He served five tours in Vietnam from '71 all the way to the end of the conflict in late '74. He was wounded and sent stateside. He is a Purple Heart and a Bronze Star recipient. According to his personnel file, he spent several months at Walter Reed Army Hospital. He was recruited by Border Patrol shortly after. Outstanding background."

"Up until he resigned instead of facing federal indictment," Jack said.

"There is that," Anna admitted. "Hank and Cody had arrested the man they were accused of killing for gun violations, burglary, rape, you name it. The last arrest they made was for the rape of an eleven-year-old girl he'd taken from a library. The guy got a public defender and, because both the agents were accused regularly of excessive use of force, the rapist was deported. Their supervisors must have overlooked the use of force issues because they were making a lot of arrests, until they couldn't ignore it anymore."

"I take it there's more," Jack said.

"There is," Anna said. "The El Salvador guy didn't stay gone. He came back and killed Coté's wife and daughter. Raped them first, dismembered the daughter, and wrote a word on the wall of Coté's bedroom in blood. 'Coyote.'"

"Coyote?" Jack said. "I thought that was a moniker for guys that bring illegals into the US? Was he leaving a signature at the scene?"

"How would I know? Anyway, the accusation was that Coté and Brown retaliated by finding this guy in Mexico and killing him. The body was found in the US, but he'd been killed somewhere else and dumped on the US side of the border."

"If the Border Patrol or whoever knew all of this, why weren't they both put in prison for murder?" Jack asked.

"Angelina's still doing research on Coté's background."

"You think he's our guy?" Jack asked.

"We have to find him to ask him," Anna said. "We've got enough to pick him up for questioning, but the Department of Justice will never let us get a warrant based on just this."

Welcome to Fed-land.

Liddell came in carrying two mugs of coffee. He mouthed "From the captain," and sat down to listen.

"Anna, Liddell just got here. We'll go talk to this woman in Mt. Vernon, but have Angelina send me what she can dig up on this other guy."

Chapter 30

Coyote had called Claudine Setera's cameraman, Bart Hiller, but he didn't really expect the eager young cameraman-wannabe-reporter to get very far with his inquiries on the whereabouts of the boy. He was sure the woman reporter had already covered all the bases searching for the kid and come up blank.

But Bart hadn't been a complete disappointment. Even what Bart didn't find out told Coyote something. The fact that ICE didn't have custody of the kid meant Murphy had stashed him somewhere. Child Protective Services refused to contact the police and knew nothing about the boy, so they didn't have him. The police department gave no comment.

He lay back on the hard bed and stared at the ceiling until it became blurry. The shrink said he should write his feelings in his journal, but she also said he should go home, visit his wife and daughter, talk to them. Maybe she was right. He hadn't been home for years. How could he? He had started down this path. He would continue.

He had always been in some kind of conflict, whether it was in Vietnam or patrolling the border or doing what he was doing now. Except for marrying and having a daughter, his life would have been more of the same. He had fallen in love with Emma, and when they married he'd promised to put his anger behind him. He'd really tried. It seemed like he could overcome it by throwing himself into his work, and then his daughter was born. Olivia. She'd changed everything. Made him see what his life could be like.

But that was all a pipe dream. On some level, he'd always known it. He wasn't meant to be a husband or a father. He hadn't even been a good son. He was good at one thing. Violence.

His shrink said he'd inherited his temper from his father, but he knew better. Every man makes their own choices. After what was done to Emma and Olivia, he'd made his.

He didn't feel like he'd been a bad husband, a bad father. He worked. He put a roof over their heads. He tried to make them happy. They should have known everything he did was to protect them. To build a future. One where no one would have to pay for the mistakes made by a government that had neutered law enforcement, disbanded most of the military, hamstrung any other agency that dared to try to stop the invasion by outsiders. But that wasn't going to happen by wishing it so. It wouldn't even happen by changing government leaders. It would happen when people like him stood up on their own feet and did what was right.

He came to a decision. When this leg of the mission was over, he'd go home. Visit Emma and Olivia. He'd been gone too long. He'd stayed away because it was too painful and he didn't want to feel anything. But they needed to know that he still remembered them. That he was doing all of this for them. They deserved that much.

His eyes grew moist, and an odd feeling constricted his chest and throat, a feeling he hadn't experienced since he'd been boots down on Vietnamese soil for the first time. It wasn't exactly fear. More of a feeling of hopelessness, sadness, anger, despair. A feeling that he was fighting an elephant with his bare hands even while knowing the eventual outcome. But he had fought monsters before. You went at it with all you had. If you didn't have a weapon, you used your fists, a rock, your teeth, whatever it took.

He let a tear trickle down his cheek, glad for it, knowing it meant he was still human. Life hadn't defeated him. Humanity was what separated him from his prey. He was a patriot. People would see that. Even if they didn't appreciate what he was doing now, what it was costing him, they would eventually see that he was protecting them. Keeping America safe from the outsiders that threatened to ruin his way of life. It was either kill or be killed. He wouldn't lose anyone else. He would keep killing until he was dead.

He finally fell into a fitful sleep, felt ghost pain in his chest and neck where the bayonet had skewered him, and woke up several times clamping his mouth shut against a scream.

Coyote woke at sunup, took a scalding hot shower, and shaved. He felt better than he'd felt in months. He would get this done and go home. He dressed in dirty jeans, a faded red sweatshirt, and combat boots. He'd bought an army fatigue jacket with sergeant stripes last night from a derelict outside the homeless shelter down the street. The guy claimed he was a veteran. Coyote didn't believe him, but he'd given the guy four crisp twenty-dollar bills to buy another jacket. More likely the money was used to buy liquor.

He rummaged in his bag and took out a Saints baseball cap and a pair of cheap reading glasses. He put all this on and affected a slight limp. He needed two things. To find the boy and end this. It was time for a different approach.

Chapter 31

"Shit!" Liddell said as they drove past Bristol-Myers, heading west out of the city.

"What? You don't like the way I drive?" At the speed Jack was driving, they would make the thirty-five-minute trip from downtown Evansville to Mt. Vernon in fifteen minutes.

Liddell said, "I think you just passed a State Police car."

"That's their problem," Jack said. He hadn't seen a police car.

"I think I heard a sonic boom," Liddell persisted.

"That was your stomach, Bigfoot. Relax. We'll get there in one piece."

"That's why I'm worried, pod'na. The whole car and us being in one piece. Smashed into a Rubik's Cube. Can you slow down to subsonic? You're going to get us killed."

"Maybe you should quit front-seat driving and load the shotguns," Jack said sarcastically. "Get back in the game. A distracted yeti is a dead yeti."

"I'm not a dead yeti, and I intend to stay that way. You expecting to shoot it out?" Liddell asked. They had taken Remington twelve-gauge shotguns from the weapons locker in the detectives' office. These were now propped up between Liddell's knees. Four boxes of twelve-gauge shotgun shells were in Liddell's lap, and he was loading shells into the breaches.

The Remington 870 shotguns had a pistol grip instead of the shoulder stock and were capable of holding seven shells in the feeder and one in the chamber. Liddell had loaded the shotguns, alternating deer slugs and double-aught buckshot.

"I don't know anything about this militia group, Bigfoot. They might be pro-police or paranoid," Jack said.

"Maybe we should show our Evansville badges. Most of these kinds of people distrust the Feds. They might not worry about us if we don't tell them we're part of a task force. You think?"

"Excellent idea, Bigfoot. This Karen Stenger might welcome us with open arms. Bake you a pie even. Give you a free membership."

"No matter how she tempts me, I won't join them," Liddell said.

Jack laughed, but in truth was he was nervous about dealing with a militia. Those groups didn't have a reputation for cooperation or giving hugs. He didn't disagree with their right to create a survival group, but many of these groups were extremely anti-government. They didn't want to pay taxes. Didn't think they owed society anything even though they used the same roads and grocery stores and clothing stores as the average law-abiding citizen. They were autonomous as long as their supplies lasted.

Jack heard a siren bleep twice behind them, and in his rearview mirror he saw a Posey County Sheriff cruiser come up fast behind them.

"Busted," Liddell said, and Jack pulled off on the shoulder of Highway 62 and stopped.

The deputy exited the car and came running to the driver's door, huddled in his jacket, holding his Smokey Bear hat on his head against the cold wind.

"Detective Murphy," the deputy said when Jack cracked the window. "Remember me?"

The deputy's face was familiar to Jack, and he remembered where they'd met. "Last time I saw you a burning man was hanging from a burning grain silo," Jack said.

The deputy asked, "You on your way to another fire?"

Jack said, "We need to talk to someone in your county, Deputy Stevens."

"It's Corporal Stevens now," the man said, and Jack noticed the corporal chevrons pinned to his collar.

"Congratulations," Jack said.

"Are we on our way to a fire?" Stevens asked again. "I didn't hear a dispatch."

"No fire. We just wanted to get to this person's..." Jack hesitated to call it a house, and he didn't want to call it a compound. "We just need to talk to this person without making them any more nervous than necessary."

Stevens held on to the brim of his hat to keep the wind from blowing it away. "I tell you what. You give me the address, and I'll give you an escort. We won't go as fast as y'all were driving, but we'll get there."

Jack didn't want to be seen as poaching, and he didn't know exactly where the compound was located, so he agreed.

"Okay, Corporal. I'm going to tell you something, but you have to keep it under your hat for a little bit."

Stevens said nothing.

"You know my partner," Jack said.

Liddell leaned over and gave a curt wave. "Congratulations on the promotion, pod'na."

"Thanks a million," Stevens said.

Jack said, "We're part of a federal task force. You probably haven't heard of it yet." He hoped Stevens wouldn't ask to see federal credentials. "We're following up a lead to the murders in Evansville. You've heard?"

"Who hasn't?" Stevens said. "We going after the killer?"

"We're just here to ask some questions, Corporal," Jack said. "Probably nothing to it if you ask me. In fact, I'm glad you're here. Maybe you could show us where the place is?"

"Oh boy," Stevens said. "I mean, hell yeah. I'll have to call dispatch."

Jack said, "They'll be dispatching a couple of units in about five or ten minutes. I'm hoping you can get us there before they arrive. Too many cars may put their backs up. I don't want a fight." Jack gave Stevens the name and address.

Stevens grinned.

"Something funny?" Jack asked.

"I know right where that is. I know Karen personally. She goes to my church. I'm a member of the CIA. That's Citizens In Arms, not the other CIA. We're a group of patriots Karen put together, and I'm proud to be a part of it."

* * * *

Corporal Stevens escorted them to Karen Stenger's farm/compound. He had a key to the gate and quickly gained the detectives entry and an audience with Karen Stenger.

Jack expected Karen to be a cammo-wearing, rifle-toting fanatic. Instead she reminded him of his wife, Katie. She was soft spoken, intelligent, and effortlessly put him at ease.

Jack looked out of the farmhouse windows and considered what he'd seen on the drive in to the compound. The Midwest was farming country, and the Stengers lived in a simple farmhouse with barns and outbuildings and farm equipment and animals of all sorts on an enormous tract of land. He smelled something he thought might be pigs or hogs nearby.

The ICE Queen passed on the meager intelligence that had filtered into the Homeland Security database. She didn't know the real people, or their intentions.

A rifle was propped in the far corner of the kitchen, but so far Jack had seen one person who was armed. As they drove toward the farmhouse, he'd seen a man sitting on a shooting bench with a rifle propped on sandbags. He was sighting in the riflescope at around a two-hundred-yard distance from a bull's-eye target.

Nearer the house, two straw-filled dummies were tied to upright posts. The earth around the posts was worn bare. The dummies were spilling their straw guts and brains, and one had an arm missing.

He expected more members to be present. Where were they?

Corporal Stevens had introduced them, but Karen said, "I know who they are, Ed. My late husband admired both of you. When this was a working farm, he would come in from the fields with my son and they'd sit down at this table, my husband would shake the newspaper open and read it out loud to us. He said people like you made it possible for people like us to keep going."

To Corporal Stevens she said, "You didn't know him, did you, Ed?"

"No, ma'am. But I feel like I do."

Karen continued. "He always said you kept the bad guys on the run."

"Where are the rest of your people?" Jack asked.

"Everyone's at church, Detective Murphy. Everyone except Arnie, that is. He's the one you hear out there giving those targets hell. He's a recovering Baptist, according to him, so he doesn't go to church on Sunday. He says God is resting on Sunday, so he doesn't want to disturb him."

"You train with bayonets too," Jack remarked.

Karen said, "We train with whatever we need to, Detective Murphy."

"How many members do you have?" Jack asked, and Corporal Stevens answered for her.

"There's seventy-two of us, including Arnie out there. Arnie comes every Sunday to practice shooting and do whatever chores he can do," Stevens said. "I thought he might've been a sniper in the Army or Marines. Maybe some kind of hand-to-hand combat instructor. You should see him work a bayonet. Scary. And he don't talk much. I finally got him to tell me what he does, and he's a damn accountant. He's never been in the service. He said shooting and stabbing things helps him relax. Tell you what, that made me see my tax guy in a whole different light."

Jack mentally filed that tidbit away. He'd need to get more information on "Shootin-stabbin-Arnie the accountant."

"Karen, we want to ask you some questions about..." Jack said.

She interrupted him and said, "I was expecting you or someone from Homeland Security to pay a visit a long time ago."

"Why do you say that?" Jack asked.

"You'll laugh at me. I shouldn't have said anything. Go ahead and ask your questions, Detective Murphy."

"That was my first question," Jack said, and she smiled. "Why did you expect police or Homeland Security to pay you a visit?"

"They've taken a real interest in us. In me, I should say. One of my bankers is my cousin. She said a bank examiner had called and was asking questions about my business and personal accounts. She said that's not how bank examiners work."

Jack knew enough about bunco-fraud investigators to know that was true. Bank examiners weren't generally interested in just one account. Maybe Anna Whiteside could explain this. Maybe Karen Stenger was channeling other funds through her account, enough that she caught the interest of the bank.

"And last year I was audited by the IRS. First time for everything I suppose, but there are other things too. Like that guy, Arnie. He just showed up one day after I was audited and wanted to join up. I can always spot a liar, Detective Murphy. He said he was a true patriot and wanted to give something back to his country. I tried to explain to him that we weren't a militia. Just a group of citizens who believe in our Second Amendment right to bear arms. With what's going on in the country, it doesn't hurt to be prepared to defend ourselves."

"You *know* Arnie is a government agent?" Jack asked. "How?"

"I had Ed here follow him. Arnie doesn't work anywhere, but he does take a lot of trips to the Federal Building in Evansville. I told Arnie I needed an accountant. He didn't offer to take the job himself. He said he would find someone at his company for me. I asked what company. I said I would just go there and talk to someone. I like to meet the people I do business with face-to-face. Arnie danced around and finally gave me the name of his company in Evansville."

Jack said, "Did Ed find Arnie at work?"

Stevens shriveled under Jack's glare.

"Ed's a deputy sheriff. I didn't want to get him in trouble. I called the company. Told them I was thinking of hiring an accountant. The person I talked to gave Arnie a glowing recommendation, but I didn't believe them. I kind of staked out the office where he worked, and guess what, he never showed up for work all that week. I know what he drives and never saw it on their lot. I went in and asked for him, and they said he was on vacation, but he told me he was working overtime that week."

Jack made a second mental note. He would have to ask the ICE Queen if Arnie was indeed a plant. Karen was probably right. In any case, she was shrewd as hell. And she seemed to want Jack to know that she was.

Plus, she was training her members with the use of bayonets. Jack didn't peg her as a killer or someone that would allow anyone to join the group if they were bent in the head that way. But it was possible that one of her members was. Even the police department had hired a psycho or two before. People lie.

"I guess you know about the newspaper articles from a couple of years ago and aren't satisfied that I'm just a citizen that wants to be prepared. I know this must have something to do with all those bodies you found in Evansville."

"Yes, it does," Jack said.

She gazed out of the window for a long time before saying, "My son was in town to see a movie with some friends from school. Doug Jr. had a lot of friends. He was a good boy. He had the flu that night, but he wouldn't stay home in bed. He was as headstrong as his father. His friends said he started feeling worse during the show and they made him go home. He left the theater and was stabbed to death and robbed on the way to his truck. The killer couldn't have gotten more than ten dollars. That's what my son's life was worth to the man that killed him."

"Did they catch the killer?" Jack asked. He already knew the answer.

"The man that murdered my son was in this country illegally. Costa Rican. He had been deported three times in one year for violent crimes. Each time he came back, and each time he committed another violent crime. They arrested him for the murder, but the jury decided the case against him for murder was too weak. He admitted to getting into a fistfight with Doug Jr. He said Doug Jr. started it and that Doug pulled the knife. He was convicted of battery, and the judge sentenced him to be deported a fourth time."

"Was he?" Jack asked. "Deported I mean?"

"Oh yeah. He was flown back to Costa Rica on the country's dime. He was home and my son was dead. My husband was never the same. He lost interest in farming. He lost his appetite and shrunk up to nothing before we found out he had cancer. The kind you don't get better from. At least he lived long enough to see the man that murdered our son in the ground. And before you ask, no we didn't kill him. I would have..."

She caught herself and said, "I wanted him dead. But we're not that way. We're farmers. Or we were. That man took my life from me. I'm glad he's dead."

"Did you or your husband hire someone to kill him, Karen?" Jack asked.

She laughed. "If I did, I wouldn't admit it. But no, I didn't hire anyone."

Jack noticed she had said "I" and not "we." But she wasn't going to incriminate herself.

Jack said, "Is someone helping you through this? There are groups..."

Karen said, "Hell, I'm through the grieving. I keep busy. My husband's life insurance will keep me going for a long time, and I've got my group right here. They're my family. For better or worse, we're a family. It's enough."

Jack asked, "Why bayonets?" It seemed an insensitive question given the direction the interview/conversation was going, but it was one that needed answered.

"My son was beaten to death and stabbed. The bayonets are for close combat. If my son had taken combat training, maybe he'd still be alive. Maybe my husband wouldn't have just given up and his cancer wouldn't have progressed so fast. Maybe we would still be working this as a farm. But this is what we've got."

Jack waited.

"I abhor violence, Detective Murphy, but I've seen what happens when it catches you by surprise and unprepared. I'll never lose another person. My husband said you were good at reading people too. Was he right?"

"Yeah. I guess I am," Jack said.

"Okay, tell me what you think. Am I a fanatic that would kill a bunch of innocent people?"

Chapter 32

The walk from the Dream Lodge to the parking lot at Deaconess Hospital was short, and the cold helped him think. Coyote now sat in a visitor parking spot on University of Evansville's campus with the engine running. He had a clear view of the Weinbach/Lincoln Avenue intersection and the front of the Coffee Shop. A couple of hours ago he'd watched the owner pull the curtains open on the upper floor. She lived above her business. That was convenient for her. For him as well.

She'd come out in front of the shop and gone back inside. He imagined she was looking for possible customers. It was Sunday. He didn't imagine she would have any, but he'd counted two customers in the last two hours. Both had that harried academic demeanor that only college professors can carry off. One left; one was still inside.

He sat patiently watching for another half hour before he saw movement on the side of the shop. The shop owner had a dog on a leash and was letting it piss on the bricks of the neighboring business. The dog was black and white. Some kind of border collie. His daughter had wanted a border collie, but he was gone so much and he didn't think she was old enough or responsible enough to care for it. Besides, he hated dogs. Dogs scared him. He wasn't afraid of being bitten. It was a visceral response. Just seeing the mutt caused his groin to contract and a sharp pain ran down his legs. Still, he'd never hurt an animal. They couldn't help how he reacted any more than they could help biting him in the face when he was a kid. He shouldn't have gotten in the dog's face.

The dog was in the VW the night he'd killed the driver. The shop owner had a bad attitude to go with a face that would stop a train, but she had some cojones on her, and he respected that. He'd still have to kill her.

He laid his head back against the headrest and closed his eyes, bidding the pain to go away. It almost always faded immediately, but this time it didn't. Something was wrong, but he couldn't put his finger on the problem.

Chapter 33

"The Mt. Vernon lead is no good." Jack said to Anna Whiteside over the speakerphone on the drive back to Evansville. "Karen admitted she was glad her son's killer had been murdered. Even admitted to wanting to do it herself. But I don't see her as dangerous to anyone else. She's just dealing with the grief of losing her husband and son. But the group may bear watching. They claimed to have seventy-two members including a man named Arnie Johnson."

Anna said nothing. Jack continued. "The only armed and suspicious person we saw was this Arnie Johnson. Karen Stenger thinks he's a government plant."

"He's not one of mine," Anna said too quickly. "Did you talk to some of Mrs. Stenger's members?"

"Quit bullshitting, Anna. I know you can't give up an operative, but I'm telling you she's on to Arnie. His cover is blown. And one of her bankers you checked with is a relative and told her someone's going through her accounts."

Liddell added, "I think siccing the IRS on her was a little mean."

"I have my job and you have yours," Anna said defensively. "So why don't you do it. Get back out there and track down the other members and do some interviewing. If she's being so cooperative, have her give you names, addresses, that kind of stuff."

Jack said, "She says they're all at church, Anna. We'll go back if you don't get better leads. Did you know the group is called CIA for Citizens In Arms?"

"I may have heard that name."

Jack thought it was as close to an admission as Anna was capable of. "If you think this group is dangerous, you'd better get your guy out of there. The deputy sheriff we met is a member of the group. Maybe other local law enforcement is supportive if they haven't already joined," Jack said.

"I'll have Angelina call you with updates. We'll put a question mark on Mrs. Stenger for now. The Border Patrol connection looks promising."

When the call ended, Liddell said, "I think Anna just wants to say she took down the CIA."

"Yeah, she's a bitch, Bigfoot, but she's our bitch. You don't trust her?"

"Do you?"

"I trust Double Dick more. At least we know what he'll do," Jack said.

They were coming up on St. Joseph Avenue. Because Liddell was driving, the car seemed to go into auto-drive, steering itself toward Donut Bank.

"Okay. We can do the drive-through, Bigfoot, and take coffee with us," Jack said, and the car turned north on St. Joseph Avenue.

"Where we going?"

"Back to see Mrs. Rademacher," Jack said. "That's why we're getting coffee here."

"Excuse my confusion, pod'na," Liddell said, "but why exactly are we going to see Freyda?"

"I want Joe to have his dog. I know Sister Aquinas won't mind letting him have it for the short term. And Freyda might want to keep her customers from becoming dog food."

They got their coffees and headed east on Lloyd Expressway then south on Weinbach. They drove past the university with its jam-packed parking but very little foot traffic.

Liddell parked in front of the Coffee Shop. They left their coffees in the car and went inside. One older customer sat at the same table where Freyda said the customer had sat. He was most likely a professor, judging by the tweed sport jacket with patches on the elbows with matching vest and snap-brim cap. Jack could imagine him smoking a briarwood pipe if smoking were still allowed in public places. A sensible heavy coat was over the back of the booth.

Freyda Rademacher emerged from the back room carrying a bag of IAMS dog food, with the dog shadowing her every step. She put the bag of food on the countertop.

Liddell said, "The dog seems to have taken to you."

"Yeah. Her name's Shadow," Freyda replied.

"How do you know the dog's name?" Liddell asked.

"Sister Aqueduct told me."

"Do you mean Sister Aquinas?" Jack asked.

Freyda said, "Yeah, whatever. I don't plan on getting on a first name basis with some nun."

"When did you talk to Sister Aquinas?" Jack asked.

"She called a few hours ago. She said you told Joe about a dog found outside my shop. It's Joe's dog for sure. Did you know that damn woman reporter tried to interview me? Shadow run 'em off. She's a good dog."

"Claudine Setera was here?" Jack asked.

"Don't worry. That reporter don't know where you hid Joe, and neither did I until Sister Aqueduct called and asked did I have the dog. I don't know how the nun knew I kept the dog. I didn't ask. She put Joe on the phone, and he described her down to the little twist in her tail from being broke in a door. She answers to the name Shadow real good. He talked to her on the phone, and she smiled."

"The dog smiled?" Jack said.

The dog was lying on the floor beside Freyda, eyeing Jack and Liddell closely. It got to its feet and cautiously approached. "Shadow...sit," she said. The dog obeyed. "Shadow...smile," she said, and the dog bared all of its sharp teeth.

"You taught her to do that?" Liddell asked incredulously.

"You call that a smile?" Freyda asked. "The boy told me she did that. She does the same thing when someone comes in the shop. She can be a handful. If you're going to take her, you better take that food with you. I guess Sister Aqueduct don't keep that laying around a convent."

"You knew we were coming for the dog?" Jack asked.

"O' course I knew," she said. "I know how the Gestapo works. You come and take stuff from us poor people and give it to the rich. But in this case, if you're giving the dog back to the boy, I guess you're okay."

"Freyda, I need to ask you something, and I want the truth," Jack said.

"I told you the truth," she said.

"Listen up," Jack said. "We're city detectives, but we're also federal agents. We work for a federal task force. If you lie to a federal agent you can go to jail, and believe me when I tell you, I *will* take you to jail if you don't tell me the truth."

"I believe you would," she said.

"He's kind of an asshole," Liddell added.

"Okay. You got me, J. Edgar. What do you want to know?"

Jack said, "I want you to tell me what you held back."

"Okay, I'll tell you everything, and I swear to God I don't know any more," Freyda said.

Jack said to her, "Freyda, when someone says 'I swear to God,' they usually mean what?"

She grinned and patted the dog's head. "It means they're going to lie their ass off. You're smarter than you seem to be. Okay, I'll tell you, but first let's get some coffee."

"We've got coffee in the car," Jack said. "And we don't have a lot of time."

"Let's take this to the back room," she said. They followed her out of earshot of the professor, and Shadow stayed at her side. She said, "I saw Shadow in that VW that night. The engine was running. I told you a lie when I said I'd never seen the dead guy before. I saw his face that night. He was the one in the car with the dog. I had the impression he was waiting for someone."

"Go on," Jack said.

"Well, that cowboy guy was in here insulting my food, and he seemed to be waiting for someone, too. I figured he was nervous because he wasn't eating my pie. He sat there a couple of hours and just scribbled in that book of his. I wondered why the other guy didn't just come in here, but it's none of my business, is it? When the cowboy guy left that big tip, I knew something was wrong. I watched him leave and turn in the direction where the VW was at. But by the time I went out the door, the cowboy was gone. I didn't go down the alleyway because I'm not stupid. The car was still sitting with the engine running big as you please with the man and dog still inside. I was thinking it was a drug deal."

"Why didn't you tell us this?" Jack asked.

"Was it a drug deal? If it was, I'll deny I told you any of this. I'm not messing with any cartel."

"It wasn't a drug deal, Freyda," Jack said, thinking this confirmed his theory. But why stop in Evansville, steal a car, and meet with this guy on the other side of town. How did he end up here? Did someone call him? Did he call someone? So far, a phone hadn't been found.

"Is there anything else you didn't want to tell me? If we find out you had other information and didn't tell us, it's as good as a lie," Jack said.

She said nothing.

"Freyda, I'm going to have my crime scene people come out here and search again."

"They don't know squat, those guys," Freyda said. "They never checked the roof, and that's where them criminals hide stuff they don't want found."

Jack said, "I'll have them search the roof." He turned to Liddell. "Maybe we can get a fire department ladder truck?"

Freyda snorted. "You don't need to do that. You can get on the roof from inside my closet upstairs."

"Do you mind?" Jack asked.

"Help yourself, but be sure to close it up good and tight when you're done. If you don't, cold air blows right through it."

Jack said, "Bigfoot will stay down here with you, Freyda."

"You afraid I'll make a run for it, G-man?" she asked.

"Got any more of that pie, Freyda?" Liddell asked her.

Jack went up the stairs to Freyda's living quarters. Sgt. Walker hadn't said anything about searching the roofs or gutters of the Coffee Shop or nearby buildings. Jack was mad at himself that he hadn't thought of it.

The closet door was shut, but he could feel cold air leaking through the cracks. It was colder when he opened the door. Hanging inside were a few tops, two dresses that went out of style in the '30s, and one pair of sneakers. She lived more than frugally. A wooden ladder was attached to the left wall of the closet, and it led up to a wooden hatch. Jack took out his flashlight and shone the beam on the top of the ladder and the hatch. He could see where she had used rolled newspaper in an attempt to keep out the cold.

He tested his weight on a ladder rung. It squealed in protest but held. He climbed to the top and muscled the hatch open. A blast of freezing air blew through the opening and stung his cheeks and eyes. A rusty chain kept the hatch from opening and falling back against the rooftop. He held a hand out in front of his face and squinted. The roof was flat and covered with tar and splotches of silver paint.

He climbed out onto the roof, pulling his coat tight around his face. He could see the top of the beauty/barber shop next door, the intersection at both ends of the block, the tops of the houses, and Evansville University's buildings filled with parked cars.

The wind blew the hatch shut behind him. He turned at the noise and saw a black leather wallet that he'd mistaken for a roof patch. He squinted into the light wind and scanned the roof more carefully. Directly behind the hatch, he made out the shape of a flip phone. He pulled latex gloves from his pocket and tried to slip them on. It was too cold. He used the gloves to pick up the phone and wallet, wrap them in another set of gloves, and put them in his pocket. He opened the hatch and went back down into the relative warmth of the closet, being sure the hatch was completely shut and newspaper stuffed back in the cracks.

When he came back into the front of the shop, he found Liddell sitting in the booth with the customer. Liddell and the man were eating pie and conversing like old friends.

"We've got to go," Jack said to Liddell.

"Jack, this is Jim Robertson. Retired EPD officer," Liddell said.

The man Jack had thought was an academic stood. "Call me Lightning." Liddell grinned. "Tell Jack how you got that nickname."

Robertson grinned and said, "I moved slow as smoke. You know how cops are. They started calling me Lightning. Assholes."

"I told him we thought he was a college professor," Liddell told Jack, and Lightning chuckled.

"One of the professors gave me this old suit. Said he was tired of me looking like a homeless guy on my days off. I retired about the time you came on the department," he said to Jack. "I knew your old man. Good cop. Good guy. Now I work security at the university. We got a game of poker every Saturday in the Security Office if either of you are interested."

"Gambling's not really my thing," Jack said.

"Lucky at love, unlucky at cards," Lightning said and chuckled at his own joke. "Anyway, Liddell here updated me a little on your investigation. Horrible thing. This kind of thing never happened in my day. Guess the world has moved on."

"We really need to get going, Lightning, but it was good meeting an old friend of my dad's," Jack said.

"Who said we were friends?"

"I..."

"Just kidding you, Jack. He was a good cop. Smart. His gut was rarely wrong. From what I know about you, I'd say it was a family trait. I won't tie you up if you got places to go. But I was telling Liddell that I was off Friday night, Saturday, and tonight, so I don't have anything for you but gossip. But listen. If you ever need anything from the university, you call me. If they won't give it to you, I'll steal it." He gave Jack a napkin with his name and number written on it. "I don't have a home phone anymore. Can't stand all the telemarketers. That's my sister's number. Just ask for Lightning to give you a call, and she'll know it's police business. Don't talk to her, for God's sake, or she'll never shut up."

Robertson family trait.

Freyda came in with Shadow on a leash. The dog had a new collar. She handed the leash to Jack. "I'll miss the mean shit," she said, and Jack took the dog.

Jack knew he didn't have to tell Freyda to keep quiet about the dog and Joe. They thanked Lightning and went back to their car. Jack opened the back door, and Shadow jumped in and sat where she could see between the front seats.

"You drive, Bigfoot," Jack said, and when they were in the car, Jack took the glove-wrapped evidence from his pocket. "Lookie here."

"You picked up evidence, pod'na. You should have let Walker get it."

"Your point?" Jack asked.

"You gonna open the wallet?" Liddell asked.

Chapter 34

Coyote saw the two detectives enter the Coffee Shop. He'd shut his engine off. He'd been sitting there for hours and didn't want to draw any attention. He wondered if he should just leave. Leave here. Leave the city. Nah. The police didn't have much to go on. In two hours he could be in Terre Haute. In three hours he could be in Indianapolis. The next shipment would be coming through there.

He wondered if she was telling them about him being in there? She was a nosy old biddy, but he didn't think she knew anything. He'd seen Murphy on the roof of the building, but he didn't come outside first. Murphy had to have come straight up through the roof. He'd watched Murphy bend down a couple of times like he'd found something. Whatever it was, Murphy put it in his coat pocket.

The phone and wallet. I should have taken them with me or thrown them in the sewer.

Murphy was one lucky son of a bitch. Coyote had had a drill instructor in Army boot camp that said luck favored the prepared. Was Murphy prepared for him? Did Murphy know something? Did someone see him pitch the things onto the roof? Coyote knew the man was dangerous the first time he saw him on television.

He watched Murphy disappear back through the roof. He moved his car a couple of rows back where he had a better view through the front windows of the shop. The big detective was sitting with the professor. Murphy came into the room, and the big detective stood and introduced him to the man at the table. Coyote lost interest. If Murphy found the phone and wallet, he wouldn't show them to his partner with the professor at the table.

Coyote took out his notebook, what his shrink called his journal. After the fiasco at the roadside café, he'd been busting at the seams to write. Maybe his shrink was onto something. He always felt a tiny bit better when he recorded his thoughts. The shrink had called it "cathartic." He thought it was like sticking a tube into his brain and letting all the emotion and nightmare sludge flow onto the pages.

He propped the notebook on the steering wheel, keeping the shop in his peripheral vision, and wrote.

The manager of the greasy spoon said I didn't have to do this. I'd already killed her with the first strike. She was dead and didn't know it. Still begging like I could pull the blade out and say I'm sorry. I had no choice. If she blamed anyone she should blame that damn waitress. The girl shouldn't have been reading over my shoulder. No. That's not the whole reason they all died. That newswoman, Claudine something, broadcasted my failure to end everyone in that truckload. I want them to know I'm doing this for them. I want them to believe I'm not a monster. Of course, the media is going to portray me as a Hitler, committing genocide. The boy surviving has ensured the ruin of my reputation. One little mistake and all my past work is in the shitter.

That cop should have driven away. I told her the place was closed. She should have listened to me. She saw my face but it was only for a few seconds and I might have let her go if she hadn't told me the waitress inside was her daughter. I had no choice. My face would be posted all over the news and on bulletin boards in every police station and government office. Killing a state trooper made me an enemy of every cop in the world.

He saw the detective called Murphy leading a dog out to the car. The dog wasn't too happy. Murphy wasn't either for that matter, but he seemed to be in control. He put the dog in the back seat of the Crown Vic, and they got in, but they just sat with the engine running.

What were they talking about? What did they know? Murphy was showing the other detective something. Now he was sure Murphy had found the wallet and phone, and he would soon know who the dead man was. The cell phone might reveal some interesting callers, but Coyote had used a burner phone that he had destroyed on the way to St. Louis.

Let them find out what the traitorous asshole was doing, who he was working for. He deserved to die, but Coyote felt a twinge of conscience for the trooper. In any case, he was still safe for now to finish the job he'd started.

The Crown Vic pulled onto Weinbach and turned left onto Lincoln Avenue. Coyote started his car again and cranked the heat up. He moved across the front of the campus and gave the Crown Vic plenty of room before pulling out onto Lincoln Avenue.

Chapter 35

Chad Perkins, no middle initial, had a California commercial driver's license. According to the CDL, Chad Perkins was age fifty-six, with a Pasadena address. The license would expire in three months, but Chad had expired first.

"Chad Perkins from Pasadena, California," Jack said. He used the latex glove to spread the inside of the wallet open. Paper money, tens and ones mostly, and a Blue Cross Blue Shield insurance card in the same name as the driver's license. It wasn't much money. Maybe Chad hadn't been paid yet, but he hadn't been robbed either. The killer had taken just enough—the wallet and phone—to delay identification.

"Where to next, pod'na?"

"You call Angelina and see if she can run a history on this guy. I'll call the convent and see if the sister is still willing to keep the boy and the dog a while longer. Joe needs something to keep his spirits up."

Jack called the convent and told Sister Aquinas they were coming with another guest.

Liddell asked, "You want me to call Sergeant Walker to send someone by the convent to pick the evidence up, pod'na?"

"We'll bring it in, Bigfoot. The less people that know Joe's at the convent the better. I don't trust the ICE Queen to keep her side of the bargain."

Liddell called Angelina. When he hung up, he said, "I feel a little guilty for asking her to do all this when she should be on her honeymoon."

"We didn't ask her. Anna Whiteside did," Jack responded.

"Oh. Well that makes all the difference. You're losing your conscience, pod'na."

"I think our killer stole it. I'm going to find him and get it back. One wing at a time." Jack's voice didn't hold any humor.

Jack slowed the Crown Vic as they passed St. Anthony Grade School. Not all of his memories from St. Anthony's were bad. He'd had his first crush here. Kissed his first girl here. Had his nose broken here. Smoked his first cigarette in the basement with Bobby Sanders, the same kid that he'd beaten to a pulp the week before for breaking said nose. He'd learned to be tough.

"I wonder what happened to them all," Jack said.

"All who?" Liddell said.

"Nothing, Bigfoot. Nobody. Sister Aquinas damn near yanked my ear off in that little courtyard over there behind the convent. She caught me and some other kids, Bobby Sanders, Cathy Scheidel, Keith Lloyd, and someone else. We were smoking what we thought was a marijuana cigarette. Turns out it was dead grass from Keith Lloyd's yard."

"How old were you, pod'na?"

"Second grade. I had no idea what drugs were back in the day," Jack said.

"Wanted to be part of the gang, huh? Be accepted."

"Hell no," Jack said and smiled. "I had a crush on Cathy Scheidel. I think I would have smoked a dog turd to get her attention."

"Ain't love grand?" Liddell pulled to the curb in front of the convent.

They got out of the car, and Jack retrieved Shadow. The dog sniffed the air and dragged Jack to the front door of the convent, trembling and straining at the new collar and leash Freyda must have bought.

Jack didn't have to knock before the door flew open and the boy dropped to his knees, throwing his arms around the dog. Shadow knocked Joe to the ground and jumped and tromped and licked any available part of the boy's face and arms.

Liddell caught up and said, "There's no doubt this is Joe's dog, pod'na."

"Joe, we need to talk again." Jack said. "I hope this isn't an imposition, Sister?"

Joe led the way inside, and Shadow ran behind him, dragging her leash.

"I hope this isn't an imposition, Sister?" Jack said.

"Nonsense, Jack. He could hardly keep his pants in a chair after we talked to Mrs. Rademacher. I would have gone to get the dog myself, but I don't drive anymore. Eyesight is the first thing to go as you age."

"That reminds me," Liddell said and went back to the car, bringing the bag of dog food back.

"Bless her," Sister Aquinas said.

"Can we run to the store for you, Sister?" Liddell offered.

She waved the offer away. "I've got the donated food from the foodbank. If this isn't a charitable case, I don't know what is."

Jack said, "Sister, I know I don't have to tell you how important it is that you keep Joe inside. I have sort of a friend at Immigration that is searching the database for his family. Maybe there's someone in the US. You're the only one besides me and Bigfoot that know he's here. I don't want anyone..."

"You don't have to go on," the sister said. "There's a little fenced courtyard between the convent and the church where the dog can do its business. No one can see in. It's too cold for them to go out and play. I'll take good care of them. You just do what needs done."

Jack and Liddell left Shadow with his boy, and an admonition to Sister Aquinas not to call anyone else. She wasn't too happy with being given orders by a once delinquent student, but she agreed.

She stopped Jack at the front door. "You should come back to church, Jack. You need Him more than He needs you." She uncharacteristically hugged him. "You're a good man, Jack. He knows that."

In the car, Jack called Captain Franklin. "Captain, I need something, so I'm going to tell you something." He explained what he wanted and why. Franklin agreed to get it done without asking questions.

"You think that's necessary, pod'na?" Liddell asked, put the Crown Vic in gear, and pulled away from the curb, headed south on First Avenue.

"Better safe than sorry," Jack said.

"Captain Franklin is in the circle of trust now?"

"No," Jack said. "I don't trust him to keep Joe's location to himself."

"Right," Liddell said. "Some patrolmen are going to be pissed at having to pull guard duty all day and not know why."

"Pissed about what?" Jack said. "I didn't put a guard on Joe at the hospital, and Joe left without anyone noticing. Besides, it'll be overtime pay."

Sergeant Walker was inside the detectives' office when Jack and Liddell arrived on station.

"Let's see what you've got, Jack," Walker said.

Jack handed Walker the evidence from the roof he'd wrapped in the latex gloves. "I didn't have evidence bags with me."

"Didn't I teach you anything when we were partners?" Walker asked.

"No," Jack said. "You didn't."

Liddell said, "We just peeked at the driver's license, Tony. The picture looks like our dead guy. Good thing Jack found it, since nothing came back on the fingerprints."

"You want a copy of everything here and the originals sent to Whiteside?" Walker asked.

"Might as well," Jack answered. "I'll call her and make the arrangements to have it picked up."

"I'm embarrassed that we didn't check the roofs, Jack," Walker said.

"I'm surprised we got as much done as we have. It's not every day you have a mass murder. Don't blame yourself, Tony," Jack said.

"I'm not, Jack. I'm blaming you. But I forgive you, since you found it," Walker said and left.

Jack asked Liddell, "Do you blame me, too?"

"You are the lead investigator on this, pod'na. Heavy is the head that wears the crown."

"And shit rolls downhill," Jack said.

Jack and Liddell went back to the detectives' office and spent the rest of the daylight going through the files Sanchez had given them on the other cases. This time they went slowly, page by page, photo by photo, keeping in mind the information on this driver, Chad Perkins, and the one identified by St. Louis, Hank Brown.

It was dark again. Another day of running around like a chicken with its head cut off, gone but not a waste. This time they had something to show for their pains. The wallet and the phone would yield results. He could feel it. There comes a point in every investigation when you get a sensation in your gut that spreads into your throat. It was like riding a zip line, or bungee jumping, or facing down a gunman. The exhilaration of nearing the prize.

* * * *

Coyote was feeling an exhilaration of his own. The detectives had led him to the boy. The kid was hidden at the convent a block from where Coyote was staying all the time. His drill sergeant when he was in basic training in the service had given him some wise pieces of advice to take with him to Vietnam. One piece was "Keep your knife sharp and ready," and the other was "Chance favors the prepared." He was prepared, and it was pure chance that had prodded him to follow the detectives instead of finishing his business with the old woman in the Coffee Shop.

His original plan was to kill her and use it to draw the detectives away, but Murphy had shown up before he could put the plan into effect. It was still broad daylight at the time, and his odds of getting away were slim.

Not bad, but still a risk. When Murphy and the big one showed up, he'd considered taking them out as well, which would have surely slowed down any pursuit, but he still wouldn't have known where the boy was being kept.

Now that he knew for certain where the boy was, he could do things a little more to his liking. Darkness was an old friend. He'd be finished here and on his way to Indianapolis, where he would take a few weeks off to plan the next mission. Miles had better come through with the information.

Chapter 36

Jack put the last file folder back in the box. "I'm going to call Angelina and see what she's come up with on Perkins."

Liddell's head was down on the desk.

Jack said, "Why don't you go home and get some rest. I'll be leaving shortly."

Liddell raised his head and rubbed at his eyes.

"Tomorrow is another day. Be back in here at five."

Liddell was stuffing files inside his desk drawer when his phone rang. He answered and put it on speakerphone. "Angelina," he said.

"We were just about to call you," Jack said.

"Chad Perkins. Two arrests for car theft. One for drug trafficking," Angelina said.

Liddell said, "Sergeant Walker ran his prints through IAFIS and AFIS. Why didn't we get anything?"

"Because Chad Perkins is in the Witness Protection Program. He turned state's evidence on the trafficking charge. The two auto theft charges were dismissed. I guess it was part of the deal. Chad dropped off the radar two months ago. They were expecting him to testify in a federal case. Guess he won't be there. His fingerprints are flagged in the system by WITSEC."

Jack asked, "If his fingerprints are flagged, why didn't they contact us when we made an inquiry?"

"That, I didn't ask. Let me text someone?" Angelina said. She came back on the line and said, "My friend says they contacted EPD but got no response."

"Who did they contact?" Jack asked. It was the first he'd heard of this.

"Double Dick was contacted yesterday," Angelina said.

"What the hell?" Jack said.

"My friend said there's a note on Chad's file that says several messages were left yesterday for Dick, asking him to contact them immediately. Dick is apparently the main contact person on their list since he's commander of the Investigations Unit. He hasn't called them as far as my friend knows."

Double Dick, as commander of the Investigations Unit, was the main contact person for a couple of things. No one knew a moron was running the insane asylum. He wondered what else Dick had screwed up.

"I told my contact that Chad was driving a truck full of illegals when he was killed. He said it didn't surprise him."

"Thanks, Angelina," Jack said.

When Jack hung up, Liddell asked, "Why wouldn't Dick call Witness Protection back?"

"He was probably too busy doing interviews," Jack said. "But we know he didn't call them, because the name of our driver would already be on television."

Jack was punching in the buttons for Captain Franklin's phone when his own cell phone rang. He didn't recognize the number. "Murphy," he said into the phone.

"I was just messing with you yesterday, Detective Murphy. You didn't have to go to my sergeant and get me in hot water," the voice said angrily.

"You did it to yourself, Officer Hurt."

"Hell I did," Hurt said. "I just got a call ordering me to work some chicken shit detail. I know you have it in for me, but you'd better back off. I've got friends."

"You failed to patrol your sector the night the murder was committed," Jack said. When Hurt tried to talk, he continued, "Just shut it, patrolman. I can have the dispatch records pulled and produce witnesses that you never drove past the area where a suspicious vehicle was reported, or past the Coffee Shop. We even have video to back it up," he lied. "And I don't like you calling me to chew me out. You'll know when I come after you. If you pull something like that again, I'll have you spayed. Are we clear?"

"Spaying is for females, Murphy," Hurt said smugly.

"Exactly," Jack said and hung up.

"Not in a good mood, pod'na?" Liddell asked.

"He'll be the next Double Dick if he gets any rank at all, Bigfoot. You mark my words. That asshole is nothing but a mistake waiting to happen."

"I'll type up the report on Chad Perkins," Liddell offered. "Go home to Katie. Marcie and the baby are already asleep."

"I'm going to call Captain Franklin," Jack said. "You call the ICE Queen."

Captain Franklin stuck his head in the office. "With me," he said to the men.

* * * *

The fluorescent lights overhead flickered and hummed as the detectives followed the captain down the hall.

Liddell whispered, "What'd you do now, pod'na?"

Captain Franklin used a key fob to unlock the doors. His mood was pensive and he said nothing as he led them to the conference room.

"Why do I feel like we're going to get a spanking?" Liddell said quietly.

Captain Franklin turned. "None of that in there, gentlemen. Don't say anything you don't have to. Understand?"

"Got it," Jack said.

"Oui mon, Capitaine," Liddell said under his breath.

Jack entered the room first. Chief Marlin Pope, Deputy Chief Richard Dick, Assistant Deputy Director Toomey, and US Marshal Pete Swaim were seated at the table.

Jack and Liddell took seats near the door.

"I won't keep you. I just wanted us all on the same page," Toomey said, and cast a sideways glance at Deputy Chief Dick. "You should remember Marshal Swaim." He didn't give them a chance to answer. "Part of the US Marshal duties is the Witness Protection Program."

Jack didn't know that, but he knew what was coming next.

"Chad Perkins, the driver you've just identified, was in the program," Toomey said.

"You're shitting me?" Jack said convincingly. He didn't want to get Angelina in trouble in case she'd broken any federal laws to get the information for him.

"It seems," Toomey continued, "that WITSEC tried to hand that information off to Deputy Chief Dick and, for whatever reason, the information was delayed getting into the hands of the investigators. I know the Evansville Police Department doesn't operate like the Department of Justice does. And I know you think we're all a bunch of paper pushers and glory hounds. But I want to dispel that notion right now."

Dick was staring straight ahead with his hands clasped in his lap like a pouting child.

Marshal Swaim said, "When no one called my office back, we knew there was a snafu. This happens sometimes."

Jack asked the expected question, "Why did you get a hit on his fingerprints and we didn't?"

Swaim explained, "Your department ran the fingerprints, and ICE ran them again. You both got nothing. The system flags any inquiry into one of our protectees, and we are notified. You won't get anything unless we want you to get it. We take the security of our program seriously. We have never had a witness compromised and killed."

"How did Perkins end up driving a load of illegals and getting himself killed?" Liddell asked, and Swaim's face flushed.

"I didn't say one or two hadn't run off on us," Swaim said. "Before you ask, Detective Murphy, Perkins wasn't working undercover. He was supposed to testify in court, and we think he got scared and ran. We don't know why he was driving for the people he was supposed to testify against."

"You mean you don't know why he wasn't dead before now?" Jack said.

Captain Franklin cleared his throat. That was his signal to drop it.

"The people we protect are felons. Most are assholes who never learn a lesson. Perkins was working for traffickers in drugs, weapons, and now humans. We turned him. We got him a job and a place to stay. But he considered regular work beneath him. I guess he went back to work for them because the money was better. He was going to get killed sooner or later. If I can speak plainly," he said, "I wanted to kill him myself when he was first unloaded on us. If the guy you're after wasn't a murderous psycho, I'd shake his hand for saving the government a bunch of money and trouble."

"Do you think his people killed him. Killed all these people in the truck, too?" Jack asked.

"No," Swaim said. "They'd lose too much money. They could have just killed Perkins and called it a day."

"I still don't understand how we weren't told this until now. You say you tried to notify us. What happened?" Jack asked, knowing the answer but wanting to twist the knife a little more.

Dick kept quiet, but Jack could see his neck muscles working.

"I guess it doesn't matter now," Swaim said. "No real harm done."

Toomey wasn't satisfied with that. "I hope I'm not coming off like I'm scolding any of you." He cast a sideways glance at Double Dick again.

Chief Pope said, "Not at all. We screwed up. We'll do better next time. I'm sure no one sat on the information on purpose."

"How are we going to avoid miscommunications in the future?" Toomey asked. "And I mean both ways, Marshal."

"I admit my people should have followed up in a timelier fashion," Swaim said and handed business cards around the table. "You may not have been told, Jack, but I'm part of the overall USOC task force. If you ever need assistance, don't hesitate to call me. My personal cell is on those cards."

"Any other questions?" Toomey asked the group.

Dick was silently fuming.

Pope said, "From this point forward I will be the direct contact person for any information coming in from USOC or any other federal agency. I'll be solely responsible for any glitch in the communications, Director Toomey. In this current situation, I'm making Detectives Murphy and Blanchard my second and third in command. Jack is the lead detective on this. I've already provided you with their direct numbers. Anything you have to say to me, you can say to them."

"Do you have anything to say, Jack?" Captain Franklin asked.

Jack stood and said, "I'm just happy to be here."

"That's all. You're dismissed," Pope said and asked Toomey and the marshal to stay.

Jack and Liddell left.

Outside the conference room, Liddell smirked and said, "I'm just happy to be here?"

"I was," Jack said. "Happy to see Dick squirming. I'm a little concerned at how everyone keeps information from us though. Angelina's having a hell of a time getting useful information or a picture of Cody Coté. We're supposed to catch this guy, but the Feds keep all the information we need compartmented."

Jack and Liddell went back to their office. Jack called the Crime Scene office and talked to Sergeant Walker. "Anything jump out of that wallet or phone?"

"Nada," Walker said. "I'll call you if I get anything usable. It's still early days."

Jack told him about the US Marshal and Dick's screw-up. Walker was unaware of the WITSEC procedures, but he wasn't surprised either.

Jack hung up and called Lieutenant Sanchez's personal cell and put him on speakerphone for Liddell.

"I thought I told you never call me at work, honey," Sanchez said.

Liddell said. "I think I'm pregnant. Jack is, too. Damn you to hell, Lou."

Sanchez chuckled. "I heard about Chad Perkins from the ICE Queen. She knew the marshal was at your headquarters and had his panties in a twist. Man oh man, you guys weren't kidding about Double Dick."

And so the rumor spreads, Jack thought.

"Have you got something for me," Sanchez asked, "or are you just checking your trotline?"

"I *was* going to tell you about Chad Perkins and some other stuff."

Sanchez asked, "You think Perkins was killed before he could testify? He opened himself up when he fled protective custody."

"Nah. The marshal doesn't think so either. I think it was our guy that killed him. And I've got some news on that front," Jack said.

"If you're going to tell me about Cody Coté, you're too late. The ICE Queen filled me in on that, too."

"So, I wasted my dime calling you," Jack said.

"I guess all you have to do now is figure out a way to find Cody Coté," Sanchez said.

"All *I* have to do? What will *you* be doing?"

Jack could hear a beer can being crumpled and Sanchez saying, "Good girl. Now get me another."

"Let me change the subject," Jack said. "What's the word on Lieutenant Battle?" Jack couldn't help but think he'd been in her exact situation a time or two.

"Major Maddox put her on admin leave. But Maddox's reputation is that he's fair. She'll probably be back at work after a little grief counseling. I told you I took her out once. Well, she was too intense for me. Always watching everyone. I don't need that shit. I'm paranoid enough."

"Speaking of watching someone, is Kim still watching your witness?" Jack asked.

"She's not my witness, Jack. Kim is ready to defect. I think I'll get Toomey to have her reassigned here by next week. Say what you will about the Feds, Toomey takes care of his guys."

Jack said, "Anna is taking the Border Patrol connection more serious."

"The dead driver's ex-partner is the best suspect we have so far. But how are we going to track him down? You said your computer expert isn't having any luck. Kim's tied up babysitting."

"Couldn't hurt, Lieutenant," Jack said.

"I'll ask. It'll give her something to take her mind off babysitting. I don't think we'll have much luck though. If this is the guy and he follows the same pattern from all the other cases, he's long gone. He's never hit a state twice until he got our state trooper."

Jack said, "She may have just been unlucky enough to come upon him. Maybe he was cleaning his bayonet in public?"

Sanchez chuckled. "In Missouri it's not against the law to do anything in public."

"I've heard that. After all, it is the Show-Me state," Jack said.

"Major Maddox told me earlier that his Crime Scene Unit thinks the people inside were killed first. The trooper was just unlucky to stop there."

"Maybe he didn't like the food," Jack said absentmindedly. "Did he leave a tip for the waitress?"

Jack heard notebook pages riffling.

Sanchez said, "The waitress had a new twenty-dollar bill in her pocket. They think they have a fingerprint. Could be the dead waitress's though."

"Lieutenant, be sure they get that fingerprint to Anna as soon as they can. Now that we have a possible suspect, she may be able to get a match," Jack said, thinking that Freyda had been given a new twenty-dollar bill also.

"Yeah, unless this Coté guy is in Witness Protection too. But I'll do it now," Sanchez said. "And Jack."

"Yes."

"Stop with the Lieutenant stuff, okay?"

"Okay, Lieutenant," Jack said and hung up.

Liddell had been listening. He said, "I guess we wait."

"We wait."

Chapter 37

The Dodge Dart was parked in the University of Evansville campus lot again. Coyote had been careful to avoid any surveillance cameras. He'd had to avoid most of the main streets and take a circuitous route. His plan was to strike and move and strike again somewhere else. That had been his mantra for several years. It had served him well. But he couldn't afford to fail tonight. Failing showed weakness. It didn't serve his cause.

Coyote left the car and found what he wanted in an unlocked pickup truck. The windows were down, and a Purple Aces hooded jacket was on the passenger seat. He pulled it on over the Indianapolis Colts jacket he was wearing and pulled a black sock hat over his ears. A tartan scarf covered the bottom half of his face.

He crossed the street and walked with his gloved hands jammed in the jacket pockets. Two college students were walking south on Weinbach, and he fell in twenty feet behind them, matching their quick pace. They paid him no attention as he slipped into the alleyway beside the Coffee Shop. He peeked around the front and saw the lights were off, the CLOSED sign in the front window. No one was moving inside.

He went to the back and climbed onto a chain-link fence that separated the back of the property from the one behind it. He walked the fence until he got close to the building next door, jumped up and caught the edge of the flat roof, and pulled himself onto it. The distance between the roof he was on and the Coffee Shop's roof was less than six feet. He could easily make that. His big concern was noise. He saw a semitruck coming down Weinbach and waited until it began rumbling to a stop for the red light. As it passed in front of the Coffee Shop, he took a step back and leaped. He landed as softly as possible and lay flat for a minute, two minutes, three.

He didn't hear sirens, so he got up and made his way to the part of the roof where he'd seen Murphy earlier and found a square hatch. He lay flat again and listened. Nothing.

He slowly lifted the tarpaper-covered hatch and, ignoring the ladder, dropped silently to the floor. He didn't need to wait for his night vision to adjust. He could see he was in a musty closet. The door was cracked open. He could hear footsteps leaving the room. He eased the door further open and saw a shadow of a figure on the wall outside of the room.

He went to the bedroom door and saw the old woman going down the stairs. She was still in that nasty robe or dress or whatever she had on. The lights were now on in the storage room. The lights came on in the front seating area. She went behind the counter, lit the gas stove, and was filling a steel coffee maker when Coyote stepped into the room.

She didn't scream. She set the pot down and stared at him.

"You're him," she said in an even tone.

He grabbed her by the front of her faded gown and pulled her into the storage room. "Yeah. You got me," he said, and in one deft motion pulled the bayonet and plunged it into her throat, driving it downward.

She didn't struggle. She reached up and pulled at his scarf.

"You want to see me?" he asked.

Her expression didn't change. Blood poured from the side of her mouth, and he helped her to a sitting position.

"I don't think so," he said, and yanked the blade free, plunging it down again in a killing blow. "I'll give you a quick death. You never done anything to me."

Her eyes remained staring up into his, but he could see she was gone.

"I know you don't understand, but you're a part of my mission. You can help me finish here and get on with my work. You're doing this for your country. For that, I thank you." He yanked the bayonet free, wiped the blood on her front, and slid it back into the holster at his waist.

He dragged her to the storage door and flipped the light switch, turning the lights in the front off again. He dragged her to one of the booths and leaned her in a sitting position against the wall facing the front door and windows.

He left her there and took the stairs back to her bedroom. An old rotary-dial telephone was on a tiny table beside her bed. He picked the receiver up and heard a dial tone. He put the end of his scarf over the mouthpiece and dialed 9-1-1.

"Police and Fire Emergency Dispatch," came the voice on the phone. "What is your emergency?"

"A woman has been injured." He hung up. He was going to leave when he spotted the VHS recorder on a table in the corner. He ejected the tape, stuck it down in his shirt, and climbed back to the roof.

Chapter 38

The Crown Vic slid to the curb behind the crime scene wagon. Three police cars were in front of the Coffee Shop, parked nose-in, and the officers were setting up a perimeter. Traffic was blocked for two square blocks surrounding the scene. The cold had driven most of those living in the area inside, but some had come out to watch the Christmas-light show of the police response.

Captain Franklin beat Jack and Liddell to the scene and stood beside the crime scene log officer at the front of the Coffee Shop. The inside was brightly lit with portable floodlights. As usual, Captain Franklin was dressed in a black suit, starched white shirt, red tie, and black wing tip shoes. His tie was uncharacteristically loosened.

"It's him, Jack," Captain Franklin said. "He was here. Sergeant Walker is calling people in to work the scene, and I have every available uniformed officer and detective dispatched to scour the area. The crime scene techs think it just happened. Please tell me you have something."

"Who called it in?" Jack asked.

Franklin said, "Dispatch got the 9-1-1 call from her phone. A man said a woman was hurt and hung up. What can you tell me, Jack?"

"ICE is working on something, Captain," Jack said. "A guy, ex-Border Patrol, matches the profile I had in mind. He was partnered with the dead driver in the St. Louis case. That guy was ex-Border Patrol too."

"I was aware of that, Jack," the captain said.

"I didn't tell you yet because I didn't want certain people to know."

"I understand, Jack, but now is not the time to keep me in the dark. If we have a suspect or a photo, I need to get it out to our people."

Rick Reed

"We don't have a photo yet, but Angelina is working on it," Jack said, without mentioning his frustration with the Feds. "This guy and his partner were involved in the killing of an illegal alien from El Salvador. The Border Patrol officers' names are Hank Brown—that's the St. Louis driver—and Cody S. Coté. The guy from El Salvador was suspected of killing Coté's wife and daughter. DOJ thought the murder of Coté's family was a revenge killing because Coté had arrested this particular Salvadoran several times. Coté had a reputation for roughing illegals up. They suspected this guy of killing Coté's family, but they couldn't find him. A week after the murder, he turned up dead on our side of the border. Both Border Patrol officers were allowed to resign, and the record was sealed by the Department of Justice. No charges against the officers, no further investigation. The Salvadoran was stabbed just like our victims."

"Can you prove any of that?" Franklin asked.

"I have it on good authority, Captain," Jack said.

"Go on," Franklin said.

"Hank Brown went to work for the same traffickers he had been arresting. Coté just disappeared, but his military experience and law enforcement records suggest he had the knowledge and skill needed to pull this off. The thing is, Captain, all the DOJ records on this incident are sealed."

"But you can get them," Captain Franklin said. "Don't tell me. I don't want to know how you know this. What can I do to help?"

"Maybe Marshal Swaim can get the records for us," Jack suggested. "We would have fingerprints, photos, everything we need to make a good case. It's a political issue, I know, but what's more important?"

"I assume ICE knows all of this?" Captain Franklin said.

"If they do, they can't get the records opened."

"I'll see what I can do," Franklin said. "But if I do, and if this Coté guy has an inside source..."

"I've thought that over," Jack said. "He has to have someone giving him the routes and dates for these trucks, but maybe we can get the information on Coté without him finding out. It's a chance we have to take. I just want Coté. Let Border Patrol clean their own house."

"I agree, Jack."

"Captain, if you don't mind, I'd like to see inside," Jack said.

Franklin moved aside, and Jack reached for the sign-in log. The log officer said, "I already put you and Detective Blanchard on the log, Jack."

Jack and Liddell put latex gloves on, and Jack tapped on the glass. Joanie Ryan was working the scene. She came to the door and said, "I'm nearly finished taking pictures, Detective Murphy. Give me two minutes, and I'll walk you through."

Jack could see Freyda's thin frame leaned against the wall near a booth. Her skinny arms were drooped at her sides. Her faded gown was soaked in blood.

Joanie Ryan was a civilian EPD employee with forensic training. Jack had worked several high-profile cases with her, and she was as good or better than some of the old-timers.

Jack gave her a thumbs-up and waited.

Franklin said, "I haven't been inside. Officer Thompson was first on scene. He didn't find a pulse and just did a sweep inside to check for other victims and backed out."

"He did the right thing, Captain," Jack said. "I'm going to make a call while we wait." Jack walked a short distance away and sheltered at the corner of the alleyway to block the wind.

"Angelina," Jack said when the call was picked up.

"This is Mark. I'll get her." The phone was handed off, and Angelina's sleepy voice said, "Jack."

"Sorry to wake you, but we've got another murder. The woman at the Coffee Shop. I need to get a picture of Cody Coté to broadcast to the troops. Anything you can get."

"I thought Anna gave you his photo and information. She said she'd send it to your phone."

Jack checked his text messages. Whiteside had sent one that he hadn't opened.

"Shit. Can you send the picture and physical descriptors to dispatch? I'd do it, but I have a hard time with this..."

"Don't worry, Jack, I'll get it now. I couldn't find a vehicle registered to that name. He doesn't have a driver's license associated with his name. The last address I have is in Bisbee, Arizona, from his personnel file from Border Patrol. You want me to have dispatch send it down the wire to the other agencies?" Angelina asked.

"You're an angel. Please and thank you. And can you send his personnel file records to my phone?"

"For all the good it will do," Angelina said and was gone.

He opened the photo Anna had sent an hour ago. The name attached to the picture was Cody Samuel Coté. *Cody Coté?* The photo was from his days as a Border Patrol agent. He was in uniform, wearing a cowboy-style cream-colored hat. His expression was all business with a face heavily lined and skin like leather. He reminded Jack of a Western cowboy. Same leathery, Marlboro-smoking type.

Jack thought of Freyda Rademacher's take-no-prisoner sense of humor that was rare these days. She was a tough old bird, but not tough enough.

"Did anyone know Mrs. Rademacher's surveillance camera was operational?" Jack asked Franklin.

"Just the ones in the meeting earlier. You two, Walker, me, Toomey, the chief, and..."

"Deputy Chief Dick," Jack finished the sentence for him.

"I know what you're thinking, Jack, but none of that was released to the news media. I don't think Deputy Chief Dick would talk to anyone about evidence," Franklin said, but he didn't sound convincing or convinced. "Especially after what happened earlier with Witness Protection."

"If it's our killer, why else did he come back and do this?" Jack asked.

Franklin said, "Maybe he was worried that she might have seen his face. Channel Six said something about a witness in one of their broadcasts. I thought Claudine Setera was talking about the boy. Joe."

"The boy!" Jack said and grabbed Liddell's arm. "Come on."

Joanie Ryan came to the door and called out, "You can come through now." Seeing Jack's and Liddell's retreating figures, she said, "Or not."

Captain Franklin said, "I'll have a detective here shortly. Did you see how the killer gained entry?"

"Officer Thompson said he had to force the front door. He swept the place in case the killer was still here," Joanie said, "but he didn't say anything about unlocked doors or windows, sir."

Franklin called Jack's cell phone and gave him that information.

Jack and Liddell were already on Lincoln Avenue, Liddell driving, speeding west when Jack talked to Captain Franklin.

"They didn't find an entry point, Bigfoot," Jack said and put the phone in his pocket.

"Think she let him in?" Liddell suggested.

"That café in St. Louis was open for business when he killed them. He locked the front door and turned off the OPEN sign."

"The CLOSED sign was in Freyda's front door," Liddell said. "Maybe she was still open?"

"Maybe," Jack admitted. "She was wearing night clothes. I don't think she'd be working the shop dressed like that." Jack called Captain Franklin again and asked if the heat was on downstairs. He heard the captain pass the question on to Joanie Ryan.

He came back on and said, "Turned off, but still a little warm. The heat was on upstairs."

"Thanks, Captain," Jack said.

Franklin said quickly, "Don't hang up, Jack. Where are you going? This is *your* crime scene."

"We're going to check on Joe, Captain. I've got to go." He disconnected the call and checked for recent calls on his cell phone. One had come in whose number he didn't recognize earlier. He touched that number and heard a ringing.

It rang half a dozen times and went to voice mail. "You have reached Evansville Police Officer Hurt. I'm busy fighting crime right now, so leave a message."

Jack tried two more times with the same result.

"Didn't Hurt say he was working this detail tonight?" Jack asked.

"I don't know, pod'na. You talked to him."

"If he's sleeping, I'll kill him," Jack said.

Jack pulled up Sister Aquinas's phone number. No answer. He tried again and still no answer.

"Shit! Step on it, Bigfoot. No one's answering their phones."

Liddell stomped down on the gas pedal and took Highway 41 to the Division Street ramp. "Should we call backup, pod'na?"

"We'll see," Jack said, drew his .45, checked the action, and didn't reholster.

They were on First Avenue, a block from the church, in less than a minute. Officer Hurt's marked police cruiser was in the parking lot of Hacienda Restaurant, the front pointed toward the church. A cloud of mist came from the exhaust.

Liddell flashed his bright lights several times to get Hurt's attention, but Hurt didn't respond.

"You check him. I'm going across," Jack said and was out of the car and running across First Avenue, gun in hand.

Liddell approached the police car and saw a spray of blood on the driver's window. Hurt's head was against the window, a black sock hat covering his face. Liddell opened the car door, and Hurt's body slid toward him. Liddell pushed the body back up in the seat, checked for a pulse, and got on his portable radio.

He keyed the mic and said, "Signal ten traffic, Signal ten." Without waiting for dispatch to respond, he gave his location, requested an ambulance and backup. He heard dispatch acknowledge and begin the dispatches as he was running across First Avenue after Jack.

Jack ran up the steps to the convent and, ignoring proper police procedure, he tried the front door, found it unlocked, and entered into a dark hallway. He shut the door behind himself to avoid being backlit and held the .45 at shoulder height, finger on the trigger, trying to control his breathing, and listening. He could hear the *slap-slap* of shoes on pavement. *Bigfoot.*

Jack heard the front door opening behind him and said, "Go to the back, Bigfoot."

As the door closed, Jack had a sick feeling that they were too late. The place felt empty of life. He saw a beam of light splash against the end of the hallway. Liddell was in the back door. They now had both ends covered, so the need to be quiet was outweighed by the urgency of checking for life.

"Sister," Jack called out. "It's Jack. Sister."

Not a sound. Jack moved forward to the stairway and took the Vipertek flashlight from his coat pocket. He held it away from his body and flipped it on. The hallway lit up like somebody had turned on the sun.

"Check down here, Liddell. I'm going up," Jack said, and trained the light at the top of the stairway as he climbed. His thoughts turned to the weapon of choice, a twenty-two-inch-blade bayonet, and he wished this asshole preferred a gun. Jack had gone against a large knife before and almost lost his life. He still carried the long scar from his ear to his nipple.

At the top of the stairs he peeked around the corner, trained the beam down that hall and then turned it off. The light was bright enough that it was like throwing a flash-bang without the explosion. No response. He found the light switch on the wall and turned the lights on upstairs.

The rooms along the hall were all empty until he came to the small bedroom at the front of the convent. He opened the door and said, "Aw shit!"

Liddell called from the bottom of the stairs, "All clear."

"Joe," Jack called out and could hear Liddell doing the same downstairs.

Jack checked the closet in the bedroom. It contained a few items of clothing and some boxes stacked in one corner. This was all Sister Aquinas had to show for a life of generosity and service to her God and her community.

He went back to the dresser by the bed. Sister Aquinas was on her knees, propped against the dresser, palms together and held that way by a rosary. Her head was leaning forward as if in prayer. The white nightgown she'd gone to bed in was soaked in blood at the shoulders and down her front, and some puddled on the floor around her legs.

He called out, "Joe!"

No response.

He started to leave the bedroom when he heard a muffled whine.

"Joe!"

He heard the whine coming from the closet. He opened the door. The dog had knocked down a stack of boxes that were hiding a cubbyhole off to the side. The dog pushed her head between two boxes and bared her teeth at Jack. He still didn't see the boy.

"Joe, you can come out," Jack said. Joe didn't answer. "Joe? Are you okay?"

Jack pulled the top boxes off onto the floor and found Joe scrunched down against the back wall, his eyes and mouth clenched into straight lines. The dog's leash was pulled up short in a tight grip, but its eyes were on Jack, and it was smiling.

"Liddell," Jack yelled. "Up here." He could hear Liddell bounding up the stairs.

Liddell came in the bedroom and turned the lights on.

"Turn the lights back off, Bigfoot," Jack said, and Liddell did. Jack didn't want the boy to have to see Sister Aquinas like that. How the killer hadn't found Joe was a mystery, but then Jack remembered, he himself had checked the closet and missed the hiding place.

Jack got to one knee in the closet to talk to Joe. "You're safe now. I need you to come with me." He held a hand out to the boy. Shadow growled but didn't bite. Joe took Jack's hand and was coaxed to his feet. "Come on, Joe. You're alive. Shadow is here with you. I'm here too. I won't let anything else happen."

Joe said in a quiet voice, "Grandfather promised me we would have a better life here. Now he is dead. Everyone that cared for me is dead, and it's all my fault. I should have stayed with those men. Maybe I would be with my sister?" He lifted his eyes to Jack's, and Jack could see the pain in them.

"Let's go downstairs. I'll let you make me some coffee, and I'll tell you what I know. Agreed?"

"Shadow goes too? She's hungry," Joe said.

"We'll find something for Shadow. Come on."

Jack led the way past Liddell, past two burly uniformed officers coming up the stairs wearing grim expressions, past a crime scene tech struggling with two large cases of forensic equipment, past the boxes of clothes stacked in the hallway that would be delayed in finding homes now. The clothes made him wonder how he would find Sister Aquinas's next of kin. The nun had to be in her nineties.

But he had to worry about the living right now. Joe needed him. He wanted to promise that he could protect him, but he had failed to protect Freyda and Sister Aquinas. He'd almost lost the boy. Maybe it was time to get someone else involved.

"I'm calling a friend," Jack said. "She will help you and keep you safe."

"You are giving me to them," Joe said. "To ICE. Sending me back."

Jack was surprised to hear that word come from this boy's mouth, but how could he not know the terminology. His grandfather had warned him.

"No. My friend will find a place for you here. She will try to help you stay. If that's what you want?" Jack said.

In the kitchen, the boy sat on the floor with Shadow cradled between his legs while Jack called Anna Whiteside and filled her in on the night's happenings.

"We know who he is now, Jack. He can run, but he can't hide for long," Anna said.

"I've got to ask for another favor." Jack asked the favor without much hope it would be given.

"I have a local agent in Evansville as it so happens. She'll pick the boy up and take him to a safe house. Hang on," Anna said. She came back on the line. "She's been notified. Where are you?"

Jack told her, and she gave an ETA—estimated time of arrival—of ten minutes.

Joe, who had been listening to the one-sided conversation, said, "I will never see you again, so thank you for helping me, Detective Murphy."

The boy held a hand out to shake, and Jack felt his throat constrict at the boy's bravery. Jack took his hand and pulled him into a hug. "I will see you again if I can. I can at least promise that, Joe. And there's always email."

Joe smiled. "Bigfoot said you suck at using computers. If I see you again, I will teach you."

Jack noticed Joe had been clutching something in one hand the whole time. "What's that, Joe?"

"He dropped it."

"Who dropped it?" Jack asked.

Joe said, "The sister came into the room and hid me and Shadow in the closet. She said be very quiet. I heard the man come in the room, and the sister told him she would pray for him. It was quiet, and then I heard the closet open, and the man was looking for me. I hurt Shadow keeping her quiet, I think, but she didn't make a sound until she heard you. When the man was in the closet, I think he dropped this." Joe held out a small and very worn spiral notebook.

Jack took the notebook. The cover was rough and warn and wouldn't produce any usable fingerprints. He asked Joe, "Did you open it?"

Joe said he hadn't. Jack slid the notebook into his pocket and helped Joe into a seat at the table. They talked about Joe's life in Honduras until the ICE agent showed up. She introduced herself, bundled Joe into her heavy parka, and took him out the front to her car.

Liddell joined Jack and watched the too-thin boy getting into a black Suburban.

"He set us up, pod'na," Liddell said to Jack. "This guy is slick."

"I didn't expect him to go after Freyda," Jack said. "I didn't even think he would come back to Evansville."

"He's done St. Louis twice, pod'na."

"You're right, Bigfoot. But I don't think the trooper's killing was intentional. I think that was an escape route and she was in the wrong place. He surprised her while she was still in her car. I think he was on his way back here to kill Joe."

"Why would a little boy be a threat to him?" Liddell asked.

"Maybe he wasn't a threat. Who knows how this sick bastard thinks. Maybe he was just making sure everyone from that truck was dead," Jack said. "Like pride in his work."

Chapter 39

Coyote had staged the woman's body so that Murphy would be called to the Coffee Shop. He'd kept the 9-1-1 call short and disguised his voice, but it was a mistake to make the call from her phone. He had barely made it before the police arrived. He hadn't counted on such a quick response.

When he'd hurried across town to the convent, he could hear sirens getting closer, and the police cars had passed him going the other direction. He didn't know if he'd have time to complete his mission when he spotted the police car sitting on the parking lot of the Mexican restaurant across from the convent. The officer inside had a sock hat covering his face. He'd quietly put the cop to sleep permanently.

Gaining entry to the convent had been easy enough. The locks were old, and there weren't any deadbolts. He'd been quiet enough getting in, but he hadn't counted on the old nun's hearing being so good. He'd seen her with the boy when Murphy brought the dog to them, and she was at least in her nineties. Old people were supposed to have poor hearing.

He'd been prepared for the dog. When he'd killed the old woman, he found some ground beef in her fridge. He'd taken some of it to the convent for the dog, but he hadn't needed it. He found the nun, but she wouldn't give the boy up.

He had searched the convent, and she'd quietly followed him around. She hadn't tried to stop him. She wasn't afraid. Instead she had blessed him and asked him to pray with her. She said no matter what he'd done, he would be forgiven. For just a moment he'd felt different. Like when he was a boy and his parents had told him about the power of prayer. But he was beyond prayer. He'd had no choice but to kill her. If she was right, He would forgive him that too. She said she'd pray for him. That was when he'd killed her.

Murphy must have moved the boy. Murphy reminded him of himself. That was bad.

The whole night had been for nothing. He didn't have a plan, and when you didn't know what to do, you just moved and kept on moving. He had to go forward. Cut his losses. After what he'd done tonight, Murphy would have to turn the boy over to the Feds for protection. From what he'd read about the detective at the library, Murphy would come after him with everything he had. Like him, Murphy wasn't squeamish about killing.

After he got a safe distance away, he could call his source to find out where they were keeping the boy, just in case. If he had another shot, he'd go back. That would most likely burn his source, and that would put Coyote out of business.

He'd made it to Interstate 64 and gone west instead of east toward Indianapolis like he'd planned earlier. Zig when you planned to zag, but keep moving. It had served him well in the Border Patrol and saved his butt more than once in Vietnam.

Another hour or so of driving and he could spend the day at a real hotel if he wanted. Get a decent meal for a change. In the morning he would move on. Head home. He regretted what he'd had to do tonight. He didn't intend to kill civilians or innocents, but his country was asleep to the danger they were in. As a people, they were incapable of stopping the waves of illegal immigrants washing over this country, stripping it of its resources, changing its way of life to something he no longer recognized. Instead of being angry with the illegals, American citizens were angry with their law enforcers, their military, always limiting and restricting their ability to carry out the job. He felt sorry for the ignorance, whether it was deliberate or caused by an ill-informed news media. Everyone likes to eat chicken, but sometimes to eat, you have to be the one to kill the chicken. They had forgotten that.

He crossed the Mississippi for the third time in two days and took the first exit. He drove back roads, not knowing where he was going, not needing to, just moving, needing time to think.

He needed to record the day's events in his journal. Maybe he could discover what had gone so wrong? He had hesitated to kill the nun. That was the first time he'd hesitated since he was boots down in Vietnam. Back then he'd learned a lesson; you hesitate, you die. He hadn't hesitated to kill the woman trooper at the café this morning, but her death was gnawing at him. He rationalized that he was protecting American citizens and that she was sworn to do the same thing. She hadn't died in vain.

He spotted a red neon sign ahead, pulled in and parked outside the last run-down room of yet another dump motel. It wouldn't have surveillance systems, hence no need to kill again. Maybe now he could have privacy, write until he got it all out, and maybe tonight he would sleep.

The clerk had zits on his face and was more interested in the titty magazine he was perusing than in Coyote. He paid cash for the room with new twenty-dollar bills, plus one for a tip. The kid hadn't thanked him for the extra. Things had changed.

He took the key, got a Diet Coke from the machine outside his room, and opened the door to his home for the night. The smell of disinfectant hit him so hard he thought he'd ask zit-face for another room. It wouldn't matter. All the rooms probably smelled the same.

He left the door open. He'd rather be cold than suffocate on the smell. He sat at a small table with a stubby shadeless lamp and reached in his coat pocket for the notebook. It was gone!

Chapter 40

Jack stood in the front door of the convent, watching the pulsing blue-and-white emergency lights, and felt like a fool for being played so easily. There were three more dead tonight because he couldn't get a handle on the killer, and he wondered what he should have done. Was it his fault? Sister Aquinas's death was on him. He knew that for sure. If he'd done what everyone else had suggested and given Joe over to ICE, maybe the guy wouldn't have come back? But he hadn't. A gentle soul had been savagely taken. *Coté killed a nun!*

Jack watched as Officer Hurt was removed from his police cruiser and placed in a body bag. This was placed on a gurney and loaded into the back of the black Suburban that would ferry the policeman to the morgue.

Joe had been examined by the paramedics that arrived but refused to be taken back to the hospital to be seen by an ER doctor. He had glued himself to Jack, and Shadow had done likewise to the boy. The arriving ICE agent had been gentle with Joe and cautious with Shadow, but both had been taken peacefully, leaving Jack with the memory of the last words he heard the boy say. "I'll never see you again, Detective Murphy."

Liddell cut into Jack's thoughts. "Crime Scene is done up there, pod'na. They said they're ready to turn the body over to the coroner's crew."

Sister Aquinas was still in her room. Jack had requested they not move her until he could be present.

"Let's do this," Jack said, and he and Liddell climbed the stairs. Every light in the convent was turned on, and Jack's mind flashed back to grade school again when the convent had been a spooky place. It was still spooky, but now empty of any mystery.

Jack took in the threadbare carpet in the hallway upstairs, the worn-through carpet entryways to the rooms; the paint was as old and faded as the building itself, every inch spotless. The sisters had taken a vow of poverty and service. They never complained; they cleaned, they taught, and they prayed.

It was with these thoughts and feelings he reentered the crime scene and saw the pitiable, emaciated body of the little nun. The killer had posed her, propped her up, buttocks on heels, hands folded in her lap in a prayer position with a rosary around her hands. Blood spattered the front and pooled around the hem of the faded white gown.

"Joe said she was praying for the asshole when he killed her," Jack said.

Jack saw the big man's fists clenched. There would be a "come to Jesus" when they caught up with this guy.

Jack and Liddell made a quick walk-through of the upstairs, found nothing, and went downstairs. They walked out the front door and logged out of the crime scene with the officer guarding the entrance.

"Joe gave me this," Jack said and showed the notebook to Liddell. "He said the killer must have dropped it in the closet. Freyda said the customer was writing in a notebook."

"Oh yeah. You going to open it?" Liddell asked.

"To borrow one of your Bigfoot-isms, 'Does the Pope shit in the Vatican?'"

"I don't say that," Liddell corrected him. "It's 'shit in the woods,' pod'na."

They crossed First Avenue to their car. There were coroner seals on the doors of Hurt's police cruiser, and it was being loaded on the back of a flatbed wrecker to be taken to the garage for processing. Hurt wasn't a great cop, not even a good one, but he was a cop nonetheless.

They got in their car, and Jack took the notebook out of his pocket and turned on the dome light. He folded the cover back. The lined page was written in a very neat hand. Jack read the first page and closed the cover.

Liddell said, "What's it say?"

Jack said, "I'll read it to you on the way to the office."

Liddell drove down First Avenue toward the Civic Center, and Jack read the first few pages out loud. Jack skipped forward and read another page, and skipped to the last pages of writing.

"Listen to this," Jack said and read the last entry out loud. "She should have driven away when I told her the place was closed. She should have listened to me. She saw my face, but I might have let her go if she hadn't told me the waitress inside was her daughter. I had no choice. My face would be posted all over the news and on bulletin boards in every police station and government office. Killing a state trooper made me an enemy of every cop in the world."

Jack closed the notebook and put it back in the evidence bag. "I'm going to call Sanchez."

* * * *

"We need to call Anna or Toomey," Liddell said when they got into their office.

"Do you think they'll do anything but talk and put out bulletins? How long does it take for the Feds to screw in a light bulb, Bigfoot?"

"I get ya," Liddell said. "But we should tell them anyway. We can still work on this. Maybe he's still in the area?"

"You call Anna," Jack said. "I don't accept that this guy got away. And I sure as hell don't want Toomey or Anna or anyone else shutting us down. Now that we know who the killer is, they will take the case and screw it up. They might as well give it to Double Dick."

Jack was thinking about the last words Joe had said to him. "I'll never see you again." He'd promised Joe, and he'd promised Trooper Battle that he'd find the killer and bring him in. He still meant it. He had an idea where this guy was going. He needed a little time.

"One day, Bigfoot. Then we'll call everyone. I promise."

"You got it. Where do we go now?"

"You don't go anywhere," Jack said. "I'm going to see Sanchez and Lieutenant Battle. She deserves to know who killed her sister and her niece. Sanchez needs to have the opportunity to be in on this because it started with him. I need you here. Will you do that?"

"You want me here so the brass won't know you're gone. Is that the idea?" Liddell asked.

"You don't even know I've gone. Get it?" Jack said.

"What do you want me to tell the captain or whoever asks what we're doing? They'll want some answers. Hell, the news media will be all over this. A cop and a nun are dead."

"That's what I'm saying, Bigfoot. I know we can't keep a lid on something like this, but let's get our hands on him before he digs a hole and disappears for good. Okay?"

"Hey, you don't have to convince me, pod'na. Where do you think he's going? At least tell me that because you didn't let me read the notebook."

"Not exactly," Jack lied. He hated to lie to his partner, but it was meant to protect the big man's job. Liddell had a wife and a child to support. He wouldn't get his friend caught up in what was going to happen. "If you call me, let it ring twice, hang up, wait five seconds and call again. If I can, I'll answer. I'm not taking calls from anyone else. Don't call unless it's life or death, Bigfoot. I'm serious."

"Tell me where you're really going," Liddell said.

"I'm going to see Sanchez. That's the truth."

"Have you got your phone with you?"

Jack patted his pocket.

"Is it charged? Do you have a charger cord?" Liddell asked.

"Yes, Mother," Jack said.

"If someone important wants to know, I'll say you're getting together with Sanchez. If they want to know more, I'll tell them that you never tell me anything. How's that?"

"Perfect, the truth always works," Jack said and pulled on his coat. "Listen. I haven't told Katie what's going on. If she calls..."

"I'll take care of it, pod'na. I'll fill Marcie in, and she can help."

Jack took a twelve-gauge pump shotgun from a rack beside the desk and a box of deer slugs and one of double-aught buck. "Tell Double Dick to bite me," he said to Liddell and left the office.

He took Liddell's Crown Vic because it had a full tank of gas. He called Sanchez's personal cell phone. It rang several times before Sanchez answered.

"Jack. I'm glad you called," Sanchez said.

"Have you already heard?" Jack asked. He wasn't surprised.

"Heard what? What are you talking about?"

"That he was just here," Jack said.

"He was there?"

"Yeah. About an hour ago he killed a police officer and went after the boy. He killed the nun that was keeping Joe for me," Jack said.

"An hour ago?" Sanchez asked.

"Yeah. Do I need to repeat everything twice, Lou? He was here about an hour ago. He killed the old lady that owned the coffee shop to create a diversion and went after the boy."

"You're not making any sense, Jack. Are you saying the killer—our killer—was just in Evansville an hour ago?"

"What the hell is wrong with you, Lieutenant? Are you drunk? If you are, get sober quick. I'm on my way."

Sanchez said, "Kim's in the hospital. She's hurt real bad, Jack, and the witness is missing. There's a lot of blood, but we don't know if he took the witness or what. Kim was stabbed. If he was there an hour ago, how could he be here?"

It was Jack's turn to be confused. Kim was in the hospital and she'd been stabbed, but she was still alive. Cody had never left anyone alive before. "Who took the witness? Do you think it's our guy? When did this happen?"

Sanchez's voice was thick with emotion. "About two hours ago. I called Kim, and when she didn't pick up I went over there and found her in the bathtub. There'd been a hell of a fight. Kim's head was bleeding, and she was stabbed in the neck. I didn't wait for an ambulance. I took her to the hospital, and I've been here ever since. I didn't see the witness, but blood was all over the place. I don't think she's going to make it, Jack."

It was at least a three-hour drive between St. Louis and Evansville. Jack thought he could cut the time in half if he didn't get pulled over.

"Lou, I'm sorry about Kim. I'm on my way there. Send me the hospital's address so I can get it on my phone's GPS. I hate these damn things."

"Will do. Jack, when was he in Evansville? You said about an hour ago." Sanchez sounded a little more with it. His cop sense must have kicked in and blocked out some of the anxiety over Kim.

"Freyda Rademacher owns the Coffee Shop. I told you about her. She's the one that told us about the strange customer. The one that left her a new twenty-dollar bill as payment for a cup of coffee. An hour ago she was found dead in her shop. A 9-1-1 call came from her phone, and a man reported an injured woman. She was killed just like all the others, deep stab wounds.

"While I was at that scene, he went to St. Anthony's convent, where I was keeping Joe stashed. He killed a cop that was posted across the street from the convent, then went in and killed the nun that was watching Joe."

"You're sure it's our guy?"

"Yeah. And remember me telling you the woman at the Coffee Shop said that the customer was writing in a spiral-bound notebook the whole time he was there? I found the notebook at the convent. He dropped it while he was searching for Joe, and Joe picked it up. The boy was hiding, but he heard the nun being killed."

"Where is he now? Joe?"

"With the ICE Queen's minion," Jack said not meaning to be funny, but it got a tiny chuckle from Sanchez. Jack's phone buzzed. "I just got your text. I'm about two and a half hours out. I'll get there as quick as I can. The last entry in the notebook talks about killing the state trooper and the people in the café. There's personal stuff in there too. I think I know where he's going."

Jack's phone buzzed. He was getting another call. It was the ICE Queen. He ignored it.

"I'll give you everything I've got when I get there, Lou. We need to talk."

"Yeah," Sanchez said, and they hung up.

It was late on a Sunday night, traffic was light, and the roads were clear. He could see intermittent patches of black ice between the lanes. The weather had at least given him a chance to drive on autopilot and think.

He retrieved the address and name of the hospital from Sanchez's text and brought up the directions. He relaxed his grip on the steering wheel and took a deep breath as Siri directed him to the hospital. He hoped.

Chapter 41

When Coyote discovered his notebook wasn't in his pocket, he felt numb. He stripped his coat off and went through the pockets, squeezed it to be sure it hadn't slipped into the lining, retraced his steps to the office, back to his room and back to the car. He searched under the seats, between the seats, the glove box, under the floor mats. He carried his bag into the room and went through the extra clothing and jackets. The notebook was gone.

He was sure it was in his pocket when he went to the convent. He was pretty sure it was still there when he left town. He mentally traced his steps in Evansville. There were a couple of places he could have lost it. On the roof of the Coffee Shop. Or it had fallen out of his pocket on his way to or from his car. A steel donation box was near the entrance to the St. Anthony Homeless Shelter. He'd thrown the army jacket in the bin, but he would have searched the pockets. He was sure he had. He'd never be that careless.

But he must have. It didn't matter how. It mattered that his real name, Cody Samuel Coté, was in it. It mattered that it was a goldmine of information if it was discovered. It might even lead some smart detective straight to him.

No chance of getting the notebook back, and nothing he could do about it. Nothing but be aware the notebook was out there and his anonymity was no longer intact. If they knew who he was, it was just a matter of time before they asked themselves how he had gotten all of his information. How did he know exactly where the trucks were going, where they could be stopped, how to get in touch with the drivers, how he was able to kill so many and still remain invisible. They would figure out who his source was, and his source would give him up. The Feds were good at making deals that no one could refuse.

He could eliminate his source before the Feds got him, but even if he eliminated the possibility of his source talking to the Feds, he still had the issue of the notebook. But—one problem at a time. Maybe all was not lost. Maybe no one had the notebook yet. Maybe, if he was lucky, it wouldn't be found at all. And maybe pigs could fly.

He wondered if he should have taken the dead cop's gun, waited at the convent and killed Murphy. It was partly Murphy's fault he'd had to kill the nun. He regretted that. But, of course, Murphy wouldn't have come alone. There would have been one hell of a firefight. At least he could die with some semblance of honor. That was something sadly missing in today's world. Honor.

He wouldn't run if they came for him. He would stand and fight. He'd faced death before. He wasn't afraid to die. If they came for him, they were his enemy, and therefore enemies of his country. He would kill them all, or die trying.

Chapter 42

The dispatcher had tried to raise him on the police radio until he was out of range of the tower, but his cell phone rang repeatedly. He felt bad leaving Bigfoot behind to take all the heat, but he needed to do this, and Bigfoot had a wife and a new baby to think about.

The female voice on his phone announced, "You've arrived at your destination."

"Screw you, Siri. Just shut the hell up," Jack said. She'd been announcing every damn little bend in the road. It made him nervous to hear a voice in the car while he was trying to think.

"I'm sorry, Supreme Commander. I don't understand that command."

Jack parked in the hospital garage and went to the emergency entrance, where he knew a security guard or off-duty cop would be easier to convince to let him in after visiting hours. He was in luck. The cop on duty not only let him in, he accompanied him to the room so he wouldn't get lost. Another uniformed policeman stood outside the door to Intensive Care.

The cop asked, "Who the hell are you?" He was big enough to tear the head off a bull.

Jack showed his EPD detective credentials, and the cop's eyebrow went up.

"You want to talk to Sanchez?" the cop asked.

"Does the Pope shit in the Vatican," Jack said, and the cop laughed and seemed to relax.

"No one goes in but doctors and nurses."

"Can you tell him Jack Murphy is here?"

"No one in or out. You will stay here," the cop said to Jack and cracked the door wide enough to call a nurse over. "Tell him Murphy is here."

The door had just shut when a pale Lt. Sanchez came out.

"Hey, Lou," Jack said. "Sorry about Kim."

"He damn near killed her," Sanchez said. "I couldn't put word out because Toomey said Anna wasn't sure we had the right guy."

Jack pulled up a photo on his cell phone. "We know who he is now. His real name is Cody Samuel Coté. He goes by Coyote."

Sanchez took the cell phone and stared at the photo.

Jack said, "He resigned from Border Patrol five years ago. He and his partner—the driver here—were being investigated for the murder of an illegal immigrant. I called Angelina on the drive here. It was buried in the DHS files."

"In other words, hidden to cover someone's ass?" Sanchez said.

"Yeah. Hank and Cody had arrested the illegal several times for felonies, deported him, and he made his way back to the US, where he continued his criminal activities. Cody and his partner took exception to this, and the next time they caught up with him, they gave him an ass-whipping before he was deported. He came back, and this time he found Cody's family. He raped and murdered the wife and daughter."

"Son of a bitch!"

Jack continued, "Cody's wife was raped, stabbed, and sliced open. His daughter was found the same way. She was nine years old. Their killer wrote 'COYOTE' in blood on the wall beside the daughter's body.

"The journal I found at the convent was Cody's. He wrote that his Border Patrol buddies called him 'Coyote' because he would illegally transport the ones he and his partner captured back across the border into Mexico. They made a lesson of some of these people as a warning not to come back. Angelina couldn't find any records to back that up, but it sounds like our guy's personality."

"Yeah. It does," Sanchez said.

Jack went quiet. His hatred for Cody, or Coyote, was fighting with his conscience. The man's family had been sexually abused and slaughtered. Jack felt he might have done the same thing to the guy that had done that to his family. He'd ended a freak that was holding a knife to Katie's throat, threatening to kill her in front of Jack. He hadn't hesitated giving him a lead lobotomy. The difference between him and Cody Coté was that Jack had ended it there. He hadn't gone after other scumbags, killed hundreds in retaliation. Cody was definitely a mad dog.

Sanchez asked, "Why would the Border Patrol cover all of this up?"

"Covering their ass. The Border Patrol didn't need the bad press. Angelina said they were under scrutiny for several shootings of illegals along the border. This wasn't the first time a Border Patrol officer had killed someone. But the attention from something like Cody's situation would bring congressional hearings and all hell would break loose."

"I guess I can see their reasoning," Sanchez said. "The illegal had gotten what he deserved. The government was happy to let Cody and his partner resign rather than go to court."

Jack said, "When Cody's partner—the driver you had here in St. Louis—I forget his name..."

"Hank Brown," Sanchez said.

"Yeah, when Hank, his old partner, went to work for the traffickers, it must have sent Cody over the edge. He was a decorated soldier in Vietnam, and that war ended badly for him. He was already angry with a system that would let a convicted violent felon back into the country to kill Cody's wife and kid. To top that, he was facing criminal charges for killing the scumbag and had to resign. I think that's what set off the chain of events we're dealing with. Cody feels betrayed by his partner and his country. Psycho 101."

Jack thought Sanchez looked tired, wasted. Like he'd been on an all-night drunk and was trying to keep it together.

"So why are you here?" Sanchez asked. "Do you think this guy is here again?"

Jack said, "I'm not sure where he is right at this minute, but I know where he's going to be. I'm going to get him. I thought you might want to come?"

"Come where?"

"Bisbee, Arizona. If you're coming, we need to leave tonight. Now." Jack hoped Sanchez would come with him, but he could see the man didn't have it in him.

"Why there?"

"Angelina told me something interesting," Jack said. "Cody's from Tucson, but he was living in Bisbee. That's where his family was slaughtered. His wife and daughter are buried just outside of Bisbee. One of the last entries in his diary talked about going home."

"That's all you've got?" Sanchez asked.

"It's a combination of things, Lou," Jack said. "I'm close. I'm going to end this."

Sanchez said, "I don't think so."

"Okay," Jack said. "I understand. I'll let you know what happens."

Sanchez put a hand on Jack's arm. "No. You misunderstood me. I don't think you'll be going to Bisbee. It's outside our jurisdiction, Jack. You need to call Toomey. He'll send another team."

"Okay. I'll call Toomey," Jack lied. Toomey had never explained jurisdictional limits. Jack assumed something like this covered the whole United States. "I'll call him on my way back to Evansville. You need to get back in there with her. I hope Kim pulls through this. I'll see you."

"You'll be in prison. Or dead," Sanchez said. "I won't call Toomey. I didn't even see you tonight. I'm not going, but you need to take *someone* with you."

"Thanks for the advice, Lieutenant," Jack said and pulled his arm away.

"There you go with that Lieutenant shit again. I *would* go, you know I would, but Kim..."

Jack gripped Sanchez hand. "If I ever get in a bar fight, I want you and Cutie to back me up."

"You're one crazy son of a bitch. You know that?"

"So I've heard," Jack said and walked toward the elevator.

Sanchez called out to him. "Hey. Call Battle."

Jack waved a goodbye without turning around. He'd already thought of calling Battle. She would want to be there. She was going to get fired anyway, so better to go out guns blazing than give up your gun and go home crying in your Scotch. He pulled out his cellphone and the business card Battle had given him.

Chapter 43

Lieutenant Battle met Jack at the door. She was living in a mobile home. As it turned out, the mobile home was parked on land jointly owned with her sister. Her sister had lived in a small farmhouse a stone's throw away from the lieutenant.

"Like I told you on the phone, just give me the name and location. No need for both of us going, and excuse me for saying this, but you'll just get in my way," she said by way of greeting.

It was well after midnight, the temperatures had dropped into the negative figures, and Battle stood blocking the doorway not inviting Jack inside.

"Not going to happen," Jack said. "I'll call and let you know what happened. Or you can watch the news." He stepped off the little deck and headed toward his car.

"You shouldn't go alone," she said.

Jack turned. "*You* were going alone."

"Apology accepted," Battle said.

Jack asked, "Can I come in and show you what I found? If you're coming with me, we need to have a plan. And we need to establish some ground rules."

"You mean like who's in charge? I outrank you," she said.

"And I'm a federal agent, plus I know where he's going."

Battle opened the door wider and disappeared inside without inviting him in. Jack entered and shut the door. The kitchen and living room were separated by an eat-in counter with three bar stools on the living room side. The furniture was old and worn and didn't match. Typical yard sale stuff. The counter and the tops of the barstools were covered with stacks of papers and file folders and eight-by-ten glossy photos of the crime scene where her family was slain.

Despite the clutter on the counter, the trailer was neatly made up and smelled of cinnamon. There were half a dozen pictures on the walls of her and her sister, her sister at her swearing-in ceremony being hugged by the niece. The niece as a baby. The niece about Joe's age, and another one of her as a young teen. No men. No animals. Battle led a simple life. Now it was even simpler. He could relate to being alone. He'd spent the last four years of his life that way. He resisted the urge to excuse himself, go back to the car, and call Katie. Death had a way of making life your priority.

Battle sat on one end of the sofa and patted beside her. "Sit down. I don't bite."

Jack sat and took Coyote's journal from his pocket.

"So that's the diary you told me about on the phone?"

"This is his confession," Jack said. "Every crime he's committed, from beating illegal immigrants and dumping them on the Mexican side of the border, to the murders and slaughters here."

Battle held the notebook like it was a snake that might bite her. "Confession to the café? He say what he did to my sister and Benny? Benny's my niece. Bernice."

"And to several hundred others. There's enough in there to get him the death penalty a hundred times over," Jack said. "The victims will get justice."

"Justice. Huh," Battle mouthed the words. "Will justice bring them back?"

"Will what you're planning to do to him bring them back?" Jack asked. "We need to get on the same page here, Lieutenant. I need to know if you can't control your feelings. I need to know if I can trust you."

"Let me look at the damn thing," Battle said, and Jack handed over the diary.

Jack had the report on her sister's and niece's murders, courtesy of Sanchez. He was beginning to question the wisdom of bringing her into this, but he needed a partner with nothing to lose. That described her. That was why he couldn't bring Bigfoot along.

Battle read the diary without talking. Jack waited to answer questions, but she never asked. He closed his eyes knowing he had a very long drive ahead, and must have drifted off because the next thing he knew Battle was kicking the bottom of his foot.

"Coffee's on the stove, milk's in the refrigerator, sugar and spoons on the counter. I rinsed out some paper Hardees cups with lids. They'll have to do. Let's get going."

It was three in the morning. Jack said, "Good morning back at you." He rose and filled a coffee-stained paper cup with fresh black coffee, fitted the lid on, and noticed it had lipstick on it. *Oh well.*

Battle was stuffing a gun bag with extra ammo and gear. On top of this she put a wicked hunting knife that was bigger than a Marine KaBar and smaller than a machete, but not by much.

Battle had the physique of a basketball player, tall, not a pound of extra weight, toned, giving the impression of a tensed spring. She wore tight-fitting blue jeans, and had layered a brown wool shirt over a gray long john top. She had on sensible winter boots laced to mid-calf. She pulled a hand-tooled leather belt from the bag, threaded it through the waistband of her jeans, securing the 3-way holster that held her Glock 9mm, handcuff case, knife sheath, and double ammo pouch. She slipped the knife in the sheath, zipped the gun bag, and pulled on a loose-fitting Carhartt jacket.

"All that's missing is Arnold Schwarzenegger," Jack said.

Battle said, "Wipe the drool off your mouth, get your stuff, and let's do this."

Jack checked his Glock and put it back in its holster. He had two extra magazines of .45 caliber ammo in his coat pocket. If he needed more firepower, he had the shotgun in the car. He grabbed his coffee and was ready. They took Jack's Crown Vic, thinking that if they ran into any law enforcement obstacles, the Crown Vic looked more like an official vehicle than her Jeep. They stopped at a Shell station just outside St. Louis. Jack gassed up while Battle went inside and bought some provisions.

From there they drove five hours, covering three hundred and ninety-five miles, without talking. "Pit stop," Jack said, and took the exit to Broken Arrow in Oklahoma. They did their business, gassed up, and headed toward Interstate 44 West. On their way out of town they passed a sign that said, "Leaving Broken Arrow" and "Mayor Craig Thurmond." Underneath was another sign depicting locked seat belts. An occupied police car sat off the road near the sign. On the other side of the underpass, an Oklahoma State Police vehicle was stationed.

"Friendly little place," Jack said.

Battle finally broke her silence. "You always talk this much?"

Jack laughed out loud. "You always this quiet?"

"When I'm thinking. Deciding," she said.

Jack said nothing.

"I admit when I agreed to come on this trip I was hoping to gut the bastard's carcass and put his head on my wall."

Jack said, "And yet you seem so laid-back."

She finally grinned. "You're not going to get in my way, are you?"

"No," Jack said.

"Liar," Battle said. "I'll play by the rules if Coyote does. He seems to be proud of that stupid name."

"Don't underestimate him, Lieutenant Battle. He got that name for a reason," Jack said and told her about the cases in Florida, Texas, and Louisiana. The body count was nearing two hundred and fifty innocent souls, two of them being law enforcement, and one a nun.

With the exception of gas stops, it was silent in the car for the next several hours until they saw the exit for Amarillo. They'd been on the road ten hours. Jack said, "We need gas again. I saw a sign for a Hyatt near the interstate if you want to stop and get some rest?"

"I want to push on. I'll drive for a while, and you can rest. You can spell me again when we get close," Battle said.

"I've been up a while. You can drive after we get gas." Jack took the exit. "It's at least another ten or eleven hours to Bisbee. I doubt he's driving straight through." Jack didn't believe that when he said it. He believed Coyote was insane. He probably didn't need sleep. He probably thrived on deprivation and hate.

"Let's take turns, Jack," she said. "When we get to Bisbee, we'll see what's what. If he's there, we don't want to miss our chance. If he's not, we can watch for him. Maybe set a Coyote trap." She had said it without mirth.

Jack said, "Why don't I go ahead and drive for the next few hours, and you get some sleep and not think about ways to kill this guy. I don't need you half-alert when we get there. Emotions will screw you up. I know."

"I can't do that," she said. "But I'll try to sleep for a bit."

Jack found a gas station. He gassed up and went inside. He bought several bottles of Gatorade, water, and two black coffees. The sausage biscuits in the display case were cold, but he bought six. They needed to eat something besides power bars and candy.

When he came back to the car, Battle's seat was leaned back, her eyes were closed, and she was snoring like a wooly mammoth. The diary was in her lap. He put the bag of biscuits and Gatorade on the back floorboard and the coffees in the front holder. She needed sleep.

* * * *

While Jack was pumping gas, Coyote passed the exit to Amarillo and continued west. He'd stopped an hour earlier, gassed up, and bought another notebook. He would have preferred a spiral-bound one, but beggars can't be choosers. He'd sat in the Taco Bell attached to the gas station and ate half a dozen tacos. He'd bought four burritos to go and an extra-large coffee. The food was pretty good. With some real food in his stomach, he seemed to be thinking clearer. His anger had abated. Best of all, he had a plan.

He would talk with his source in Bisbee. He needed to be sure Miles would never talk to Murphy or anyone else about their project. He shouldn't have to worry; after all, Miles was partly to blame for all of this and complicit in the first killing. He was the one who had located the illegal who killed Coyote's wife and daughter. And Miles was complicit in destroying evidence that would have put all three of them, Coyote, Hank, and Miles, away for life. Because Miles was a coward, afraid of being discovered as corrupt, he agreed to feed Coyote whatever information he needed for his missions. Including locating and rerouting the drivers to meet him.

He'd felt nothing for the killing of Hank Brown, his ex-partner. The traitor was a true disappointment. Both Coyote and Miles had tried to warn Hank that he was going down a dark path, but greed and a misguided sense of "freedom for all" had consumed the man. Now Cody and Miles were the two left standing from the original trio.

The three of them had graduated together from FLETC, the Federal Law Enforcement Training Center, and worked for Border Patrol. Hank and Cody patrolled the border while Miles, ever the social climber, worked his way up the ladder to an inside job. Miles never wanted to get his hands dirty. He preferred to stay in an office far from the action, play at the intelligence game. Coyote had known guys like this in the Army. Sometimes their intelligence was dead on, sometimes it led troops into an ambush. Intelligence was an oxymoron. Maybe what he was doing now wasn't any more intelligent or sane. He knew he'd never stop the influx of illegal immigrants. It was like trying to empty the ocean with a spoon.

Coyote hadn't been home for—was it four years now? The last time he'd seen Emma, he was on his way to work with Hank. He and Emma had been fighting all day over something. Money mostly. She had spent too much having her hair colored and cut. He cut his own hair and thought spending money just to put some streaks in her hair was crazy, and he told her so. He hadn't told her how pretty she was. He hadn't told her he loved her. She had kissed him anyway and told him to be safe.

He'd thought about that many times over the years. Replayed every word, every look, every angry gesture—mostly on his part. He remembered thinking at her graveside that he would have spent all their savings just to take the hurtful words back. He remembered thinking what an odd thought it was to be standing beside the graves of his wife and his little girl thinking about a fight, an argument, over money. He remembered feeling much like he felt every time he thought of it. Little. Low. Angry. Disappointed. Dying inside and wishing he could magically make it different. But he couldn't. He had said what he'd said, she had kissed him anyway, and he'd left for work that night, never to see them alive again.

He wasn't a good husband. He wasn't a good father. He wasn't even a good man. His family was dead because of him. Dead because he couldn't protect them. The harsh words he'd said to his wife sat on his heart like a hot stone. He gripped the steering wheel tighter and pushed his feelings aside.

On Interstate 40 he saw a sign declaring "Santa Rosa, One Mile." He took the cloverleaf and hit Route 66 heading west. He had been through here hundreds of times over the years, and it had changed little in the four years he was gone.

He passed up the Best Western and the LaQuinta Inn where he and Emma and Olivia would stay when they could afford it. His daughter, Olivia, would just about live in the pool at the LaQuinta. He had teased her that if she stayed in any longer she'd grow gills and a tail.

Coming up on his right was a wide flat adobe building that resembled the old mud huts people lived in hundreds of years ago. This one had been fitted with central heating and air, but he remembered the bar really smelled like a bar—cigar smoke, stale puke, and even staler patrons. He needed to make two stops before Bisbee.

He pulled into the dirt lot of the Pecos Bar and Grocery. They carried Foster's beer. The thermostat on the dash read forty-eight degrees. He shucked his coat, put his Stetson on, and went inside. Two drunks and a bartender. The bartender must have recognized him when he came in the door. Two six-packs of cold Foster's were sitting on top of the bar.

"You back to stay?" the bartender asked.

Coyote paid without answering.

"I was real sorry to hear about your family," the bartender called after him as he left the bar.

Coyote took a deep breath and shoved the bartender's condolence in the mental box. He wasn't worried the bartender had recognized him. This wasn't the kind of place that talked to the cops. It was the kind of place you went to get out of the world.

Santa Rosa was just a spot in the road with two traffic lights. Just before the second traffic light, he stopped at a Phillips 66 gas station and topped the tank off.

Chapter 44

Battle's cell phone trilled, jerking her awake. She looked at the phone and held the screen so Jack could see. "Should I answer?"

"Let it ring twice. If they hang up, they should call back. That's when you answer."

"Your partner?"

"It should be."

The phone rang twice and stopped.

"You told him you'd be with me. Did you tell him where we're going?"

Before Jack could answer, his own cell phone rang. He pulled it from his pocket. It was Toomey. He punched a button to end the call, and it rang again. The screen said "ICE QUEEN" this time. He punched the button to end that call as well and turned his ringer off.

"I gave your number to my researcher, too," Jack said to Battle. "Her name is Angelina Garcia. Find my contacts and put Bigfoot's and Angelina's numbers in your phone so you'll answer."

"You give my number to your wife, too?" she asked.

"My ex-wife actually. We live together and—well, it's complicated. She'll call Bigfoot if she needs something."

"Bigfoot? Is that what you call your partner?"

"That's complicated too."

"What's your nickname for me?" Battle persisted.

"You've said two words this whole trip and now you want my life story?" Jack said.

Battle's demeanor changed. She crossed her arms and stared out the side window. Jack was saved from further discussion when her phone rang again. It was the Evansville number. She put the phone on speaker and said, "Who's this?"

"Yeti," came the response.

"What do you want, Yeti?"

"I'm here," Jack said before Battle could make another sarcastic remark.

"Listen, pod'na. The kettle is boiling here. DD is cranked up on high, and I don't think the lid will stay on the pot much longer."

"I think we're safe to talk, Bigfoot."

"Okay. Sanchez called. A St. Louis patrolman found Libby working the street by the warehouse where she was supposedly afraid the killer would find her. She was trying to score drugs. They have her in detox at the same hospital Kim's in. She confessed to bashing Kim in the head with an iron and stabbing her in the neck. She even cut herself to make it look like there was a struggle. We can rule Cody out of Kim's attack. You still doing this?" Liddell asked, and Jack could hear the concern in his voice.

The truth was, Jack was concerned too. *But in for a penny, in for a pound.* "We'll be in Arizona by nightfall. If we don't catch this guy, you'll be needing a new partner to carry you, Bigfoot."

"You want me to call Katie?"

"Not yet. She'll call you if she gets worried. She knows I'm working, and I don't always call."

"She doesn't know you're with another woman on your way to Arizona to confront a psychotic mass murderer though. Your call, pod'na," Liddell said. "You there, Lieutenant?"

"No. I'm running alongside the car to give you two some privacy," she said.

"Take care of him, Lieutenant."

She punched a button and hung up.

"I had a partner like that once," she said to Jack.

"What happened? You get promoted?"

"Nah. Divorced. He was my supervisor, and you know how that goes. I'll never marry another cop. I have enough on my plate taking care of myself. I don't have the energy or desire to stroke some man's ego."

"Is that your subtle way of telling me you're single and available?"

She laughed for the first time since Jack had known her. "In your dreams, Murphy."

"Are you rested enough to take over driving?" Jack asked.

"Yeah. My butt has gone to sleep, but I'm awake. I need to stretch my legs a little."

Jack found a clump of scrub trees and pulled off on the dirt shoulder. They got out and stretched. It was a little warmer than Indiana or Missouri, but still cold enough to wear a jacket.

"How far?" Battle asked.

"We'll run out of gas again before we get to Las Cruces, New Mexico. Maybe we can get something to eat at our next stop. It's about another nine hours to Bisbee according to the GPS on my phone."

"Do you have the address of the cemetery?" she asked.

"Yes. Angelina texted it to me. We'll put it in the GPS when we get to Bisbee, but I think we should ask directions somewhere in town to see how they are with strangers. For all we know, Coyote is a local hero."

Battle punched some icons on her cell phone and said, "Bisbee. Five thousand people, a couple of silver mines, a rock quarry, and maybe electricity and indoor plumbing."

"Sounds like a good place to retire," Jack said.

"Yeah. I'll bet the cost of living will save me enough to buy a nice coffin."

"Maybe I should drive?"

"Give me the damn keys," she said.

They got back on the road. Jack put his seat back and fell asleep. He slept through a stop in Las Cruces, where she gassed up again, and slept on until she entered Bisbee proper. They'd been on the road an entire day.

She nudged him awake.

"You drool," Battle said.

"Good morning to you too," Jack said and wiped at his mouth with the back of his hand.

"On the way back home, I'll tie a towel around your neck," Battle continued.

"You can stop now," Jack said. She was starting to sound like Bigfoot.

Battle braked the car hard enough to skid.

"I didn't mean that literally, Battle," Jack said, using her name for the first time.

"I stopped because we're a block from the cemetery."

Jack saw the arched iron gates down the street. One side stood open.

"Your friend Angelina called while you slept, princess," she said. "There's a third guy involved with Coyote."

"What did she say?" Jack asked.

"There was Hank, Cody, and a guy named Miles that were suspects in the murder case. Miles wasn't in the field. They never proved he was present when the illegal was killed, but he had a hand in it somehow. He wasn't forced to resign. He was promoted. She said his name is Miles Lyman. He works in their intelligence unit."

"Is he here?" Jack asked.

"That's where we're going after we check the cemetery," she said.

* * * *

Jack took over driving. They didn't see any activity around or in the cemetery, but it was two o'clock in the morning. Nothing would be going on. He cruised by Miles Lyman's house to see where it was and to see if Coyote might stop there to say hello to his old friend. Maybe spend the night.

"We passed this street on our way to the cemetery," Battle said.

Miles Lyman lived on the other side of town and just outside the city limits. The house was a one-story adobe with arched walkways and beautifully landscaped bare soil. A pair of ten-foot-tall yucca plants stood on each side of the arched front. Lyman's house sat on several acres of scrub land, and behind it was a view of the mountains with the moon above like it was dotting an *i*.

"Let's go back to the cemetery," Jack said. "I don't want to talk to Lyman yet, or even let him know we are here. Coyote's had more than enough time to get here. Maybe I was wrong."

"You're not wrong," Battle said. "You're driving."

Jack headed back to the cemetery.

* * * *

As soon as the Crown Vic's taillights were in the distance, the Dodge Dart pulled out of The Inn at Castle Rock. He'd stopped there to collect his thoughts, and the best way to do that was to write in his new notebook. Luckily, he saw the Crown Vic drive by heading north—toward Miles Lyman's residence. Ten minutes later it came back south. He couldn't see who was in the car, but it was Murphy's car. Murphy was here. But he was alone unless he was with the big partner of his.

Murphy didn't have time to talk to Miles, but that didn't mean he hadn't called him. Or maybe Miles was coming to meet them. It was time to pay a visit to his old friend.

Chapter 45

Coyote had driven past Lyman's house. The car he'd seen heading into town was a Crown Vic with Indiana plates. Murphy had somehow put it together, and now he was here. Maybe that was good. It had all begun here. It should end here.

He sat on an adjacent block and watched Lyman's house between two houses on this block. He didn't want to sit too long. He'd lived here and knew how alert people were. It was one of the things he missed about home. People out East had gotten complacent. That's why there were so many murders there as opposed to here.

He saw the garage door coming up at Lyman's place. Lyman had a two-car garage, from what he remembered, and lived alone. Lyman was a neat freak. The extra car bay would be empty. He was right. The bay in front of him was empty and Lyman's car, a Lexus SUV, was in the other bay. Lyman was in the process of getting into the SUV when Coyote pulled in next to him.

"Hello, Miles," Coyote said.

"What the hell are you doing at my house, Cody Coyote?" Lyman asked. He was grinning. It was an old joke between them.

Lyman was taller than Coyote but not by much. He was heavier than when Coyote had last seen him. His face was puffy like an alcoholic, which wasn't surprising. Betraying your country could do that to a man. Betraying Coyote would do worse.

"I saw you had a cop here," Coyote said.

Lyman's hands went into his jean pockets for his keys.

"I was on my way to the store. I just got up. No one's been here, Cody."

"Liquor stores open this time of morning? I don't remember that. Things must have really changed," Coyote said.

"The world has moved on, man. Things are different everywhere. If you don't mind me saying it, 'cause we're friends, you should move on too. You've made your point. You've evened the score."

Coyote said nothing.

Lyman shifted from foot to foot and stopped. "I asked you why you came to my house? If I'm seen with you, it can spell real trouble for you and me both, Cody."

"What did you tell that cop from Indiana?" Coyote asked in an even tone. "He was here. I saw him leaving."

Lyman just stood, hands in pockets, silent.

"You betrayed me once, Miles, and I had to resign. You're part of the reason for what I'm doing now. You helped create this situation. Tell me the truth about the detective, and I'll leave."

"Honest to God, Cody. No cop from Indiana or anywhere else has been here. And I haven't talked to anyone on the phone about you. As far as most people are concerned, I don't know you anymore. I guess I don't know you anymore. You've become someone else. Please—friend to friend—you've got to stop this. There's already talk at the office that Homeland Security is sniffing around for a mole."

"Asking about me?" Coyote asked.

"No. No. I swear... I don't know... Maybe." He took the keys from his pocket. "Maybe they're asking about me. No one's coming to me directly, but I'm hearing things. You know how it is."

Coyote did know. Rumors were like breathing to cops. Most were bullshit, but there was always a tad of truth that started them. He'd been doing this for a while. Of course DHS was sniffing around. Soon they would be sniffing around Miles if they weren't already.

Lyman must have come to the same conclusion. His hands came out of his pockets, and he grabbed at Coyote and caught part of his jacket. Coyote slammed the heel of his hand under Lyman's chin, popping his head backward, and with his other hand struck Lyman in the throat.

Lyman staggered back, holding his throat and trying to breathe. Coyote struck him in the nose with the heel of his hand and then slapped his palms against Lyman's ears with all his strength. Lyman's eyes bulged, and his hands came up to protect his face, but Coyote brought his left palm into the side of Lyman's throat. The blow shut off the flow of blood from the heart to the brain, and Lyman's legs turned to rubber and he went down to his knees.

Coyote stepped behind him, drew the bayonet and, using both hands, shoved it through the top of Lyman's skull.

Coyote stood on Lyman's throat, wrenched the bayonet loose, and wiped the blade clean on Lyman's face and shirt collar. He felt good.

He patted Lyman's clothes down and found his cell phone. He took Lyman's 9mm semi-automatic handgun from the hand-tooled belt holster Lyman had been so proud of. The coward had never used the gun on anything but targets, but he wanted people to think he was John Wayne. Coyote shoved the gun in the back of his own jeans.

The door to the SUV was still open, and Coyote hit the garage remote to open the door. He got in the Dart and backed into the driveway. Lyman's body was visible next to the open door of the SUV. That was good.

Coyote punched in the number for the Bisbee Police dispatcher. The call was answered, "Bisbee Police Department. What is your emergency?"

"A guy's been shot here. I think the gunman is still in the garage. Hurry." Coyote hung up. He knew once the dispatcher found the address, the whole of the Bisbee Police Department would respond. He pitched the cell phone in the driveway and backed onto the street.

On the way to the Evergreen Cemetery where his wife and daughter were buried, he was passed by two police cruisers traveling at a high rate of speed. They didn't give his car a second look; after all, the gunman was still in the garage.

Now he knew for sure that Murphy had found his journal and had figured out where he was going. Lyman hadn't lied about not getting a visit from Murphy. It didn't matter. Coyote was relaxed. He didn't even need the damn journal anymore. It was fitting it would end where it began. Evergreen Cemetery. He could finally be at peace. See his family one more time.

Chapter 46

Jack drove past the cemetery and around its perimeter. Evergreen Cemetery wasn't large, it was monstrous. The gates to the cemetery entrance were a twelve-foot-tall arch made of wrought-iron bars. A five-foot wall of stacked quarry stones surrounded the cemetery as far as the eye could see. Jack had spotted two entrances, a main entrance and one in the very back that was used by workers. The grounds were so spacious it would be impossible to watch both entrances. They'd have to find Coté's wife's and daughter's graves.

Jack drove around the outside perimeter of the cemetery again and slowed about a hundred feet from the main entrance on Old Douglas Street. He parked between two cars that resembled the Crown Vic. He backed up against the front bumper of the car behind to hide the Indiana plates.

"I think we should do another drive-by of this Lyman guy's house," Battle said.

"It's early yet."

"Think about it, Jack. Coyote killed an ex-Border Patrol officer in St. Louis. His ex-partner. What if some of the drivers in the other states were ex-law enforcement? Maybe that's why he's targeting certain trucks? Maybe he's killing dirty cops? Regardless, we need to talk to Lyman. We're just assuming he's giving information to Coyote. Maybe he's not? Maybe he's a target?"

"And maybe he's working with Coyote, and when he asks why we're there, we just say we drove from St. Louis to see how he's doing? We can't go after him until we get Coyote, and I don't want to scare Coyote off."

"So, let me go in alone. I promise he won't warn anyone," she said.

Jack said, "You don't have any authority here at all. I'm on shaky ground as far as jurisdiction, but I lie better than you. We're not talking to Lyman yet, and that's that."

"We stay here and watch the cemetery."

It was still dark out. Battle checked her phone. "The sun comes up here at about seven thirty. That's a couple of hours. You watch, I'm going to try and shut my eyes if you quit talking me into a coma."

Jack said nothing. She was obviously pissed off, but at least she'd stopped arguing. In Arizona it was cold at night and extremely hot during the day. The temperature since they arrived had already risen twenty or more degrees. It was hot enough Jack had to open the windows. They sat quietly, neither one wanting to talk. What was the point. Either Coyote was there, or he wasn't and Jack had wasted a career on a hunch.

Jack was just about to start the car and turn the air conditioning on when a huge truck came rumbling down the street and its headlights washed over the inside of the Crown Vic. Battle ducked down, but it was too late to hide from anyone. The truck didn't slow as it passed them and pulled into the cemetery through the front gates. Another truck came from the same direction and pulled into the cemetery following the first one.

Jack saw the first one was a vault truck. The kind that carried the concrete container to hold the casket in the ground. The second truck was pulling a trailer with a back hoe. They drove several hundred feet and pulled off to the side. Two men got out of the vault truck and helped a third man unload the backhoe.

"Another death in paradise," Battle said. "I've never seen a grave being dug. Thank you for giving me the opportunity to be doing this instead of trying to find Coyote."

The backhoe operator started the diesel engine and began excavating a fresh grave. None of them had seemed to notice the Crown Vic.

"Nothing's moving here except the grave diggers," Battle said.

"And what are you going to do at Lyman's?"

"You don't trust me?"

"No. I don't trust you. You're obsessed with taking Coyote out. I can understand that, and I want him as bad as you do. He killed a cop and a nun, and he tried to kill a nine-year-old boy. Twice. But he needs to go to prison for the rest of his miserable life."

"There's a lot of desert around here, Jack. A piece of scum like him won't be missed," Battle said.

"And what if he kills one of us?"

"You don't want your ex to be an ex-widow?" Battle said.

"You're not helping, Lieutenant."

"Why did you bring me along if we're after different outcomes? You want to bring him to justice. I want to bring him to Jesus. My way is cheaper and more permanent."

"I brought you along because you're committed to catching this guy just as much as I am. We both are hanging our asses out here, but I'm not going to throw my life away. You can either work with me or I can take you to the bus station and buy you a one-way ticket back to St. Louis. Your choice."

Battle crossed her arms and watched out the side window. Jack concentrated on the cemetery. The only movement came from the crew.

Headlights suddenly illuminated the inside of the car, and Jack saw a police car had come down the street and was sitting twenty feet away. Its bar lights came on, and the takedown lights fixed on Jack and Battle.

Jack adjusted the Glock .45 on his belt. It had been digging into his side for hours. "I'll do the talking," Jack said.

"Whatever," Battle said, but she was taking her badge case out of her pocket.

The police car's door opened, and the officer approached the Crown Vic. The officer stopped at the rear of their car and leaned down, shining his flashlight on their Indiana license plate.

The policeman was short and heavyset with jowls partially covered by a gunslinger mustache of the kind sported by Kurt Russell in the movie *Tombstone*. His forehead was heavily lined under a full head of hair. He stepped up to the driver's window and shined the light on Jack first and then Battle.

Jack kept his hands on the steering wheel in plain sight and was glad to see that Battle was doing the same with her hands on the front dash. Jack decided saying nothing was his best move.

The officer said, "Got a call from those men over there." He hitched a thumb toward the vault truck. "They said you've been sitting outside the cemetery for a while. Can I ask what your business is?"

Battle said, "You can ask."

"I'm a federal officer, and we're here on an investigation, officer," Jack said quickly. The officer's name tag read: SHEP. No last name or initial. "My badge case is in my pocket, Officer Shep."

"Why don't you step out of the car and show me?" To Battle he said, "You in on this *investigation* with him, hon?"

Before Battle could get them both arrested, Jack said, "Lieutenant Battle is with the Missouri Highway Patrol. I'm a Homicide detective with the Evansville Police Department in Indiana, but we're part of a federal task force. We're after a very dangerous individual, and our investigation has led us here to Bisbee."

"Is that right?" Shep said. "Feds. We don't get a lot of you folk through here unless you're investigating one of us for violating someone's civil rights. Why don't you both step out of the car where I can see you. You come on around to this side, hon."

Jack pulled the door latch and muttered to Battle, "We're not supposed to be here, remember." He hoped she would not want Officer Shep calling Major Maddox and getting her the next step up from suspended.

Jack got out, keeping his hands in Shep's sight. Shep had stepped back, hand on the butt of his revolver, eyes on Jack and Battle. Battle kept her hands at waist level and a little out to her sides and walked around the front of the car. They stood side by side.

"You can get your FBI badges out now, but be slow."

Jack noticed Shep still had the retaining strap snapped on the holster. Shep saw Jack checking out his gun. He unsnapped the strap and drew the big revolver halfway from the holster.

"You like my gun?" Shep asked.

"Colt .45. You loaded with Hydra-Shoks?" Jack asked.

"Federal HSTs. More stopping power. They open up like a flower," Shep said.

"My ID is inside my jacket," Jack said. He opened his jacket with one hand and used a finger and thumb to pull out the black badge case. He opened it and revealed his badge on one side, his police credentials with photo on the other.

Shep said, "I thought you was FBI. This shows you're just a policeman from Indiana."

"This is a new task force," Jack said. "We don't get sworn in and get badges until Friday. This came up, and they kidnapped me, so to speak."

Shep let out a hoot. "I can tell you got an answer for everything, but you're a smartass just like a cop. I guess you are who you say." Shep holstered. "Never be too careful. Why don't you show me yours, hon, just for good measure?"

"I will if you stop calling me hon," she said, and to Jack's relief Shep just chuckled.

"I assume since you didn't notify the Bisbee Police Department of your presence, or about this *dangerous individual,* that you prefer to do this alone. I can respect that, but I can't let you go shooting up my town. I can see you're both armed."

"We won't shoot up your town, Officer Shep," Jack said.

"This isn't the Old West, after all," Battle added and showed her police credentials.

"You're Missouri Highway Patrol?" Shep asked her.

"Yup," Battle answered.

"Shep is short for Shepard. I'm chief here. I always do the early morning rounds. You should be glad you got me instead of Buck."

"Buck?" Battle asked, and Jack wished she would just shut up.

"Buck Rogers. He's probably running radar somewhere," Shep said.

Battle snickered and said, "Good old Buck."

Chief Shepard said, "You said you're on a federal task force. I suppose you haven't got paperwork to support that and you don't want me calling your people to verify it?"

"You must be a mind reader, Shep," Battle said. "We're not supposed to be here, but we've got a hot lead on our guy, and believe me you don't want him in your town. If you help us, and I mean by staying out of our way unless we need you, we'll give you the credit for the takedown. Honest Injun."

Instead of being insulted, Shep said, "I respect plainspoken. I'll tell you what—by that I mean you don't call the shots here—Feds or not. But since you're being up front with me, I won't spoil what you've got working here. In return, I insist that you give me a phone number where I can reach you, and I'll give you my personal number. You keep in touch with me and don't go shooting anyone or anything. Agreed?"

"Agreed," Jack said.

Battle said, "Sounds like a plan. But can you keep Buck Rogers out of our way too?"

"Done," Shep said and took a business card from his pocket.

They exchanged information and Jack said, "Federal HSTs huh? I'll have to check them out. I still carry the Hydra-Shoks."

Battle said, "If I can interrupt you boys, we're supposed to be watching and not being watched."

Jack thanked the chief of police and they got back in their cars. The chief drove past and waved at the gravediggers. When he was out of eyesight, the gravediggers gave the chief the finger.

"I'll be right back, hon," Jack said and was out of the car again, crossed the street, and walked to the vault truck where the three men were sitting drinking coffee or something from a thermos.

"Sorry about that, mister," the biggest guy in the crew said.

"I didn't think you'd paid any attention. Listen we're working with the chief on something, and I hope you can help us," Jack said.

"I didn't know Shep had two new officers. What can we do? We're pretty busy getting ready for old Randy's funeral."

"Have you seen any other car in the last couple of hours?" Jack asked, not wanting to get into a discussion about Randy.

"We just got here," the man said. "But you're the first car with out-of-state plates that we've seen. We saw you driving around the back. No one's in the cemetery, if that's what you mean."

"Shep would like for you to keep an eye out for any stranger coming in here," Jack lied. "If you see someone, you can call him. We may or may not be here."

"What's going on?" the man asked, and the other two stopped slurping coffee.

"Shep said he'd tell you later. Just act normal," Jack said.

"Got it. Normal. You guys hear that? Just be normal assholes."

That earned a round of chuckles, and Jack went back to Battle and got in the car.

"Did you ask them what kind of shovels they use? Maybe compare brands," Battle asked.

"It's called personality. Soft persuasion. You should try it sometime," Jack said.

"He started it. Hon my ass."

Chapter 47

Jack heard more than one police siren in the distance. An ambulance and maybe a police car or two. A Fire Rescue Squad blew past them headed toward town. The sounds were too far away and it was still too dark for him to see the smoke from a fire.

Battle's .45 was in her hand, the muzzle pointed down.

"Don't shoot my car," Jack warned her.

"Shut up, Murphy," she said. "I know what I'm doing. You should be following the sirens."

"The chief said he'd call us," Jack said.

"And you believed him?"

"No, but until we know different, I'm betting Coyote will come here. He killed an old woman in Evansville to distract us. I'm not going to make that mistake again."

Battle said, "Get out of the car, Jack."

"Are you going to shoot me? Do you see what is happening to you? Are you really going down that road?" Jack said in a calm voice.

"I will if I have to. I'm taking this guy down. No one else. No one! Now get out of the car or so help me..."

A car pulled slowly past them, and the driver rolled the passenger window down, checking them out, pointing something at them.

"Coyote," Jack said just as his window exploded.

Jack's ears were still ringing, and his right ear felt on fire. Battle had her 9mm pointed past his face out the window. He grabbed Battle's gun hand and slammed a fist into her nose, making her release the gun. Her gun hit the floor, and Jack slammed the gas down. The Crown Vic rocketed forward, shearing off the left quarter panel of the car in front of them as he swerved into the street.

Battle was leaned forward. Blood was gushing from her nose, her hands scrabbling for her gun.

Jack kept Coyote's car in sight and backhanded Battle across the forehead, knocking her back in the seat. "You're going to get us killed."

Battle put bloody hands on the dash, trying to steady herself while Jack swerved back and forth to keep her off balance while trying to keep up with the car ahead. Coyote was leaving them behind but suddenly turned in to the cemetery entrance.

Jack veered into the entrance a hundred yards behind Coyote and closing the distance.

"He's getting away," Battle said and wiped at her face with the back of her coat sleeve. "Damn you, Murphy."

"He's not getting away," Jack said. "There's two ways in or out of here, and he's not heading toward the back entrance. Just keep an eye on which way he turns." Jack hit pothole after teeth-jarring pothole.

Coyote was two hundred yards ahead and pulling away fast. His car disappeared in a copse of trees at the same time Jack's right front wheel hit a deep pothole and the car slewed sideways down the gravel and into a large gravestone.

The Crown Vic's back wheels were off the ground and spinning. Battle was out and running with the Bowie knife in her hand. Jack's teeth and jaw hurt. He could feel something running down his chin. He'd bitten his tongue.

Her 9mm was on his side of the car. He picked it up and went after Battle. She reached the trees first and stopped to search for a target. She was wide open, too angry and caught up in the moment to care about caution. Jack was crouched low when the first shot rang out.

Battle's hand went to her stomach, and she turned slowly toward Jack with a curious look on her face. Her hand came away from her stomach and a flower of red that bloomed on her shirt. Her mouth moved but nothing came out. She crumpled to the ground.

Jack didn't wait for Coyote to take a second shot. He was too far away to help Battle. He dove for the ground and rolled behind a headstone. It was thick but not tall. Another shot rang out, and he saw the dirt fly up two feet to his right. He needed better cover. He spotted a statue of the Virgin Mary marking a grave ten feet away to his left. He rolled toward it. He felt the bullet rip into his foot before he heard the shot. He continued to roll until he was behind the statuary and sat up against its side with his legs drawn up. He still had his gun in his hand, but he was dazed. His foot didn't hurt so much as it burned like a hot poker was piercing it. He saw a perfectly round hole in the top of the shoe. He risked a peek around the side. Battle still wasn't moving. If she wasn't dead, she soon would be. Him too.

He had been near death before and a strange thing happens. Your mind says, "You're going to die," but a calmness comes over you. It came over him now. Time slowed down. He could see, hear, feel, taste everything all at once. Fight or flight panic left his body. He was going to kill Coyote and end this.

He peeked around the statue's side and yelled, "It's over, Cody. Everyone knows who you are. What you did. We know about your wife and daughter. We know everything, and no matter where you go you'll be caught. Prison isn't a good place for someone like you. Dead is better. Let's do this man to man. See which of us is better."

"Of course I'm better, Murphy. I have the angels on my side. I am my country. Everything I do I've done for my family and my country. My country took everything from me, but I still love it more than life itself."

"I'm going to stand up and meet you, face-to-face," Jack said. "If you're a coward, you'll shoot me. If you're the patriot you say you are, you'll face me like a man. My gun is holstered," he lied. "Let's see who's faster. Let God judge the loser."

"A gunfight," Coyote mused. "Like at the O.K. Corral. You know there were no good guys or bad guys in that fight. Just men who hated each other. Like us, in a way. Go on. Finish your little speech."

"Yeah. Like the O.K. Corral. I hear your brothers-in-arms call you Coyote. To me a coyote is a sneaky animal that can't be trusted. Is that why they called you that?"

"You're trying to make me mad. Sorry. I had hoped I wouldn't have to kill you, Murphy. You remind me of me in the old days."

"You're nothing like me. Nothing! You're psychotic. A killer of women and children. A diseased animal that needs to be put down."

"That's good, Murphy. I know I shot you at least one time. I guess you were surprised that I used a gun when I seem to favor my bayonet. Wherever I hit you won't hurt for a bit, but when it does, it'll hurt like hell. I'll tell you something. I prefer my bayonet, but I am very proficient with a gun."

"Sure you are," Jack said under his breath.

"I'll take your challenge, Murphy. Stand where I can see you with your weapon holstered. I'll step out with mine holstered—well, stuck in my belt. It's not my gun, you see. As they say in the movies, let's get it on."

Jack listened for sirens, hoping the gravediggers had called the chief, but there was nothing. It didn't matter. Battle was down and Coyote had shot him. That had to be answered.

Jack got to his knees and to his feet. He had to hop to the side, into the open, and stood with his arm stretched to the side, gun in hand. He slowly holstered the .45, took his jacket off, and dropped it to the ground.

Coyote stepped out of the trees and into the open beside Battle's body and came forward a few paces. Jack could see the butt of a handgun sticking out of the waistband of Coyote's jeans. It was light enough Jack could see Coyote's eyes were blue, and see the wrinkles that ran like sunrays from the corners of them. He could see Coyote's expression wasn't one of stress but of complete relaxation. He could smell the dry grass and the dirt from a fresh grave. He heard the backhoe revving its engine. He saw the body behind Coyote move.

Coyote held his left hand in front of his waist, his eyes never leaving Jack's. He said, "You first."

Jack never drew. A hole opened in Coyote's throat where Battle had plunged the Bowie knife in the back of his neck. The blade exited and came down again between his shoulders, buried deep. Coyote dropped the gun. The blade came down a third time, and Coyote dropped to his knees. His eyes didn't show shock. They were clear, unafraid. Battle held Coyote's head with one hand and drove the knife downward into the nexus of his neck and shoulder. The blade all but disappeared. She let go of the knife, and Coyote fell face-forward on the brittle grass.

In the distance, the sound of sirens broke the stillness.

Chapter 48

"I should have known," Bisbee Chief of Police Shepard said to Jack.

Jack sat in the back of an ambulance having his foot tended to. The bullet had punched a clean hole through his shoe and his foot, but nothing seemed to be broken. Coyote was right about it not hurting right away. Even with meds on board, it hurt like shit now.

Battle was taken by Life Flight to Sierra Vista Regional Medical Center. According to Jack's medic, this was a new 100-bed facility and she would get the best of care. By helicopter it was about ten minutes west of the cemetery. Jack hoped it had a mental facility, too.

The 9mm bullet had struck her squarely in the stomach and exited through her back, leaving a small hole going in and coming out. The initial trauma had knocked her down, but she had rallied long enough to get up and do what she had vowed to do.

Coyote was still where he'd dropped to the ground. Bisbee City Police, Cochise County deputies, and Arizona Highway Patrol were crawling all over the scene. Jack told them all he would only give his statement to Chief Shepard of the Bisbee Police Department. The other agencies hadn't liked his attitude, but they respected his wishes.

"Did you know he'd be armed?" Shep asked.

"Bayonet," Jack said. "He always used a bayonet before."

"The gun belonged to Miles Lyman," Shep said. "He's with Department of..."

Jack said, "Homeland Security. I know. Is that where all the sirens were headed earlier?"

"He stabbed Lyman and took his gun," Shepard said. "He used Lyman's phone to call in a murder. We found the phone in the yard. I guess he came here while we were there. Pretty slick."

"He fooled me like that yesterday," Jack said. "Guess he thought it would work twice."

"Well," Shepard said, "he isn't fooling anyone now."

"I guess not," Jack said and felt his strength draining. The adrenaline dump was gone. Now he had to deal with the consequences of what it did to his body and mind.

Shepard persisted in asking questions. "If you knew he was going after Lyman, why didn't you say something to me?"

It was difficult to think. He took a breath, let it out, and said, "We didn't know he was going to kill Lyman. Coyote accidentally left his journal at the last murder scene I had in Evansville. He killed a nun and a cop." He didn't mention the boy, Joe. "I thought he was headed here to visit his wife's and daughter's graves. He makes mention of a 'source' that was helping him by giving him information. I put two and two together, Chief. Lyman was probably his partner. And before you ask, no you can't have the journal. It's evidence in my case in Evansville."

"I read about that case," Shepard said. "You made national news."

"There's more than my case in Evansville," Jack said. "That's why Lieutenant Battle was with me. She lost people too. He's killed hundreds that we are aware of right now."

"Shit," Shepard said. "You hear that, Rodney?" he asked the medic.

"I didn't hear anything, Shep," the medic answered.

"Good boy. I'll buy you a coffee later," Shepard said. "I'll take your statement at the police station, but I want to know one thing right here and right now."

Jack tried to put his foot down to get up and winced at the sudden pain.

Shepard continued. "You both thought he was going to kill you? Right? He'd already ambushed your partner and shot you. He was going to kill you both. Your girl's the one that stabbed him in defense of your life. Am I right, Detective Murphy?"

"Correct. He wanted to see who was the fastest draw, Chief," Jack said.

Shepard moved closer to Jack and said in a low voice, "You might not want to tell anyone else that last part. You hear? Like your girl said, this isn't the Old West. We don't have shootouts in the streets. Or in cemeteries either. Just say he was pointing that gun at you, and your partner stabbed him in self-defense. Okay?"

"We both wanted to take him alive," Jack lied. "I thought she was dead. I still don't know how she got up. I don't know why he didn't shoot her again." He didn't have to add, "I would have."

"Let me tell you something," Shepard said to Jack. He said to the medic, "And don't you repeat any of this, Rodney."

"Did you say something, Chief?" Rodney started putting equipment away.

Shepard said, "You don't know how lucky you are, Detective Murphy. His gun was empty. I guess he didn't take any of the ammo Lyman still had on his body. He was going to shoot it out with you with an unloaded gun. That's why you don't want to repeat what you just tried to tell me, and I didn't pay it no attention."

Jack asked, "When can I go and see Battle? My partner."

The medic said, "They'll be in Sierra Vista by now. Might be a while before you can talk to her, Detective."

"That girl's got grit," Shep said. "Guess I'm lucky she didn't come after me for calling her hon. I didn't mean anything by it. You tell her that for me, will you? I'm scared of knives."

"Me too. I'll tell her," Jack said. He was feeling better. The dizziness was passing, and he felt clearer. "Can we go get that statement done, Chief? You haven't called my bosses yet, have you?"

"Woman named Anna Whiteside called me. She said to tell you that you did a good job but your ass is still on fire," Shepard said. "I'm going to add my two cents to that and try to help you out. You don't have jurisdiction in Arizona, but if push comes to shove I'll swear I deputized you and you were working for the Bisbee Police Department in the apprehension of a murder suspect."

"Thanks, Chief, but I don't want you to get in hot water."

"I'm the chief here. I don't get in hot water. I'll probably get a pay raise. You helped the police department stop a mad dog killer, and no one else got killed. Except for Lyman of course. But if he's dirty like you said, I say good riddance to him."

Jack said, "I'll follow you to the police station."

"You ain't going to be driving for a while," Shepard said and pointed at Jack's bandaged foot. "Your car's beat up pretty good. Probably tore the undercarriage all to hell and back."

Murphy's Law says: "When it rains, it pisses on you."

Jack let the chief help him to the chief's car. A wrecker pulled in front of Jack's Crown Vic. Jack looked once more at the body of the man who was responsible for all this. Coyote had started a gunfight knowing he would lose. He had wanted to die, and Jack was happy to oblige.

Jack said softly, "You're with your family now, but I hope you rot in hell."

Shepard said, "What?"

"Nothing, Chief."

Chapter 49

Jack had called Katie and spent that night and the next at the hospital in Sierra Vista. Battle was pulling through, but the bullet had done a lot of damage. She remained conscious and as sarcastic and bullying as ever. It was a good sign.

Jack had let her deal with Major Maddox and her own conscience, and Chief Shepard himself had taken Jack to the airport, where he caught a flight to Evansville. Katie, Liddell, Marcie, baby Jane, and Captain Franklin had greeted him.

Franklin said, "Don't expect any favors just because you got shot, Jack." Franklin was a swell guy. Not.

Anna Whiteside and Assistant Deputy Director Toomey made a special trip to visit Jack at home and tell him what he expected. He was not only suspended from the Evansville Police Department pending an investigation and possible ling of criminal charges, but he was suspended from federal service. They wouldn't be getting sworn in on Friday. He could survive the latter half.

Toomey had delivered the bad news with a barely disguised grin on his face that said he was just mouthing political talk. The stuff supervisors had to say when you screwed up but they were on your side.

Anna had waited until Toomey left the room and sat on the sofa beside Jack. They had the room to themselves.

"I've got good news for you," she said.

"I thought getting fired from USOC was good news," Jack said, but she ignored the remark.

"We found Joe's cousin. Second cousin really, but still a relative. She's living in Florida and is a US citizen. I've already contacted her and offered to bring Joe to her, but she insisted on coming here to thank you and Liddell."

"That's great news about Joe!" Jack said. "What made you change your mind about sending him back to that hellhole he came from? Sorry, that came out wrong. I mean, thank you for helping him out. He's been through a lot."

"Don't thank me yet," Anna said. "He's applied for SIJS and has to go before a federal judge to start the process."

"You guys love your acronyms, don't you? What's SIJS?"

"Special Immigrant Juvenile Status allows children who are brought into the US illegally to stay with a lawful resident and apply for citizenship. There's a bunch of hoops, but I'm trying to help the cousin get it all done."

"That's a kind thing you're doing, Anna," Jack said, and he meant it.

"So, you don't think I'm the ICE Queen now?"

Jack didn't tell her she was still a bitch, but she was his bitch. It didn't seem the right thing to say.

"What about Lieutenant Battle?" Jack asked. He'd been in touch with Sanchez and was relieved that Kim was on the mend. She'd suffered some brain damage, but according to Sanchez it wasn't anything she didn't already have. Jack figured Sanchez would marry her, they'd have a half dozen little Sanchezes, and all of them would carry guns and drink beer.

"Major Maddox recommended Battle be fired, but it hasn't been decided yet. The governor is still getting Facebook praise for having the smarts to send his best trooper to catch Coyote. The public loves a hero. And they love the ironic nickname for the killer."

"The Roadrunner finally caught up with him," Jack said and winced at sounding like Bigfoot.

"Toomey likes her for USOC. He hinted that if she was fired, he was going to hire her for Sanchez's group."

"Sanchez will be grateful, I'm sure," Jack said, knowing just the opposite was true. A woman scorned is bad enough. A woman scorned *and* carrying a Bowie knife meant it was time to run for the hills.

"Feel up to a little trip?" Anna asked.

"Taking me to Gitmo?" Jack asked.

"You wish."

* * * *

Anna took him to the chief's conference room at the police station. Liddell and Marcie were there. Katie had taken the morning off and came over and wrapped him in a hug under his crutches. Captain Franklin, Detective Chapman, Chief Pope, and even Double Dick were there too. Double Dick wasn't scowling. In fact, he was as happy as a toad eating flies, because also present were Claudine Setera, her cameraman, attorney Dave Wires, and someone else Jack didn't know. He figured it was an attorney, because Jack couldn't see his hands.

The crowd of well-wishers parted, and sitting at the table was the little boy that had started all this. Joe came forward and hugged Jack so fiercely Jack almost lost his balance.

"Detective Murphy, this is my cousin, Sayda. She is taking me to Florida to live with her. There is fishing there and baseball. I was a baby when she came to this country, and Grandfather never told me about her."

"What about Shadow?" Jack asked. The dog wasn't in the conference room.

"She is in his office," Joe said and pointed to Chief Pope, who shrugged like it was nothing to have a dog peeing on the chief's carpet.

"Sayda will let me take Shadow, and I can keep her," Joe said excitedly. "She will have to go in a crate. She will not like that. But we will fly to Florida."

Joe started to say something but stopped.

"What is it, Joe?" Jack asked.

Joe rubbed the back of his hand across his eyes. "I was thinking of Grandfather."

Jack hugged Joe and said, "I'm sure he is happy. He'll always be with you, Joe."

"Will I see you again, Detective Murphy?" Joe asked.

"Of course," Jack said. "My mother lives in Florida. I'll come and see you sometime. You can make Shadow smile for me."

Sayda hugged Jack, more carefully than the others, and kissed him on the cheek.

Chief Pope said, "Jack, we told Channel Six they would have the exclusive when we caught this guy."

Jack replied, "If I had known I was going to be on television, I would have worn my other crutch. Is this really necessary?"

"The public loves a hero, Jack. And the mayor loves public approval."

Claudine oozed over, a microphone clipped to her too-tight sweater, and said, "Ready?"

"Let's get it over with," Jack replied.

Jack answered the questions he could, including his knowledge that the murderer had killed hundreds of people over five different states. He was asked about the apprehension of the man called Coyote, and he gave the credit to Lieutenant Battle, Lieutenant Sanchez, Liddell, and Chief Shepard of the Bisbee Police Department. He stressed Joe's precarious situation and the trauma the boy had had to endure both in Honduras and here in America.

He knew Claudine would put her own spin to his remarks, but he really didn't care. He'd gotten the asshole, and Joe was safe.

After the news conference was over, Double Dick approached Claudine Setera, and Jack heard him say, "Miss Setera, I can add to your story if you like? As Commander of the Investigations Unit I was directly involved."

Jack didn't need to hear any more.

Epilogue

The funeral for Trooper Jeanie Battle and her daughter was attended by a contingent of law enforcement officers from several counties. The procession of police vehicles stretched for half a mile. Jack had been requested to play bagpipes for the graveside service by Major Maddox. Liddell had driven, since Jack was still using one crutch. Jack was out of practice and it was cold, but the wind was cooperating and Jack sat up on a small hill, under a leafless tree.

Jeanie Battle's casket was covered with an American flag. The casket with her daughter was adorned with a simple bouquet of flowers. The caskets were beside the open graves, ready to be lowered into the icy earth. Mounds of freshly dug earth were covered with tarps, and someone had laid several bouquets of flowers on them.

After a short service, taps were played while two Honor Guard state troopers folded the flag. The Honor Guard riflemen presented a twenty-one-gun salute, and the flag was presented to Lt. Battle, who had been flown home for the service against medical advice. She had agreed to hire a caretaker.

Jack began playing "Amazing Grace" and the sound rolled down the hill and washed across the crowd of mourners. He finished, came to parade rest, cradling the pipes across his arm. He made his way down to the others, wishing he'd worn long johns under the uniform or heated underwear.

"Lieutenant Battle," Jack said. "My condolences."

"Thank you for coming. And thank you for playing so beautifully."

"Lieutenant, I understand Director Toomey has been talking to you," Jack said.

"He has, and I haven't made my mind up yet. I'm still on suspension, and I think I just need some time. I don't know if I'll stay with Highway Patrol even if they want me. Too many things have happened. I don't know if I'd even want me." She gripped Jack's hand. "Am I a bad person, Jack? Was what I did wrong?"

"If you hadn't, I would have," Jack said. He didn't know whether that was true or not, but his comment seemed to reassure her.

She freed his hand and asked, "Was Lyman involved or was he just another victim?"

That was a question Jack couldn't answer with any proof. DHS and Angelina Garcia were tearing apart his computer, phone, phone records, internet usage, and any other data source. They hadn't come up with anything conclusive yet, but Lyman did seem to have an unusual amount of classified Border Patrol and Homeland Security files on his computer at home. He had complete access to all the databases because he worked in Intelligence.

"They're still trying to find something. My gut tells me he was working with Coyote, and when we got close to him, he became a liability to Coyote."

"He was dirty," Battle said. "Your gut is always right, Jack. But don't let it go to your head."

"I think you need to go and rest, Lieutenant," Jack suggested. She was turning pale, and she wasn't making sarcastic remarks.

"Jill will do. You earned the right to call me by my first name. I'll go in a few minutes. I just want to sit a spell. Keep in touch, will you?"

"You bet," Jack said. "If you take the job from Toomey, and they get over being mad at me, we might be working together again—Jill."

"Oh. Just shoot me! Again," Battle said, and they smiled at each other. She was feeling better.

Liddell waited a short distance away and let Jack talk to Battle alone. Jack crutched back to meet him, and Liddell took the bagpipes. "That was beautiful, pod'na."

"You should hear me play when I'm about four Scotches over the limit," Jack said.

"Better?" Liddell asked.

"Have you ever heard 'Amazing Grace' slurred?"

Battle was sitting alone near the caskets, coat pulled around her face, shivering.

"Will she be okay?" Liddell asked Jack.

"I think she'll be just fine. She was scary in Arizona, but she's coping now."

"Is Maddox protecting her job?" Liddell asked.

"Why the interest, Bigfoot?"

"I hate to say this, pod'na, but I don't think she's a good fit with police work."

"I agree, but then I don't think your big feet are a good fit for the car," Jack said.

"Bite me, pod'na."

"You first."

Liddell put a hand on Jack's shoulder and said, "I saw the ring on Katie's finger, pod'na. Are you going to make me best man?"

Acknowledgments

I would like to thank some special people who have allowed me the use their real names as characters in this story: Peter Swaim, Tony Walker, Karen Stenger-Walker, and Alfreda Cote'.

Peter Swaim is a real-life US Marshal (now retired). Tony Walker has retired from the Evansville Police Department as a crime scene detective, but still plays a key role in my stories. Thank you, Tony. His wife, Karen, found her way into the story as the founder of a homegrown militia in Indiana. This is not true in any way, according to her husband. Thank you for allowing me to put you in the story, Karen. Alfreda Cote Pietka is a friend who lives in Maine. She gave permission to use her name for my evil bad guy. Thank you, Alfreda.

If I have not mentioned you, I hope I have thanked you in some way and you will forgive my omission.

I thank all my readers, the end-users of my stories, and I ask you to please remember this is a work of fiction. Creating a character means taking what you see around you and molding it into a personality. If that personality is abrasive to some, it is still just a character. We live in a world with differing opinions and varied behaviors, so characters in books should be allowed the same latitude. Characters are not in reality racist, or misogynist, or evil or some other -ist. They are what they need to be to create a story.

Last but not least, I thank my beautiful wife, Jennifer, for giving me space and understanding, not to mention reminding me it's time to eat, go to bed, and bringing me a Scotch from time to time when I look needy. I swear she can read my mind.

This novel is a work of fiction and is not intended to reflect negatively on any law enforcement agency. Any resemblance to people, groups of people, businesses, or agencies is purely coincidental. I sincerely hope readers will understand my taking poetic license.

USOC, or Unsolved Serial and Organized Crime, is not a real FBI task force and is solely my creation.

Don't miss the next exciting Jack Murphy thriller

The Cleanest Kill

Coming soon from Lyrical Underground, an imprint of Kensington Publishing Corp.

Keep reading to enjoy a sample excerpt . . .

Chapter 1

Thirty-seven years earlier

Two days before the Thanksgiving championship game, Maximillian Alexander Day, varsity wide receiver for the Monarchs, Rex Mundi High School's football team, stood behind the bleachers before practice. This weekend would be the playoff game against their rival, the Central Bears. He was supposed to be in the locker room with the rest of the team, checking equipment, gearing up. He didn't care. He was waiting for cheerleading practice to take a break. He was waiting for Ginger. He could hear the raucous noise coming from school fans and die-hard parents sitting above him in the bleachers.

He was small for an offensive wide receiver and a defensive corner back, but he was fast and strong and gave as good as he got. Last year he'd sacked Rex Mundi's quarterback, Richard Dick, three times. This year he was supposed to protect the prick.

In his senior year, Max had transferred from Central High School to Rex Mundi Catholic High School at the insistence of his parents. His father's reasoning was Catholic high schools had less violence, more supervision, and discipline was enforced by the Catholic nuns. Max knew kids from Catholic high schools that swore the crucifixes hanging around the nun's necks were actually throwing stars. According to Max's parents, he was sorely lacking in discipline.

His little sister, Reina, younger by one year, had been allowed to stay at Central. She was a junior this year. She was the perfect child, whereas he was the defect child. She excelled at scholarly things and etiquette.

He excelled at physical confrontations and getting attention from girls. Max was known at both schools as Mad Max because of his temper and aggressive manner—and because his initials spelled M.A.D.

Even before the ink dried on his transfer, the Rex Mundi football coach had approached him and asked if he could play as hard against the Bears as he'd played against the Monarchs. Max had said yes. He didn't care who he creamed on the field. Truth be told, he didn't care for sports, but he liked hitting people—hard—and he liked the varsity football letter jacket. It was a chick magnet.

The girl he currently had his eye on was cheerleader Ginger Purdie, with her copper-colored ringlets bouncing around her shoulders and sweeping across perfect breasts as she led the cheers, urging them to victory. Max felt an urge too. He didn't know her name last year when he was with Central, but he had noticed her. He was sure she'd noticed him, too.

In addition to being head cheerleader, Max heard she was the queen of Rex Mundi's junior prom and was to be queen again at the end of this semester. No surprise there. She was the prettiest girl in school. And of course, the king of the prom would be the quarterback of the varsity team, her longtime boyfriend, Richard Dick, aka Greased Lightning. Max was determined to change the buffoon's name to Greased Monkey because Ginger would slip right through the quarterback's hands and be picked off by wide receiver Mad Max.

The cheers ended. Clapping and shouts and hoots came from above. Max stepped forward in time to watch Ginger bounce and jiggle and whip her curls around until she spotted him. She smiled at him and scurried off the field with every blue-blooded male's eyes following her, but her eyes flirted only with Max. She ran to the sidelines and joined the usual team enthusiasts. Max waited for her to turn around so he could motion her over.

The tunnel leading to the locker room where the team was gearing up was just behind him, but Max wasn't worried about Greased Lightning. In fact, he wished the arrogant asshole was watching Ginger brazenly flirting with him. Suddenly Ginger turned, stopped bouncing, and held out one of her pom-poms toward him. The smile had faded from her face. Max smiled and motioned her to come over, and something hard struck him in the back of the head. He fell down face-first but cushioned himself with his hands and arms. He'd taken harder hits both on and off the field.

Max lifted his face and pushed himself up to his knees. Richard "Greased Lightning" Dick stood looming over him, helmet in one hand, the other bunched into a fist.

Chickenshit hit me with his helmet.

Dick was tall, with blond hair combed into bangs down into his blue eyes. For a quarterback, he appeared less strong and solidly built than stringy and rangy. He had earned the name "Greased Lightning" because of his uncanny ability to hit the receiver with every pass and slip through any offense.

"Better stay down, *Max-I-mill-Yun*," Dick said, stretching Max's name out insultingly. "That's some lame shit name. Your mom must've been on drugs."

"Maybe she was on the end of my dick," Dennis James said. Dennis was one of Dick's sidekicks. "I've been doing her since I was a baby. Maybe Mad Max is my kid," James taunted.

Carl Needham piped in, "Have you seen his mom, Den? I wouldn't let my dog do her. She's a sow."

Carl wasn't on the team, but he might as well have been because the only way you could separate him from Dick was with a crowbar. Dennis James was a loser, but Carl was clever.

Bullies never travel alone. While Max was still doubled over, Dennis and Carl hurled more insults, one grunting like a pig, the other repeatedly making motions like he was rooting in the mud. Needham hawked up some snot and spat it on the ground beside Max.

Max stood, brushed some grit from the front of his letter jacket and his knees, smiled, and deftly broke Dick's nose.

Only Dennis James made a move forward but was halted by a shake of Max's head. "Dennis, you're such a dumb shit. If my mom was on the end of your dick when I was a baby, that means you were still in your mama's belly. Come to think of it, your dick is probably still that small. If you talk about my mother again, I'll tear your head off and shit down your neck." Max walked away without a challenge.

Dick was bent over, hands covering his nose, blood running between his fingers and down the front of his red football jersey.

A small crowd had gathered around Dick, some pretending sympathy and shock while others were holding their own noses and dancing around gaily. Max was sorry he'd let his temper show, but Dick had it coming. Max knew he'd be kicked off the team for punching Dick out. Hell, he'd probably be kicked out of school. If that happened, his parents would ground him for the rest of the year and take away his Camaro.

He was just about to the parking lot when he felt a strong hand on his shoulder. He spun around and kicked Dick in the crotch. Dick fell to the ground. The only noises he made were squeaks that came out like whispers. Carl and Dennis stood with their mouths hanging open. Dennis had his hands cupped protectively over his own genitals.

Max turned and headed for his car. What the hell. He'd have one last night of freedom. This time he made it to the parking lot and brushed the remainder of grit from the knees of his jeans and from his elbows.

It was a cool November night, but his temper kept him from feeling it. Max mimicked a game announcer, declaring loudly, "Oh my! The quarterback has been sacked. Looks like his nose is broke. Looks like Dick's dick is broken, too. The game is forfeited. The game is over, folks. Max one, Grease Monkey zero."

He reached his car and tried to open the door. It was locked. "Shit!" he muttered. His bravado was fading, and reality was setting in. His keys were back in the locker room.

A hand grabbed his wrist. He instinctively ducked, turned, arm cocked, ready to trade punches when he recognized his sister.

"Are you going to hit me, too?" Reina asked.

"Let go," he said and shook her hand off.

"You can't leave, dummy," Reina said and rummaged in her purse. She handed Max the extra set of keys to the Camaro. She wasn't driving yet, but she was the only one he trusted to keep the spare set. He'd come back for his stuff tomorrow.

"Come on, sis. I'm going for a little ride to cool off. I'll give you a lift home."

Reina's arms crossed her chest. "Mom and Dad aren't going to be happy. Why do you always do this, Max?"

"Do what?" He sounded hurt. "You mean defend myself? Should I have let him knock me in the dirt and make fun of me? Let them insult Mom? He had it coming, and you know it."

"And *you* know what I mean, Maximillian Day," Reina said. She only called him by his full name when she was seriously pissed. "You go back and apologize. Talk to the coach. Maybe you won't be in trouble if you..."

Ginger Purdie came prancing up and caressed his face. "Are you okay, Max? Did he hurt you?"

Max grinned at her, keeping a cautious eye on Reina. "You should've seen the other guy," he said and put a hand on her waist. "I'm not hurt. You'd better get back. They need you."

Ginger said in a pout, "You don't need me?"

"Of course I do. But I'm fine. The team needs your particular talents to give them encouragement, babe," he said and gave her a firm slap on the rear.

She giggled and bounced away.

Reina said, "You'd better stay away from that one, Max. Mom won't approve, and you're already going to be grounded for the rest of your life."

"Grounded only works if you get caught sneaking out."

"Uh oh!" She pointed across the parking lot where Dick, Needham, and James were jogging toward them. Two or three other seniors had joined them. "You can't fight all of them. Get out of here." She moved off toward the approaching boys. "I'll slow them down," she said. "As usual."

"Thanks, sis," Max said, got in his car, fired up the Hemi engine, and threw a rooster tail of gravel behind as he accelerated out of the lot.

Max took back roads to Kratzville Road, where he stopped, debating where he would go. Home was northwest. He could take Kleitz Road, but he didn't want to go home. He would maybe go downtown to the riverfront. He could sit in his car, watch the water, calm his mind. His thoughts turned to Ginger. She was pretty, but he didn't really care for her. She was just a way to get at Dick and the rest of the "popular" kids. Snobs. Every one of them. And he truly hated that smug asshole, Richard Dick. He sacked Dick every chance he got during previous practices. Dick needed to be brought down a peg or two. Punching him in the nose was worth missing the championship. Kicking him in the balls was priceless.

Max turned south on Kratzville Road. The back of his head was smarting. His fingers found a painful knot on his skull where the helmet had hit him. It hurt, but he smiled at the memory of Dick's nose exploding under his fist. "Bet you didn't expect that, Dick," he said out loud and chuckled.

He was approaching Gloria's Corral Club at Allens Lane. The normally bustling crowd was elsewhere on Sundays. He considered running the red light, but with his luck tonight, a cop would be sitting in the parking lot of the convenience store across the street. It was dark-thirty, and the streets were deserted.

Headlights flashed in his rearview mirror. He recognized the black Chevy Impala SS coming up fast. He let it come up beside him. Dick was behind the wheel. His nose was still bleeding. Needham was up front and giving him the bird while Dick laid on the horn. Dennis James was hanging out of the passenger window, hurling insults and threats about what they would do to him if he got out of the car.

Max ran the red light, cut sharp right, narrowly missed the Impala's front quarter panel, and sped down Allens Lane. The Impala peeled out and made a sharp right, but it was a boat compared to the Camaro and swayed side to side before gaining purchase of the road. Dick stamped on the gas. The Impala was fast, but it was no match for the Camaro.

Max slowed to let them catch up. He let the Impala kiss his rear bumper before he braked hard and swerved into the oncoming lane. His tires smoked as he skidded forward, but the Impala whizzed past. He could see Dick's shocked expression before the Impala went airborne over the railroad tracks and into the section of road the kids had dubbed the "double dipper." Max's car came to a stop just feet from the first dip. Some of his classmates had gotten drunk one night and found out about the dangerous railroad crossing the hard way. Max had counted on Dick forgetting in the heat of the chase.

He watched the Impala fly through the air, all four tires off the ground on the first drop, and by the time the car bottomed out on the second set of railroad tracks it was airborne again. This time the Impala came down even harder. Sparks of metal shot from beneath its chassis, and it slewed side to side, running off the right side of the road. Dick steered sharply to the left, overcorrecting, and slid sideways into a shallow ditch on the left side of the road. The Impala slammed into the Railroad Crossing sign and sheared it off.

Max slowly drove past and watched his pursuers clamber out of Dick's car. He pumped a fist in the air, yelling, "Yeah! Who's your daddy? Whose mom is stupid now, ya' bunch o' dicks?" He circled back to Kratzville Road and pulled into Locust Hill Cemetery to check his own front end. Even crawling over the tracks at the double dipper, his front end had scraped the pavement. He was at the front of his car when saw a single headlight turn in to the cemetery and come at him.

Dick's car rolled to a stop in the grass beside him. The front bumper of the Impala was canted like a lopsided grin, and one headlight was missing. He laughed.

Richard Dick and Dennis James emerged from the Impala with beer bottles in their hands. Needham got out with a tire iron.

"You think that's funny, asshole?" Dick yelled and flung a full beer bottle. It busted on the Camaro's hood and splattered Max with beer and fragments of glass. Max was on him in a flash. He didn't care if there were three or five or a hundred. Loudmouths were cowards. He was going to kick some ass.

* * * *

Car 34 cruised west on Diamond Avenue. Officer Ted Mattingly had worked third shift, West District-One for two years. He liked the hours, liked the job, and liked being out from under the glare of supervisors. He had a patrol routine, and this was part of it: shining his spotlight on the fronts of the few businesses, looking for signs of break-ins or drunks passed out on the parking lots.

He made a circuit going north on First Avenue from Dunkin' Donuts, left on Diamond Avenue, and north on Kratzville. The only deviation in his patrol tonight was to cruise through Locust Hill Cemetery. There were no gates barring the way. Young and old couples alike sometimes parked behind the mausoleum to smoke dope and do "other things."

He wouldn't normally care where people got naked, but there were reports lately of vandalism and break-ins to some of the vaults. Last week someone had started to dig up a grave. They got about two feet down and abandoned the project. That was the problem with kids today. They were too lazy to even finish a job. The crazy little bastards were probably doing black magic or summoning up demons with the bones.

Mattingly saw the front end of a Camaro parked in the middle of a cemetery lane and hit his bright lights to illuminate the interior. The lights caught a shape in the driver's seat. It didn't move, so he tapped his siren a few times. He could only make out a shoulder, and there was something splattered across the windows. He hoped it wasn't a drunk. He'd just had his car cleaned by a jail trustee from the last go-round with a vomiting drunk.

Mattingly radioed dispatch to report his location and bleeped his siren several more times. He got on the intercom and called out to the occupant. Nothing. He radioed dispatch again.

"Car 34."

"Car 34, go ahead with your traffic."

"Car 34, I'm going to be out of the car checking on this vehicle. Send me a backup."

The dispatcher asked, "Do you want that Code 3?" Code 3 means emergency lights and siren and busting ass.

"Code 3," he confirmed. He had just left Dunkin' Donuts on First Avenue and knew there were three police units there drinking free coffee and eating their way through a mountain of donuts. He also knew that unless he called a Code 3 run they would still be sitting there until he called dispatch to give them a disregard.

"Ten-four, Car 34," dispatch said and put his request for a Code 3 backup on the air. Car 32 and Car 37 responded immediately.

Mattingly kept an eye on the Camaro for any movement. The driver appeared to be slumped over the steering wheel. The windshield and the driver's window were coated with something dark. Maybe vomit, but maybe blood. He wasn't looking forward to going up there, but he knew he'd take a chiding for a month if he was wrong about needing backup. Someone might be hurt. Better safe than sorry.

He got out of the car, flashlight in one hand, Model 10 Smith and Wesson .38 revolver in the other, and eased up to the driver's side of the Camaro. Bits of something white mixed with the stuff coating the windows. He tapped on the window with his flashlight before opening the driver's door.

"Jesus," Mattingly said and vomited across the hood of the car.

Chapter 2

Deputy Chief of Police Richard Dick was in full dress blues, sitting in his personal Lexus sedan, scribbling notes on a yellow pad. He had driven his own car to work this morning, dismissed his driver, Captain Dewey Duncan, and was now parked in the lot of Rural King on the west side of Evansville. He wasn't worried about someone recognizing him, but he'd parked on the far side of the lot just in case. He dreaded what he was about to do but knew it needed to be done in person. He was totally out of his element.

His palms sweated, and his iPhone was slick in his hand. He thought back to the night that brought him to this situation. It wasn't his fault things had totally gotten out of hand. He pinched the sides of his nose, remembering how it had bled all over his football uniform. He remembered the feeling of humiliation. He could still feel the crunch of cartilage, the nostrils swelling shut, and the way his nose still canted from the little bastard's sucker punch. He'd had raccoon eyes for days, but Max had gotten much worse when they caught up with him in that cemetery. The thought of what they'd done to Max brought him out of his reverie.

He'd read the case file of Max Day's murder a thousand times since. There was nothing new, or at least nothing that would tank his chances for appointment to chief. He'd meet with Mrs. Day, be honest, forthright, confident with just the right mix of compassion, sadness, and regret. He reminded himself to take it slow. Let her ask all her questions. Listen politely. Slow and steady wins the race every time.

Dick took a deep breath, released it slowly, and wiped his hand and iPhone on a handkerchief. He punched in the telephone number he'd already typed into his phone.

"Hello," a woman's voice said.

"Hello, Mrs. Day. May I speak with you?" Dick asked.

"Who is this?"

"Deputy Chief of Police, Richard Dick," he said confidently. The title sounded impressive. "I want to..."

"You have some nerve," Mrs. Day scolded him.

"Mrs. Day, I think it's time we talked. I'm willing to tell you everything that happened that night. Everything." He had no intention of telling her all of it. No one knew all of it except for a few trusted friends.

He was surprised when she said, "You'll have to come here. I don't drive much anymore. You come here and face me. Come to Max's home. You know where. I've seen you drive by from my window. We'll see about talking."

"That's agreeable," Dick said. "I know the address. I'm five minutes away."

"Make it thirty," Mrs. Day said and hung up.

Chapter 3

Present day

"Can you believe she's already talking? She's smart, like her old man," Liddell Blanchard said.

Jack Murphy responded, "That's called babbling, but she does take after you, Bigfoot. You never shut up."

Janie Blanchard was eleven months old. She was born a month premature but had caught up fast.

"Hey. I'm a proud father. You should be proud too, Uncle Jack."

Detective Jack Murphy was just shy of six feet tall and solidly built with a shock of dark hair spiked in front. His gray eyes could turn dark when he was angry or threatened, and soft as a cloud when he was happy.

His partner, Liddell Blanchard, was a Cajun transplant from the Iberville Parish Sheriff Department, where he'd worked River Patrol until he'd met his wife, Marcie, and settled down in her hometown, Evansville. Jack called his partner Bigfoot because Liddell stood over six and a half feet tall and had the physique of a full-grown Yeti.

Detective Sergeant Wolf opened the door and stuck his head in. "The chief wants the two of you. Right now."

"Do you know what it's about?" Jack asked the sergeant.

Sergeant Wolf held the fingertips of one hand to his forehead and closed his eyes. "Hmm. I'm getting nothing, Murphy. Now take your pet Cajun and get your asses up there."

"Sarge is in a good mood today," Liddell said. Sergeant Wolf was a fair supervisor and made coffee when he emptied a carafe, but he had a dark side you didn't want to cross. "Maybe we're going to get an office big enough to smile without hitting the walls."

"Or maybe Double Dick's on a tear again," Jack said. Double Dick was the nickname Jack had bestowed on Deputy Chief Richard Dick. It became popular. Dick was known department-wide as Double Dick because of his two first names and because of his propensity to punish a policeman more than once. He was like a velociraptor with rank.

"You're gonna get a spanking," came one of the detective's voice through the open door. Everyone laughed at that.

"I've got dibs on their office," a detective named Phil shouted.

Captain Franklin had given Jack and Liddell, who were officially the Homicide Squad, what was once the lieutenant's office in the detectives' area. It was barely big enough for two desks, two chairs, and two men, but they could shut the door and block out some of the incessant clattering of keyboards, joking, farting on command, and cursing.

"You guys should start a comedy club," Jack said as they passed through to the hallway. "I hate meetings. We've got a bank robbery and a stabbing to work."

"Maybe it's something good, pod'na. You should be positive like me."

Jack said, "Okay. I'm positive it's going to be bad news."

"Hey. Maybe we got another case from the Feds?"

"If it's like the last one, I'll resign," Jack said. Earlier in the year he and Liddell had been recruited/conscripted by the FBI for a federal task force called USOC. Unsolved Serial and Organized Crime. There were other task forces working the same type of cases, but USOC was only called in on the ones deemed unsolvable. A US Marshall had sworn Jack and Liddell in as federal agents, and Liddell was beaming with pride when he'd finally received his FBI badge and credentials. Jack wasn't so happy. Working with the Feds as a police detective was one thing. Working as a Fed was quite another. They had too many rules and too many bosses.

"We caught the bad guy, saved the girl, became national heroes. Not bad for two local yokels if you ask me," Liddell said.

"Actually many people died, the girl you're talking about is a Missouri State Highway Lieutenant, and she saved me," Jack corrected his partner. "Sergeant Wolf isn't accompanying us. Not good."

Liddell put the fingertips of both hands together and held them up in a meditation pose. "Positive thoughts, grasshopper. Positive thoughts. Positive..."

"Just shut up," Jack said. "I've got a bad feeling."

They were buzzed into the chief's complex. Jack tried to read Judy Mangold, the chief's longtime secretary. Her face was as expressionless as that of a poker player in a high-stakes game.

"Morning, Judy," Liddell said.

She didn't respond.

The door to the chief's conference room was closed, and Jack heard voices raised. Jack knocked on the door. It flew open, and Deputy Chief Richard Dick stormed out. "Watch where you're going, Murphy," Dick said.

"Excuse you," Liddell said under his breath. "He didn't tell me to watch where I was going. How rude."

They entered to find the chief of police, Marlin Pope, and Captain Charles Franklin sitting at the end of the conference table with an open laptop in front of them. Marlin Pope was Jack's height, late-fifties, with skin the color of yellow coal and the physique of a serious runner.

Captain Franklin, Jack's direct supervisor, was sporting the tan he'd brought back from his Miami vacation. He was slightly taller than Jack, late forties, square-jawed, and had perfectly groomed dark hair with streaks of silver at the temples. He looked like George Clooney but without the millionaire cockiness.

A thin file folder was on the table next to the captain. It was worn at the edges and paperclipped shut.

Captain Franklin said to the detectives, "Have a seat."

Jack could hear the secretary clacking the keys on her laptop down the hall. She would normally be eavesdropping, so whatever was going on in here, she didn't want to hear it.

"If you're going to fire us, he can explain everything," Liddell offered only half-jokingly.

Captain Franklin said, "You might wish you were fired."

Shit!

Jack and Liddell sat.

Chief Pope said, "You are not to discuss anything you hear in this room outside of the four of us. Understood?"

Jack nodded.

"Yes, Chief," Liddell said. "What are we not discussing?"

Chief Pope said, "As you know, Benet Cato will be replacing Thatcher Hensley as mayor on January first."

The mayoral race hadn't even been close. Benet Cato had no previous political experience and had run a "clean sweep" campaign. She said Evansville's citizens were tired of the "good ol' boy system" where they were treated like they were not capable of understanding the operation of the city. She said the people's voice should be listened to and there would be more transparency in local government. She must have read the public's pulse correctly, because she had beat Hensley hands down. She would be sworn in January first, and there would be many changes in government.

Chief Pope said, "I have it on good authority that I'm to be replaced."

Cato would be the first female Mayor of Evansville, but this wasn't the first time Marlin Pope's position as Chief of Police was on the chopping block. Each new mayor had the option of appointing the Chief of Police. Politics was loads of laughs.

"There's a rumor going around that Deputy Chief Dick is being considered," Liddell said.

The outgoing mayor, Thatcher Hensley, had tried to replace Chief Pope with Dick, but because Pope was the first black policeman to ever attain the position of Chief of Police, replacing him with Richard Dick, a blond-haired blue-eyed Aryan Brotherhood poster child, was unthinkable. Dick had gotten in hot water over taking evidence away from a murder scene on a high-profile case. Dick skated on the Obstruction of Justice charge, the mayor's job was safe, and Chief Pope was retained. Everything was hunky-dory in E-ville, until now.

Chief Pope took a thumb drive from his pocket and slipped it in the computer's USB port. "You need to hear this." Pope tapped the keyboard. The sound of knocking, a door opening, and Double Dick's unmistakable, condescending voice came through the computer speakers.

"Mrs. Day?"

"What do you want to see me for?" A woman's voice. Presumably Mrs. Day.

"You know who I am. What I do now." The arrogant voice of Richard Dick.

"I know who you're hoping to be. You want to be chief of police," Mrs. Day said.

"That's right. That's why I'm here. I want to answer your questions. See if we can make this right. I know I haven't been forth—"

"You haven't spoken to me, to my family, for thirty-seven years. You were there, and you wouldn't tell us what happened. If your father hadn't been who he was, you would be in prison right now for what you did."

"Now, Mrs. Day. You know that's not true. I was never charged with anything. I wasn't a suspect. None of my friends were. We had alibis for that night, Mrs. Day. You know all of that."

"My husband died four years after Max's murder. He never heard a word of explanation from you or your friends about that night. You refused to talk to us, and heaven knows we tried to meet with you. The police refused to let us see the reports. And now here you are. How convenient."

"I'm here, Mrs. Day, because I want to explain myself. I can't speak for the others, but I'll answer all your questions to the best of my knowledge. I know now that it was wrong not to do this a long time ago. And it was long ago. I just want to ask you not to oppose my appointment as chief of police."

Chief Pope stopped the audio.

Captain Franklin said, "You probably won't know who Mrs. Day is. You heard Deputy Chief Dick's voice on the recording?"

"Was he recording the conversation?" Jack asked.

"No, not Richard. Mrs. Day's daughter recorded it," Pope said. "Mrs. Day received a call from Richard two days ago. He asked to meet with her, and she told him to come to her home. She didn't trust him, and we'll explain why, but the point is that their conversation was recorded when he came to her house."

Jack said, "I take it this involves the incoming mayor's selection of a chief of police?"

It was ironic that the last time Double Dick was a candidate for appointment to the highest position on the Evansville Police Department his hopes had come crashing down because of a recording. The man was his own worst enemy.

Chief Pope explained, "The woman on the recording is Mrs. Amelia Day. Her son, Max, was sixteen when he was murdered in 1980. Thirty-seven years ago this month in fact. The deputy chief was seventeen years old at the time and an acquaintance of the victim. They played football together for Rex Mundi High School."

Jack couldn't imagine Dick in a football uniform unless it had a chest full of medals and rank insignia. "Was he involved in some way with Max's death?"

Captain Franklin said, "He was a suspect. Still is. The case is unsolved."

"Holy shit, Batman!" Liddell said. Then, "Sorry, Chief. Sorry, Captain."

Jack asked, "You want us to investigate the deputy chief for a thirty-seven-year-old murder?"

"There's more," Chief Pope said.

Jack waited.

Pope pushed the thin file folder across to Jack. "This audio file was played for Benet Cato. She called me at home last night. She is aware of the deputy chief's predicament and wants this case solved before she takes office. I assume she needs the case to be put to rest before she selects a new chief. She wants total transparency as to our findings. I explained to her that we couldn't release details of an ongoing investigation, but she will have her way."

"How in the hell did she hear the recording before we did, Chief?" Jack asked.

Chief Pope said, "Mrs. Day's daughter—Max's younger sister—Reina, emailed it to her."

"So, the Days think the deputy chief was a murderer thirty-seven years ago. Why go after him now? Why didn't they raise a stink back in, what? 1980?"

Captain Franklin answered, "They did. Or at least Mr. and Mrs. Day raised hell. You can see by the very thin file that the case wasn't worked very hard. Mrs. Day said they requested meetings with Richard Dick and the other boys that were involved in whatever capacity. The parents refused. Mrs. Day claims the police department was covering for them. She said they weren't allowed to see the case file and the detective wouldn't talk to them."

Jack asked, "I wasn't here thirty-seven years ago, but is that even possible? I mean, wouldn't the news media be all over this? I have a hard time believing the assigned detective wouldn't talk to the family."

"You may be right, Jack, but we'd have to address her concerns even if the mayor-elect wasn't insisting."

Jack didn't like it. The whole thing stunk of political maneuvering. Maybe Cato was going to put Double Dick in charge and needed to get this taken care of. But why him?

"Why are you giving it to us?" Jack asked.

"Think about it," Captain Franklin said. "Benet Cato is clever. She apparently knows that you and Richard are not on...the best of terms. She also knows that you will do the right thing, even if you arrest Richard. She looks good to the voters and has an excuse to either appoint or not appoint Richard."

"She as much as said that to me when she came to my home last night," Chief Pope said.

Came to your home?

"Holy sh..." Liddell said and put a hand over his mouth.

"Yeah. Holy shit!" Chief Pope said.

Meet the Author

Photo by George Routt

Sergeant Rick Reed (Ret.), author of the Jack Murphy thriller series, is a twenty-plus-year veteran police detective. During his career, he successfully investigated numerous high-profile criminal cases, including a serial killer who claimed thirteen victims before strangling and dismembering his fourteenth and last victim. He recounted that story in his acclaimed true-crime book, *Blood Trail*.

Rick spent his last three years on the force as the commander of the police department's Internal Affairs Section. He has two master's degrees, and upon retiring from the police force, took a full-time teaching position with a community college. He currently teaches criminal justice at Volunteer State Community College in Tennessee and writes thrillers. He lives near Nashville with his wife and two furry friends, Lexie and Luthor.

Please visit him on Facebook, Goodreads, or at his website, www.rickreedbooks.com. If you'd like him to speak online for your event, contact him through his website or by going to bookclubreading.com.